Praise for TREASON AT LISSON GROVE

"Ms. Perry has always done her historical homework on the darker elements of the British ruling class, and she has outdone herself this time." —*The Washington Times*

"A fast-paced Special Branch romp from beginning to end." —Bookgasm

"Perry gives readers another top-of-the-line Victorian mystery." —*RT Book Reviews*

"Oozing atmosphere with every word, Perry brings forth the era, the ambience, the curdled dregs and rarefied airs of society in another fascinating [journey]." —*Asbury Park Press*

"Fans will find *Treason at Lisson Grove* worth their three-year wait and be anxious for more of this talented crime-fighting couple." —BookLoons

"Anne Perry takes readers on a wild ride through Victorian England. . . . Readers will be thrilled with [the book] not only for the complicated political and social relationships and fascinating twists and turns of the complex plot, but for the heart-stopping ending." —Curled Up With A Good Book

"Perry is still at the top of her form." —*Suspense Magazine*

"What a delight to travel once again with Anne Perry to Victorian England, a world she deftly shows us is so different from our own, and yet so similar." —Briar Patch Books

Treason at Lisson Grove

ANNE PERRY

TREASON AT LISSON GROVE

A CHARLOTTE AND THOMAS PITT NOVEL

BALLANTINE BOOKS TRADE PAPERBACKS • NEW YORK

2012 Ballantine Books Trade Paperback Edition

Published in the United States by Ballantine Books, an imprint of The Random House Publishing Group, a division of Random House, Inc., New York.

BALLANTINE and colophon are registered trademarks of Random House, Inc.

Originally published in hardcover in the United States by Ballantine Books, an imprint of The Random House Publishing Group, a division of Random House, Inc., in 2011.

Library of Congress Cataloging-in-Publication Data
Perry, Anne.
Treason at Lisson Grove : a Charlotte and Thomas Pitt novel / Anne Perry.
p. cm.
ISBN 978-0-345-51059-4
ISBN 978-0-345-52441-6 (ebook)
1. Pitt, Charlotte (Fictitious character)—Fiction. 2. Pitt, Thomas (Fictitious character)—Fiction. 3. Women detectives—England—London—Fiction. 4. Police spouses—Fiction. 5. Police—England—London—Fiction. I. Title.
PR6066.E693T74 2011
823'.914—dc22   2010041631

Printed in the United States of America

www.ballantinebooks.com

2 4 6 8 9 7 5 3 1

Book design by Karin Batten

To KEN SHERMAN for years of friendship

TREASON AT LISSON GROVE

CHAPTER

1

"THAT'S HIM!" GOWER YELLED above the sound of the traffic. Pitt turned on his heel just in time to see a figure dart between the rear end of a hansom and the oncoming horses of a brewer's dray. Gower disappeared after him, missing a trampling by no more than inches.

Pitt plunged into the street, swerving to avoid a brougham and stopping abruptly to let another hansom pass. By the time he reached the far pavement Gower was twenty yards ahead and Pitt could make out only his flying hair. The man he was pursuing was out of sight. Weaving between clerks in pinstripes, leisurely strollers, and the occasional early woman shopper with her long skirts getting in the way, Pitt closed the gap until he was less than a dozen yards behind Gower. He caught a glimpse of the man ahead: bright ginger hair and a green jacket. Then he was gone, and Gower turned, his right hand raised for a moment in signal, before disappearing into an alley.

Pitt followed after him into the shadows, his eyes taking a moment or two to adjust. The alley was long and narrow, bending in a dogleg a hundred yards beyond. The gloom was caused by the overhanging eaves and the water-soaked darkness of the brick, long streams of grime running down from the broken guttering. People were huddled in doorways; others made their way slowly, limping, or staggering beneath heavy bolts of cloth, barrels, and bulging sacks.

Gower was still ahead, seeming to find his way with ease. Pitt veered around a fat woman with a tray of matches to sell, and tried to catch up. Gower was at least ten years younger, even if his legs were not quite so long, and he was more used to this kind of thing. But it was Pitt's experience in the Metropolitan Police before he joined Special Branch that had led them to finding West, the man they were now chasing.

Pitt bumped into an old woman and apologized before regaining his stride. They were around the dogleg now, and he could see West's ginger head making for the opening into the wide thoroughfare forty yards away. Pitt knew that they must catch him before he was swallowed up in the crowds.

Gower was almost there. He reached out an arm to grab at West, but just then West ducked sideways and Gower tripped, hurtling into the wall and momentarily winding himself. He bent over double, gasping to catch his breath.

Pitt lengthened his stride and reached West just as he dived out into the High Street, barged his way through a knot of people, and disappeared.

Pitt went after him and a moment later saw the light on his bright hair almost at the next crossroads. He increased his pace, bumping and banging people. He had to catch him. West had information that could be vital. After all, the tide of unrest was rising fast all over Europe, and becoming more violent. Many people, in the name of reform, were actually trying to overthrow government altogether and create an anarchy in which they imagined there would be some kind of equality of justice. Some were content with blood-soaked oratory; others preferred dynamite, or even bullets.

Special Branch knew of a current plot, but not yet the leaders behind it, or—more urgently—the target of their violence. West was to provide that, at risk of his own life—if his betrayal were known.

Where the devil was Gower? Pitt swiveled around once to see if he could spot him. He was nowhere visible in the sea of bobbing heads, bowler hats, caps, and bonnets. There was no time to look longer. Surely he wasn't still in the alley? What was wrong with the man? He was not much more than thirty. Had he been more than just knocked off balance? Was he injured?

West was up ahead, seizing a break in the traffic to cross back to the other side again. Three hansoms came past almost nose-to-tail. A cart and four clattered in the opposite direction. Pitt fumed on the edge of the curb. To go out into the roadway now would only get him killed.

A horse-drawn omnibus passed, then two heavily loaded wagons. More carts and a dray went in the other direction. Pitt had lost sight of West, and Gower had vanished into the air.

There was a brief holdup in traffic and Pitt raced across the road. Weaving in and out of the way of frustrated drivers, he only just missed being caught by a long, curling carriage whip. Someone yelled at him and he took no notice. He reached the opposite side and caught sight of West for an instant as he swung around a corner and made for another alley.

Pitt raced after him, but when he got there West had disappeared. "Did you see a man with ginger hair?" Pitt demanded of a peddler with a tray of sandwiches. "Where did he go?"

"Want a sandwich?" the man asked with eyes wide. "Very good. Made this morning. Only tuppence."

Pitt fished frantically in his pocket; found string, sealing wax, a pocketknife, a handkerchief, and several coins. He gave the man a threepenny bit and took a sandwich. It felt soft and fresh, although right now he didn't care. "Which way?" he said harshly.

"That way." The man pointed into the deeper shadows of the alley.

Pitt began to run again, weaving a path through the piles of rubbish. A rat skittered from under his feet, and he all but fell over a drunken figure lying half out of a doorway. Somebody swung a punch at him; he lurched to one side, losing his balance for a moment, glimpsing West still ahead of him.

Now West disappeared again and Pitt had no idea which way he had gone. He tried one blind courtyard and alley after another. It seemed like endless, wasted moments before Gower joined him from one of the side alleyways.

"Pitt!" Gower clutched at his arm. "This way! Quickly." His fingers dug deep into Pitt's flesh, making him gasp with the sudden pain.

Together they ran forward, Pitt along the broken pavement beside the dark walls, Gower in the gutter, his boots sending up a spray of filthy water. Pace for pace, they went around the corner into the open entrance to a brickyard and saw a man crouching over something on the ground.

Gower let out a cry of fury and darted forward, half crossing in front of Pitt and tripping him up in his eagerness. They both fell heavily. Pitt was on his feet in time to see the crouched figure swing around for an instant, then scramble up and run as if for his life.

"Oh God!" Gower said, aghast, now also on his feet. "After him! I know who it is!"

Pitt stared at the heap on the ground: West's green jacket and bright hair. Blood streamed from his throat, staining his chest and already pooling dark on the stones underneath him. There was no way he could possibly be alive.

Gower was already pursuing the assassin. Pitt raced after him and this time his long strides caught up before they reached the road. "Who is it?" he demanded, almost choking on his own breath.

"Wrexham!" Gower hissed back. "We've been watching him for weeks."

Pitt knew the man, but only by name. There was a momentary break in the stream of vehicles. They darted across the road to go after Wrexham, who thank heaven was an easy figure to see. He was taller than average, and—despite the good weather—he was wearing a long, pale-colored scarf that swung in the air as he twisted and turned. It flashed through Pitt's mind that it might be a weapon; it would not be hard to strangle a man with it.

They were on a crowded footpath now, and Wrexham dropped his pace. He almost sauntered, walking easily, swiftly, with loping strides, but perfectly casual. Could he be arrogant enough to imagine he had lost them so quickly? He certainly knew they had seen him, because he had swiveled around at Gower's cry, and then run as if for his life.

They were now walking at a steady pace, eastward toward Stepney and Limehouse. Soon the crowds would thin as they left the broader streets behind.

"If he goes into an alley, be careful," Pitt warned, now beside Gower, as if they were two tradesmen bound on a common errand. "He has a knife. He's too comfortable. He must know we're behind him."

Gower glanced at him sideways, his eyes wide for an instant. "You think he'll try and pick us off?"

"We practically saw him cut West's throat," Pitt replied, matching Gower stride for stride. "If we get him he'll hang. He must know that."

"I reckon he'll duck and hide suddenly, when he thinks we're taking it easy," Gower answered. "We'd better stay fairly close to him. Lose sight of him for a moment and he'll be gone for good."

Pitt agreed with a nod, and they closed the distance to Wrexham, who was still strolling ahead of them. Never once did he turn or look back.

Pitt found it chilling that a man could slit another's throat and see him bleed to death, then a few moments after walk through a crowd with outward unconcern, as if he were just one more pedestrian about some trivial daily business. What passion or inhumanity drove him? In the way he moved, the fluidity—almost grace—of his stride, Pitt could not detect even fear, let alone the conscience of a brutal murderer.

Wrexham wove in and out of the thinning crowd. Twice they lost sight of him.

"That way!" Gower gasped, waving his right hand. "I'll go left." He swerved around a window cleaner with a bucket of water, almost knocking the man over.

Pitt went the other way, into the north end of an alley. The sudden shadows momentarily made him blink, half blind. He saw movement and charged forward, but it was only a beggar shuffling out of a doorway. He swore under his breath and sprinted back to the street just in time to see Gower swiveling around frantically, searching for him.

"That way!" Gower called urgently and set off, leaving Pitt behind.

The second time it was Pitt who saw him first, and Gower who had to catch up. Wrexham had crossed the road just in front of a brewer's dray and was out of sight by the time Pitt and Gower were able to follow. It took them more than ten minutes to close on him without drawing attention. There were fewer people about, and two men running would have been highly noticeable. With fifty yards' distance between them, Wrexham could have outrun them too easily.

They were in Commercial Road East, now, in Stepney. If Wrexham did not turn they would be in Limehouse, perhaps the West India Dock Road. If they went that far they could lose him among the tangle of wharves with cranes, bales of goods, warehouses, and dock laborers. If he went down to one of the ferries he could be out of sight between the ships at anchor before they could find another ferry to follow him.

Ahead of them, as if he had seen them, Wrexham increased his pace, his long legs striding out, his jacket scarf flying.

Pitt felt a flicker of nervousness. His muscles were aching, his feet sore despite his excellent boots—his one concession to sartorial taste. Even well-cut jackets never looked right on him because he weighted the pockets with too many pieces of rubbish he thought he might need. His ties never managed to stay straight; perhaps he knotted them too tightly, or too loosely. But his boots were beautiful and immaculately cared for. Even though most of his work was of the mind, out-thinking, out-guessing, remembering, and seeing significance where others didn't, he still knew the importance of a policeman's feet. Some habits do not die. Before he had been forced out of the Metropolitan Police and Victor Narraway had taken him into Special Branch, he had walked enough miles to know the price of inattention to physical stamina, and to boots.

Suddenly Wrexham ran across the narrow road and disappeared down Gun Lane.

"He's going for the Limehouse Station!" Gower shouted, leaping out of the way of a cart full of timber as he dashed after him.

Pitt was on his heels. The Limehouse Station was on the Blackwall Railway, less than a hundred yards away. Wrexham could go in at least three possible directions from there and end up anywhere in the city.

But Wrexham kept moving, rapidly, right, past the way back up to the station. Instead, he turned left onto Three Colts Street, then swerved right onto Ropemaker's Field, still loping in an easy run.

Pitt was too breathless to shout, and anyway Wrexham was no more than fifteen yards ahead. The few men and one old washerwoman on the path scattered as the three running men passed them. Wrexham was going to the river, as Pitt had feared.

At the end of Ropemaker's Field they turned right again into Narrow Street, still running. They were only yards from the river's edge. The breeze was stiff off the water, smelling of salt and mud where the tide was low. Half a dozen gulls soared lazily in circles above a string of barges.

Wrexham was still ahead of them, moving less easily now, tiring. He passed the entrance to Limehouse Cut. Pitt figured that he must be making for Kidney Stairs, the stone steps down to the river, where, if they were lucky, he would find a ferry waiting. There were two more sets of stairs before the road curved twenty yards inland to Broad Street. At the Shadwell Docks there were more stairs again. He could lose his pursuers on any of them.

Gower gestured toward the river. "Steps!" he shouted, bending a moment and gasping to catch his breath. He gestured with a wild swing of his arm. Then he straightened up and began running again, a couple of strides ahead of Pitt.

Pitt could see a ferry coming toward the shore, the boatman pulling easily at the oars. He would get to the steps a moment or two after Wrexham—in fact Pitt and Gower would corner him nicely. Perhaps they could get the ferry to take them up to the Pool of London. He ached to sit down even for that short while.

Wrexham reached the steps and ran down them, disappearing as if he had slipped into a hole. Pitt felt an upsurge of victory. The ferry was still twenty yards from the spot where the steps would meet the water.

Gower let out a yell of triumph, waving his hand high.

They reached the top of the steps just as the ferry pulled away, Wrexham sitting in the stern. They were close enough to see the smile on his face as he half swiveled on the seat to gaze at them. Then he faced forward, speaking to the ferryman and pointing to the farther shore.

Pitt raced down the steps. His feet slithered on the wet stones. He waved his arms at the other ferry, the one they had seen. "Here! Hurry!" he shouted.

Gower shouted also, his voice high and desperate.

The ferryman increased his speed, throwing his full weight behind his oars, and in a matter of seconds had swung around next to the pier.

"Get in, gents," he said cheerfully. "Where to?"

"After that boat there," Gower gasped, choking on his own breath and pointing to the other ferry. "An extra half crown in it for you if you catch up with him before he gets up Horseferry Stairs."

Pitt landed in the boat behind him and immediately sat down so they could get under way. "He's not going to Horseferry," he pointed out. "He's going straight across. Look!"

"Lavender Dock?" Gower scowled, sitting in the seat beside Pitt. "What the hell for?"

"Shortest way across," Pitt replied. "Get up to Rotherhithe Street and away."

"Where to?"

"Nearest train station, probably. Or he might double back. Best place to get lost is among other people."

They were pulling well away from the dock now and slowly catching up with the other ferry.

There were fewer ships moored here, and they could make their way almost straight across. A string of barges was still fifty yards downstream, moving slowly against the tide. The wind off the water was colder. Without thinking what he was doing, Pitt hunched up and pulled his collar higher around his neck. It seemed like hours since he and Gower had burst into the brickyard and seen Wrexham crouched over West's blood-soaked body, but it was probably little more than ninety minutes. Their source of information about whatever plot West had known of was gone with his death.

He thought back to his last interview with Narraway, sitting in the office with the hot sunlight streaming through the window onto the piles of books and papers on the desk. Narraway's face had been intensely serious under its graying mane of hair, his eyes almost black. He had spoken of the gravity of the situation, the rise of the passion to reform Europe's old imperialism, violently if necessary. It was no longer a matter of a few sticks of dynamite, an assassination here and there. Rather, there were whispers of full governments overthrown by force.

"Some things need changing," Narraway had said with a wry bitterness. "No one but a fool would deny that there is injustice. But this would result in anarchy. God alone knows how wide this spreads, at least as far as France, Germany, and Italy, and by the sounds of it here in England as well."

Pitt had stared at him, seeing a sadness in the man he had never before imagined.

"This is a different breed, Pitt, and the tide of victory is with them now. But the violence . . ." Narraway had shaken his head, as if awakening himself. "We don't change that way in Britain, we evolve slowly. We'll get there, but not with murder, and not by force."

The wind was fading, the water smoother.

They were nearly at the south bank of the river. It was time to make a decision. Gower was looking at him, waiting.

Wrexham's ferry was almost at the Lavender Dock.

"He's going somewhere," Gower said urgently. "Do we want to get him now, sir—or see where he leads us? If we take him we won't know who's behind this. He won't talk, he's no reason to. We practically saw him kill West. He'll hang for sure." He waited, frowning.

"Do you think we can keep him in sight?" Pitt asked.

"Yes, sir." Gower did not hesitate.

"Right." The decision was clear in Pitt's mind. "Stay back then. We'll split up if we have to."

The ferry hung back until Wrexham had climbed up the narrow steps and all but disappeared. Then, scrambling to keep up, Pitt and Gower went after him.

They were careful to follow from more of a distance, sometimes together but more often with a sufficient space between them.

Yet Wrexham now seemed to be so absorbed in his own concerns that he never looked behind. He must have assumed he had lost them when he crossed the river. Indeed, they were very lucky that he had not. With the amount of waterborne traffic, he must have failed to realize that one ferry was dogging his path.

At the railway station there were at least a couple of dozen other people at the ticket counter.

"Better get tickets all the way, sir," Gower urged. "We don't want to draw attention to ourselves from not paying the fare."

Pitt gave him a sharp look, but stopped himself from making the remark on the edge of his tongue.

"Sorry," Gower murmured with a slight smile.

Once on the platform they remained close to a knot of other people waiting. Neither of them spoke, as if they were strangers to each other. The precaution seemed unnecessary. Wrexham barely glanced at either of them, nor at anyone else.

The first train was going north. It drew in and stopped. Most of the waiting passengers got on. Pitt wished he had a newspaper to hide his face and appear to take his attention. He should have thought of it before.

"I think I can hear the train . . . ," Gower said almost under his breath. "It should be to Southampton—eventually. We might have to change . . ." The rest of what he said was cut off by the noise of the engine as the train pulled in, belching steam. The doors flew open and passengers poured out.

Pitt struggled to keep Wrexham in sight. He waited until the last moment in case he should get out again and lose them, and, when he didn't, he and Gower boarded a carriage behind him.

"He could be going anywhere," Gower said grimly. His fair face was set in hard lines, his hair poking up where he had run his fingers through it. "One of us better get out at every station to see that he doesn't get off at the last moment."

"Of course," Pitt agreed.

"Do you think West really had something for us?" Gower went on. "He could have been killed for some other reason. A quarrel? Those revolutionaries are pretty volatile. Could have been a betrayal within the group? Even a rivalry for leadership?" He was watching Pitt intently, as if trying to read his mind.

"I know that," Pitt said quietly. He was by far the senior, and it was his decision to make. Gower would never question him on that. It was little comfort now, in fact rather a lonely thought. He remembered Narraway's certainty that there was something planned that would make the recent random bombings seem trivial. In February of last year, 1894, a French anarchist had tried to destroy the Royal Observatory at Greenwich with a bomb. Thank heaven he had failed. In June, President Carnot of France had been assassinated. In August, a man named Caserio had been executed for the crime. Everywhere there was anger and uncertainty in the air.

It was a risk to follow Wrexham, but to seize on an empty certainty was a kind of surrender. "We'll follow him," Pitt replied. "Do you have enough money for another fare, if we have to separate?"

Gower fished in his pocket, counted what he had. "As long as it isn't all the way to Scotland, yes, sir. Please God it isn't Scotland." He smiled with a twisted kind of misery. "You know in February they had the coldest temperature ever recorded in Britain? Nearly fifty degrees of frost! If the poor bastard let off a bomb to start a fire you could hardly blame him!"

"That was February, this is April already," Pitt reminded him. "Here, we're pulling into a station. I'll watch for Wrexham this time. You take the next."

"Yes, sir."

Pitt opened the door and was only just on the ground when he saw Wrexham getting out and hurrying across the platform to change trains for Southampton. Pitt turned to signal Gower and found him already out and at his elbow. Together they followed, trying not to be conspicuous by hurrying. They found seats, but separately for a while, to make sure Wrexham didn't double back and elude them, disappearing into London again.

But Wrexham seemed to be oblivious, as if he no longer even considered the possibility of being followed. He appeared completely carefree, and Pitt had to remind himself that Wrexham had followed a man in the East End only hours ago, then quite deliberately cut his throat and watched him bleed to death on the stones of a deserted brickyard.

"God, he's a cold-blooded bastard!" he said with sudden fury.

A man in pin-striped trousers on the seat opposite put down his newspaper and stared at Pitt with distaste, then rattled his paper loudly and resumed reading.

Gower smiled. "Quite," he said quietly. "We had best be extremely careful."

One or the other of them got out briefly at every stop, just to make certain Wrexham did not leave this train, but he stayed until they finally pulled in at Southampton.

Gower looked at Pitt, puzzled. "What can he do in Southampton?" he said. They hurried along the platform to keep pace with Wrexham, then past the ticket collector and out into the street.

The answer was not long in coming. Wrexham took an omnibus directly toward the docks, and Pitt and Gower had to race to jump onto the step just as it pulled away. Pitt almost bumped into Wrexham, who was still standing. Deliberately he looked away from Gower. They must be more careful. Neither of them was particularly noticeable alone. Gower was fairly tall, lean, his hair long and fair, but his features were a trifle bony, stronger than average. An observant person would remember him. Pitt was taller, perhaps less than graceful, and yet he moved easily, comfortable with himself. His hair was dark and permanently untidy. One front tooth was a little chipped, but visible only when he smiled. It was his steady, very clear gray eyes that people did not forget.

Wrexham would have to be extraordinarily preoccupied not to be aware of seeing them in London, and now again here in Southampton, especially if they were together. Accordingly, Pitt moved on down the inside of the bus to stand well away from Gower, and pretended to be watching the streets as they passed, as if he were taking careful note of his surroundings.

As he had at least half expected, Wrexham went all the way to the dockside. Without speaking to Gower, Pitt followed well behind their quarry. He trusted that Gower was off to the side, as far out of view as possible.

Wrexham bought a ticket on a ferry to St. Malo, across the channel on the coast of France. Pitt bought one as well. He hoped fervently that Gower had sufficient money to get one too, but the only thing worse than ending up alone in France, trying to follow Wrexham without help, would be to lose the man altogether.

He boarded the ferry, a smallish steamship called the *Laura*, and remained within sight of the gangplank. He needed to see if Gower came aboard, but more important to make sure that Wrexham did not get off again. If Wrexham were aware of Pitt and Gower it would be a simple thing to go ashore and hop the next train back to London.

Pitt was leaning on the railing with the sharp salt wind in his face when he heard footsteps behind him. He swung around, then was annoyed with himself for betraying such obvious alarm.

Gower was a yard away, smiling. "Did you think I was going to push you over?" he said amusedly.

Pitt swallowed back his temper. "Not this close to the shore," he replied. "I'll watch you more closely out in mid-channel!"

Gower laughed. "Looks like a good decision, sir. Following him this far could get us a real idea of who his contacts are in Europe. We might even find a clue as to what they're planning."

Pitt doubted it, but it was all they had left now. "Perhaps. But we mustn't be seen together. We're lucky he hasn't recognized us so far. He would have if he weren't so abominably arrogant."

Gower was suddenly very serious, his fair face grim. "I think whatever he has planned is so important his mind is completely absorbed in it. He thought he lost us in Ropemaker's Field. Don't forget we were in a totally separate carriage on the train."

"I know. But he must have seen us when we were chasing him. He ran," Pitt pointed out. "I wish at least one of us had a jacket to change. But in April, at sea, without them we'd be even more conspicuous." He looked at Gower's coat. They were not markedly different in size. Even if they did no more than exchange coats, it would alter both their appearances slightly.

As if reading this thought, Gower began to slip off his coat. He passed it over, and took Pitt's from his outstretched hand.

Pitt put on Gower's jacket. It was a little tight across the chest.

With a rueful smile Gower emptied the pockets of Pitt's jacket, which now sat a little loosely on his shoulders. He passed over the notebook, handkerchief, pencil, loose change, half a dozen other bits and pieces, then the wallet with Pitt's papers of identity and money.

Pitt similarly passed over all Gower's belongings.

Gower gave a little salute. "See you in St. Malo," he said, turning on his heel and walking away without looking back, a slight swagger in his step. Then he stopped and turned half toward Pitt, smiling. "I'd keep away from the railing if I were you, sir."

Pitt raised his hand in a salute, and resumed watching the gangway.

IT WAS JUST PAST the equinox, and darkness still came quite early. They set out to sea as the sun was setting over the headland, and the wind off the water was distinctly chill. There was no point in even wondering where Wrexham was, let alone trying to watch him. If he met with anyone they would not know unless they were so close as to be obvious, and it might look like no more than a mere casual civility between strangers anyway. It would be better to find a chair and get a little sleep. It had been a long day, full of exertion, horror, hectic running through the streets, and then sitting perfectly still in a railway carriage.

As he sat drifting toward sleep, Pitt thought with regret that he had not had even a chance to tell Charlotte that he would not be home that night, or perhaps even the next. He had no idea where his decision would take him. He had only a little money with him—sufficient for one or two nights' lodging now that he had bought a train ticket and a ferry ticket. He had no toothbrush, no razor, certainly no clean clothes. He had imagined he would meet West, learn his information, and then take it straight back to Narraway at his office in Lisson Grove.

Now they would have to send a telegram from St. Malo requesting funds, and saying at least enough for Narraway to understand what had happened. Poor West's body would no doubt be found, but the police might not know of any reason to inform Special Branch of it. No doubt Narraway would find out in time. He seemed to have sources of information everywhere. Would he think to tell Charlotte?

Pitt wished now that he had made some kind of a provision to see she was informed, or even made a telephone call from Southampton. But to do that, he would have had to leave the ship, and perhaps lose Wrexham. He thought with surprise that he did not even know if Gower was married, or living with his parents. Who would be waiting for him to get home? This thought in his mind, Pitt drifted off to sleep.

He awoke with a jolt, sitting upright, his mind filled with the image of West's body, head lolling at an angle, blood streaming onto the stones of the brickyard, the air filled with the smell of it.

"Sorry, sir," the steward said automatically, passing a glass of beer to the man in the seat next to Pitt. "Can I get you something? How about a sandwich?"

Pitt realized with surprise that he had not eaten in twelve hours and was ravenous. No wonder he could not sleep. "Yes," he said eagerly. "Yes, please. In fact, may I have two, and a glass of cider?"

"Yes, sir. How about roast beef, sir. That do you?"

"Please. What time do we get into St. Malo?"

"About five o'clock, sir. But you don't need to go ashore until seven, unless o' course you'd like to."

"Thank you." Inwardly Pitt groaned. They would have to be up and watching from then on, in case Wrexham chose to leave early. That meant they would have to be half awake all night.

"Better bring me two glasses of cider," he said with a wry smile.

Pitt slept on and off, and he was awake and on edge when he saw Gower coming toward him on the deck as the ferry nosed its way slowly toward the harbor of St. Malo. It was not yet dawn but there was a clear sky, and he could see the outline of medieval ramparts against the stars. Fifty or sixty feet high at the least, they looked to be interspersed with great towers such as in the past would have been manned by archers. Perhaps on some of them there would have been men in armor, with cauldrons of boiling oil to tip on those brave enough, or foolish enough, to scale the defenses. It was like a journey backward in time.

He was jerked back to reality by Gower's voice behind him.

"I see you are awake. At least I assume you are?" It was a question.

"Not sure," Pitt replied. "That looks distinctly like a dream to me."

"Did you sleep?" Gower asked.

"A little. You?"

Gower shrugged. "Not much. Too afraid of missing him. Do you suppose he's going to make for the first train to Paris?"

It was a very reasonable question. Paris was a cosmopolitan city, a hotbed of ideas, philosophies, dreams both practical and absurd. It was the ideal meeting place for those who sought to change the world. The two great revolutions of the last hundred years had been born there.

"Probably," Pitt answered. "But he could get off anywhere." He was thinking how hard it would be to follow Wrexham in Paris. Should they arrest him while they still had the chance? In the heat of the chase yesterday it had seemed like a good idea to see where he went and, more important, whom he met. Now, when they were cold, tired, hungry, and stiff, it felt a lot less sensible. In fact it was probably absurd. "We'd better arrest him and take him back," he said aloud.

"Then we'll have to do it before we get off," Gower pointed out. "Once we're on French soil we'll have no authority. Even the captain here is going to wonder why we didn't do it in Southampton." His voice took on a note of urgency, his face grave. "Look, sir, I speak pretty good French. I've still got a reasonable amount of money. We could send a telegram to Narraway to have someone meet us in Paris.

Then we wouldn't be just the two of us. Maybe the French police would be pleased for the chance to follow him?"

Pitt turned toward him, but he could barely make out his features in the faint light of the sky and the dim reflection of the ship's lights. "If he goes straight for the town, we'll have no time to send a telegram," he pointed out. "It'll take both of us to follow him. I don't know why he hasn't noticed us already.

"We should arrest him," he continued with regret. He should have done this yesterday. "Faced with the certainty of the rope, he might feel like talking."

"Faced with the certainty of the rope, he'd have nothing to gain," Gower pointed out.

Pitt smiled grimly. "Narraway'll think of something, if what he says is worth enough."

"He might not go for the train," Gower said quickly, moving his weight to lean forward a little. "We were assuming he'll go to Paris. Perhaps he won't? Maybe whoever he's going to meet is here. Why come to St. Malo otherwise? He could have gone to Dover, and taken the train from Calais to Paris, if that was where he wanted to be. He still doesn't know we're on to him. He thinks he lost us in Rope-maker's Field. Let's at least give it a chance!"

The argument was persuasive, and Pitt could see the sense in it. It might be worth waiting a little longer. "Right," he conceded. "But if he goes to the railway station, we'll take him." He made a slight grimace. "If we can. He might shout for help that he's being kidnapped. We couldn't prove he wasn't."

"Do you want to give up?" Gower asked. His voice was tight with disappointment, and Pitt thought he heard a trace of contempt in it.

"No." There was no uncertainty in the decision. Special Branch was not primarily about justice for crimes; it was about preventing civil violence and the betrayal, subversion, or overthrow of the government. They were too late to save West's life. "No, I don't," he repeated.

WHEN THEY DISEMBARKED IN the broadening daylight it was not difficult to pick Wrexham out from the crowd and follow him. He didn't go, as Pitt had feared, to the train station, but into the magnificently walled old city. They could not risk losing sight of him, or Pitt would have taken time to look with far more interest at the massive ramparts as they went in through an entrance gate vast enough to let several carriages pass abreast. Once inside, narrow streets crisscrossed one another, the doors of the buildings flush with footpaths. Dark walls towered four or five stories high in uniform gray-black stone. The place had a stern beauty Pitt would have liked to explore. Knights on horseback would have ridden these streets, or swaggering corsairs straight from plunder at sea.

But they had to keep close to Wrexham. He was walking quickly as if he knew precisely where he was going, and not once did he look behind him.

It was perhaps fifteen minutes later, when they were farther to the south, that Wrexham stopped. He knocked briefly on a door, and was let into a large house just off a stone-paved square.

Pitt and Gower waited for nearly an hour, moving around, trying not to look conspicuous, but Wrexham did not come out again. Pitt imagined him having a hot breakfast, a wash and shave, clean clothes. He said as much to Gower.

Gower rolled his eyes. "Sometimes it's easier being the villain," he said ruefully. "I could do very well by bacon, eggs, sausages, fried potatoes, then fresh toast and marmalade and a good pot of tea." He grinned. "Sorry. I hate to suffer alone."

"You're not!" Pitt responded with feeling. "We'll do something like that before we go and send a telegram to Narraway, then find out who lives in number seven." He glanced up at the wall. "Rue St. Martin."

"It'll be hot coffee and fresh bread," Gower told him. "Apricot jam if you're lucky. Nobody understands marmalade except the British."

"Don't they understand bacon and eggs?" Pitt asked incredulously.

"Omelet, maybe?"

"It isn't the same!" Pitt said with disappointment.

"Nothing is," Gower agreed. "I think they do it on purpose."

After another ten minutes of waiting, during which Wrexham still did not emerge, they walked back along the way they had come. They found an excellent café from which drifted the tantalizing aroma of fresh coffee and warm bread.

Gower gave him a questioning look.

"Definitely," Pitt agreed.

There was, as Gower had suggested, thick, homemade apricot jam, and unsalted butter. There was also a dish of cold ham and other meats, and hard-boiled eggs. Pitt was more than satisfied by the time they rose to leave. Gower asked the *patron* for directions to the post office. He also inquired, as casually as possible, where they might find lodgings, and if number 7 rue St. Martin was a house of that description, adding that someone had mentioned it.

Pitt waited. He could see from the satisfaction in Gower's face as they left and strode along the pavement that the answer had pleased him.

"Belongs to an Englishman called Frobisher," he said with a smile. "Bit of an odd fellow, according to the *patron*. Lot of money, but eccentric. Fits the locals' idea of what an English upper-class gentleman should be. Lived here for several years and swears he'll never go home. Give him half a chance, and he'll tell anyone what's wrong with Europe in general and England in particular." He gave a slight shrug and his voice was disparaging. "Number seven is definitely not a public lodging house, but he has guests more often than not, and the *patron* does not like the look of them. Subversives, he says. But then I gathered he was pretty conservative in his opinions. He suggested we would find Madame Germaine's establishment far more to our liking, and gave me the address."

In honesty, Pitt could only agree. "We'll send a telegram to Narraway, then see if Madame Germaine can accommodate us. You've done very well."

"Thank you, sir." He increased very slightly the spring in his step and even started to whistle a little tune, rather well.

At the post office Pitt sent a telegram to Narraway.

Staying St. Malo. Friends here we would like to know better.
Need funds. Please send to local post office, soonest. Will
write again.

Until they received a reply, they would be wise to conserve what
money they had left. However, they would find Madame Germaine,
trusting that she had vacancies and would take them in.

"Could be awhile," Gower said thoughtfully. "I hope Narraway
doesn't expect us to sleep under a hedge. Wouldn't mind in August,
but April's a bit sharp."

Pitt did not bother to reply. It was going to be a long, and probably boring, duty. He was thinking of Charlotte at home, and his children Jemima and Daniel. He missed them, but especially Charlotte,
the sound of her voice, her laughter, the way she looked at him. They
had been married for fourteen years, but every so often he was still
overtaken by surprise that she had apparently never regretted it.

It had cost her her comfortable position in Society and the financial security she had been accustomed to, as well as the dinner parties,
the servants, the carriages, the privileges of rank.

She had not said so—it would be heavy-handed—but in return
she had gained a life of interest and purpose. Frequently she had been
informally involved in his cases, in which she had shown considerable skill. She had married not for convenience but for love, and in
dozens of small ways she had left him in no doubt of that.

Dare he send her a telegram as well? In this strange French street
with its different sounds and smells, a language he understood little
of, he ached for the familiar. But the telegram to Narraway was to a
special address. If Wrexham were to ask the post office for it, it would
reveal nothing. If Pitt allowed his loneliness for home to dictate his
actions, he would have to give his home address, which could put his
family in real danger. He should not let this peaceful street in the
April sun, and a good breakfast, erase from his mind the memory of
West lying in the brickyard with his throat slashed open and his blood
oozing out onto the stones.

"Yes, we'll do that," he said aloud to Gower. "Then we will do what we can, discreetly, to learn as much as possible about Mr. Frobisher."

IT WAS NOT DIFFICULT to observe number 7 rue St. Martin. It was near the towering wall of the city, on the seaward side. Only fifty yards away a flight of steps climbed to the walkway around the top. It was a perfect place from which to stand and gaze at the ever-changing horizon out to sea, or watch the boats tacking across the harbor in the wind, their sails billowing, careful to avoid the rocks, which were picturesque and highly dangerous. In turning to talk to each other, it was natural for them to lean for a few minutes on one elbow and gaze down at the street and the square. One could observe anybody coming or going without seeming to.

In the afternoon of the first day, Pitt checked at the post office. There was a telegram from Narraway, and arrangements for sufficient money to last them at least a couple of weeks. There was no reference to West, or the information he might have given, but Pitt did not expect there to have been. He walked back to the square, passing a girl in a pink dress and two women with shopping baskets. Ascending the steps on the wall again, he found Gower leaning against the buttress at the top. His face was raised to the westering sun, which was gold in the late afternoon. He looked like any young Englishman on holiday.

Pitt stared out over the sea, watching the light on the water. "Narraway replied," he said quietly, not looking at Gower. "We'll get the money. The amount he's sending, he expects us to learn all we can."

"Thought he would."

Gower did not turn either, and barely moved his lips. He could have been drifting into sleep, his weight relaxed against the warm stone. "There's been some movement while you were gone. One man left, dark hair, very French clothes. Two went in." His voice became a little higher, more tightly pitched. "I recognized one of them—Pieter Linsky. I'm quite sure. He has a very distinctive face, and a limp from having been shot escaping from an incident in Lille. The man with him was Jacob Meister."

Pitt stiffened. He knew the names. They were both men active in socialist movements in Europe, traveling from one country to another fomenting as much trouble as they could, organizing demonstrations, strikes, even riots in the cause of various reforms. But underneath all the demands was the underlying wish for violent revolution. Linsky in particular was unashamedly a revolutionary. Interesting, though, was that the two men did not hold the same viewpoints, but instead represented opposing sides of the socialist movement.

Pitt let out his breath in a sigh. "I suppose you're sure about Meister as well?"

Gower was motionless, still smiling in the sun, his chest barely rising and falling as he breathed. "Yes, sir, absolutely. I'll bet that has something to do with what West was going to tell us. Those two together has to mean something pretty big."

Pitt did not argue. The more he thought of it the more certain he was that it was indeed the storm Narraway had seen coming, and which was about to break over Europe if they did not prevent it.

"We'll watch them," Pitt said quietly, also trying to appear as if he were relaxed in the sun, enjoying a brief holiday. "See who else they contact."

Gower smiled. "We'll have to be careful. What do you think they're planning?"

Pitt considered in silence, his eyes almost closed as he stared down at the painted wooden door of number 7. All kinds of ideas teemed through his head. A single assassination seemed less likely than a general strike, or even a series of bombings; otherwise they would not need so many men. In the past assassinations had been accomplished by a lone gunman, willing to sacrifice his own life. But now . . . who was vulnerable? Whose death would really change anything permanently?

"Strikes?" Gower suggested, interrupting his thought. "Europewide, it could bring an industry to its knees."

"Possibly," Pitt agreed. His mind veered to the big industrial and shipbuilding cities of the north. Or the coal miners of Durham, Yorkshire, or Wales. There had been strikes before, but they were always broken and the men and their families suffered.

"Demonstrations?" Gower went on. "Thousands of people all out at once, in the right places, could block transport or stop some major event, like the Derby?"

Pitt imagined it, the anger, the frustration of the horse-racing and fashionable crowd at such an impertinence. He found himself smiling, but it was with a sour amusement. He had never been part of the Society that watched the Sport of Kings, but he had met many members during his police career. He knew their passion, their weaknesses, their blindness to others, and at times their extraordinary courage. Forcible interruption of one of the great events of the year was not the way to persuade them of anything. Surely any serious revolutionary had long ago learned that.

But what was?

"Meister's style, maybe," Pitt said aloud. "But not Linsky's. Something far more violent. And more effective."

Gower shivered very slightly. "I wish you hadn't said that. It rather takes the edge off the idea of a week or two in the sun, eating French food and watching the ladies going about their shopping. Have you seen the girl from number sixteen, with the red hair?"

"To tell you the truth, it wasn't her hair I noticed," Pitt admitted, grinning broadly.

Gower laughed outright. "Nor I," he said. "I rather like that apricot jam, don't you? And the coffee! Thought I'd miss a decent cup of tea, but I haven't yet." He was silent again for a few minutes, then turned his head. "What do you really think they have planned in England, sir—beyond a show of power? What do they want in the long run?"

The *sir* reminded Pitt of his seniority, and therefore responsibility. It gave him a sharp jolt. There were scores of possibilities, a few of them serious. There had been a considerable rise in political power of left-wing movements in Britain recently. They were very tame compared with the violence of their European counterparts, but that did not mean they would remain that way.

Gower was still staring at Pitt, waiting, his face puzzled and keen.

"I think a concerted effort to bring about change would be more likely," Pitt said slowly, weighing the words as he spoke.

"Change?" Gower said quizzically. "Is that a euphemism for over-throwing the government?"

"Yes, perhaps it is," Pitt agreed, realizing how afraid he was as he said it. "An end to hereditary privilege, and the power that goes with it."

"Dynamiters?" Gower's voice was a whisper, the amusement completely vanished. "Another blowing up, like the gunpowder plot of the early 1600s?"

"I can't see that working," Pitt replied. "It would rally everyone against them. We don't like to be pushed. They'll need to be a lot cleverer than that."

Gower swallowed hard. "What, then?" he said quietly.

"Something to destroy that power permanently. A change so fundamental it can't be undone." As he said the words they frightened him. Something violent and alien waited ahead of them. Perhaps they were the only ones who could prevent it.

Gower let out his breath in a sigh. He looked pale. Pitt watched his face, obliquely, as if he were still more absorbed in enjoying the sun, thinking of swiveling around to watch the sailing boats in the harbor again. They would have to rely on each other totally. It was going to be a long, tedious job. They dare not miss anything. The slightest clue could matter. They would be cold at night, often hungry or uncomfortable. Always tired. Above all they must not look suspicious. He was glad he liked Gower's humor, his lightness of touch. There were many men in Special Branch he would have found it much harder to be with.

"That's Linsky now, coming out of the door!" Gower stiffened, and then deliberately forced his body to relax, as if this sharp-nosed man with the sloping forehead and stringy hair were of no more interest than the baker, the postman, or another tourist.

Pitt straightened up, put his hands in his pockets quite casually, and went down the steps to the square after him.

CHAPTER

2

On the late afternoon of the day that Pitt and Gower had followed Wrexham to Southampton, Victor Narraway was sitting in his office at Lisson Grove. There was a knock on his door, and as soon as he answered one of his more junior men, Stoker, came in.

"Yes?" Narraway said with a touch of impatience. He was waiting for Pitt to report on the information from West, and the man was late. Narraway had no wish to speak to Stoker now.

Stoker closed the door behind him and came to stand in front of Narraway's desk. His lean face was unusually serious. "Sir, there was a murder in a brickyard off Cable Road in Shadwell in the middle of the day—"

"Are you sure I care about this, Stoker?" Narraway interrupted.

"Yes, sir," Stoker said without hesitation. "The victim had his throat cut, and the man who did it was caught almost in the act, knife still in his hand. He was chased by two men who seem to have followed him to Limehouse, according to the investigation by the local police. Then—"

Narraway interrupted him again impatiently. "Stoker, I'm waiting for information about a major attack of some sort by socialist revolutionaries, possibly another spate of dynamitings." Then suddenly he was chilled to the bone. "Stoker . . ."

"West, sir," Stoker said immediately. "The man with his throat cut was West. It looks as if Pitt and Gower went after the man who did it, at least as far as Limehouse, probably across the river to the railway station. From there they could have gone anywhere in the country. There's been no word. No telephone call."

Narraway felt the sweat break out on his body. It was almost a relief to hear something. But where the hell was Pitt now? Why had he not at least placed a telephone call? The train could have gone anywhere. Even on an all-night train to Scotland he could have gotten off at one of the stations and called.

Then another thought occurred to him: Dover—or any of the other seaports. Folkestone, Southampton. If he were on a ship, then calls would be impossible. That would explain the silence.

"I see. Thank you," he said aloud.

"Sir."

"Say nothing to anyone, for the time being."

"Yes, sir."

"Thank you. That's all."

After Stoker had gone Narraway sat still for several minutes. To have lost West, with whatever information he had, was serious. There had been increased activity lately, known troublemakers coming and going more often than usual, a charge of expectancy in the air. He knew all the signs; he just did not know what the target was this time. There were so many possibilities. Specific assassination, such as a government minister, an industrialist, a foreign dignitary on British soil—that would be a serious embarrassment. Or the dynamiting of a major landmark. He had relied on Pitt to find out. Perhaps he still might, but without West it would be more difficult.

And of course it was not the only issue at hand. There were always whispers, threats, the air breathing of suspicion and betrayal. It was the purpose of Special Branch to detect such things before they happened, and prevent at least the worst.

But if Pitt had gone to Scotland after the murderer of West, or worse still, across the channel, and had had no time to tell Narraway, then certainly he would not have had time to tell his wife either. Charlotte would be at home in Keppel Street waiting for him, expecting him, and growing more and more afraid with each passing hour as the silence closed in on her.

Narraway glanced at the longcase clock standing against the wall of his office. Its ornate hands pointed at quarter to seven. On a usual day Pitt would be home by now.

He thought of her in the kitchen, preparing the evening meal, probably alone. Her children would be occupied with studies for the following day's school. He could picture her easily; in fact the picture was already there in his mind, unbidden.

Some would not have found Charlotte beautiful. They might have preferred a face more traditional, daintier, less challenging. Narraway found such faces boring. There was a warmth in Charlotte, a laughter he could never quite forget—and he had tried. She was quick to anger at times, far too quick to react. Many of her judgments were flawed, in his opinion, but never her courage, never her will.

Someone must tell her that Pitt had gone in hot pursuit of West's murderer—no, better leave out the fact that West had been murdered. Pitt had gone in hot pursuit of a man with vital information, possibly across the channel, and had been unable to telephone her to let her know. He could call Stoker back and send him, but she did not know him. She did not know anyone else at Lisson Grove Headquarters. It would be the courteous thing to tell her himself. It would not be far out of his way. Well, yes it would, but it would still be the better thing to do.

Pitt, for all his initial ignorance of Special Branch ways, and his occasional political naïveté, was one of the best men Narraway had ever known. A gamekeeper's son, he had been educated in the household of the manor, which had produced a man who was by nature a gentleman, and yet possessing an anger and a compassion Narraway admired. He found himself puzzlingly protective of Pitt. Now he must tell Charlotte that her husband had disappeared, probably to France.

He tidied his desk, locked away anything that might be confidential, left his office, and caught a hansom within minutes. He gave him Pitt's address on Keppel Street.

Narraway saw the fear in Charlotte's eyes as soon as she opened the door to him. He would never have called merely socially, and she knew that. The strength of her emotion gave him a startling twinge of envy. It was a long time since there had been anyone who would have felt that terror for him.

"I'm sorry to disturb you," he said with rather stiff formality. "Events did not go according to plan today, and Pitt and his assistant were obliged to pursue a suspected conspirator without the opportunity to inform anyone of what was happening."

Warmth returned to her face, flushing the soft honey color of her skin. "Where is he?" she asked.

He decided to sound more certain than he was. West's murderer might have fled to Scotland, but France was far more likely. "France," he replied. "Of course he could not telephone from the ferry, and he would not have dared leave in case the man got off as well, and he lost him. I'm sorry."

She smiled. "It was very thoughtful of you to come tell me. I admit, I was beginning to be concerned."

The April evening was cold, a sharp wind carrying the smell of rain. He was standing on the doorstep staring at the light beyond. He stepped back, deliberately, his thoughts, the temptation, the quickening of his heart frightening him.

"There is no need," he said hastily. "Gower is with him; an excellent man, intelligent and quite fluent in French. And I daresay it will be warmer there than it is here." He smiled. "And the food is excellent." She had been preparing dinner. That was clumsy. Thank goodness he was far enough into the darkness that she could not see the blush rise up his face. "I will let you know as soon as I hear from him. If this man they are following goes to Paris, it may not be easy for them to be in contact, but please don't fear for him."

"Thank you. I won't now."

He knew that was a polite lie. Of course she would fear for Pitt, and miss him. Loving always included the possibility of loss. But the emptiness of not loving was even greater.

He nodded very slightly, just an inclination of his head, then wished her good night. He walked away, feeling as if he were leaving the light behind him.

IT WAS THE MIDDLE of the following morning when Narraway received the telegram from Pitt in St. Malo. He immediately forwarded him sufficient money to last both men for at least two weeks. He thought about it as soon as it had been sent, and knew he had been overgenerous. Perhaps that was an indication of the relief he felt to know Pitt was safe. He would have to go back to Keppel Street to tell Charlotte that Pitt had been in touch.

He had returned to his desk after lunch when Charles Austwick came in and closed the door behind him. He was officially Narraway's next in command, although in practical terms it had come to be Pitt. Austwick was in his late forties with fair hair that was receding a little, and a good-looking but curiously unremarkable face. He was intelligent and efficient, and he seemed to be always in control of whatever feelings he might have. Now he looked very directly at Narraway, deliberately so, as if he was uncomfortable and attempting not to show it.

"An ugly situation has arisen, sir," he said, sitting down before he was invited to. "I'm sorry, but I have no choice but to address it."

"Then do so!" Narraway said a little hastily. "Don't creep around it like a maiden aunt at a wedding. What is it?"

Austwick's face tightened, his lips making a thin line.

"This has to do with informers," Austwick said coldly. "Do you remember Mulhare?"

Narraway recognized the name with a rush of sadness. Mulhare had been an Irishman who risked his life to give information to the English. It was dangerous enough that he would have to leave Ireland, taking his family with him. Narraway had made sure there were funds provided for him.

"Of course I do," he said quietly. "Have they found who killed him? Not that it'll do much good now." He knew his voice sounded bitter. He had liked Mulhare, and had promised him that he'd be safe.

"That is something of a difficult question," Austwick replied. "He never got the money, so he couldn't leave Ireland."

"Yes, he did," Narraway contradicted him. "I dealt with it myself."

"That's rather the point," Austwick said. He moved position slightly, scuffing the chair leg on the carpet.

Narraway resented being reminded of his failure. It was a loss that would continue to hurt. "If you don't know who killed him, why are you spending time on that now, instead of current things?" he asked abruptly. "If you have nothing to do, I can certainly find you something. Pitt and Gower are away for a while. Somebody'll have to pick up Pitt's case on the docks."

"Oh really?" Austwick barely masked his surprise. "I didn't know. No one mentioned it!"

Narraway gave him a chill look and ignored the implied rebuke.

Austwick drew in his breath. "As I said," he resumed, "this is something I regret we have to deal with. Mulhare was betrayed—"

"We know that, for God's sake!" Narraway could hear his own voice thick with emotion. "His corpse was fished out of Dublin Bay."

"He never got the money," Austwick said again.

Narraway clenched his hands under the desk, out of Austwick's sight. "I paid it myself."

"But Mulhare never received it," Austwick replied. "We traced it."

Narraway was startled.

"To whom? Where is it?"

"I have no idea where it is now," Austwick answered. "But it was in one of your bank accounts here in London."

Narraway froze. Suddenly, with appalling clarity, he knew what Austwick was doing here, and held at least a hazy idea of what had happened. Austwick suspected, or even believed, that Narraway had taken the money and intentionally left Mulhare to be caught and killed. Was that how little he knew him? Or was it more a measure of his long-simmering resentment, his ambition to take Narraway's place and wield the razor-edged power that he now held?

"And out again," he said aloud to Austwick. "We had to move it around a little, or it would have been too easily traceable to Special Branch."

"Oh yes," Austwick agreed bleakly. "Around to several places. But the trouble is that in the end it went back again."

"Back again? It went to Mulhare," Narraway corrected him.

"No, sir, it did not go to Mulhare. It went back into one of your special accounts. One that we had believed closed," Austwick said. "It is there now. If Mulhare had received it, he would have left Dublin, and he would still be alive. The money went around to several places, making it almost untraceable, as you said, but it ended up right back where it started, with you."

Narraway drew in his breath to deny it, and saw in Austwick's face that it would be pointless. Whoever had put it there, Austwick believed it was Narraway himself, or he chose to pretend he believed it.

"I did not put it there," Narraway said, not because he thought it would change anything, but because he would not admit to something of which he was not guilty. The betrayal of Mulhare was repugnant to him, and betrayal was not a word he used easily. "I paid it to Terence Kelly. He was supposed to have paid it to Mulhare. That was his job. For obvious reasons, I could not give it directly to Mulhare, or I might as well have painted a bull's-eye on his heart."

"Can you prove that, sir?" Austwick asked politely.

"Of course I can't!" Narraway snapped. Was Austwick being deliberately obtuse? He knew as well as Narraway himself that one did not leave trails to prove such things. What he would be able to prove now, to justify himself, anyone else could have used to damn Mulhare.

"You see it calls into question the whole subject of your judgment," Austwick said half apologetically, his bland face grave. "It would be highly advisable, sir, for you to find some proof of this, then the matter could be let go."

Narraway's mind raced. He knew what was in his bank accounts, both personal and for Special Branch use. Austwick had mentioned one that had been presumed closed. No money had passed through it for some time, but Narraway had deliberately left a few pounds in it, in case he ever wished to use it again. It was a convenience.

"I'll check the account," he said aloud, his voice cold.

"That would be a good idea, sir," Austwick agreed. "Perhaps you will be able to find some proof as to why it came back to you, and a reason poor Mulhare never received it."

Narraway realized that this was not an invitation, but rather a warning. It was even possible that his position at Special Branch was in jeopardy. Certainly he had created enemies over the years, both in his rise to leadership and even more so in the time since then. There were always hard decisions to make; whatever you did could not please everyone.

He had employed Pitt as a favor, when Pitt had challenged his own superiors and been thrown out of the Metropolitan Police. And initially he had found Pitt unsatisfactory, lacking the training or the inclination for Special Branch work. But the man had learned quickly, and he was a remarkably good detective: persistent, imaginative, and with a moral courage Narraway admired. And he liked the man, despite his own resolution not to allow personal feelings into anything professional.

He had protected Pitt from the envy and the criticism of others in the branch. That was partly because Pitt was more than worthy of the place, but also to defend Narraway's own judgment. Yet—he admitted it now—it was also for Charlotte's sake. Without Pitt, he would have no excuse to see her again.

"I'll attend to it," he answered Austwick at last. "As soon as I have a few more answers on this present problem. One of our informants was murdered, which has made things more difficult."

Austwick rose to his feet. "Yes, sir. That would be a good idea. I think the sooner you put people's minds at rest on the issue, the better it will be. I suggest before the end of this week."

"When circumstances allow," Narraway replied coolly.

CIRCUMSTANCES DID NOT ALLOW. Early the following morning Narraway was sent for to report to the Home Office, directly to Sir

Gerald Croxdale, his political superior, the one man to whom he was obliged to answer without reservation.

Croxdale was in his early fifties, a quiet, persistent politician who had risen in the ranks of the government with remarkable swiftness, not having made great speeches or introduced new laws, nor apparently having used the benefit of patronage from any of the more noted ministers. Croxdale seemed to be his own man. Whatever debts he collected or favors he owed were too discreet for even Narraway to know of, let alone the general public. He had made no individual initiatives that were remarkable but—probably far more important—he had also made no visible mistakes. Insiders spoke his name with respect.

Narraway had never seen in him the passion that marked an ambitious man, but he noted the quick rise to greater power and it earned in him a deeper, if reluctant, respect.

"Morning, Narraway," Croxdale said with an easy smile as he waved him to a brown leather armchair in his large office. Croxdale was a big man, tall and solid. His face was far from handsome in any traditional sense, but he was imposing. His voice was soft, his smile benign. Today he was wearing his usual well-cut but unostentatious suit, and perfectly polished black leather boots.

Narraway returned the greeting and sat down, not comfortably, but a little forward, listening.

"Bad business about your informant West being killed," Croxdale began. "I presume he was going to tell you a great deal more about whatever it is building up among the militant socialists."

"Yes, sir," Narraway said bleakly. "Pitt and Gower were only seconds too late. They saw West, but he was already terrified of something and took to his heels. They caught up with him in a brickyard in Shadwell, only moments after he was killed. The murderer was still bending over him." He could feel the heat of the blood in his cheeks as he said it. It was partly anger at having been so close, and yet infinitely far from preventing the death. One minute sooner and West would have been alive, and all his information would be theirs. It was also a sense of failure, as if losing him were an incompetence on the part of his men, and so of himself. Deliberately he met Croxdale's eyes, refusing to look away. He never made excuses, explicit or implicit.

Croxdale smiled, leaning back and crossing his long legs. "Unfortunate, but luck cannot always be on our side. It is the measure of your men that they kept track of the assassin. What is the news now?"

"I've had a couple of telegrams from Pitt in St. Malo," Narraway answered. "Wrexham, the killer, seems to have more or less gone to ground in the house of a British expatriate there. The interesting thing is that they have seen other socialist activists of note."

"Who?" Croxdale asked.

"Pieter Linsky and Jacob Meister," Narraway replied.

Croxdale stiffened, straightening up a little, his face keen with interest. "Really? Then perhaps not all is lost." He lowered his voice. "Tell me, Narraway, do you still believe there is some major action planned?"

"Yes," Narraway said without hesitation. "I think West's murder removes any doubt. He would have told us what it was, and probably who else was involved."

"Damn! Well you must keep Pitt there, and the other chap, what's his name?"

"Gower."

"Yes, Gower too. Give them all the funds they need. I'll see to it that that meets no opposition."

"Of course," Narraway said with some surprise. He had always had complete authority to disburse the funds in his care as he saw fit.

Croxdale pursed his lips and leaned farther forward. "It is not quite so simple, Narraway," he said gravely. "We have been looking into the matter of past funds and their use, in connection with other cases, as I daresay you know." He interlaced his fingers and looked down at them a moment, then up again quickly. "Mulhare's death has raised some ugly questions, which I'm afraid have to be answered."

Narraway was stunned. He had not realized the matter had already gone as far as Croxdale, and before he had even had a chance to look into it more deeply, and prove his own innocence. Was that Austwick's doing again? Damn the man.

"It will be," he said now to Croxdale. "I kept certain movements of the funds secret, to protect Mulhare. They'd have killed him instantly if they'd known he received English money."

"Isn't that rather what happened?" Croxdale asked ruefully.

Narraway thought for a moment of denying it. They knew who had killed Mulhare, but it was only proof they lacked; the deduction was certain in his own mind. But he did not need another moral evasion. His life was too full of shadows. He would not allow Croxdale to provoke him into another. "Yes."

"We failed him, Narraway," Croxdale said sadly.

"Yes."

"How did that happen?" Croxdale pressed.

"He was betrayed."

"By whom?"

"I don't know. When this socialist threat is dealt with, I shall find out, if I can."

"If you can," Croxdale said gently. "Do you doubt it? You have no idea who it was here in London?"

"No, I haven't."

"But you used the word *betrayed*," Croxdale persisted. "I think advisedly so. Does that not concern you urgently, Narraway? Whom can you trust, in any Irish issue?—of which, God knows, there are more than enough."

"The European socialist revolutionaries are our most urgent concern now, sir." Narraway also leaned forward. "There is a high degree of violence threatened. Men like Linsky, Meister, la Pointe, Corazath, are all quick to use guns and dynamite. Their philosophy is that a few deaths are the price they have to pay for the greater freedom and equality of the people. As long, of course, as the deaths are not their own," he added drily.

"Does that take precedence over treachery among your own people?" He left it hanging in the air between them, a question that demanded answering.

Narraway had seen the death of Mulhare as tragic, but less urgent than the threat of the broader socialist plot that loomed. He knew how he had guarded the provenance of the money, and did not know how someone had made the funds appear to return to Narraway's own personal account. Above all he did not know who was responsible, or whether it was done through incompetence—or deliberately in order to make him look a thief.

"I'm not yet certain it was betrayal, sir. Perhaps I used the word hastily." He kept his voice as level as he could; still, there was a certain roughness to it. He hoped Croxdale's less sensitive ear did not catch it.

Croxdale was staring at him. "As opposed to what?"

"Incompetence," Narraway replied. "And this time we covered the tracks of the transfers very carefully, so no one in Ireland would be able to trace it back to us. We made it seem like legitimate purchases all the way."

"Or at least you thought so," Croxdale amended. "But Mulhare was still killed. Where is the money now?"

Narraway had hoped to avoid telling him, but perhaps it had always been inevitable that Croxdale would have to know. Maybe he did, and this was a trap. "Austwick told me it was back in an account I had ceased using," he replied. "I don't know who moved it, but I shall find out."

Croxdale was silent for several moments. "Yes, please do, and with indisputable proof, of course. Quickly, Narraway. We need your skills on this wretched socialist business. It seems the threat is real."

"I'll look into the money as soon as we have learned what West's killers are planning," Narraway answered. "With a little luck, we'll even catch some of them and be able to put them away."

Croxdale looked up, his eyes bright and sharp. Suddenly he was no longer an amiable, rather bearlike man but tigerish, the passion in him like a coiled spring, masked only by superficial ease. "Do you imagine that a few martyrs to the cause will stop anything, Narraway? If so, I'm disappointed in you. Idealists thrive on sacrifice, the more public and the more dramatic the better."

"I know that." Narraway was stung by the misjudgment. "I have no intention of giving them martyrs. Indeed, I have no intention of denying them social reform and a good deal of change, but in pace with the will of the majority of the people in the country, not ahead of it, and not forced on them by a few fanatics. We've always changed, but slowly. Look at the history of the revolutions of 1848. We were about the only major country in Europe that didn't have an uprising. And by 1850, where were all the idealists from the barricades? Where were all the new freedoms so bloodily won? Every damn one of them gone, and all the old regimes back in power."

Croxdale was looking at him intensely, his expression unreadable.

"We had no uprising," Narraway went on, his voice dropped a level but the heat still there. "No deaths, no grand speeches, just quiet progress, a step at a time. Boring, perhaps unheroic, but also blood-less—and more to the point, sustainable. We aren't back under the old tyrannies. As governments go, ours is not bad."

"Thank you," Croxdale said drily.

Narraway gave one of his rare, beautiful smiles. "My pleasure, sir."

Croxdale sighed. "I wish it were so simple. I'm sorry, Narraway, but you will solve this miserable business of the money that should have gone to Mulhare immediately. Austwick will take over the so-cialist affair until you have it dealt with, which includes inarguable proof that someone else placed it in your account, and you were un-aware of it until Austwick told you. It will also include the name of whoever is responsible for this, because they have jeopardized the ef-fectiveness of one of the best heads of Special Branch that we have had in the last quarter century, and that is treason against the country, and against the queen."

For a moment Narraway did not grasp what Croxdale was saying. He sat motionless in the chair, his hands cold, gripping the arms as if to keep his balance. He drew in his breath to protest but saw in Croxdale's face that it would be pointless. The decision was made, and final.

"I'm sorry, Narraway," Croxdale said quietly. "You no longer have the confidence of Her Majesty's government, or of Her Majesty her-self. I have no alternative but to remove you from office until such time as you can prove your innocence. I appreciate that that will be more difficult for you without access to your office or the papers in it, but you will appreciate the delicacy of my position. If you have access to the papers, you also have the power to alter them, destroy them, or add to them."

Narraway was stunned. It was as if he had been dealt a physical blow. Suddenly he could barely breathe. It was preposterous. He was head of Special Branch, and here was this government minister telling him he was dismissed, with no warning, no preparation: just his decision, a word and it was all over.

"I'm sorry," Croxdale repeated. "This is a somewhat unfortunate way of having to deal with it, but it can't be helped. You will not go back to Lisson Grove, of course."

"What?"

"You cannot go back to your office," Croxdale said patiently. "Don't oblige me to make an issue of it."

Narraway rose to his feet, horrified to find that he was a trifle unsteady, as if he had been drinking. He wanted to think of something dignified to say, and above all to make absolutely certain that his voice was level, completely without emotion. He drew in his breath and let it out slowly.

"I will find out who betrayed Mulhare," he said a little hoarsely. "And also who betrayed me." He thought of adding something about keeping this as a Special Branch fit to come back to, but it sounded so petty he let it go. "Good day."

Outside in the street everything looked just as it had when he went in: a hansom cab drawn up at the curb, half a dozen men here and there dressed in striped trousers.

He started to walk without a clear idea of where he intended to go. His lack of direction was immediate, but he thought with a sense of utter emptiness that perhaps it was eternal as well. He was fifty-eight. Half an hour ago he had been one of the most powerful men in Britain. He was trusted absolutely; he held other men's lives in his hands, he knew the nation's secrets; the safety of ordinary men and women depended on his skill, his judgment.

Now he was a man without a purpose, without an income—although that was not an immediate concern. The land inherited from his father supported him, not perhaps in luxury, but at least adequately. He had no family alive now, and he realized with a gathering sense of isolation that he had acquaintances, but no close friends. His profession had made it impossible during the years of his increasing power. Too many secrets, too much need for caution.

It would be pathetic and pointless to indulge in self-pity. If he sank to that, what better would he deserve? He must fight back. Someone had done this to him. The only person he would have trusted to help was Pitt, and Pitt was in France.

He was walking quickly up Whitehall, looking neither right nor left, probably passing people he knew and ignoring them. No one would care. In time to come, when it was known he was no longer in power, they would probably be relieved. He was not a comfortable man to be with. Even the most innocent tended to attribute ulterior motive to him, imagining secrets that did not exist.

Whitehall became Parliament Street, then he turned left and continued walking until he was on Westminster Bridge, staring eastward across the wind-ruffled water.

He could not even return to his office. He could not properly investigate who had betrayed Mulhare. Then another thought occurred to him, which was far uglier. Was Mulhare the one who was incidental damage, and Narraway himself the target of the treachery?

As that thought took sharper focus in his mind he wondered bitterly if he really wanted to know the answer. Who was it that he had trusted, and been so horribly mistaken about?

He turned and walked on over the bridge to the far side, and then hailed a hansom, giving the driver his home address.

When he reached his house he poured himself a quick shot of single-malt whiskey, his favorite Macallan. Then went to the safe and took out the few papers he had kept there referring to the Mulhare case. He read them from beginning to end and learned nothing he did not already know, except that the money for Mulhare had been returned to the account within two weeks. He had not known because he had assumed the account closed. There was no notification from the bank.

It was close to midnight and he was still sitting staring at the far wall without seeing it when there came a sharp double tap on the window of the French doors opening onto the garden. It startled him out of his reverie, and he froze for an instant then got to his feet.

The tap came again, and he looked at the shadow outside. He could just see the features of a man's face beyond, unmoving, as if he wished to be recognized. Narraway thought for a moment of Pitt, but he knew it was not him. He was in France, and this man was not as tall.

It was Stoker. He should have known that straightaway. It was ridiculous to be standing here in the shadows as if he were afraid. He went forward, unlocked the French doors, and opened them wide.

Stoker came in, holding a bundle of papers in a large envelope, half hidden under his jacket. His hair was damp from the slight drizzle outside, as if he had walked some distance. Narraway hoped he had, and taken more than one cab, to make following or tracing him difficult.

"What are you doing here, Stoker?" he said quietly, for the first time this evening drawing the curtains closed. It had not mattered before, and he liked the presence of the garden at twilight, the birds, the fading of the sky, the occasional movement of leaves.

"Brought some papers that might be useful, sir," Stoker replied. His voice and his eyes were perfectly steady, but the tension in his body, in the way he held his hands, betrayed to Narraway that he knew perfectly well the risk he was taking.

Narraway took the envelope from him, pulled out the papers, and glanced down at them, riffling through the pages swiftly to see what they were. Then he felt the breath tighten in his chest. They referred to an old case in Ireland, twenty years ago. The memory of it was powerful, for many reasons, and he was surprised how very sharply it returned.

It was as if he had last seen the people only a few days ago. He could remember the smell of the peat fire in the room where he and Kate had talked long into the night about the planned uprising. He could almost bring back the words he had used to persuade her it could only fail, and bring more death and more bitterness with it.

Even with his eyes open in his mind he could see Cormac O'Neil's fury, and then his grief. He understood it. But for all its vividness, it had been twenty years ago.

He looked up at Stoker. "Why these?" he asked. "This case is old, it's finished."

"The Irish troubles are never finished," Stoker said simply.

"Our more urgent problem is here now," Narraway replied. "And possibly in Europe."

"Socialists?" Stoker said drily. "They're always grumbling on."

"It's a lot more than that," Narraway told him. "They're fanatic. It's the new religion, with all the fire and evangelism of a holy cause. And just like Christianity in its infancy, it has its apostles and its dogma—and its splinter groups, quarrels over what is the true faith."

Stoker looked puzzled, as if this were all true but irrelevant.

"The point," Narraway said sharply, "is that they each consider the others to be heretics. They fight one another as much as they fight anyone else."

"Thank God," Stoker said with feeling.

"So when we see disciples of different factions meeting in secret, working together, then we know it is something damn big that has patched the rifts, temporarily." Narraway heard the edge in his own voice, and saw the sudden understanding in Stoker's eyes.

Stoker let out his breath slowly.

"How close are we to knowing what they're planning, sir?"

"I don't know," Narraway admitted. "It all rests on Pitt now."

"And you," Stoker said softly. "We've got to sort this money thing out, sir, and get you back."

Narraway drew in his breath to answer, and felt a sudden wave of conviction, a helplessness, a loss, an awareness of fear so profound that no words were adequate.

Stoker held out the papers he had brought. "We can't afford to wait," he said urgently. "I looked through everything I could that had to do with informants, money, and Ireland, trying to work out who's behind this. This case seemed the most likely. Also, I'm pretty sure someone else has had these papers out recently."

"Why?"

"Just the way they were put back," Stoker answered.

"Untidy?"

"No, the opposite. Very neat indeed."

Now Narraway was afraid for Stoker. He would lose his job for this; indeed, if he were caught, he could even be charged with treason himself. Regardless, he wanted to read the pages, but not with Stoker present. If this were the act of personal loyalty it seemed, or even loyalty to the truth, he did not want Stoker to take such a risk. It would be better for both of them not to be caught.

"Where did you get them?" he asked.

Stoker looked at him with a very slight smile. "Better you don't know, sir."

Narraway smiled back. "Then I can't tell," he agreed wryly.

Stoker nodded. "That too, sir."

There was something about Stoker calling him *sir* that was stupidly pleasing, as if he were still who he had been this morning. Did he value such respect so much? How pathetic!

He swallowed hard and drew in his breath. "Leave them with me. Go home, where everyone expects you to be. Come back for them when it's safe."

"Sorry, sir, but they have to be back by dawn," Stoker replied. "In fact, the sooner the better."

"It will take me all night to read these and make my own notes," Narraway argued, knowing even as he said it that Stoker was right. To have them absent from Lisson Grove, even for one day, was too dangerous. Then they could never be returned. Anyone with two wits to rub together would look to Narraway for them, and then to whoever had brought them to him. He had no right to jeopardize Stoker's life with such stupidity.

"All right," he said, "I'll have them read before dawn. Three o'clock. You can return then and I'll give them to you. You can be at the Grove before light, and away again. Or you can go and sleep in my spare room, if you prefer. It would be wiser. No chance then of being caught in the street."

Stoker did not move.

"I'll stay here, sir. I'm pretty good at not being seen, but no risk at all is better. Wouldn't do if I couldn't get back."

Narraway nodded. "Up the stairs, across the landing to the left," he said aloud. "Help yourself to anything you need."

Stoker thanked him and left, closing the door softly.

Narraway turned up the gas a little more brightly, then sat down in the big armchair by the fireplace and began to read.

The first few pages were about the Mulhare case: the fact that a large sum of money had been promised to Mulhare if he cooperated. It was paid not as reward so much as a means for him to leave Ireland and go—not as might be expected, to America, but to Southern France, a less likely place for his enemies to seek him.

As Narraway was painfully aware, Mulhare had not received the money. Instead he had remained in Ireland and been killed. Narraway still did not know exactly what had gone wrong. He had arranged the money, passed it through one of his own accounts. It had been kept in a different name so that it could not be traced back to him, and thus to Special Branch.

But now, inexplicably, it had reappeared.

The papers Stoker had brought referred to a twenty-year-old case that Narraway would like to have forgotten. It was at a time when the passion and the violence were even higher than usual.

Charles Stewart Parnell had just been elected to Parliament. He was a man of fire and eloquence, a highly active member in the council of the Irish Home Rule League, and everything in his life was dedicated to that cause. Indeed, if he'd had his way, Ireland might at last throw off the yoke of domination and govern itself again. The horrors of the great potato famine could be put behind them. Freedom beckoned.

Of course 1875 was before Narraway had become head of Special Branch. He was simply an agent in the field at that time, in his midthirties; wiry, strong, quick thinking, and with considerable charm. With his black hair and eyes, and his dry wit, he could easily have passed for an Irishman himself. When that assumption was made, as it often was, he did not deny it.

One of the leaders of the Irish cause then had been a man called Cormac O'Neil. He had a dark, brooding nature, like an autumn landscape, full of sudden shadows, storms on the horizon. He loved history, especially that handed down by word of mouth or immortalized in old songs. He was a man built to yearn for what he could not have.

Narraway thought of that wryly, remembering still with regret and guilt Cormac's brother Sean, and more vividly Kate. Beautiful

Kate, so fiercely alive, so brave, so quick to see reason, so blind to the wounded and dangerous emotions of others.

In the silence of this comfortable London room with its very English mementos, Ireland seemed like the other side of the world. Kate was dead; so was Sean. Narraway had won, and their planned uprising had failed without bloodshed on either side.

Even Charles Stewart Parnell was dead now, just three and a half years ago, October 1891, of a heart attack.

And Home Rule for Ireland was still only a dream, and the anger remained.

Narraway shivered here in his warm, familiar sitting room with the last of the embers still glowing, the pictures of trees on the wall, and the gas lamp shedding a golden light around him. The chill was inside, beyond the reach of any physical ease, perhaps of any words either, any thoughts or regrets now.

Was Cormac O'Neil still alive? There was no reason why he should not be. He would barely be sixty, perhaps less. If he were, he could be the one behind this. God knew, after the failed uprising and Sean's and Kate's deaths, he had cause enough to hate Narraway, more than any other man on earth.

But why wait twenty years to do it? Narraway could have died of an accident or of natural causes anytime between then and now, and robbed the man of his revenge.

Could something have prevented him in the meantime? A debilitating illness? Not twenty years long. Time in prison? Surely Narraway would have heard of anything serious enough for such a term. And even from prison there was communication.

Perhaps this case had nothing to do with the past. Or perhaps it was simply that this was the time when Special Branch would be most vulnerable if Narraway was taken from it and his work discredited?

He closed the papers and put them back in the envelope Stoker had brought, then sat quietly in the dark and thought about it.

The old memories returned easily to his mind. He was walking again with Kate in the autumn stillness, fallen leaves red and yellow, frozen and crunching under their feet. She had no gloves, and he had lent her his. He could feel his hands ache with the cold at the memory. She had laughed at him for it, smiling, eyes bright, all the while making bitter jokes about warming the hands of Ireland with English wool.

When they had returned to the tavern Sean and Cormac had been there, and they had drunk rye whiskey by the fire. He could recall the smell of the peat, and Kate saying it was a good thing he didn't want vodka because potatoes were too scarce to waste on making it.

There were other memories as well, all sharp with emotion, torn loyalties, and regret. Wasn't it Wellington who had said that there was nothing worse than a battle won—except a battle lost? Or something like that.

Was the record accurate, as far as he had told anyone? Sanitized, of course, robbed of its passion and its humanity, but the elements that mattered to Special Branch were correct and sufficient.

Then something occurred to him, maybe an anomaly. He stood up, turned the gaslight higher again, and took the papers back out of the envelope. He reread them from beginning to end, including the marginal notes from Buckleigh, his superior then.

Narraway found what he feared. Something had been added. It was only a word or two, and to anyone who did not know Buckleigh's turn of phrase, his pedantic grammar, it would be undetectable. The hand looked exactly the same. But the new words added altered the meaning. Once it was only the addition of a question mark that had not been there originally, another time it was a few words that were not grammatically exact, a phrase ending with a preposition. Buckleigh would have included it in the main sentence.

Who had done that, and when? The why was not obscure to him at all: It was to raise the question of his role in this again, to cause the old ghosts to be awakened. Perhaps this was the deciding factor that had forced Croxdale to remove him from office.

He read through the papers one more time, just to be certain, then replaced them in the envelope and went upstairs to waken Stoker so he could leave well before dawn.

By the time he had opened the door Stoker was standing beside the bed. In the light from the landing it was clear that the quilt was barely ruffled. One swift movement of the hand and it was as if he had never been there.

Stoker looked at Narraway questioningly.

"Thank you," Narraway said quietly, the emotion in his voice more naked than he had meant it to be.

"It told you something," Stoker observed.

"Several things," Narraway admitted. "Someone else has been judiciously editing it since Buckleigh wrote his marginal notes, altering the meaning very slightly, but enough to make a difference."

Stoker came out of the room, and Narraway handed him the envelope. Stoker put it under his jacket where it could not be seen, but he did not fold it, or tuck it into his belt so the edges could be damaged. It was a reminder of the risk he was taking in having it at all. He looked very directly at Narraway.

"Austwick has taken your place, sir."

"Already?"

"Yes, sir. Mr. Pitt's over the channel, and you've no friends at Lisson Grove anymore. At least not who'll risk anything for you. It's every man for himself," Stoker said grimly. "I'm afraid there's no one for sure who'll help Mr. Pitt either, if he gets cut off or in any kind of trouble."

"I know that," Narraway said with deep unhappiness.

Stoker hesitated as if he would say something else, then changed his mind. He nodded silently and went down the stairs to the sitting room. He felt his way across the floor without lighting the gas lamps. He opened the French doors and slipped out into the wind and the darkness.

Narraway locked the door behind him and went back upstairs. He undressed and went to bed but lay awake staring up at the ceiling. He had left the curtains open, and gradually the faintest softening of the spring night made a break in the shadows across the ceiling. The glimmer was almost invisible, just enough to tell him there was movement, light beyond.

Only a matter of hours had passed since Austwick had come into Narraway's office. Narraway had thought little enough of it: a nuisance, no more. Then Croxdale had sent for him, and everything had changed. It was like going down a steep flight of stairs, only to find that the last one was not there.

He lay until daylight, realizing with a pain that amazed him how much of himself he had lost. He was used to getting up whether he had slept or not. Duty was a relentless mistress, but suddenly he knew also that she was a constant companion, loyal, appreciative, and above all, never meaningless.

Without her he was naked, even to himself. Narraway was accustomed to not particularly being liked. He'd had too much power for that, and he knew too many secrets. But never before had he not been needed.

CHAPTER

3

CHARLOTTE SAT BY THE fire in the parlor alone in her armchair opposite Pitt's. It was early evening. The children were in bed. There was no sound except now and then the settling of ashes as the wood burned through. Occasionally she picked up a piece of the mending that was waiting to be done—a couple of pillowcases, a pinafore of Jemima's. More often she simply stared at the fire. She missed Thomas, but she understood the necessity of his having pursued whoever it was to France. She also missed Gracie, the maid who had lived with them since she was thirteen and now, in her twenties, had finally married the police sergeant who had courted her so diligently for years.

Charlotte picked up the pinafore and began stitching up the hem where it had fallen, doing it almost as much by feel as by sight. The needle clicked with a light, quick sound against her thimble. Jemima was thirteen and growing tall very quickly. One could see the young woman that she would shortly become. Daniel was nearly three years younger, and desperate to catch up.

Charlotte smiled as she thought of Gracie, so proud in her white wedding gown, walking down the aisle on Pitt's arm as he gave her away. Tellman had been desperately nervous waiting at the altar, then so happy he couldn't control the smile on his face. He must have thought that day would never come.

But Charlotte missed Gracie's cheerfulness, her optimism, her candor, and her courage. Gracie never admitted to being beaten in anything. Her replacement, Mrs. Waterman, was middle-aged and dour as a walk in the sleet. She was a decent woman, honest as the day, kept everything immaculately clean, but she seemed to be content only if she was miserable. Perhaps in time she would gain confidence and feel better. It was sincerely to be hoped.

Charlotte did not hear the doorbell ring and was startled when Mrs. Waterman knocked on the parlor door. The older woman immediately came in, her face pinched with displeasure.

"There's a gentleman caller, ma'am. Shall I tell him that Mr. Pitt is not at home?"

Charlotte was startled, and her first thought was to agree to the polite fiction. Then her curiosity intruded. Surely at this hour it must be someone she knew?

"Who is it, Mrs. Waterman?"

"A very dark gentleman, ma'am. Says his name is Narraway," Mrs. Waterman replied, lowering her voice, although Charlotte could not tell if it were in disgust or confidentiality. She thought the former.

"Show him in," she said quickly, putting the mending out of sight on a chair behind the couch. Without thinking, she straightened her skirt and made sure she had no badly straying hairs poking out of her rather loose coiffure. Her hair was a rich dark mahogany color, but it slithered very easily out of control. As the pins dug into her head during the day, she was apt to remove them, with predictable results.

Mrs. Waterman hesitated.

"Show him in, please," Charlotte repeated, a trifle more briskly.

"I'll be in the kitchen if you need me," Mrs. Waterman said with a slight twist of her mouth that was definitely not a smile. She withdrew, and a moment later Narraway came in. When Charlotte had seen him a few days ago he had looked tired and a little concerned, but that was not unusual. This evening he was haggard, his lean face hollow-eyed, his skin almost without color.

Charlotte felt a terrible fear paralyze her, robbing her of breath. He had come to tell her terrible news of Pitt; even in her own mind she could not think the words.

"I'm sorry to disturb you so late," he said. His voice was almost normal, but she heard in its slight tremor the effort that it cost him. He stood in front of her. She could see from his eyes that he was hurt; there was an emptiness inside him that had not been there before.

He must have read her fear. How could he not? It filled the room.

He smiled thinly. "I have not heard from Thomas, but there is no reason to believe he is other than in excellent health, and probably having better weather than we have," he said gently. "Although I daresay he finds it tedious hanging about the streets watching people while trying to look as if he is on holiday."

She swallowed, her mouth dry, relief making her dizzy. "Then what is it?"

"Oh dear. Am I so obvious?"

It was more candid than he had ever been with her, yet it did not feel unnatural.

"Yes," she admitted. "I'm afraid you look dreadful. Can I get you something? Tea, or whiskey? That is, if we have any. Now that I've offered it, I'm not sure we do. The best of it might have gone at Gracie's wedding."

"Oh yes, Gracie." This time he did smile, and there was real warmth in it, changing his face. "I shall miss seeing her here. She was magnificent, all five feet of her."

"Four feet eleven, if we are honest," Charlotte corrected him with answering warmth. "Believe me, you could not possibly miss her as much as I do."

"You do not care for Mrs. . . . Lemon?"

"Waterman," she corrected him. "But Lemon would suit her. I don't think she approves of me. Perhaps we shall become accustomed to each other one day. She does cook well, and you could eat off the floors when she has scrubbed them."

"Thank you, but the table will do well enough," Narraway observed.

She sat down on the sofa. Standing so close to him in front of the fire was becoming uncomfortable. "You did not come to inquire after my domestic arrangements. And even if you had known Mrs. Waterman, she is not sufficient to cause the gravity I see in your face. What has happened?" She was holding her hands in her lap, and realized that she was gripping them together hard enough to hurt. She forced herself to let go.

There was a moment or two with no sound in the room but the flickering of the fire.

Narraway drew in his breath, then changed his mind.

"I have been relieved of my position in Special Branch. They say that it is temporary, but they will make it permanent if they can." He swallowed as if his throat hurt, and turned his head to look at her. "The thing concerning you is that I have no more access to my office at Lisson Grove, or any of the papers that are there. I will no longer know what is happening in France, or anywhere else. My place has been taken by Charles Austwick, who neither likes nor trusts Pitt. The former is a matter of jealousy because Pitt was recruited after him, and has received preferment in fact, if not in rank, that has more than equaled his. The latter is because they have little in common. Austwick comes from the army, Pitt from the police. Pitt has instincts Austwick will never understand, and Pitt's untidiness irritates Austwick's orderly, military soul." He sighed. "And of course Pitt is my protégé . . . was."

Charlotte was so stunned her brain did not absorb what he had said, and yet looking at his face she could not doubt it.

"I'm sorry," he said quietly.

She understood what he was apologizing for. He had made Pitt unpopular by singling him out, preferring him, confiding in him. Now, without Narraway, he would be vulnerable. He had never had any other profession but the police, and then Special Branch. He had been forced out of the police and could not go back there. It was Narraway who had given him a job when he had so desperately needed it. If Special Branch dismissed him, where was there for him to go? There was

no other place where he could exercise his very particular skills, and
certainly nowhere he could earn a comparable salary.

They would lose this house in Keppel Street and all the comforts
that went with it. Mrs. Waterman would certainly no longer be a
problem. Charlotte might well be scrubbing her own floors; indeed, it
might even come to scrubbing someone else's as well. She could imagine it already, see the shame in Thomas's face for his own failure to
provide for her, not the near luxury she had grown up in, nor even the
amenities of a working-class domesticity.

She looked up at Narraway, wondering now about him. She had
never considered before if he was dependent upon his salary or not.
His speech and his manner, the almost careless elegance of his dress,
said that he was born to a certain degree of position, but that did not
necessarily mean wealth. Younger sons of even the most aristocratic
families did not always inherit a great deal.

"What will you do?" she asked.

"How like you," he replied. "Both to be concerned for me, and to
assume that there is something to be done."

Now she felt foolish.

"What are you going to do?" she asked again.

"To help Pitt? There's nothing I can do," he replied. "I don't know
the circumstances, and to interfere blindly might do far more harm."

"Not about Thomas, about yourself." She had not asked him what
the charge was, or if he was wholly or partially guilty.

The ashes settled even further in the fire.

Several seconds passed before he answered. "I don't know," he admitted, his voice hesitant for the first time in her knowledge. "I am
not even certain who is at the root of it, although I have at least an
idea. It is all . . . ugly."

She had to press onward, for Pitt's sake. "Is that a reason not to
look at it?" she said quietly. "It will not mend itself, will it?"

He gave the briefest smile. "No. I am not certain that it can be
mended at all."

"Would you like a cup of tea?" she asked.

He was startled. "I beg your pardon?"

"I don't have anything better," she apologized. "But you look uncomfortable standing there in front of the fire. Wouldn't sitting down with a hot cup of tea be better?"

He turned slightly to look behind him at the hearth and the mantel. "You mean I am blocking the heat," he said ruefully.

"No," she replied with a smile. "Actually I meant that I am getting a crick in my neck staring up and sideways at you."

For a moment the pain in his face softened. "Thank you, but I would prefer not to disturb Mrs. . . . whatever her name is. I can sit down without tea, unnatural as that may seem."

"Waterman," she supplied.

"Yes, of course."

"I was going to make it myself, provided that she would allow me into the kitchen. She doesn't approve. The ladies she is accustomed to working for do not even know where the kitchen is. Although how I could lose it in a house this size, I have no idea."

"She has come down in the world," Narraway observed. "It can happen to the best of us."

She watched as he sat down, elegantly as always, crossing his legs and leaning back as if he were comfortable.

"I think it may concern an old case in Ireland," he began, at first meeting her eyes, then looking down awkwardly. "At the moment it is to do with the death of a present-day informant there, because the money I paid did not reach him in time to flee those he had . . . betrayed." He said the word crisply and clearly, as if deliberately exploring a wound: his own, not someone else's. "I did it obliquely, so it could not be traced back to Special Branch. If it had been it would have cost him his life immediately."

She hesitated, seeking the right words, but watching his face, she had no impression that he was being deliberately obscure. She waited. There was silence beyond the room, no sound of the children asleep upstairs, or of Mrs. Waterman, who was presumably still in the kitchen. She would not retire to her room with a visitor still in the house.

"My attempts to hide its source make it impossible to trace what actually happened to it," Narraway continued. "To the superficial investigation, it looks as if I took it myself."

He was watching her now, but not openly.

"You have enemies," she said.

"Yes," he agreed. "I have. No doubt many. I thought I had guarded against the possibility of them injuring me. It seems I overlooked something of importance."

"Or someone is an enemy whom you did not suspect," she amended.

"That is possible," he agreed. "I think it is more likely that an old enemy has gained a power that I did not foresee."

"You have someone in mind?" She leaned forward a little. The question was intrusive, but she had to know. Pitt was in France, relying on Narraway to back him up. He would have no idea Narraway no longer held any office.

"Yes." The answer seemed to be difficult for him.

Again she waited.

He leaned forward and put a fresh log on the fire. "It's an old case. It all happened more than twenty years ago." He had to clear his throat before he went on. "They're all dead now, except one."

She had no idea what he was referring to, and yet the past seemed to be in the room with them.

"But one is alive?" she probed. "Do you know, or are you guessing?"

"I know Kate and Sean are dead," he said so quietly she had to strain to hear him. "I imagine Cormac is still alive. He would be barely sixty."

"Why would he wait this long?"

"I don't know," he admitted.

"But you believe he hates you enough to lie, to plan and connive to ruin you?" she insisted.

"Yes. I have no doubt of that. He has cause."

She realized with surprise, and pity, that he was ashamed of his part in whatever had happened.

"So what will you do?" she asked again. "You have to fight. Nurse your wound for a few hours, then gather yourself together and think what you wish to do."

Now he smiled, showing a natural humor she had not seen in him before. "Is that how you speak to your children when they fall over and skin their knees?" he asked. "Quick sympathy, a hug, and then briskly get back up again? I haven't fallen off a horse, Charlotte. I have fallen from grace, and I know of nothing to get me back up again."

The color was hot in her cheeks. "You mean you have no idea what to do?"

He stood up and straightened the shoulders of his jacket. "Yes, I know what to do. I shall go to Ireland and find Cormac O'Neil. If I can, I shall prove that he is behind this, and clear my name. I shall make Croxdale eat his words. At least I hope I will."

She stood also. "Have you anyone to help you, whom you can trust?"

"No." His loneliness was intense. Just the one, simple word. Then it vanished, as if self-pity disgusted him. "Not here," he added. "But I may find someone in Ireland."

She knew he was lying.

"I'll come with you," she said impulsively. "You can trust me because our interests are the same."

His voice was tight with amazement, as if he did not dare believe her. "Are they?"

"Of course," she said rashly, although she knew it was the absolute truth. "Thomas has no other friend in Special Branch than you. The survival of my family may depend upon your being able to prove your innocence."

The color was warm in his cheeks also, or perhaps it was the firelight. "And what could you do?" he asked.

"Observe, ask questions, go where you will be recognized and cannot risk being seen. I am quite a good detective—at least I was in the past, when Thomas was in the police force and his cases were not so secret. At least I am considerably better than nothing."

He blushed and turned away. "I could not allow you to come."

"I did not ask your permission," she retorted. "But of course it would be a great deal pleasanter with it," she added.

He did not answer. It was the first time she had seen him so uncertain. Even when she had realized some time ago, with shock, that he found her attractive, there had always been a distance between them. He was Pitt's superior, a seemingly invulnerable man: intelligent, ruthless, always in control, and aware of many things that others knew nothing about. Now he was unsure, able to be hurt, no more in control of everything than she was. She would have used his Christian name if she had dared, but that would be a familiarity too far.

"We need the same thing," she began. "We have to find the truth of who is behind this fabrication and put an end to it. It is survival for both of us. If you think that because I am a woman I cannot fight, or that I will not, then you are a great deal more naïve than I assumed, and frankly I do not believe that. You have some other reason. Either you are afraid of something I will find out, some lie you need to protect; or else your pride is more important to you than your survival. Well, it is not more important to me." She took a deep breath. "And should I be of assistance, you will not owe me anything, morally or otherwise. I care what happens to you. I would not like to see you ruined, because you helped my husband at a time when we desperately needed it."

"Every time I think I know something about you, you surprise me," he observed. "It is a good thing you are no longer a part of high Society; they would never survive you. They are unaccustomed to such ruthless candor. They would have no idea what to do with you."

"You don't need to be concerned for them. I know perfectly well how to lie with the best, if I have to," she retorted. "I am coming to Ireland with you. This needs to be done, and you cannot do it alone because too many people already know you. You said as much yourself. But I had better have some reasonable excuse to justify traveling with you, or we shall cause an even greater scandal. May I be your sister, for the occasion?"

"We don't look anything alike," he said with a slightly twisted smile.

"Half sister then, if anybody asks," she amended.

"Of course you are right," he conceded. His voice was tired, the banter gone from it. He knew it was ridiculous to deny the only help he had been offered. "But you will listen to me, and do as I tell you. I cannot afford to spend my time or energy looking after you or worry-ing about you. Is that understood, and agreed?"

"Certainly. I want to succeed, not prove some kind of point."

"Then I shall be here at eight o'clock in the morning the day after tomorrow to take us to the train, and then the boat. Bring clothes suitable for walking, for discreet calling upon people in the city, and at least one gown for evening, should we go to the theater. Dublin is famous for its theaters. No more than one case."

"I shall be waiting."

He hesitated a moment, then let out his breath. "Thank you."

After he had gone Charlotte went back to the front parlor. A mo-ment later there was a knock on the door.

"Come in," she said, expecting to thank Mrs. Waterman for wait-ing up, tell her that nothing more was needed and she should go to bed.

Mrs. Waterman came in and closed the door behind her. Her back was ramrod-stiff, her face almost colorless and set in lines of rigid disapproval. One might imagine she had found a blocked drain.

"I'm sorry, Mrs. Pitt," she said before Charlotte had had time to say anything. "I cannot remain here. My conscience would not allow it."

Charlotte was stunned. "What are you talking about? You've done nothing wrong."

Mrs. Waterman sniffed. "Well, I daresay I have my faults. We all do. But I've always been respectable, Mrs. Pitt. There wasn't ever any-one who could say different."

"Nobody has." Charlotte was still mystified. "Nobody has even suggested such a thing."

"And I mean to keep it like that, if you understand me." Mrs. Waterman stood, if possible, even straighter. "So I'll be going in the morning. I'm sorry, about that. I daresay it'll be difficult for you, which I regret. But I've got my name to think of."

"What are you talking about?" Charlotte was growing annoyed. Mrs. Waterman was not particularly agreeable, but they might learn to accept each other. She was certainly hardworking, diligent, and to-tally reliable—at least she had been so far. With Pitt away for an indefinite period of time, and now this disastrous situation with Nar-raway, the last thing Charlotte needed was a domestic crisis. She had to go to Ireland. If Pitt were without a job they would lose the house and in quite a short time possibly find themselves scraping for food. He might have to learn a new trade entirely, and that would be diffi-cult for a man in his forties. Even with all the effort he would put into it, it would still take time. It was barely beginning to sink in. How on earth would Daniel and Jemima take the news? No more pretty dresses, no more parties, no more hoping for a career for Daniel. He would be fortunate not to start work at anything he could find, in a year or two. Even Jemima could become somebody's kitchen maid.

"You can't leave," Charlotte said, her tone angry now. "If you do, then I cannot give you a letter of character." That was a severe threat. Without a recommendation no servant could easily find another position. Their reason for leaving would be unexplained, and most people would put the unkindest interpretation on it.

Mrs. Waterman was unmoving. "I'm not sure, ma'am, if your rec-ommendation would be of any service to me, as to character, that is— if you understand me."

"No, I do not understand you," she said tartly.

"I don't like having to say this," Mrs. Waterman replied, her face wrinkling with distaste. "But I've never before worked in a household where the gentleman goes away unexpectedly, without any luggage at all, and the lady receives other gentlemen, alone and after dark. It isn't decent, ma'am, and that's all there is to it. I can't stay in a house with 'goings-on.'"

Charlotte was astounded. "'Goings-on'! Mrs. Waterman, Mr. Pitt was called away on urgent business, without time to come home or pack any luggage. He went to France in an emergency, the nature of which is not your business. Mr. Narraway is his superior in the government, and he came to tell me, so I would not be concerned. If you see it as something else, then the 'goings-on,' as you put it, are entirely in your own imagination."

"If you say so, ma'am," Mrs. Waterman answered, her eyes un-wavering. "And what did he come for tonight? Did Mr. Pitt give a message to him, and not to you, his lawful wedded wife—I assume?"

Charlotte wanted to slap her. With a great effort she forced herself to become calm.

"Mrs. Waterman, Mr. Narraway came to tell me further news concerning my husband's work. If you choose to think ill of it, or of me, then you will do so whatever the truth is, because that is who you are . . ."

Now it was Mrs. Waterman's face that flamed. "Don't you try to cover it with nice words and high-and-mighty airs," she said bitterly. "I know a man with a fancy for a woman when I see one."

It was on the edge of Charlotte's tongue to ask sarcastically when Mrs. Waterman had ever seen one, but it was perhaps an unnecessarily cruel thought. Mrs. Waterman was exactly what her grandmama used to call a vinegar virgin, despite the courteous *Mrs.* in front of her name.

"You have an overheated and somewhat vulgar imagination, Mrs. Waterman," she said coldly. "I cannot afford to have such a person in my household, so it might be best for both of us if you pack your belongings and leave first thing in the morning. I shall make breakfast myself, and then see if my sister can lend me one of her staff until I find someone satisfactory of my own. Her husband is a member of Parliament, and she keeps a large establishment. I shall see you to say good-bye in the morning."

"Yes, ma'am." Mrs. Waterman turned for the door.

"Mrs. Waterman!"

"Yes, ma'am?"

"I shall say nothing of you to others, good or ill. I suggest that you return that courtesy and say nothing of me. You would not come out of it well, I assure you."

Mrs. Waterman's eyebrows rose slightly.

Charlotte smiled with ice in her eyes. "A servant who will speak ill of one mistress will do so of another. Those of us who employ servants are well aware of that. Good night."

Mrs. Waterman closed the door without replying.

Charlotte went to the telephone to speak to Emily and ask for her help, immediately. She was a little surprised to see her hand shaking as she reached for the receiver.

When the voice answered she gave Emily's number.

It rang at the other end several times before the butler picked it up.

"Mr. Radley's residence. May I help you?" he said politely.

"I'm sorry to disturb you so late," Charlotte apologized. "It is Mrs. Pitt calling. Something of an emergency has arisen. May I speak with Mrs. Radley, please?"

"I'm very sorry, Mrs. Pitt," he replied with sympathy. "Mr. and Mrs. Radley have gone to Paris and I do not expect them back until next weekend. Is there something I may do to assist you?"

Charlotte felt a sort of panic. Who else could she turn to for help? Her mother was also out of the country, in Edinburgh, where she had gone with her second husband, Joshua. He was an actor, and had a play running in the theater there.

"No, no thank you," she said a little breathlessly. "I'm sure I shall find another solution. Thank you for your trouble. Good night." She hung up quickly.

She stood in the quiet parlor, the embers dying in the fire because she had not restoked it. She had until tomorrow evening to find someone to care for Daniel and Jemima, or she could not go with Narraway. And if she did not, then she could not help him. He would be alone in Dublin, hampered by the fact that he was known there, by friend and enemy alike.

Pitt had been Narraway's man from the beginning, his protégé and then his second in command—perhaps not officially, that was Austwick, but in practice. It had bred envy, and in some cases fear. With Narraway gone it would be only a matter of time before Pitt too was dismissed, demoted to an intolerable position, or—worse than that—met with an accident.

Then another thought occurred to her, ugly and even more imperative. If Narraway was innocent, as he claimed, then someone had deliberately reorganized evidence to make him look guilty. They could do the same to Pitt. In fact it was quite possible that if Pitt had had anything whatever to do with the case, he might already be implicated. As soon as he was home from France he would walk straight into the trap. Only a fool would allow him time to mount a defense, still less to find proof of his innocence and, at the same time, presumably their guilt.

But why? Was it really an old vengeance against Narraway? Or did Narraway know something about them that they could not afford to have him pursue? Whatever it was, whatever Narraway had done or not done, she must protect her husband. Narraway could not be guilty, that was the only thing of which she had no doubt.

Now she must find someone to look after Jemima and Daniel while she was away. Oh, damn Mrs. Waterman! The stupid creature!

CHARLOTTE WAS TIRED ENOUGH to sleep quite well, but when she woke in the morning it all flooded back to her. Not only did she have to make breakfast herself—not an unfamiliar task—but she also had to see Mrs. Waterman on her way, and explain to Daniel and Jemima at least something of what had happened. It might be easier for Jemima, since she was thirteen, but how would Daniel, at ten, grasp enough of the idea at least to believe her? She must make sure he did not imagine it was in any way his fault.

Then she must tackle the real task of the day: finding someone trustworthy with whom to leave her children. Put in such simple words, the thought overwhelmed her. She stood in her nightgown in the center of the bedroom floor, overcome with anxiety.

Still, standing here stalling would achieve nothing. She might as well get dressed while she weighed it up. A white blouse and a plain brown skirt would be fine. She was going to do chores, after all.

When she went down the stairs Mrs. Waterman was waiting in the hall, her one suitcase by the door. Charlotte was tempted to be sorry for her, but the moment passed. There was too much to do for her to relent, even if Mrs. Waterman wanted her to. This was an inconvenience. There were disasters on the horizon.

"Good morning, Mrs. Waterman," she said politely. "I am sorry you feel it necessary to go, but perhaps in the circumstances it is better. You will forgive me if I do not draw this out. I have to find someone to replace you by this evening. I hope you find yourself suited very soon. Good day to you."

"I'm sure I will, ma'am," Mrs. Waterman replied, and with such conviction that it flashed across Charlotte's mind to wonder if perhaps she already had. Sometimes domestic staff, especially cooks, found a cause to give notice in order to avail themselves of a position they preferred, or thought more advantageous for themselves.

"Yes, I imagine you will land on your feet," Charlotte said a trifle brusquely.

Mrs. Waterman gave her a cold look, drew breath to respond, then changed her mind and opened the front door. With some difficulty she dragged her case outside, then went to the curb to hail a cab.

Charlotte closed the door as Jemima came down the stairs. She was getting tall. From the looks of it, she would grow to her mother's height, with Charlotte's soft lines and confident air. The day was not far off.

"Where's Mrs. Waterman going?" she asked. "It's breakfast time."

There was no point in evading it. "She is leaving us," Charlotte replied quietly.

"At this time in the morning?" Jemima's eyebrows rose. They were elegant, slightly winged, exactly like Charlotte's own.

"It was that, or last night," Charlotte answered.

"Did she steal something?" Jemima reached the bottom stair. "Are you sure? She's so terribly good I can't believe she'd do that. She'd never be able to face herself in the glass. Come to think of it, perhaps she doesn't anyway. She might crack it."

"Jemima! That is rude, and most unkind," Charlotte said sharply. "But true," she added. "I did not ask her to leave. It is actually very inconvenient indeed . . ."

Daniel appeared at the top of the stairs, considered sliding down the banister, saw his mother at the bottom, and changed his mind. He came down the steps in a self-consciously dignified manner, as if that had always been his intention.

"Is Mrs. Waterman going?" he asked hopefully.

"She's already gone," Charlotte answered.

"Oh good. Is Gracie coming back?"

"No, of course she isn't," Jemima put in. "She's married. She's got to stay at home and look after her husband. We'll get someone else, won't we, Mama?"

"Yes. As soon as we've had breakfast and you've gone to school, I shall begin looking."

"Where do you look?" Daniel asked curiously as he followed her down the passage to the kitchen. It was shining clean after last night's dinner. Mrs. Waterman had left it immaculate, but not a thing was started for breakfast. Not even the stove was lit. It was still full of yesterday's ashes and barely warm to the touch. It would take some time to rake it out and lay it, light it, and wait for it to heat—too long for a hot breakfast of any sort before school. Even tea and toast required the use of the stove.

Charlotte controlled her temper with difficulty. If she could have been granted one wish, other than Pitt being home, it would have been to have Gracie back. Just her cheerful spirit, her frankness, her refusal ever to give in, would have made things easier.

"I'm sorry," she said to Daniel and Jemima, "but we'll have to wait until tonight for something hot. It'll be bread and jam for us all this morning, and a glass of milk." She went to the pantry to fetch the milk, butter, and jam without waiting for their response. She was already trying to find words to tell them that she had to leave and go to Ireland. Except that she couldn't, if she didn't find someone totally trustworthy to care for them, and how could she do that in half a day? As an absolutely final resort she knew she could take them to Emily's home for the servants to look after.

She came back with the milk, butter, and jam, and put them on the table. Jemima was setting out the knives and spoons; Daniel was putting the glasses out one at a time. She felt a sudden tightening in her chest. How could she have contemplated leaving them with the disapproving Mrs. Waterman? Blast Emily for being away now, when she was so badly needed!

She turned and opened the bread bin, took out the loaf, and set it on the board with the knife.

"Thank you," she said, accepting the last glass. "I know it's a little early, but we had better begin. I knew Mrs. Waterman was going. I should have been up sooner and lit the stove. I didn't even think of it. I'm sorry." She cut three slices of bread and offered them. They each took one, buttered it, and chose the jam they liked best: gooseberry for Jemima, blackcurrant for Daniel—like his father—and apricot for Charlotte. She poured the milk.

"Why did she go, Mama?" Daniel asked.

For once Charlotte did not bother to tell him not to speak with his mouth full. His question deserved an honest answer, but how much would he understand? He was looking at her now with solemn gray eyes exactly like his father's. Jemima waited with the bread halfway to her mouth. Perhaps the whole truth, briefly and without fear, was the only way to avoid having to lie later, as more and more emerged. If they ever found her lying to them, even if they understood the reason, their trust would be broken.

"Mr. Narraway, your father's superior, called a few evenings ago to tell me that your father had to go to France, without being able to let us know. He didn't want us to worry when he didn't come home . . ."

"You told us," Jemima interrupted. "Why did Mrs. Waterman go?"

"Mr. Narraway came again yesterday evening, quite late. He stayed for a little while, because something very bad had happened to him. He has been blamed for something he didn't do, and he is no longer your father's superior. That matters rather a lot, so he had to let me know."

Jemima frowned. "I don't understand. Why did Mrs. Waterman go? Can't we pay her anymore?"

"Yes, certainly we can," Charlotte said quickly, although that might not always be true. "She went because she didn't approve of Mr. Narraway coming here and telling me in the evening."

"Why not?" Daniel put his bread down and stared at her. "Shouldn't he have told you? And how does she know? Is she in the police as well?"

Pitt had not explained to his children the differences between the police, detecting any type of crime, and Special Branch, a force created originally to deal with violence, sometimes treason, or any other threat to the safety of the country. This was not the time to address it.

"No," she said. "It is not her concern at all. She thought I should not have received any man after dark when your father was not here. She said it wasn't decent, and she couldn't remain in a house where the mistress did not behave with proper decorum. I tried to explain to her that it was an emergency, but she did not believe me." If she did not have more urgent problems, that would still have rankled.

Daniel still looked puzzled, but it was clear that Jemima understood.

"If she hadn't left anyway, then you should have thrown her out," she said angrily. "That's impertinent." She was immediately defensive of her mother, and *impertinent* was her new favorite word of condemnation.

"Yes it was," Charlotte agreed. She had been going to tell them about her need to go to Ireland, but changed her mind. "But since she did leave of her own will, it doesn't matter. May I have the butter, please, Daniel?"

He passed it to her. "What's going to happen to Mr. Narraway? Is Papa going to help him?"

"He can't," Jemima pointed out. "He's in France." She looked questioningly at Charlotte to support her, if she was right.

"Well, who is, then?" Daniel persisted.

There was no escape, except lies. Charlotte took a deep breath. "I am, if I can think of a way. Now please finish your breakfast so I can get you on your way to school, and begin looking for someone to replace Mrs. Waterman."

BUT WHEN SHE PUT on an apron and knelt to clear the ashes out of the grate in the stove, then laid a new fire ready to light when she returned, finding a new maid did not seem nearly as simple a thing to accomplish as she had implied to Daniel and Jemima. It was not merely a woman to cook and clean that she required. It was someone who would be completely reliable, kind, and, if any emergency arose, would know what to do.

If she were in Ireland, who would they ask for help? Was she even right to go? Which was the greater emergency? Should she ask any new maid, if she could find one, to call Great-Aunt Vespasia, if she needed help? Vespasia was close to seventy, although she might not look it, and certainly had not retired from any part of life. Her passion, courage, and energy would put to shame many a thirty-year-old, and she had always been a leader in the highest Society. Her great beauty had changed, but not dimmed. But was she the person to make decisions should a child be ill, or there be some other domestic crisis such as a blocked drain, a broken faucet, a shortage of coal, a chimney fire, and so on?

Gracie had risen to all such occasions, at one time or another.

Charlotte stood up, washed her hands in water that was almost cold, and took off her apron. She would ask Gracie's advice. It was something of a desperate step to disturb her newfound happiness so soon, but it was a desperate situation.

It was an omnibus ride, but not a very long one, to the small red-brick house where Gracie and Tellman lived. They had the whole of the ground floor to themselves, including the front garden. This was quite an achievement for a couple so young, but then Tellman was twelve years older than Gracie, and had worked extremely hard to gain promotion to sergeant in the Metropolitan Police. Pitt still missed working with him.

Charlotte walked up to the front door and knocked briskly, holding her breath in anticipation. If Gracie was not in, she had no idea where she could turn next.

But the door opened and Gracie stood just inside, five feet tall with her smart boots on, and wearing a dress that for once was nobody else's cast-off taken up and in to fit her. There was no need to ask if she was happy; it radiated from her face like heat from a stove.

"Mrs. Pitt! Yer come ter see me! Samuel in't 'ere now, 'e's gorn already, but come in an 'ave a cup o' tea." She pulled the door open even wider and stepped back.

Charlotte accepted, forcing herself to think of Gracie's new house, her pride and happiness, before she said anything of her own need. She followed Gracie inside along the linoleum-floored passage, polished to a gleaming finish, and into the small kitchen at the back. It too was immaculately clean and smelled of lemon and soap, even this early in the morning. The stove was lit and there was well-kneaded bread sitting in pans on the sill, rising gently. It would soon be ready to bake.

Gracie pulled the kettle over onto the hob and set out a teapot and cups, then opened the pantry cupboard to get milk.

"I got cake, if yer like?" she offered. "But mebbe yer'd sooner 'ave toast an' jam?"

"Actually, I'd rather like cake, if you can spare it," Charlotte replied. "I haven't had good cake for a while. Mrs. Waterman didn't approve of it, and the disfavor came through her hands. Heavy as lead."

Gracie turned around from the cupboard where she had been getting the cake. Plates were on the dresser. Charlotte noted with a smile that it was set out exactly like the one in her own kitchen, which Gracie had kept for so long: cups hanging from the rings, small plates on the top shelf, then bowls, dinner plates lowest.

"She gorn, then?" Gracie said anxiously.

"Mrs. Waterman? Yes, I'm afraid so. She gave notice and left all at the same time, yesterday evening. Or to be exact, she gave notice late yesterday evening, and was in the hall with her case when I came down this morning."

Gracie was astounded. She put the cake—which was rich and full of fruit—on the table, then stared at Charlotte in dismay. "Wot she done? Yer din't never throw 'er out fer nothin'!"

"I didn't throw her out at all," Charlotte answered. "She really gave notice, just like that—"

"Yer can't do that!" Gracie waved her hands to dismiss the idea. "Yer won't never get another place, not a decent one."

"A lot has happened," Charlotte said quietly.

Gracie sat down sharply in the chair opposite and leaned a little across the small wooden table, her face pale. "It in't Mr. Pitt . . ."

"No," Charlotte assured her hastily. "But he is in France on business and cannot come home until it is complete, and Mr. Narraway has been thrown out of his job." There was no use, and no honor, in concealing the truth from Gracie. After all, it was Victor Narraway who had placed her as a maid in Buckingham Palace when Pitt so desperately needed help in that case. The triumph had been almost as much Gracie's as his. Narraway himself had praised her.

Gracie was appalled. "That's wicked!"

"He thinks it is an old enemy, perhaps hand in glove with a new one, possibly someone after his job," Charlotte told her. "Mr. Pitt doesn't know, and is trusting Mr. Narraway to support him in his pursuit now and do what he can to help from here. He doesn't know he will be relying on someone else, who may not believe in him as Mr. Narraway does."

"Wot are we goin' ter do?" Gracie said instantly.

Charlotte was so overwhelmed with gratitude, and with emotion at Gracie's passionate and unquestioning loyalty, that she felt the warmth rise up in her and the tears prickle her eyes.

"Mr. Narraway believes that the cause of the problem lies in an old case that happened twenty years ago in Ireland. He is going back there to find his enemy and try to prove his own innocence."

"But Mr. Pitt won't be there to 'elp 'im," Gracie pointed out. "'Ow can 'e do that by 'isself? Don't this enemy know 'im, never mind that 'e'll expect 'im ter do it?" She looked suddenly quite pale, all the happy flush gone from her face. "That's just daft. Yer gotter tell 'im ter think afore 'e leaps in, yer really 'ave!"

"I must help him, Gracie. Mr. Narraway's enemies in Special Branch are Mr. Pitt's as well. For all our sakes, we must win."

"Yer goin' ter Ireland? Yer goin' ter 'elp 'im . . ." She reached out her hand, almost as if to touch Charlotte's where it lay on the table, then snatched it back self-consciously. She was no longer an employee, but it was a liberty too far, for all the years they had known each other. She took a deep breath. "Yer 'ave gotta!"

"I know. I mean to," Charlotte assured her. "But since Mrs. Waterman has walked out—in disgust and outraged morality, because Mr. Narraway was alone in the parlor with me after dark—I have to find someone to replace her before I can leave."

A succession of emotions passed across Gracie's face: anger, indignation, impatience, and a degree of amusement. "Stupid ol' 'aporth," she said with disgust. "Got minds like cesspits, some o' them ol' vinegar virgins. Not that Mr. Narraway don't 'ave a soft spot for yer, an' all." The smile lit her eyes for an instant, then was gone again. She might not have dared say that when she worked for Charlotte, but she was a respectable married woman now, and in her own kitchen, in her own house. She wouldn't have changed places with the queen—and she had met the queen, which was more than most could say.

"Gracie, Emily is away and so is my mother," Charlotte told her gravely. "I can't go and leave Jemima and Daniel until I find someone to look after them, someone I can trust completely. Where do I look? Who can recommend someone without any doubt or hesitation at all?"

Gracie was silent for so long that Charlotte realized she had asked an impossible question.

"I'm sorry," she said quickly. "That was unfair."

The kettle was boiling and began to whistle. Gracie stood up, picked up the cloth to protect her hands, and pulled it away from the heat. She swirled a little of the steaming water around the teapot to warm it, emptied it down the sink, and then made the tea. She carried the pot carefully over to the table and set it on a metal trivet to protect the wood. Then she sat down again.

"I can," she said.

Charlotte blinked. "I beg your pardon?"

"I can recommend someone," Gracie said. "Minnie Maude Mudway. I knowed 'er since before I ever met you, or come to yer 'ouse. She lived near where I used ter, in Spitalfields, just 'round the corner, couple o' streets along. 'Er uncle were killed. I 'elped 'er find 'oo done it, 'member?"

Charlotte was confused, trying to find the memory, and failing.

"You were riding the donkey, for Christmas," Gracie urged. "Minnie Maude were eight then, but she's growed up now. Yer can trust 'er, 'cos she don't never, ever give up. I'll find 'er for yer. An' I'll go ter Keppel Street meself an' check on them every day."

Charlotte looked at Gracie's small, earnest face, the gently steaming teapot, and the homemade cake with its rich sultanas, the whole lovingly immaculate kitchen.

"Thank you," she said softly. "That would be excellent. If you call in every day then I shan't worry."

Gracie smiled widely. "Yer like a piece o' cake?"

"Yes please," Charlotte accepted.

By three o'clock in the afternoon, Charlotte was already packed to leave with Narraway on the train the following morning, should it prove possible after all. She could not settle to anything. One moment she wanted to prepare the vegetables for dinner, then she forgot what she was intending to cook, or thought of something else to pack. Twice she imagined she heard someone at the door, but when she looked there was no one. Three times she went to check that Daniel and Jemima were doing their homework.

Then at last the knock on the door came, familiar in the rhythm, as if it were a person she knew. She turned and almost ran to open it.

On the step was Gracie, her smile so wide it lit her whole face with triumph. Next to her stood another young woman, several inches taller, slender, and with unruly hair she had done her best to tame, unsuccessfully. But the thing that caught Charlotte's attention was the intelligence in her eyes, even though now she looked definitely nervous.

"This is Minnie Maude," Gracie announced, as if she were a magician pulling a rabbit out of a top hat.

Minnie Maude dropped a tiny curtsy, obviously not quite sure enough to do it properly.

Charlotte could not hide her smile—not of amusement, but of relief. "How do you do, Minnie Maude. Please come in. If Gracie has explained my difficulty to you, then you know how delighted I am to see you." She opened the door more widely and turned to lead the way. She took them into the kitchen because it was warmer, and it would be Minnie Maude's domain, if she accepted the position.

"Please sit down," Charlotte invited them. "Would you like tea?" It was a rhetorical question. One made tea automatically.

"I'll do it," Gracie said instantly.

"You will not!" Charlotte told her. "You don't work here, you are my guest." Then she saw the startled look on Gracie's face. "Please," she added.

Gracie sat down suddenly, looking awkward.

Charlotte set about making the tea. She had no cake to offer, but she cut lacy-thin slices of bread and butter, and there was fine-sliced cucumber and hard-boiled egg. Of course there was also jam, although it was a little early in the afternoon for anything so sweet.

"Gracie tells me that you have known each other for a very long time," Charlotte said as she worked.

"Yes, ma'am, since I were eight," Minnie Maude replied. "She 'elped me when me uncle Alf were killed, an' Charlie got stole." She drew in her breath as if to say something more and then changed her mind.

Charlotte had her back to the table, hiding her face and her smile. She imagined that Gracie had schooled Minnie Maude well in not saying too much, not offering what was not asked for.

"Did she also explain that my husband is in Special Branch?" she asked. "Which is a sort of police, but dealing with people who are trying to cause war and trouble of one sort or another to the whole country."

"Yes, ma'am. She said as 'e were the best detective in all England," Minnie Maude replied. There was a warmth of admiration in her voice already.

Charlotte brought the plate of bread and butter over and set it on the table.

"He is very good," she agreed. "But that might be a slight exaggeration. At the moment he has had to go abroad on a case, unexpectedly. My previous maid left without any notice, because she misunderstood something that happened, and felt she could not stay. I have to leave tomorrow morning very early, because of another problem that has arisen." It sounded peculiar, even to her own ears.

"Yes, ma'am." Minnie Maude nodded seriously. "A very important gentleman, as Gracie speaks very 'ighly of too. She said as someone is blaming 'im fer summink as 'e didn't do, an' you're going to 'elp 'im, 'cos it's the right thing ter do."

Charlotte relaxed a little. "Exactly. I'm afraid we are a household of unexpected events, at times. But you will be in no danger at all. However, your job will involve considerable responsibility, because although I am here most of the time, I am not always."

"Yes, ma'am. I bin in service before, but the lady I were with passed on, an' I in't found a new place yet. But Gracie said as she'll come by every day, just ter make certain as everything's all right, like." Minnie Maude's face was a little tense, her eyes never leaving Charlotte's face.

Charlotte looked at Gracie and saw the confidence in her eyes, because she was sitting at the table sideways to her, the small hands knotted, knuckles white, in her lap. She made her decision.

"Then Minnie Maude, I would be very happy to engage you in the position of housemaid, starting immediately. I apologize for the urgency of the situation, and you will be compensated for the inconvenience by a double salary for the first month, to reflect also the fact that you will be alone at the beginning, which is always the most difficult time in a new place."

Minnie Maude gulped. "Thank you, ma'am."

"After tea I shall introduce you to Jemima and Daniel. They are normally well behaved, and the fact that you are a friend of Gracie's will endear you to them from the beginning. Jemima knows where most things are. If you ask her, she will be happy to help you. In fact she will probably take a pride in it, but do not allow her to be cheeky. And that goes for Daniel as well. He will probably try your patience, simply to test you. Please do not let him get away with too much."

The kettle was boiling and she made the tea, bringing it over to the table to brew. While they were waiting she explained some of the other household arrangements, and where different things were kept.

"I shall leave you a list of the tradesmen we use, and what they should charge you, although I daresay you are familiar with prices. But they might take advantage, if they think you don't know." She went on to tell her of the dishes Daniel and Jemima liked best, and the vegetables they were likely to refuse if they thought they could get away with it. "And rice pudding," she finished. "That is a treat, not more than twice a week."

"Wi' nutmeg on the top?" Minnie Maude asked.

Charlotte glanced at Gracie, then smiled, the ease running through her like a warmth inside. "Exactly. I think this is going to work very well."

GRACIE AND MINNIE MAUDE returned early in the evening, accompanied by Tellman, who carried Minnie Maude's luggage. He took it up to the room that not long ago had been Gracie's, then excused himself to take Gracie home. Minnie Maude began to unpack her belongings and settle in, helped by Jemima, and watched from a respectful distance by Daniel. Clothes were women's business.

Once she had made certain that all was well, Charlotte telephoned her great-aunt Vespasia. Immensely relieved to find her at home, she asked if she might visit.

"You sound very serious," said Vespasia across the rather crackly wire.

Charlotte gripped the instrument more tightly in her hand. "I am. I have a great deal to tell you, and some advice to seek. But I would much prefer to tell you in person rather than this way. In fact some of it is most confidential."

"Then you had better come to see me," Vespasia replied. "I shall send my carriage for you. Are you ready now? We shall have supper. I was going to have Welsh rarebit on toast, with a little very good Hock

I have, and then apple flan and cream. Apples at this time of year are not fit for anything except cooking."

"I would love it," Charlotte accepted. "I shall just make certain that my new maid is thoroughly settled and aware of what to cook for Daniel and Jemima, then I shall be ready."

"I thought you had had her since Gracie's wedding," Vespasia exclaimed. "Is she still not able to decide what to prepare?"

"Mrs. Waterman gave notice last night and left this morning," Charlotte explained. "Gracie found me someone she has known for years, but the poor girl has only just arrived. In fact she is still unpacking."

"Charlotte?" Now Vespasia sounded worried. "Has something happened that is serious?"

"Yes. Oh . . . we are all alive and well, but yes, it is serious, and I am in some concern as to whether the course of action I plan is wise or not."

"And you are going to ask my advice? It must be serious indeed if you are willing to listen to someone else." Vespasia was vaguely mocking, though anxiety clearly all but overwhelmed her.

"I'm not," Charlotte told her. "I have already given my word."

"I shall dispatch my coachman immediately," Vespasia responded. "If Gracie recommends this new person then she will be good. You had better wear a cape. The evening has turned somewhat cooler."

"Yes, yes I will," Charlotte agreed, then she said good-bye and replaced the receiver on its hook.

Half an hour later Vespasia's coachman knocked on the door. Minnie Maude seemed confident enough for Charlotte to leave her, and Daniel and Jemima were not in the least concerned. Indeed, they seemed to be enjoying showing her the cupboards and drawers, and telling her exactly what was kept in each.

Charlotte answered the door, told the coachman that she would be ready in a moment, then went to the kitchen. She stopped for a moment to stare at Jemima's earnest face explaining to Minnie Maude which jugs were used to keep the day's milk and where the milkman was to be found in the morning. Daniel was moving from foot to foot in his urgency to put in his advice as well, and Minnie Maude was smiling at first one, then the other.

"I may be late back," Charlotte interrupted. "Please don't wait up for me."

"No, ma'am," Minnie Maude said quickly. "But I'll be happy to, if you wish?"

"Thank you, but please make yourself comfortable," Charlotte told her. "Good night."

She went straight out to the carriage, and for the next half hour rode through the streets to Vespasia's house in Gladstone Park— which was really not so much a park as a small square with flowering trees. She sat and tried to compose in her mind exactly how she would tell Vespasia what she meant to do.

At last Charlotte sat in Vespasia's quiet sitting room. The colors were warm, muted to a familiar gentleness. The curtains were drawn across the window onto the garden, and the fire burned in the hearth with a soft whickering of flames. She looked into Vespasia's face, and it was not so easy to explain to her the wild decision to which Charlotte had already committed herself.

Vespasia had been considered by many to be the most beautiful woman of her generation, as well as the most outrageous in her wit and her political opinions—or maybe *passions* would be a more fitting word. Time had marked her features lightly and, if anything, liberated her temperament even more. She was secure enough in her financial means and her social preeminence not to have to care what other people thought of her, as long as she was certain in her own mind that a course of action was for the best. Criticism might hurt, but it was a long time since it had deterred her.

Now she sat stiff-backed—she had never lounged in her life—her silver hair coiffed to perfection. A high lace collar covered her throat, and the lamplight gleamed on the three rows of pearls.

"You had better begin at the beginning," she told Charlotte. "Supper will be another hour."

At least Charlotte knew what the beginning was. "Several evenings ago Mr. Narraway came to see me at home, to tell me that

Thomas had been in pursuit of a man who had committed a murder, almost in front of him. He and his junior had been obliged to follow this person and had not had the opportunity to inform anyone of what they were doing. Mr. Narraway knew that they were in France. They sent a telegram. He told me of it so that I would not worry when Thomas did not come home or call me."

Vespasia nodded. "It was courteous of him to come himself," she observed a trifle drily.

Charlotte caught the tone in her voice, and her eyes widened.

"He is fond of you, my dear," Vespasia responded. Her amusement was so slight it could barely be seen, and was gone again the second after. "What has this to do with the maid?"

Charlotte looked at the drawn curtains, the pale design of flowers on the carpet. "He came again last evening," she said quietly. "And stayed for much longer."

Vespasia's voice changed almost imperceptibly. "Indeed?"

Charlotte raised her eyes to meet Vespasia's. "There appears to have been a conspiracy within Special Branch to make it look as if he embezzled a good deal of money." She saw Vespasia's look of disbelief. "They have dismissed him, right there on the spot."

"Oh dear," Vespasia said. "I see why you are distressed. This is very serious indeed. Victor may have his faults, but financial dishonesty is not one of them. Money does not interest him. He would not even be tempted to do such a thing."

Charlotte did not find that comforting. What faults was Vespasia implying? It seemed she knew him better than Charlotte had appreciated, even though Vespasia had interested herself in many of Pitt's cases, and therefore Narraway's. Then the moment after, studying Vespasia's expression, Charlotte realized that Vespasia was deeply concerned for him and believed in his innocence.

Charlotte found the tension in her body easing, and she smiled. "I did not believe it of him either, but there is something in the past that troubles him very much."

"There will be a good deal," Vespasia said with the ghost of a smile. "He is a man of many sides, but the most vulnerable one is his work, because that is what he cares about."

"Then he wouldn't jeopardize it, would he?" Charlotte pointed out.

"No. Someone finds it imperative that Victor Narraway be driven out of office, and out of credit with Her Majesty's government. There are many possible reasons, and I have no idea which of them it is, so I have very little idea where to begin."

"We have to help him." Charlotte hated asking this of Vespasia, but the need was greater than the reluctance. "Not only for his sake, but for Thomas's. In Special Branch, Thomas is regarded as Mr. Narraway's man. I know this because, apart from my own sense, Thomas has told me so himself, and so has Mr. Narraway. Aunt Vespasia, if Mr. Narraway is gone, then whoever got rid of him may try to get rid of Thomas as well—"

"Of course," Vespasia cut across her. "You do not need to explain it to me, my dear. And Thomas is in France, not knowing what has happened, or that Victor can no longer give him the support from London that he needs."

"Have you friends—" Charlotte began.

"I do not know who has done this, or why," Vespasia answered even before the question was finished. "So I do not know whom I can trust."

"Victor . . . Mr. Narraway . . ." Charlotte felt a faint heat in her cheeks. ". . . said he believed it was an old case in Ireland, twenty years ago, for which someone now seeks revenge. He didn't tell me much about it. I think it embarrassed him."

"No doubt." Vespasia allowed a bleak spark of humor into her eyes for an instant. "Twenty years ago? Why now? The Irish are good at holding a grudge, or a favor, but they don't wait on payment if they don't have to."

"'Revenge is a dish best served cold'?" Charlotte suggested wryly.

"Cold, perhaps, my dear, but this would be frozen. There is more to it than a personal vengeance, but I do not know what. By the way, what has this to do with your maid leaving? Clearly there is something you have . . . forgotten . . . to tell me."

Charlotte found herself uncomfortable. "Oh . . . Mr. Narraway called after dark, and clearly since the matter was of secrecy, for obvious reasons he closed the parlor door. I'm afraid Mrs. Waterman thought I was . . . am . . . a woman of dubious morals. She doesn't feel she can remain in a household where the mistress has 'goings-on,' as she put it."

"Then she is going to find herself considerably restricted in her choice of position," Vespasia said waspishly. "Especially if her disapproval extends to the master as well."

"She didn't say." Charlotte bit her lip, but couldn't conceal her smile. "But she would be utterly scandalized, so much so that she might have left that night, out into the street alone, with her suitcase in her hand, if she had known that I promised Mr. Narraway that I would go to Ireland with him, to do whatever I can to find the truth and help him clear his name. I have to. His enemies are Thomas's enemies, and Thomas will have no defense against them without Mr. Narraway there. Then what shall we do?"

Vespasia was silent for several moments. "Be very careful, Charlotte," she said gravely. "I think you are unaware of how dangerous that could become."

Charlotte clenched her hands. "What would you have me do? Sit here in London while Mr. Narraway is unjustly ruined, and then wait for Thomas to be ruined as well? At best he will be dismissed because he was Mr. Narraway's man, and they don't like him. At worst he may be implicated in the same embezzlement, and end up charged with theft." Her voice cracked a little and she realized how tired she was, and how very frightened. "What would you do?"

Vespasia reached across and touched her very gently, just fingertip-to-fingertip. "Just the same as you, my dear. That's not the same thing as saying that it is wise. It is simply the only choice you can live with."

There was a tap on the door, and the maid announced that supper was ready. They ate in the small breakfast room. Slender-legged Georgian mahogany furniture glowed dark amid golden-yellow walls, as if they were dining in the sunset, although the curtains were closed and the only light came from the mounted gas brackets.

They did not resume the more serious conversation until they had returned to the sitting room and were assured of being uninterrupted.

"Do not forget for a moment that you are in Ireland," Vespasia warned. "Or imagine it is the same as England. It is not. They wear their past more closely wound around themselves than we do. Enjoy it while you are there, but don't let your guard down for a second. They say you need a long spoon to sup with the devil. Well; you need a strong head to dine with the Irish. They'll charm the wits out of you, if you let them."

"I won't forget why I'm there," Charlotte promised.

"Or that Victor knows Ireland very well, and the Irish also know him?" Vespasia added. "Do not underestimate his intelligence, Charlotte, or his vulnerability. By the way, you have not mentioned how you intend to carry this off without causing a scandal that might not damage Narraway's good name any further, but would certainly ruin yours. I assume your sense of fear and injustice did not blind you to that?" There was no criticism in her voice, only concern.

Charlotte felt the blood hot in her face. "Of course not. I can't take a maid, I don't have one, or the money to pay her fare if I did. I am going to say I am Mr. Narraway's sister—half sister. That will make it decent enough."

A tiny smile touched the corners of Vespasia's lips. "Then you had better stop calling him Mr. Narraway and learn to use his given name, or you will certainly raise eyebrows." She hesitated. "Or perhaps you already do."

Charlotte looked into Vespasia's steady silver-gray eyes, and chose not to respond.

NARRAWAY CAME EARLY THE following morning in a hansom cab. When she answered the door he hesitated only momentarily. He did not ask her if she were certain of the decision. Perhaps he did not want to give her the chance to waver. He called the cabdriver to put her case on the luggage rack.

"Do you wish to go and say good-bye?" he asked her. His face looked bleak, with shadows under his eyes as if he had not slept in many nights. "There is time."

"No thank you," she answered. "I have already done so. And I hate long good-byes. I am quite ready to go."

He nodded and walked behind her across the footpath. Then he helped her up onto the seat, going around to the other side to sit next to her. The cabbie apparently knew the destination.

She had already decided not to tell him that she had visited Vespasia. He might prefer to think Vespasia did not know of his dismissal. She also chose not to let him know of Mrs. Waterman's suspicions. It could prove embarrassing, even as if she herself had considered the journey as something beyond business herself.

"Perhaps you would tell me something about Dublin," she requested. "I have never been there, and I realize that beyond the fact that it is the capital of Ireland, I know very little."

The idea seemed to amuse him. "We have a long train journey ahead of us, even on the fast train, and then a crossing of the Irish Sea. I hear that the weather will be pleasant. I hope so, because if it is rough, then it can be very violent indeed. There will be time for me to tell you all I know, from 7500 BC until the present day."

She was amazed at the age of the city, but she would not allow him to see that he had impressed her so easily. It might look as if she were being deliberately gentle with the grief she knew he must be feeling.

"Really? Is that because our journey is enormously long after all, or because you know less than I had supposed?"

"Actually there is something of a gap between 7500 BC and the Celts arriving in 700 BC," he said with a smile. "And after that not a great deal until the arrival of Saint Patrick in AD 432."

"So we can leap eight thousand years without further comment," she concluded. "After that surely there must be something a little more detailed?"

"The building of Saint Patrick's Cathedral in AD 1192?" he suggested. "Unless you want to know about the Vikings, in which case I would have to look it up myself. Anyway, they weren't Irish, so they don't count."

"Are you Irish, Mr. Narraway?" she asked suddenly. Perhaps it was an intrusive question, and when he was Pitt's superior she would not have asked it, but now the relationship was far more equal, and she might need to know. With his intensely dark looks he easily could be.

He winced slightly. "How formal you are. It makes you sound like your mother. No, I am not Irish, I am as English as you are, except for one great-grandmother. Why do you ask?"

"Your precise knowledge of Irish history," she answered. That was not the real reason. She asked because she needed to know more about his loyalties, the truth about what had happened in the O'Neil case twenty years ago.

"It is my job to know," he said quietly. "As it was. Would you like to hear about the feud that made the King of Leinster ask Henry the Second of England to send over an army to assist him?"

"Is it interesting?"

"The army was led by Richard de Clare, known as Strongbow. He married the king's daughter and became king himself in 1171, and the Anglo-Normans took control. In 1205 they began to build Dublin Castle. 'Silken' Thomas led a revolt against Henry the Eighth in 1534, and lost. Do you begin to see a pattern?"

"Of course I do. Do they burn the King of Leinster in effigy?"

He laughed, a brief, sharp sound. "I haven't seen it done, but it sounds like a good idea. We are at the station. Let me get a porter. We will continue when we are seated on the train."

The hansom pulled up as he spoke, and he alighted easily. There was an air of command in him that attracted attention within seconds, and the luggage was unloaded into a wagon, the driver paid, and Charlotte walked across the pavement into the vast Paddington railway station for the Great Western rail to Holyhead.

It had great arches, as if it were some half-finished cathedral, and a roof so high it dwarfed the massed people all talking and clattering their way to the platform. There was a sense of excitement in the air, and a good deal of noise and steam and grit.

Narraway took her arm. For a moment his grasp felt strange and she was about to object, then she realized how foolish that would be. If they were parted in the crowd they might not find each other again until after the train had pulled out. He had the tickets, and he must know which platform they were seeking.

They passed groups of people, some greeting one another, some clearly stretching out a reluctant parting. Every so often the sound of belching steam and the clang of doors drowned out everything else. Then a whistle would blast shrilly, and one of the great engines would come to life beginning the long pull away from the platform.

It was not until they had found their train and were comfortably seated that they resumed any kind of conversation. She found him courteous, even considerate, but she could not help being aware of his inner tensions, the quick glances, the concern, the way his hands were hardly ever completely still.

It would be a long journey to Holyhead on the west coast. It was up to her to make it as agreeable as possible, and also to learn a good deal more about exactly what he wanted her to do.

Sitting on the rather uncomfortable seat, upright, with her hands folded in her lap, she realized she must look very prim. It was not an image she liked, and yet now that they were embarked on this adventure together, each for their own reasons, she must be certain not to make any irretrievable mistakes, first of all in the nature of her feelings. She liked Victor Narraway. He was highly intelligent, and he could be very amusing at rare times, but she knew only one part of his life.

Still, she knew that there must be more, the private man. Somewhere beneath the pragmatism there had been dreams.

"Thank you for the lesson on ancient Irish history," she began, feeling clumsy. "But I need to know far more than I do about the specific matter that we are going to investigate; otherwise I may not recognize something important if I hear it. I cannot possibly remember everything to report it accurately to you."

"Of course not." He was clearly trying to keep a straight face, and not entirely succeeding. "I will tell you as much as I can. You understand there are aspects of it that are still sensitive . . . I mean politically."

She studied his face, and knew that he also meant they were personally painful. "Perhaps you could tell me something of the political situation?" she suggested. "As much as is public knowledge—to those who were interested," she added. Now it was her turn to mock herself very slightly. "I'm afraid I was more concerned with dresses and gossip at the time of the O'Neil case." She would have been about fifteen. "And thinking whom I might marry, of course."

"Of course," he nodded. "A subject that engages most of us, from time to time. All you need to know of the political background is that Ireland, as always, was agitating for Home Rule. Various British prime ministers had attempted to put it through Parliament, and it proved their heartbreak, and for some their downfall. This is the time of the spectacular rise of Charles Stewart Parnell. He was to become leader of the Home Rule Party in '77."

"I remember that name," she agreed.

"Naturally, but this was long before the scandal that ruined him."

"Did he have anything to do with what happened with the O'Neil family?"

"Nothing at all, at least not directly. But the fire and hope of a new leader was in the air, and Irish independence at last, and everything was different because of it." He looked out the window at the passing countryside, and she knew he was seeing another time and place.

"But we had to prevent it?" she assumed.

"I suppose it came to that, yes. We saw it as the necessity to keep the peace. Things change all the time, but how its done must be controlled. There is no point in leaving a trail of death behind you in order merely to exchange one form of tyranny for another."

"You don't have to justify it to me," she told him. "I am aware enough of the feeling. I only wish to understand something of the O'Neil family, and why one of them should hate you personally so much that twenty years later you believe he would stoop to manufacturing evidence that you committed a crime. What sort of a man was he then? Why has he waited so long to do this?"

Narraway turned his head away from the sunlight coming through the carriage window. He spoke reluctantly. "Cormac? He was a good-looking man, very strong, quick to laugh, and quick to anger—but it was usually only on the surface, and gone before he would dwell on it. But he was intensely loyal, to Ireland above all, then to his family. He and his brother Sean were very close." He smiled. "Quarreled like Kilkenny cats, as they say, but let anyone else step in and they'd turn on them like furies."

"How old was he then?" she asked.

"Close to forty," he replied without hesitation.

She wondered if he knew that from records, or if he had been close enough to Cormac O'Neil that such things were open between them. She had the increasing feeling that this was far more than a Special Branch operation. There was deep, many-layered personal emotion as well, and Narraway would only ever tell her what he had to.

"Were they from an old family?" she pursued. "Where did they live, and how?"

He looked out the window again. "Cormac had land to the south of Dublin—Slane. Interesting place. Old family? Aren't we all supposed to go back to Adam?"

"He doesn't seem to have bequeathed the heritage to us equally," she answered.

"I'm sorry. Am I being evasive?"

"Yes," she replied.

"Cormac had enough means not to have to work more than in an occasional overseeing capacity. He and Sean between them owned a brewery as well. I daresay you know the waters of the Liffey River are famous for their softness. You can make ale anywhere, but nothing else has quite the flavor of that made with Liffey water. But you want to know what they were like."

"Yes," she answered. "Don't you need me to seek him out? Because if he hates you as deeply as you think, he will tell you nothing that could help."

The light vanished from his face. "If it's Cormac, he's thought this out very carefully. He must have known all about Mulhare and the whole operation: the money, the reason for paying it as I did, and how any interference would cost Mulhare his life."

"And he must also have been able to persuade someone in Lisson Grove to help him," she pointed out.

He winced. "Yes. I've thought about that a lot." Now his face was very somber indeed. "I've been piecing together all I know: Mulhare's connections; what I did with the money to try to make certain it would never be traced back to Special Branch, or to me personally, all the past friends and enemies I've made, where it happened. It always comes back to O'Neil."

"Why would anyone at Lisson Grove be willing to help O'Neil?" she asked. It was like trying to take gravel out of a wound, only far deeper than a scraped knee or elbow. She thought of Daniel's face as he sat on one of the hard-backed kitchen chairs, dirt and blood on his legs, while she tried to clean where he had torn the skin off, and pick out the tiny stones. There had been tears in his eyes and he had stared resolutely at the ceiling, trying to stop them from spilling over and giving him away.

"Many reasons," Narraway replied. "You cannot do a job like mine without making enemies. You hear things about people you might very much prefer not to know, but that is a luxury you sacrifice when you accept the responsibility."

"I know that," she told him.

His eyes wandered a little. "Really? How do you know that, Charlotte?"

She saw the trap and slipped around it. "Not from Thomas. He doesn't discuss his cases since he joined Special Branch. And anyway, I don't think you can explain to someone else such a complicated thing."

He was watching her intently now. His eyes were so dark it was hard to read the expression in them. The lines in his face showed all the emotions that had passed over them through the years: the anxiety, the laughter, and the grief.

"My eldest sister was murdered, many years ago now," she explained. "But perhaps you know that already. Several young women were at that time. We had no idea who was responsible. In the course of the investigation we learned a great deal about each other that would have been far more comfortable not to have known, and we cannot unlearn such things." She remembered it with pain now, even though it was fourteen years ago.

She looked up at him and saw his surprise. The only way to cover the discomfort was to continue talking.

"After that, when Thomas and I were married, I am afraid I meddled a good deal in many of his cases, particularly those where Society people were involved. I had an advantage in being able to meet them socially, and observe things he never could. One listens to gossip as a matter of course. It is largely what Society is about. But when you do it intelligently, actually trying to learn things, comparing what one person says with what another does, asking questions obliquely, weighing answers, you cannot help but learn much that is private to other people, painful, vulnerable, and absolutely none of your affair."

He moved his head very slightly in assent, but he knew it was not necessary to speak.

For a little while they rode in silence. The rhythmic clatter of the wheels over the railway ties was comfortable, almost somnolent. It had been a difficult and tiring few days and she found herself drifting into a daze, then woke with a start. She hoped she had not been lolling there with her mouth open!

Still, she did not yet know enough about what she could do to help and asked, "Do you know who it was at Lisson Grove who betrayed you?"

"No, I don't," he admitted. "I have considered several possibilities. In fact the only people I am certain it is not are Thomas and a man called Stoker. It makes me realize how incompetent I have been that I suspected nothing. I was always looking outward, at the enemies I knew. In this profession I should have looked behind me as well."

She did not argue. "So we can trust no one in Special Branch, apart from Stoker," she concluded. "Then I suppose we need to concentrate on Ireland. Why does Cormac O'Neil hate you so much? If I am to learn anything, I need to know what to build upon."

This time he did not look away from her, but she could hear the reluctance in his voice. He told her only because he had to. "When he was planning an uprising I was the one who learned about it and prevented it. I did it by turning to his sister-in-law, Sean's wife, and using the information she gave me to have his men arrested and imprisoned."

"I see."

"No, you don't," he said quickly, his voice tight. "And I have no intention of telling you any further. But because of it Sean killed her, and was hanged for her murder. It is that which Cormac cannot forgive. If it had simply been a battle he would have considered it the fortunes of war. He might have hated me at the time, but it would have been forgotten, as old battles are. But Sean and Kate are still dead, still tarred as a betrayer and a wife murderer. I just don't know why he waited so long. That is the one piece of it I don't understand."

"Perhaps it doesn't matter," she said somberly. It was a tragic story, ugly even, and she was certain he had edited it very heavily in the telling. "What do you want me to do?"

"I still have friends in Dublin, I think," he answered. "I cannot approach Cormac myself. I need someone I can trust, who looks totally innocent and unconnected with me. I . . . I can't even go anywhere with you, or he would suspect you immediately. Bring me the facts. I can put them together." He seemed about to add something more, then changed his mind.

"Are you worried that I won't know what is important?" she asked. "Or that I won't remember and tell you accurately?"

"No. I know perfectly well that you can do both."

"Do you?" She was surprised.

He smiled, briefly. "You tell me about helping Pitt when he was in the police, as if you imagined I didn't know."

"You said you didn't know about my sister Sarah," she pointed out. "Or was that . . . discretion rather than truth?"

"It was the truth. But perhaps I deserved the remark. I learned about you mostly from Vespasia. She did not mention Sarah, perhaps out of delicacy. And I had no need to know."

"You had some need to know the rest?" she said with disbelief.

"Of course. You are part of Pitt's life. I had to know exactly how far I could trust you. Although given my present situation, you cannot be blamed for doubting my ability in that."

"That sounds like self-pity," she said tartly. "I have not criticized you, and that is not out of either good manners or sympathy—neither of which we can afford just at the moment, if they disguise the truth. We can't live without trusting someone. It is an offense to betray, not to be betrayed."

"As I said, it is a good thing you did not marry into Society," he retorted. "You would not have survived. Or on the other hand, perhaps Society would not have, and that might not have been so bad. A little shake-up now and then is good for the constitution."

Now she was not sure if he was laughing at her or defending himself. Or possibly it was both.

"So you accepted my assistance because you believe I can do what you require?" she concluded.

"Not at all. I accepted it because you gave me no alternative. Also, since Stoker is the only other person I trust, and he did not offer, nor has he the ability, I had no alternative in any case."

"Touché," she said quietly.

They did not speak again for quite some time, and when they did it was about the differences between Society in London and Dublin. He described the city and surrounding countryside with such vividness that she began to look forward to seeing it herself. He even spoke of the festivals, saints' days, and other occasions people celebrated.

When the train drew into Holyhead they went straight to the boat. After a brief meal, they returned to their cabins for the crossing. They would arrive in Dublin before morning, but were not required to disembark until well after daylight.

DUBLIN WAS UTTERLY DIFFERENT from London, but at least to begin with Charlotte was too occupied with getting ashore at Dun Laoghaire to have time to stare about her. Then there was the ride into the city itself, which was just waking up to the new day; the rain-washed streets were clean and filling with people about their business. She saw plenty of horse traffic—mostly trade at this hour; the carriages and broughams would come later. The few women were laundresses, maids going shopping, or factory workers wearing thick skirts and with heavy shawls wrapped around them.

Narraway hailed a cab, and they set out to look for accommodation. He seemed to know exactly where he was going and gave very precise directions to the driver, but he did not explain them to her. They rode in silence. He stared out the window and she watched his face, the harsh early-morning light showing even the smallest lines around his eyes and mouth. It made him seem older, far less sure of himself.

She thought of Daniel and Jemima, and hoped Minnie Maude was settling in. They had seemed to like her, and surely anyone Gracie vouched for would be good. She could not resent Gracie's happiness, but she missed her painfully at times like this.

That was absurd. There had never been another time like this, when a case took her out of London and away from her children. Here she was in a foreign country, with Victor Narraway, riding around the streets looking for lodgings. Little wonder Mrs. Waterman was scandalized. Perhaps she was right to be.

And Pitt was in France pursuing someone who thought nothing of slitting a man's throat in the street and leaving him to die as if he were no more than a sack of rubbish. Pitt didn't even have a clean shirt, socks, or personal linen. Narraway had sent him money, but he would need more. He would need help, information, probably the assistance of the French police. Would Narraway's replacement provide all this? Was he loyal? Was he even competent?

And worse than any of that, if he was Narraway's enemy, then he was almost certainly Pitt's enemy as well, only Pitt would not know that. He would go on communicating as if it were Narraway at the other end.

She turned away and looked out the window on her own side. They were passing handsome Georgian houses and every now and then public buildings and churches of classical elegance. There were glimpses of the river, which she thought did not seem to curve and wind as much as the Thames. She saw several horse-drawn trams, not unlike those in London, and—in the quieter streets—children playing with spinning tops, or jumping rope.

Twice she drew in breath to ask Narraway where they were going, but each time she looked at the tense concentration on his face, she changed her mind.

Finally they stopped outside a house in Molesworth Street in the southeastern part of the city.

"Stay here." Narraway came suddenly to attention. "I shall be back in a few moments." Without waiting for her acknowledgment he got out, strode across the footpath, and rapped sharply on the door of the nearest house. After less than a minute it was opened by a middle-aged woman in a white apron, her hair tied in a knot on top of her head. Narraway spoke to her and she invited him in, closing the door again behind him.

Charlotte sat and waited, suddenly cold now and aware of how tired she was. She had slept poorly in the night, aware of the rather cramped cabin and the constant movement of the boat. But far more than anything physical, it was the rashness of what she was doing that kept her awake. Now alone, waiting, she wished she were anywhere but here. Pitt would be furious. What if he had returned home to find the children alone with a maid he had never seen before? They would tell him Charlotte had gone off to Ireland with Narraway, and of course they would not even be able to tell him why!

She was shivering when Narraway came out again and spoke to the driver, then at last to her.

"There are rooms here. It is clean and quiet and we shall not be noticed, but it is perfectly respectable. As soon as we are settled I shall go to make contact with the people I can still trust." He looked at her face carefully. She was aware that she must look rumpled and tired, and probably ill-tempered into the bargain. A smile would help, she knew, but in the circumstances it would also be idiotic.

"Please wait for me," he went on. "Rest if you like. We may be busy this evening. We have no time to waste."

He held out his arm to assist her down, meeting her eyes earnestly, questioningly, before letting go. He was clearly concerned for her, but she was glad that he did not say anything more. Though they would both feel terrible doubt and strain in the days to come, she should not forget that, after all, it was his career that was ruined, not hers. It was he who would in the end have to bear it alone; he was the one accused of theft and betrayal. No one would blame her for any of this.

But of course there was every likelihood that they would blame Pitt.

"Thank you," she said with a quick smile, then turned away to look at the house. "It seems very pleasant."

He hesitated, then with more confidence he went ahead of her to the front door. When the landlady opened it for them, he introduced Charlotte as Mrs. Pitt, his half sister, who had come to Ireland to meet with relatives on her mother's side.

"How do you do, ma'am," Mrs. Hogan said cheerfully. "Welcome to Dublin, then. A fine city it is."

"Thank you, Mrs. Hogan. I look forward to it very much," Charlotte replied.

NARRAWAY WENT OUT ALMOST immediately. Charlotte began by unpacking her case and shaking the creases out of the few clothes she had brought. There was only one dress suitable for any sort of formal occasion, but she had some time ago decided to copy the noted actress Lillie Langtry and add different effects to it each time: two lace shawls, one white, one black; special gloves; a necklace of hematite and rock crystals; earrings; anything that would draw the attention from the fact that it was the same gown. At least it fit remarkably well. Women might be perfectly aware that it was the same one each time she wore it, but with luck men would notice only that it became her.

As she hung it up in the wardrobe along with a good costume with two skirts, and a lighter-weight dress, she remembered the days when Pitt had still been in the police, and she and Emily had tried their own hands at helping with detection. Of course that had been particularly when the victims had been from high Society, to which they had access, and Pitt could observe them only as a police officer, when behavior was unnatural and everyone very much on their guard.

At that time his cases had been rooted in human passions, and

occasionally social ills, but never secrets of state. There had been no
reason why he would not discuss them with her and benefit from her
greater insight into Society's rules and structures, and especially the
subtler ways of women whose lives were so different from his own he
could not guess what lay behind their manners and their words.

At times it had been dangerous. But she had loved the adventure
of both heart and mind, the cause for which to fight. She had never
for an instant been bored, or suffered the greater dullness of soul that
comes when one does not have a purpose one believes in passionately.

Charlotte laid out her toiletries both on the dressing table and in
the very pleasant bathroom that she shared with another female
guest. Then she took off her traveling skirt and blouse, removed the
pins from her hair, and lay down on the bed in her petticoat.

She must have fallen asleep because she woke to hear a tap on
the door. She sat up, for a moment completely at a loss as to where she
was. The furniture, the lamps on the walls, the windows were all unfamiliar. Then it came back to her and she rose so quickly she was
dragging the coverlet with her.

"Who is it?" she asked.

"Victor," he replied quietly, perhaps remembering he was supposed to be her brother, and Mrs. Hogan might have excellent hearing.

"Oh." She looked down at herself in her underclothes, hair all
over the place. "A moment, please," she requested. There was no
chance in the world of redoing her hair, but she must make herself decent. She was suddenly self-conscious about her appearance. She
seized her skirt and jacket and pulled them on, misbuttoning the latter in her haste and having then to undo it all and start anew. He
must be standing in the corridor, wondering what on earth was the
matter with her.

"I'm coming," she repeated. There was no time to do more than
put the brush through her hair, then pull the door open.

He looked tired, but it did not stop the amusement in his eyes
when he saw her, or a flash of appreciation she would have preferred
not to be aware of. Perhaps she was not beautiful—certainly not in a

conventional sense—but she was a remarkably handsome woman with fair, warm-toned skin and rich hair. And she had never, since turning sixteen, lacked the shape or allure of womanhood.

"You are invited to dinner this evening," he said as soon as he was inside the room and the door closed. "It is at the home of John and Bridget Tyrone, whom I dare not meet yet. My friend Fiachra McDaid will escort you. I've known him a long time, and he will treat you with courtesy. Will you go . . . please?"

"Of course I will," she said instantly. "Tell me something about Mr. McDaid, and about Mr. and Mrs. Tyrone. Any advantage I can have, so much the better. And what do they know of you? Will they be startled that you suddenly produce a half sister?" She smiled slightly. "Apart from someone looking for distant family in Ireland. And how well do you and I know each other? Do I know you work with Special Branch? We had better have grown up quite separately, because we know too little of each other. Even one mistake would arouse suspicion."

He leaned against the doorjamb, hands in his pockets. He looked completely casual, nothing like the man she knew professionally. She had a momentary vision of how he must have been twenty years ago: intelligent, elusive, unattainable—but to some women that in itself was an irresistible temptation. Before her marriage, and occasionally since, she had known women for whom that was an excitement far greater than the thought of a suitable marriage, even than a title or money.

She stood still, waiting for his reply, conscious of her traveling costume and extremely untidy hair.

"My father married your mother after my mother died," he began.

She was about to express sympathy, then realized she had no idea whether it was true, or if he was making it up for the story they must tell. Perhaps better she was not confused with the truth, whatever that was.

"By the time you were born," he continued. "I was already at university—Cambridge—you should know that. That is why we know each other so little. My father is from Buckinghamshire, but he could perfectly well have moved to London, so you may have grown up wherever you did. Always better to stay with the truth where you can. I know that area. I would have visited."

"What did he do—our father?" she asked. This all had an air of unreality about it, even ridiculousness, but she knew it mattered, perhaps vitally.

"He had land in Buckinghamshire," he replied. "He served in the Indian army. You don't need to have known him well. I didn't."

She heard the sharpness of regret in his voice. "He died some time ago. Keep the mother you have. You and I have become acquainted only recently. This trip is in part for that purpose."

"Why Ireland?" she asked. "Someone is bound to ask me."

"My mother was Irish," he replied.

"Really?" She was surprised, but perhaps she should have known it.

"No." This time he smiled fully, with both sweetness and humor. "But she's dead too. She won't mind."

She felt a strange lurch of pity inside her, an intimate knowledge of loneliness.

"I see," she said quietly. "And these relatives I am looking for— how is it that I remain here without finding them? In fact, why do I think to find them anyway?"

"Perhaps it is best if you don't," he answered. "You merely want to see Dublin. I have told you stories about it, and we have seized the excuse to visit. That will flatter them, and be easy enough to believe. It's a beautiful city and has a character that is unique."

She did not argue, but she felt that nothing very much would happen if she did not ask questions. Polite interest could be very easily brushed aside and met with polite and uninformative answers.

CHARLOTTE COLLECTED HER CAPE. They left Molesworth Street and in the pleasant spring evening walked in companionable silence the half mile to the house of Fiachra McDaid.

Narraway knocked on the carved mahogany door, and after a few moments it was opened by an elegant man wearing a casual velvet jacket of dark green. He was quite tall, but even under the drape of the fabric Charlotte could see that he was a little plump around the middle. In the lamplight by the front door his features were melancholy, but as soon as he recognized Narraway, his expression lit with a vitality that made him startlingly attractive. It was difficult to know his age from his face, but he had white wings to his black hair, so Charlotte judged him to be close to fifty.

"Victor!" he said cheerfully, holding out his hand and grasping Narraway's fiercely. "Wonderful invention, the telephone, but there's nothing like seeing someone." He turned to Charlotte. "And you must be Mrs. Pitt, come to our queen of cities for the first time. Welcome. It will be my pleasure to show you some of it. I'll pick the best bits, and the best people; there'll be time only to taste it and no more. Your whole life wouldn't be long enough for all of it. Come in, and have a drink before we start out." He held the door wide and, after a glance at Narraway, Charlotte accepted.

Inside, the rooms were elegant, very Georgian in appearance. Their contents could easily have been found in a home in any good area of London, except perhaps for some of the pictures on the walls, and a certain character to the silver goblets on the mantel. She was interested in the subtle differences, but had no time to indulge in such trivial matters anyway.

"You'll be wanting to go to the theater," Fiachra McDaid went on, looking at Charlotte. He offered her sherry, which she merely sipped. She needed a very clear head, and she had eaten little.

"Naturally," she answered with a smile. "I could hardly hold my head up in Society at home if I came to Dublin and did not visit the theater." With a touch of satisfaction she saw an instant of puzzlement in his eyes. What had Narraway told this man of her? For that matter, what did Fiachra McDaid know of Narraway?

The look in McDaid's eyes, quickly masked, told her that it was quite a lot. She smiled, not to charm but in her own amusement.

He saw it and understood. Yes, most certainly he knew quite a lot about Narraway.

"I imagine everybody of interest is at the theater, at one time or another," she said.

"Indeed." McDaid nodded. "And many will be there at dinner

tonight at the home of John and Bridget Tyrone. It will be my pleasure to introduce you to them. It is a short carriage ride from here, but
certainly too far to return you to Molesworth Street on foot, at what
may well be a very late hour."

"It sounds an excellent arrangement," she said, accepting. She
turned to Narraway. "I shall see you at breakfast tomorrow? Shall we
say eight o'clock?"

Narraway smiled. "I think you might prefer we say nine," he
replied.

CHARLOTTE AND FIACHRA MCDAID spoke of trivial things
on the carriage ride, which was, as he had said, quite short. Mostly he
named the streets through which they were passing, and mentioned a
few of the famous people who had lived there at some time in their
lives. Many she had not heard of, but she did not say so, although she
thought he guessed. Sometimes he prefaced the facts with "as you will
know," and then told her what indeed she had not known.

The home of John and Bridget Tyrone was larger than McDaid's.
It had a splendid entrance hall with staircases rising on both sides,
which curved around the walls and met in a gallery arched above the
doorway into the first reception room. The dining room was to the
left beyond that, with a table set for above twenty people.

Charlotte was suddenly aware that her inclusion, as an outsider,
was a privilege someone had bought through some means of favor.
There were already more than a dozen people present, men in formal
black and white, women in exactly the same variety of colors one
might have found at any fashionable London party. What was different was the vitality in the air, the energy of emotion in the gestures,
and now and then the lilt of a voice that had not been schooled out
of its native music.

She was introduced to the hostess, Bridget Tyrone, a handsome
woman with very white teeth and the most magnificent auburn hair,
which she hardly bothered to dress. It seemed to have escaped her attempts like autumn leaves in a gust of wind.

"Mrs. Pitt has come to see Dublin," McDaid told her. "Where better to begin than here?"

"Is it curiosity that brings you, then?" John Tyrone asked, standing at his wife's elbow, a dark man with bright blue eyes.

Sensing rebuke in the question, Charlotte seized the chance to begin her mission. "Interest," she corrected him with a smile she hoped was warmer than she felt it. "Some of my mother's family were from this area, and spoke of it with such vividness I wanted to see it for myself. I regret it has taken me so long to do so."

"I should have known it!" Bridget said instantly. "Look at her hair, John! That's an Irish color if you like, now, isn't it? What were their names?"

Charlotte thought rapidly. She had to invent, but let it be as close to the truth as possible, so she wouldn't forget what she had said or contradict herself. And it must be useful. There was no point in any of this if she learned nothing of the past. Bridget Tyrone was waiting, eyes wide.

Charlotte's mother's mother had been Christine Owen. "Christina O'Neil," she said with the same sense of abandon she might have had were she jumping into a raging river.

There was a moment's silence. She had an awful thought that there might really be such a person.

"O'Neil," Bridget repeated. "Sure enough there are O'Neils around here. Plenty of them. You'll find someone who knew her, no doubt. Unless, of course, they left in the famine. Only God Himself knows how many that'd be. Come now, let me introduce you to our other guests, because you'll not be knowing them."

Charlotte accompanied her obediently and was presented to one couple after another. She struggled to remember unfamiliar names, trying hard to say something reasonably intelligent and at the same time gain some sense of the gathering, and whom she should seek to know better. She must tell Narraway something more useful than that she had gained an entry to Dublin Society.

She introduced her fictitious grandmother again.

"Really?" a women named Talulla Lawless said with surprise, raising her thin black eyebrows as soon as Charlotte mentioned the name. "You sound fond of her," Talulla continued. Talulla was a slender woman, almost bony, but with marvelous eyes, wide and bright, and of a shade neither blue nor green.

Charlotte thought of the only grandmother she knew, and found impossibly cantankerous. "She told me wonderful stories," she lied confidently. "I daresay they were a little exaggerated, but there was a truth in them of the heart, even if events were a trifle inaccurate in the retelling."

Talulla exchanged a brief glance with a fair-haired man called Phelim O'Conor, but it was so quick that Charlotte barely saw it.

"Am I mistaken?" Charlotte asked apologetically.

"Oh no," Talulla assured her. "That would be long ago, no doubt?"

Charlotte swallowed. "Yes, about twenty years, I think. There was a cousin she wrote to often, or it may be it was her cousin's wife. A very beautiful woman, so my grandmama said." She tried rapidly to calculate the age Kate O'Neil would be were she still alive. "Perhaps a second cousin," she amended. That would allow for a considerable variation.

"Twenty years ago," Phelim O'Conor said slowly. "A lot of trouble then. But you wouldn't be knowing that—in London. Might have seemed romantic, to your grandmother, Charles Stewart Parnell and all that. God rest his soul. Other people's griefs can be like that." His face was smooth, almost innocent, but there was a darkness in his voice.

"I'm sorry," Charlotte said quietly. "I didn't mean to touch on something painful. Do you think perhaps I shouldn't ask?" She looked from Phelim to Talulla, and back again.

He gave a very slight shrug. "No doubt you'll hear anyway. If your cousin's wife was Kate O'Neil, she's dead now, God forgive her . . ."

"How can you say that?" Talulla spat the words between her teeth, the muscles in her thin jaw clenched tight. "Twenty years is nothing! The blink of an eye in the history of Ireland's sorrows."

Charlotte tried to look totally puzzled, and guilty. But in truth she was beginning to feel a little afraid. Rage sparked in Talulla as if she'd touched an exposed nerve.

"Because there's been new blood, and new tears since then," Phelim answered, speaking to Talulla, not Charlotte. "And new issues to address."

Good manners might have dictated that Charlotte apologize again and withdraw, leaving them to deal with the memories in their own way, but she thought of Pitt in France, alone, trusting in Narraway to back him up. She feared there were only Narraway's enemies in Lisson Grove now, people who might easily be Pitt's enemies too. Good manners were a luxury for another time.

"Is there some tragedy my grandmother knew nothing of?" she asked innocently. "I'm sorry if I have woken an old bereavement, or injustice. I certainly did not mean to. I'm so sorry."

Talulla looked at her with undisguised harshness, a slight flush in her sallow cheeks. "If your grandmother's cousin was Kate O'Neil, she trusted an Englishman, an agent of the queen's government who courted her, flattered her into telling him her own people's secrets, then betrayed her to be murdered by those whose trust she gave away."

O'Conor winced. "I daresay she loved him. We can all be fools for love," he said wryly.

"I daresay she did!" Talulla snarled. "But that son of a whore never loved her, and with half a drop of loyalty in her blood she'd have known that. She'd have won his secrets, then put a knife in his belly. He might have been able to charm the fish out of the sea, but he was her people's enemy, and she knew that. She got what she deserved." She turned and moved away sharply, her dark head high and stiff, her back ramrod-straight, and she made no attempt to offer even a glance backward.

"You'll have to forgive Talulla," O'Conor said ruefully. "Anyone would think she'd loved the man herself, and it was twenty years ago. I must remember never to flirt with her. If she fell for my charm I might wake up dead of it." He shrugged. "Not that it'd be likely, God help me!" He did not add anything more, but his expression said all the rest.

Then with a sudden smile, like spring sun through the drifting rain, he told her about the place where he had been born and the little town to the north where he had grown up and his first visit to Dublin when he had been six.

"I thought it was the grandest place I'd ever seen," he said. "Street after street of buildings, each one fit to be the palace of a king. And some so wide it was a journey just to cross from one side to another."

Suddenly Talulla's hatred seemed no more than a lapse in manners. But Charlotte did not forget it. O'Conor's charm was clearly masking great shame. She was certain that he would find Talulla afterward and, when they were alone, berate her for allowing a foreigner—an Englishwoman at that—to see a part of their history that should have been kept private.

The party continued. The food was excellent, the wine flowed generously. There was laughter, sharp and poignant wit, even music as the evening approached midnight. But Charlotte did not forget the emotion she had seen, and the hatred.

She rode home in the carriage with Fiachra McDaid, and despite his gentle inquiries she said nothing except how much she had enjoyed the hospitality.

"And did anyone know your cousin?" he asked. "Dublin's a small town, when it comes to it."

"I don't think so," she answered easily. "But I may find trace of her later. O'Neil is not a rare name. And anyway, it doesn't matter very much."

"Now, there's something I doubt our friend Victor would agree with," he said candidly. "I had the notion it mattered to him rather a lot. Was I wrong, then, do you suppose?"

For the first time in the evening she spoke the absolute truth. "I think maybe you know him a great deal better than I do, Mr. McDaid. We have met only in one set of circumstances, and that does not give a very complete picture of a person, don't you think?"

In the darkness inside the carriage she could not read his expression.

"And yet I have the distinct idea that he is fond of you, Mrs. Pitt," McDaid replied. "Am I wrong in that too, do you suppose?"

"I don't do much supposing, Mr. McDaid . . . at least not aloud," she said. And as she spoke, her mind raced, remembering what

Phelim O'Conor had said of Narraway, and wondering how much she really knew him. The certainty was increasing inside her that it was Narraway of whom Talulla had been speaking when she referred to Kate O'Neil's betrayal—both of her country, and of her husband—because she had loved a man who had used her, and then he allowed her to be murdered for it.

Pitt had believed in Narraway; she knew that without doubt. But she also knew that Pitt thought well of most people, even if he accepted that they were complex, capable of cowardice, greed, and violence. But had he ever understood any of the darkness within Narraway, the human man beneath the fighter against his country's enemies? They were so different. Narraway was subtle, where Pitt was instinctive. He understood people because he understood weakness and fear; he had felt need and knew how powerful it could be.

But Pitt also understood gratitude. Narraway had offered him dignity, purpose, and a means to feed his family when he had desperately needed it. He would never forget that.

Was he also just a little naïve?

She remembered with a smile how disillusioned her husband had been when he had discovered the shabby behavior of the Prince of Wales. She had felt his shame for a man he thought should have been better. He had believed more in the honor of his calling than the man did himself. She loved Pitt intensely for that, even in the moment she understood it.

Narraway would never have been misled; he would have expected roughly what he eventually found. He might have been disappointed, but he would not have been hurt.

Had he ever been hurt?

Could he have loved Kate O'Neil, and still used her? Not as Charlotte understood love.

But then perhaps Narraway always put duty first. Maybe he was feeling a deep and insuperable pain for the first time, because he was robbed of the one thing he valued: his work, in which his identity was so bound up.

Why on earth was she riding through the dark streets of a strange city, with a man she had never seen before tonight, taking absurd risks, telling lies, in order to help a man she knew so little? Why did she ache with a loss for him?

Because she imagined how she would feel if he were like her—and he was not. She imagined he cared about her, because she had seen it in his face in unguarded moments. It was probably loneliness she saw, an instant of lingering for a love he would only find an encumbrance if he actually had it.

"I hear Talulla Lawless gave you a little display of her temper," McDaid said, interrupting her thoughts. "I'm sorry for that. Her wounds are deep, and she sees no need to hide them; it is hardly your fault. But then there are always casualties of war, the innocent often as much as the guilty."

She turned to look at his face in the momentary light of a passing carriage's lamp. His eyes were bright, his mouth twisted in a sad little smile. Then the darkness shadowed him again and she was aware of him only as a soft voice, a presence beside her, the smell of fabric and a faint sharpness of tobacco.

"Of course," she agreed very quietly.

They reached Molesworth Street and the carriage stopped.

"Thank you, Mr. McDaid," she said with perfect composure. "It was most gracious of you to have me invited, and to accompany me. Dublin's hospitality is all that has been said of it, and believe me, that is high praise."

"We have just begun," he replied warmly. "Give Victor my regards, and tell him we shall continue. I won't rest until you think this is the fairest city on earth, and the Irish the best people. Which of course we are, despite our passion and our troubles. You can't hate us, you know." He said it with a smile that was wide and bright in the lamplight.

"Not the way you hate us, anyway," she agreed gently. "But then we have no cause. Good night, Mr. McDaid."

CHAPTER

5

CHARLOTTE FACED NARRAWAY ACROSS the breakfast table in Mrs. Hogan's quiet house the next morning, still in conflict as to what she would say to him.

"Very enjoyable," she answered his inquiry as to the previous evening. And she realized with surprise how much that was true. It was a long time since she had been at a party of such ease and sophistication. Although this was Dublin, not London, Society did not differ much.

There were no other guests in the dining room this late in the morning. Most of the other tables had already been set with clean, lace-edged linen ready for the evening. She concentrated on the generous plate of food before her. It contained far more than she needed for good health. "They were most kind to me," she added.

"Nonsense," he replied quietly.

She looked up, startled by his abruptness.

He was smiling, but the sharp morning light showed very clearly the tiredness in his face. Her resolve to lie to him wavered. There were many ways in which he was unreadable, but not in the deep-etched lines in his face or the hollows around his eyes.

"All right," she conceded. "They were hospitable and a certain glamour in it was fun. Is that more precise?"

He was amused. He gave nothing so obvious as a smile, but it was just as plain to her.

"Whom did you meet, apart from Fiachra, of course?"

"You've known him a long time?" she asked, remembering McDaid's words with a slight chill.

"Why do you say that?" He took more toast and buttered it. He had eaten very little. She wondered if he had slept.

"Because he asked me nothing about you," she answered. "But he seems very willing to help."

"A good friend," he replied, looking straight at her.

She smiled. "Nonsense," she said with exactly the same inflection he had used.

"Touché," he acknowledged. "You are right, but we have known each other a long time."

"Isn't Ireland full of people you have known a long time?"

He put a little marmalade on his toast.

She waited.

"Yes," he agreed. "But I do not know the allegiances of most of them."

"If Fiachra McDaid is a friend, what do you need me for?" she asked bluntly. Suddenly an urgent and ugly thought occurred to her: Perhaps he did not want her in London where Pitt could reach her. Just how complicated was this, and how ugly? Where was the embezzled money now? Was it really about money, and not old vengeances at all? Or was it both?

He did not answer.

"Because you are using me, or both of us, with selected lies?" she suggested.

He winced as if the blow had been physical as well as emotional. "I am not lying to you, Charlotte." His voice was so quiet, she had to lean forward a little to catch his words. "I am . . . being highly selective about how much of the truth I tell you . . ."

"And the difference is?" she asked.

He sighed. "You are a good detective—in your own way almost as good as Pitt—but Special Branch work is very different from ordinary domestic murder."

"Domestic murder isn't always ordinary," she contradicted him. "Human love and hate very seldom are. People kill for all sorts of reasons, but it is usually to gain or protect something they value passionately. Or it is in outrage at some violation they cannot bear. And I do not mean necessarily a physical one. The emotional or spiritual wounds can be far harder to recover from."

"I apologize," he responded. "I should have said that the alliances and loyalties stretch in far more complicated ways. Brothers can be on opposite sides, as can husband and wife. Rivals can help each other, even die for each other, if allied in the cause."

"And the casualties are the innocent as well as the guilty," she said, echoing McDaid's words. "My role is easy enough. I would like to help you, but I am bound by everything in my nature to help my husband, and of course myself . . ."

"I had no idea you were so pragmatic," he said with a slight smile.

"I am a woman, I have a finite amount of money, and I have children. A degree of pragmatism is necessary." She spoke gently to take the edge from her words.

He finished spreading his marmalade. "So you will understand that Fiachra is my friend in some things, but I will not be able to count on him if the answer should turn out to be different from the one I suppose."

"There is one you suppose?"

"I told you: I think Cormac O'Neil has found the perfect way to take revenge on me, and has taken it."

"For something that happened twenty years ago?" she questioned.

"The Irish have the longest memories in Europe." He bit into the toast.

"And the greatest patience too?" she said with disbelief. "People take action because something, somewhere has changed. Crimes of state have that in common with ordinary, domestic murders. Something new has caused O'Neil, or whoever it is, to do this now. Perhaps it has only just become possible. Or it may be that for him, now is the right time."

He ate the whole of his toast before replying. "Of course you are right. The trouble is that I don't know which of those reasons it is. I've studied the situation in Ireland and I can't see any reason at all for O'Neil to do this now."

She ignored her tea. An unpleasant thought occurred to her, chilling and very immediate. "Wouldn't O'Neil know that this would bring you here?" she asked.

Narraway stared at her. "You think O'Neil wants me here? I'm sure if killing me were his purpose, he would have come to London and done it. If I thought it was simply murder I wouldn't have let you come with me, Charlotte, even if Pitt's livelihood rests on my return to office. Please give me credit for thinking that far ahead."

"I'm sorry," she said. "I thought bringing someone that nobody would see as assisting you might be the best way of getting around that. You never suggested it would be comfortable, or easy. And you cannot prevent me from coming to Ireland if I want to. You could simply have let me do it alone, which would be inefficient, and unlike you."

"It would have been awkward," he conceded. "But not impossible. I had to tell you something of the situation, for Pitt's sake. For your own, I cannot tell you everything. I don't know any reason why O'Neil should choose now. But then I don't know any reason why anyone should. It is unarguable that someone with strong connections in Dublin has chosen to steal the money I sent for Mulhare, so to bring about the poor man's death. Then they made certain it was evident first to Austwick, and then to Croxdale, and so brought about my dismissal."

He poured more tea for himself. "Perhaps it was not O'Neil who initiated it; he may simply have been willingly used. I've made many enemies. Knowledge and power both make that inevitable."

"Then think of other enemies," she urged. "Whose circumstances have changed? Is there anyone you were about to expose?"

"My dear, do you think I haven't thought of that?"

"And you still believe it is O'Neil?"

"Perhaps it is a guilty conscience." He gave a smile so brief it reached his eyes and was gone again. "'The guilty flee where no man pursueth,'" he quoted. "But there is knowledge in this that only people familiar with the case could have."

"Oh." She poured herself fresh tea. "Then we had better learn more about O'Neil. He was mentioned yesterday evening. I told them that my grandmother was Christina O'Neil."

He swallowed. "And who was she really?"

"Christine Owen," she replied.

He started to laugh. She said nothing, but finished her toast and then the rest of her tea.

CHARLOTTE SPENT THE MORNING and most of the afternoon quietly reading as much as she could of Irish history, realizing the vast gap in her knowledge and becoming a little ashamed of it. Because Ireland was geographically so close to England, and because the English had occupied it one way or another for so many centuries, in their minds its individuality had been swallowed up in the general tide of British history. The empire covered a quarter of the world. Englishmen tended to think of Ireland as part of their own small piece of it, linked by a common language—disregarding the existence of the Irish tongue.

So many of Ireland's greatest sons had made their names on the world stage indistinguishably from the English. Everyone knew Oscar Wilde was Irish, even though his plays were absolutely English in their setting. They probably knew Jonathan Swift was Irish, but did they know it of Bram Stoker? Did they know it of the great duke of Wellington, victor of Waterloo, and later prime minister? The fact that these men had left Ireland in their youth did not in any way alter their heritage.

Her own family was not Anglo-Irish, but in pretending to have a grandmother who was, perhaps she should be a little more sensitive to people's feelings and treat the whole subject less casually.

By evening she was again dressed in her one black gown, this time with different jewelry and different gloves, and her hair decorated with an ornament given to her years ago. She was off to the theater, and quite suddenly worried that she was overdressed. Perhaps other people would be far less formal. After all, they were a highly literate culture, educated in words and ideas but also very familiar with them. They might consider an evening at the theater not a social affair but rather an intellectual and emotional one.

She took the ornament out of her hair, and then had to restyle it accordingly. All of which meant she was late, and flustered, when Narraway knocked on the door to tell her that Fiachra McDaid was there to escort her for the evening again.

"Thank you," she said, putting the comb down quickly and knocking several loose hairpins onto the floor. She ignored them.

He looked at her with anxiety. "Are you all right?"

"Yes! It is simply an indecision as to what to wear." She dismissed it with a slight gesture.

He regarded her carefully. His eyes traveled from her shoes, which were visible beneath the hem of her gown, all the way to the crown of her head. She felt the heat burn up her face at the candid appreciation in his eyes.

"You made the right decision," he pronounced. "Diamonds would have been inappropriate here. They take their drama very seriously."

She drew in breath to say that she had no diamonds, and realized he was laughing at her. She wondered if he would have given a woman diamonds, if he loved her. She thought not. If he were capable of that sort of love, it would have been something more personal, more imaginative. A cottage by the sea, however small, perhaps; something of enduring meaning that would add joy to its owner's life.

"I'm so glad," she said, meeting his eyes. "I thought diamonds were too trivial." She accepted his arm, laying her fingers so lightly on the fabric of his jacket that he could not have felt her touch.

Fiachra McDaid was as elegant and graceful as the previous evening, although on this occasion dressed less formally. He greeted Charlotte with apparent pleasure at seeing her again, even so soon.

He expressed his willingness to help her to understand as much of Irish theater as was possible for an Englishwoman to grasp. He smiled at Charlotte as he said it, as if it were some secret aside that she already understood.

It was some time since she had been to the theater at all. It was not an art form Pitt was particularly fond of, and she did not like going without him.

Here in Dublin the event was quite different. The theater building itself was smaller; indeed there was an intimacy to it that made it less an occasion to be seen, and more of an adventure in which to participate.

McDaid introduced her to various of his own friends who greeted him. They varied in age and apparent social status, as if he had chosen them from as many walks of life as possible.

"Mrs. Pitt," he explained cheerfully. "She is over from London to see how we do things here, mostly from an interest in our fair city, but in part to see if she can find some Irish ancestry. And who can blame her? Is there anyone of wit or passion who wouldn't like to claim a bit of Irish blood in their veins?"

She responded warmly to the welcome extended her, finding the exchanges easy, even comfortable. She had forgotten how interesting it was to meet new people, with new ideas. But she did wonder exactly what Narraway had told McDaid.

She searched his face and saw nothing in it but good humor, interest, amusement, and a blank wall of guarded intelligence intended to give away nothing at all.

They were very early for the performance, but most of the audience were already present. While McDaid was talking she had an opportunity to look around and study faces. They were different from a London audience only in subtle ways. There were fewer fair heads, fewer blunt Anglo-Saxon features, a greater sense of tension and suppressed energy.

And of course she heard the music of a different accent, and now and then people speaking in a language utterly unrecognizable to her. There was in them nothing of the Latin or Norman-French about the words, or the German from which so much English was derived. She assumed it was the native tongue. She could only guess at what they said by the gestures, the laughter, and the expression in faces.

She noticed one man in particular. His hair was black with a loose, heavy wave streaked with gray. His head was narrow-boned, and it was not until he turned toward her that she saw how dark his eyes were. His nose was noticeably crooked, giving his whole aspect a lopsided look, a kind of wounded intensity. Then he turned away, as if he had not seen her, and she was relieved. She had been staring, and that was ill-mannered, no matter how interesting a person might seem.

"You saw him," McDaid observed so quietly it was little more than a whisper.

She was taken aback. "Saw him? Who?"

"Cormac O'Neil," he replied.

She was startled. Had she been so very obvious? "Was that . . . I mean the man with the . . ." Then she did not know how to finish the sentence.

"Haunted face," he said for her.

"I wasn't going to . . ." She saw in his eyes that she was denying it pointlessly. Either Narraway had told him, or he had pieced it together himself. It made her wonder how many others knew, indeed if all those involved might well know more than she, and her pretense was deceiving no one.

"Do you know him?" she asked.

"I?" McDaid raised his eyebrows. "I've met him, of course, but know him? Hardly at all."

"I didn't mean in any profound sense," she parried. "Merely were you acquainted."

"In the past, I thought so." He was watching Cormac while seeming not to. "But tragedy changes people. Or then on the other hand, perhaps it only shows you what was always there, simply not yet uncovered. How much does one know anybody? Most of all oneself."

"Very metaphysical," she said drily. "And the answer is that you can make a guess, more or less educated, depending on your intelligence and your experience with that person."

He looked at her steadily. "Victor said you were . . . direct."

She found it odd to hear Narraway referred to by his given name, instead of the formality she was used to, the slight distance that leadership required.

Now she was not sure if she was on the brink of offending McDaid. On the other hand, if she was too timid even to approach what she really wanted, she would lose the chance.

She smiled at him. "What was O'Neil like, when you knew him?"

His eyes widened. "Victor didn't tell you? How interesting."

"Did you expect him to have?" she asked.

"Why is he asking, why now?" He sat absolutely still. All around him people were moving, adjusting position, smiling, waving, finding seats, nodding agreement to something or other, waving to friends.

"Perhaps you know him well enough to ask him that?" she suggested.

Again he countered. "Don't you?"

She kept her smile warm, faintly amused. "Of course, but I would not repeat his answer. You must know him well enough to believe he would not confide in someone he could not trust."

"So perhaps we both know, and neither will trust the other," he mused. "How absurd, how vulnerable and incredibly human; indeed, the convention of many comic plays."

"To judge by Cormac O'Neil's face, he has seen tragedy," she countered. "One of the casualties of war that you referred to."

He looked at her steadily, and for a moment the buzz of conversation around them ceased to exist. "So he has," he said softly. "But that was twenty years ago."

"Does one forget?"

"Irishmen? Never. Do the English?"

"Sometimes," she replied.

"Of course. You could hardly remember them all!" Then he caught himself immediately and his expression changed. "Do you want to meet him?" he asked.

"Yes—please."

"Then you shall," he promised.

There was a rustle of anticipation in the audience and everyone fell silent. After a moment or two the curtain rose and the play began. Charlotte concentrated so that she could speak intelligently when she was introduced to people at the intermission.

But she found following it difficult. There were frequent references to events she was not familiar with, even words she did not know, and there was an underlying air of sadness.

Was that how Cormac O'Neil felt: helpless, predestined to be overwhelmed? Everybody lost people they loved. Bereavement was a part of life. The only escape was to love no one. She stopped trying to understand the drama on the stage and, as discreetly as she could, she studied O'Neil.

He seemed to be alone. He looked neither right nor left, and the people on either side seemed to be with others.

The longer she watched him, the more totally alone did he seem to be. But she was equally sure that he was never bored. His eyes never strayed from the stage, yet at times his expression did reflect the drama.

By the time the intermission came Charlotte felt herself moved by the passion emanating from players and audience alike. But she was also confused by it. It made her feel more sharply than the lilt of a different accent, or even the sound of another language, that she was in a strange place, teeming with emotions she caught and lost again.

"May I take you to get something to drink?" McDaid asked her when the curtain fell and the lights were bright again. "And perhaps to meet one or two more of my friends? I'm sure they are dying of curiosity to know who you are, and of course how I know you."

"I would be delighted," she answered. "And how do you know me? We had better be accurate, or it will start people talking." She smiled to rob the words of offense.

"But surely the sole purpose of coming to the theater with a beautiful woman is to start people talking?" He raised his eyebrows. "Otherwise one would be better to come alone, like Cormac O'Neil, and concentrate on the play, without distraction."

"Thank you. I'm flattered to imagine I could distract you." She inclined her head a little, enjoying the trivial play of words. "Especially from so intense a drama. The actors are superb. I have no idea what they are talking about at least half the time, and yet I am conquered by their emotions."

"Are you sure you are not Irish?" he pressed.

"Not sure at all. Perhaps I am, and I should simply look harder. But please do not tell Mr. O'Neil that my grandmother's name was O'Neil also, or I shall be obliged to admit that I know very little about her, and that would make me seem very discourteous, as if I did not wish to own that part of my heritage. The truth is I simply did not realize how interesting it would be."

"I shall not tell him, if you don't wish me to," he promised.

"But you have not told me how we met," she reminded him.

"I saw you across a room and asked a mutual acquaintance to introduce us," he said. "Is that not always how one meets a woman one sees, and admires?"

"I imagine it is. But what room was it? Was it here in Ireland? I imagine not, since I have been here only a couple of days. But have you been to London lately?" She smiled at him. "Or ever, for that matter?"

"Of course I've been to London. Do you think I am some provincial bumpkin?" He shrugged. "Only once, mind you. I did not care for it—nor it for me. It was so huge, so crowded with people, and yet at the same time anonymous. You could live and die there, and never be seen."

"But I have been in Dublin only a couple of days," she said to fill the silence.

"Then I was bewitched at first sight," he said reasonably, suddenly smiling again. "I'm sorry I insulted your home. It was unforgivable. Call it my own inadequacy in the midst of three million English."

"Oh quite a few Irishmen, believe me," she said with a smile. "And none of them in the least inadequate."

He bowed.

"And I accepted your invitation because I was flattered, and irresponsible?" she challenged.

"You are quite right," he conceded. "We must have mutual friends—some highly respectable aunt, I daresay. Do you have any such relations?"

"My great-aunt Vespasia, by marriage. If she recommended you I would accompany you anywhere on earth," she responded unhesitatingly.

"She sounds charming."

"She is. Believe me, if you had met her really, you would not dare to treat me other than with the utmost respect."

"Where did I meet this formidable lady?"

"Lady Vespasia Cumming-Gould. It doesn't matter. Any surroundings would be instantly forgotten once you had seen her. But London will do."

"Vespasia Cumming-Gould." He turned the name over on his tongue. "It seems to find an echo in my mind."

"It has set bells ringing all over Europe," she told him. "You had better be aware that she is of an indeterminate age, but her hair is silver and she walks like a queen. She was the most beautiful and most outrageous woman of her generation. If you don't know that, they will know that you never met her."

"I am now most disappointed that I did not." He offered her his arm, and they began to descend the stairway.

Together they walked down to the room where refreshments were already being served, and the audience had gathered to greet friends and exchange views on the performance.

It was several minutes of pleasant exchange before McDaid introduced her to a woman with wildly curling hair named Dolina Pearse and a man of unusual height whom he addressed as Ardal Barralet. Beside them, but apparently not with them, was Cormac O'Neil.

"O'Neil!" McDaid said with surprise. "Haven't seen you for some time. How are you?"

Barralet turned as if he had not noticed O'Neil standing so close as to brush coattails with him.

"'Evening, O'Neil. Enjoying the performance? Excellent, don't you think?" he said casually.

O'Neil had either to answer or offer an unmistakable rebuff.

"Very polished," he said, looking straight back at Barralet. His voice was unusually deep and soft, as if he too were an actor, caressing the words. He did not even glance at Charlotte. "Good evening, Mrs. Pearse." He acknowledged Dolina.

"Good evening, Mr. O'Neil," she said coldly.

"You know Fiachra McDaid?" Barralet filled in the sudden silence. "But perhaps not Mrs. Pitt? She is newly arrived in Dublin."

"How do you do, Mrs. Pitt," O'Neil said politely, but without interest. McDaid he looked at with a sudden blaze of emotion.

McDaid stared back at him calmly, and the moment passed.

Charlotte wondered if she had seen it, or merely imagined it.

"What brings you to Dublin, Mrs. Pitt?" Dolina inquired, clearly out of a desire to change the subject. There was no interest in either her voice or her face.

"Good report of the city," Charlotte replied. "I have made a resolution that I will no longer keep on putting off into the future the good things that can be done today."

"How very English," Dolina murmured. "And virtuous." She added the word as if it were insufferably boring.

Charlotte felt her temper flare. She looked straight back at Dolina. "If it is virtuous to come to Dublin, then I have been misled," she said drily. "I was hoping it was going to be fun."

McDaid laughed sharply, his face lighting with sudden amusement. "It depends how you take your pleasures, my dear. Oscar Wilde, poor soul, is one of us, of course, and he made the world laugh. For years we have tried to be as like the English as we can. Now at last we are finding ourselves, and we take our theater packed with anguish, poetry, and triple meanings. You can dwell on whichever one suits your mood, but most of them are doom-laden, as if our fate is in blood. If we laugh, it is at ourselves, and as a stranger you might find it impolite to join in."

"That explains a great deal." She thanked him with a little nod of her head. She was aware that O'Neil was watching her, possibly because she was the only one in the group he did not already know, but she wanted to engage in some kind of conversation with him. This was the man Narraway believed had contrived his betrayal. What on earth could she say that did not sound forced? She looked directly at him, obliging him either to listen or to deliberately snub her.

"Perhaps I sounded a bit trivial when I spoke of fun," she said half apologetically. "I like my pleasure spiced with thought, and even a puzzle or two, so the flavor of it will last. A drama is superficial if one can understand everything in it in one evening, don't you think?"

The hardness in his face softened. "Then you will leave Ireland a happy woman," he told her. "You will certainly not understand us in a week, or a month, probably not in a year."

"Because I am English? Or because you are so complex?" she pursued.

"Because we don't understand ourselves, most of the time," he replied with the slightest lift of one shoulder.

"No one does," she returned. Now they were speaking as if there were no one else in the room. "The tedious people are the ones who think they do."

"We can be tedious by perpetually trying to, aloud." He smiled, and the light of it utterly changed his face. "But we do it poetically. It is when we begin to repeat ourselves that we try people's patience."

"But doesn't history repeat itself, like variations on a theme?" she said. "Each generation, each artist, adds a different note, but the underlying tune is the same."

"England's is in a major key." His mouth twisted as he spoke. "Lots of brass and percussion. Ireland's is minor, woodwind, and the dying chord. Perhaps a violin solo now and then." He was watching her intently, as if it were a game they were playing and one of them would lose. Did he already know who she was, and that she had come with Narraway, and why?

She tried to dismiss the thought as absurd, then remembered that someone had already outwitted Narraway, which was a considerable feat. It required not only passion for revenge, but a high level of intelligence as well. Most frightening of all, it needed connections in Lisson Grove sufficiently well placed to have put the money in Narraway's bank account.

Suddenly the game seemed a great deal more serious. She was aware that because of her hesitation, Dolina was watching her curiously as well, and Fiachra McDaid was standing at her elbow.

"I always think the violin sounds so much like the human voice," she said with a smile. "Don't you, Mr. O'Neil?"

Surprise flickered for a moment in his eyes. He had been expecting her to say something more defensive, no doubt.

"Did you not expect the heroes of Ireland to sound human?" he asked her.

"Not entirely." She avoided looking at McDaid, or Dolina, in case their perception brought them back to reality. "I had thought of something heroic, even supernatural."

"Touché," McDaid said softly. He took Charlotte by the arm, holding her surprisingly hard. She could not have shaken him off even had she wished to. "We must take our seats." He excused them and led her away after only the briefest farewell. She nearly asked him if she had offended someone, but she did not want to hear the answer. Nor did she intend to apologize.

As soon as she resumed her seat she realized that it offered her as good a view of the rest of the audience as it did of the stage. She glanced at McDaid, and saw in his expression that he had arranged it so intentionally, but she did not comment.

They were only just in time for the curtain going up, and immediately the drama recaptured their attention. Charlotte, lost in the many allusions to history and legends with which she was not familiar, began to look at the audience again, to catch something of their reaction and follow a little more.

John and Bridget Tyrone were in a box almost opposite. With the intimate size of the theater she could see their faces quite clearly. He was watching the stage, leaning a little forward as if not to miss a word. She glanced at him, then—seeing his absorption—turned away. Her gaze swept around the audience. Charlotte put up the opera glasses McDaid had lent her, not to see the stage but to hide her own eyes, and to keep watching Mrs. Tyrone.

Bridget's searching stopped when she saw a man in the audience below her, to her left. To Charlotte all that was visible was the back of his head, but she was certain she had seen him before. She could not remember where.

Bridget continued staring at him, as if willing him to look back at her.

On the stage the drama heightened. Charlotte was only dimly aware of it, for her emotional concentration was upon the audience. John Tyrone was still watching the players. At last the man Bridget was watching turned and looked back up at the boxes. It was Phelim O'Conor. As soon as she saw his profile Charlotte knew him. He remained with his eyes fixed on Bridget, his face unreadable.

Bridget looked away just as her husband became aware of her again, and switched his attention from the stage. They spoke to each other briefly.

In the audience below, O'Conor turned back to the stage. His neck was stiff, his head unmoving.

During the second intermission, McDaid took Charlotte back outside to the bar where once more refreshments were liberally served. The conversation buzzed about the play. Was it well performed? Was it true to the intention of the author? Had the main actor misinterpreted his role?

Charlotte listened, trying to fix her expression in an attitude of intelligent observation. But really she was watching to see whom else she recognized among those queueing for drinks or talking excitedly to people they knew. All of them were strangers to her, and yet in a way they were familiar. Many were so like those she had known before her marriage that she half expected them to recognize her. It was an odd feeling, pleasant and nostalgic, even though she would have changed nothing of her present life.

"Are you enjoying the play?" McDaid asked her. They drifted toward the bar counter, where Cormac O'Neil had a glass of whiskey in his hand.

"I am enjoying the whole experience," she replied. "I am most grateful that you brought me. I could not have come alone, nor would I have found it half so pleasant."

"I am delighted you enjoy it," McDaid replied with a smile. "I was not sure that you would. The play ends with a superb climax, all very dark and dreadful. You won't understand much of it at all."

"Is that the purpose of it?" she asked, looking from McDaid to O'Neil and back again. "To puzzle us all so much that we will be obliged to spend weeks or months trying to work out what it really means? Perhaps we will come up with half a dozen different possibilities?"

For a moment there was surprise and admiration in McDaid's eyes; then he masked it and the slightly bantering tone returned. "I think perhaps you overrate us, at least this time. I rather believe the playwright himself has no such subtle purpose in mind."

"What meanings did you suppose?" O'Neil asked softly.

"Oh, ask me in a month's time, Mr. O'Neil," she said casually. "There is anger in it, of course. Anyone can see that. There seems to me also to be a sense of predestination, as if we all have little choice, and birth determines our reactions. I dislike that. I don't wish to feel so . . . controlled by fate."

"You are English. You like to imagine you are the masters of history. In Ireland we have learned that history masters us," he responded. The bitterness in his tone was laced with irony and laughter, but the pain was real.

It was on her tongue to contradict him, until she realized her opportunity. "Really? If I understand the play rightly, it is about a certain inevitability in love and betrayal that is quite universal—a sort of darker and older Romeo and Juliet."

O'Neil's face tightened, and even in the lamplight of the crowded room Charlotte could see his color pale. "Is that what you see?" His voice was thick, almost choking on the words. "You romanticize, Mrs. Pitt." Now the bitterness in him was overwhelming. She was as aware of it as if he had touched her physically.

"Do I?" she asked him, moving aside to allow a couple arm in arm to pass by. In so doing she deliberately stepped close to O'Neil, so he could not leave without pushing her aside. "What harder realities should I see? Rivalry between opposing sides, families divided, a love that cannot be fulfilled, betrayal and death? I don't think I really find that romantic, except for us as we sit in the audience watching. For the people involved it must be anything but."

He stared at her, his eyes hollow with a kind of black despair. She could believe very easily that Narraway was right, and O'Neil had nursed a hatred for twenty years, until fate had given him a way to avenge it. But what was it that had changed?

"And what are you, Mrs. Pitt?" he asked, standing close to her and speaking so McDaid almost certainly would not hear him. "Audience or player? Are you here to watch the blood and tears of Ireland, or to meddle in them, like your friend Narraway?"

She was stunned. So he did know that she was linked to Narraway. The hushed anger with which he now confronted her seemed on the verge of boiling over at last. Surely to feign innocence would be ridiculous?

"I would like to be a deus ex machina," she replied. "But I imagine that's impossible."

"God in the machine?" he said with an angry shrug. "You want to descend at the last act and arrange an impossible ending that solves it all? How very English. And how absurd, and supremely arrogant. You are twenty years too late. Tell Victor that, when you see him. There's nothing left to mend anymore." He turned away before she could answer again, pushing past her and spilling what was left of his whiskey as he bumped into a broad man in a blue coat. The moment after, he was gone.

Charlotte was aware of McDaid next to her, and a certain air of discomfort about him.

"I'm sorry," she said. There was no point in trying to explain. "I allowed myself to express my opinions too freely."

He bit his lip. "You couldn't know it, but the subject of Irish freedom, and traitors to the cause, is painfully close to O'Neil. It was through his family that our great plan was betrayed twenty years ago." He winced. "We never knew for sure by whom. Sean O'Neil murdered his wife, Kate, and was hanged for it. Even though it was because she was the one who told the English our plans, some thought it was because Sean found her with another man. Either way, we failed again, and the bitterness still lasts."

"It was an uprising that you intended?" she asked quietly. She heard the chatter around her.

"Of course," McDaid replied flatly. "Home Rule was in the very air we breathed then. We could have been ourselves, without the weight of England around our necks."

"Is that how you see it?" She turned as she spoke and looked at him, searching his face.

His expression softened. He smiled back at her, rueful and a little self-deprecating. "I did at the time. Seeing Cormac brings it back. But I'm cooler-headed now. There are better places to put one's energy—causes less narrow." She was aware of the color and whisper of fabric around them, silk against silk. They were surrounded by people in one of the most interesting capital cities in the world, come out to an evening at the theater. Some of them, at least, were also men and women who saw themselves living under a foreign oppression in their own land, and some of them at least were willing to kill and to die to throw it off. She looked just like them, cast of feature, tone of skin and hair, and yet she was not; she was different in heart and mind.

"What causes?" she asked with interest.

His smile widened, as if to brush it aside. "Social injustices, old-fashioned laws to reform," he replied. "Greater equality. Exactly the same as, no doubt, you fight for at home. I hear there are some great women in London battling for all manner of things. Perhaps one day you will tell me about some of them?" He made it a question, as if he were interested enough to require an answer.

"Of course," she said lightly, trying to master facts in her mind so she could answer sensibly, if the necessity arose.

He took her arm as people milled around her, returning to their seats, courteous, hospitable, full of dry wit and a passion for life. How easy, and dangerous, it would be for her to forget that she did not belong here.

NARRAWAY WAS UNCERTAIN WHAT Charlotte would learn at the theater. As he walked along Arran Quay, on the north bank of the Liffey, his head down into the warm, damp breeze off the water, he was afraid that she would discover a few things about him that he would very much rather she not know, but he knew no way to help that.

He smiled bitterly as he pictured her probing relentlessly for the facts behind the pain. Would she be disillusioned to hear his part in it all? Or was that his vanity, his own feelings—that she cared enough for him that disillusion was even possible, let alone something that would wound her?

He would never forget the days after Kate's death. Worst was the morning they hanged Sean. The brutality and the grief of that had cast a chill over all the years since.

But he did not want Charlotte's grief for him, particularly if it was based on a misconception of who he was.

He laughed at himself; it was just a faint sound, almost drowned by his quick footsteps along the stones of the quayside. Why, at this time in his life, did he care so much for the opinion of another man's wife?

He forced his attention to where he was going, and why. If he did not learn who had diverted the money meant for Mulhare, anything else he learned about O'Neil was pointless. Someone in Lisson Grove had been involved. He blamed none of the Irish. They were fighting for their own cause, and at times he even sympathized with it. But the man in Special Branch who had done this had betrayed his own people, and that was different. He wanted to know who it was, and prove it. The damage he could cause would have no boundary. If he hated England enough to plan and execute a way of disgracing Narraway, then what else might he do? Was his real purpose to replace him? This whole business of Mulhare might be no more than a means to that end. But was it simply ambition, or was there another, darker purpose behind it as well?

Without realizing it he increased his pace, moving so softly he almost passed the alley he was looking for. He turned and fumbled in the dark. He had to feel his way along one of the walls. Third door. He knocked sharply, a quick rhythm.

He had brought Charlotte because he wanted to, but she had her own compelling reasons to be here. If he was right, that there was a traitor in Lisson Grove, then one of the first things that person would do would be to get rid of Pitt. If Pitt was fortunate, he would simply be dismissed. There were much worse possibilities.

The door opened. He was let into a small, extremely stuffy office piled high with ledgers, account books, and sheaves of loose papers. A striped cat had claimed itself a space in front of the hearth and did not stir when Narraway came in and took a seat on a chair opposite the cluttered desk.

O'Casey sat in the chair behind it, his bald head gleaming in the gaslight.

"Well?" Narraway asked, masking his eagerness as closely as he could.

O'Casey hesitated.

Narraway considered threatening him. He still had power, albeit illegal now. He drew in his breath. Then he looked at O'Casey's face again and changed his mind. He had few enough friends; he could not afford to alienate any of them.

"So what is it you expect of me, then?" O'Casey asked, cocking his head a little to one side. "I'll not help you, not more than I owe. For old times' sake. And that's little enough."

"I know," Narraway agreed. There were wounds and debts between them, some still unpaid. "I need to know what's changed for Cormac O'Neil—"

"For God's sake, leave the poor man alone! Have you not already taken all he has?" O'Casey exclaimed. "You'll not be after the child, will you?"

"The child?" For a moment Narraway was at a loss. Then memory flooded back. Kate's daughter by Sean. She had been only a child, six or seven years old when her parents died. "Did Cormac raise her?" he asked.

"A little girl?" O'Casey squinted at him contemptuously. "Of course he didn't, you fool. And what would Cormac O'Neil do with a six-year-old girl, then? Some cousin of Kate's took her, Maureen, I think her name was. She and her husband. Raised her as their own."

Narraway felt a stab of pity for the child—Kate's child. That should never have happened.

"But she knows who she is?" he said aloud.

"Of course. Cormac would have told her, if no one else." O'Casey lifted one shoulder slightly. "Although, of course, it might not be the truth as you know it, poor child. There are things better left unsaid."

Narraway felt chilled. He had not thought of Kate's daughter.

Looking back, even weeks afterward, he had known that Kate had crossed sides because she believed it was a doomed rising, and more Irishmen would die in it than English, far more. But she knew Sean as well. He had been willing enough to use her beauty to shame Narraway, even lead him to his death, but in his wildest imagination he had never considered that she might give herself willingly to Narraway or, worse, care for him.

And when she did, it was beyond Sean's mind or heart to forgive. He had said he killed her for Ireland, but Narraway knew it was for himself, just as in the end Sean knew it too.

And Cormac? He had loved Kate also. Did he feel an Irishman bested in deviousness by an Englishman, in a fight where no one was fair? Or a man betrayed by a woman he wanted and could never have: his brother's wife, who had sided with the enemy—for her own reasons, political or personal?

What had he told Talulla?

Could it possibly be anything new in the last few months? And if it were, how could she have moved the money from Mulhare's account back to Narraway's, using some traitor in Lisson Grove? Not by herself. Then with whom?

"Who betrayed Mulhare?" he asked O'Casey.

"No idea," O'Casey answered. "And if I did know, I wouldn't tell you. A man who'll sell his own people deserves to have his thirty pieces of silver slip out of his hands. Deserves to have it put in a bag o' lead around his neck, before they throw him into Dublin Bay."

Narraway rose to his feet. The cat by the fire stretched out and then curled up on the other side.

"Thank you," he said.

"Don't come back," O'Casey replied. "I'll not harm you, but I'll not help you either."

"I know," Narraway replied.

CHARLOTTE DID NOT HAVE the opportunity to speak at any length with Narraway after returning from the theater that night. She had hoped to tell him all that she had seen and learned there the following morning, but when they met for breakfast, the presence of others eating at nearby tables kept her from revealing what had transpired. Narraway said he had business to attend to, that he had heard from Dolina Pearse that Charlotte would be most welcome to attend the opening of an art exhibition, if she cared to, and to take tea with Dolina and her friends afterward. He had accepted on her behalf.

"Thank you," she said a little coolly.

He caught the intonation, and smiled. "Did you wish to decline?" he asked, eyebrows raised.

She looked at his dark face. To have taken the slightest notice of his pride now would be idiotic. He was facing disgrace, and further, his own downfall would destroy his friend's life. If he failed to exonerate himself, Pitt too might lose all the worldly possessions he had; cutting most deeply would be the loss of his ability to support his family, most particularly the wife who had stepped down so far from financial and social comfort to marry him.

"No, of course not," she replied, smiling at Narraway. "I am just a little nervous about it. I met some of them at Bridget Tyrone's party, and I am not sure that the encounter was entirely amicable."

"I can imagine," he said wryly. "But I know you, and I know something of Dolina. Tea should be interesting. And you'll like the art. It is impressionist, I think." He rose from the table.

"Victor!" She used his name for the first time without thinking, until she saw his face, the quickening, the sudden vulnerability. She wanted to apologize, but that would only make it worse. She forced herself to smile up at him where he stood, half turned to leave. He was naturally elegant; his jacket perfectly cut, his cravat tied with care.

She hardly knew how to begin, and yet certain necessity compelled her.

He was waiting.

"If I am to go to the exhibition I would like to purchase a new blouse." She felt the flush of embarrassment hot in her face. "I did not bring . . ."

"Of course," he said quickly. "We will go as soon as you have finished your breakfast. Perhaps we should get two. You cannot be seen in precisely the same costume at every function. Will you be ready in half an hour?" He glanced at the clock on the mantel.

"Good heavens! I could have luncheon as well in that time. I shall be ready in ten minutes," she exclaimed.

"Really? Then I shall meet you at the front door." He looked surprised, and quite definitely pleased.

THEY WALKED PERHAPS THREE hundred yards then quite easily found a hansom to take them into the middle of the city. Narraway seemed to know exactly where he was going and stopped at the entrance to a very elegant couturier.

Charlotte imagined the prices, and knew that they would be beyond her budget. Surely Narraway must know what Pitt earned? Why was he bringing her here?

He opened the door for her and held it.

She stood where she was. "May we please go somewhere a little less expensive? I think this is beyond what I should spend, particularly on something I may not wear very often."

He looked surprised.

"Perhaps you have never bought a woman's blouse before," she said a little tartly, humiliation making her tongue sharp. "They can be costly."

"I wasn't proposing that you should buy it," he replied. "It is necessary in pursuit of my business, not yours. It is rightly my responsibility."

"Mine also . . . ," she argued.

"May we discuss it inside?" he asked. "We are drawing attention to ourselves standing in the doorway."

She moved inside quickly, angry with both him and herself. She should have foreseen this situation and avoided it somehow.

An older woman came toward them, dressed in a most beautifully cut black gown. It had no adornment whatever; the sheer elegance of it was sufficient. She was the perfect advertisement for her establishment. Charlotte would have loved a gown that fitted so exquisitely.

She still had a very good figure, and such a garment would have flattered her enormously. She knew it, and the temptation was so sharp she could feel it like a sweet taste in her mouth.

"May we see some blouses, please?" Narraway asked. "Suitable for attending an exhibition of art, or an afternoon soirée."

"Certainly, sir," the woman agreed. She regarded Charlotte for no more than a minute, assessing what might both fit and suit her, then another mere instant at Narraway, perhaps judging what he would be prepared to pay.

Looking at his elegant and clearly expensive clothes, Charlotte's heart sank. The woman had no doubt jumped to the obvious conclusion that they were husband and wife. Who else would a respectable woman come shopping with, for such intimate articles as a blouse? She should have insisted that he take her somewhere else and wait outside. Except that she would have to borrow the money from him anyway.

"Victor, this is impossible!" she said under her breath as soon as the woman was out of earshot.

"No it isn't," he contradicted. "It is necessary. Do you want to draw attention to yourself by wearing the same clothes all the time? People will notice, which you know even better than I do. Then they will wonder what our relationship is—that I do not take better care of you."

She tried to think of a satisfactory argument, and failed.

"Or perhaps you want to give up the whole battle?" he suggested.

"No, of course I don't!" she retaliated. "But—"

"Then be quiet and don't argue." He took her arm and propelled her forward, holding her firmly. If she had pulled back she would have bumped into him, and the pressure of his fingers on her arm would have hurt. She determined to have words with him later, in no uncertain fashion.

The woman returned with several blouses, all of them beautiful.

"If madame would care to try them, there is a room available over here," she offered.

Charlotte thanked her and followed immediately. Every one of them was ravishing, but the most beautiful was one in black and bronze stripes that fitted her as if it had been both designed and cut for her personally; and one in white cotton and lace with ruffles and pearl buttons that was outrageously feminine. Even as a girl, in the days when her mother was trying to marry her to someone suitable, she had never felt so attractive, even verging on the really beautiful.

Temptation to have them both ached inside her.

The woman returned to see if Charlotte had made a decision, or if perhaps she wished for a further selection.

"Ah!" she said, drawing in her breath. "Surely madame could not wish for anything lovelier."

Charlotte hesitated, glancing at the striped blouse on its hanger.

"An excellent choice. Perhaps you would like to see which your husband prefers?" the woman suggested.

Charlotte started to say that Narraway was not her husband, but she wanted to phrase it graciously and not seem to correct the woman. Then she saw Narraway just beyond the woman's shoulder, and the admiration in his face. For an instant it was naked, vulnerable, and completely without guard. Then he must have realized, and he smiled.

"We'll take them both," he said decisively, and turned away.

Unless she should contradict him in front of the saleswoman, embarrassing them all, Charlotte had no alternative but to accept. She stepped back, closed the door, and changed into her own very ordinary blouse.

"Victor, you shouldn't have done that," she said as soon as they were outside in the street again. "I have no idea how I am going to repay you."

He stopped and looked at her for a moment.

Suddenly his anger evaporated and she remembered the expression in his eyes only a few moments before.

He reached up and with his fingertips touched her face. It was only her cheek, but it was an extraordinarily intimate gesture, with a great tenderness.

"You will repay me by helping me to clear my name," he replied. "That is more than enough."

To argue would be pointlessly unkind, not only to his very obvious emotion but also to the hope of the success they both needed so much.

"Then we had better set about it," she agreed, then moved a step away from him and started walking along the pavement again.

THE ART EXHIBITION WAS beautiful, but Charlotte could not turn her attention to it and knew that to Dolina Pearse she must have appeared terribly ignorant. Dolina seemed to know each artist at least by repute, and be able to say for what particular technique he was famous. Charlotte simply listened with an air of appreciation, and hoped she could remember enough of it to recite back later.

While they walked around the rooms looking at one picture after another, Charlotte watched the other women, who were fashionably dressed exactly as they would have been in London. Sleeves were worn large at the shoulder this season, and slender from the elbow down. Even the most unsophisticated were puffed, or flying like awkward wings. Skirts were wide at the bottom, padded and bustled at the back. It was very feminine, like flowers in full bloom—large ones, magnolias or peonies.

Tea reminded her of the days before she was married, accompanying her mother on suitable "morning calls," which were actually always made in the afternoon. Behavior was very correct, all the unwritten laws obeyed. And beneath the polite exchanges the gossip was ruthless, the cutting remark honed to a razor's edge.

"How are you enjoying Dublin, Mrs. Pitt?" Talulla Lawless asked courteously. "Do have a cucumber sandwich. Always so refreshing, don't you think?"

"Thank you," Charlotte accepted. It was the only possible thing to do, even if she had not liked them. "I find Dublin fascinating. Who would not?"

"Oh, many people," Talulla replied. "They think us very unsophisticated." She smiled. "But perhaps that is what you enjoy?"

Charlotte smiled back, utterly without warmth. "Either they were not serious, or if they were, then they missed the subtlety of your words," she replied. "I think you anything but simple," she added for good measure.

Talulla laughed. It was a brittle sound. "You flatter us, Mrs. Pitt. It is Mrs., isn't it? I do hope I have not made the most awful mistake."

"Please don't concern yourself, Miss Lawless," Charlotte replied. "It is very far from the most awful mistake. Indeed, were it a mistake, which it isn't, it could still quite easily be put right. Would that all errors were so simply mended."

"Oh dear!" Talulla affected dismay. "How much more exciting your life must be in London than ours is here. You imply dark deeds. You have me fascinated."

Charlotte hesitated, then plunged in. "I daresay the grass is always greener on the other side of the fence. After watching the play last night I imagined life was full of passion and doom-laden love here. Please don't tell me it is all just the fervor of a playwright's imagination. You will entirely ruin the reputation of Ireland abroad."

"I didn't know you had such influence," Talulla said drily. "I had better be more careful of what I say." There was mocking and anger in her face.

Charlotte cast her eyes down toward the floor. "I am so sorry. I seem to have spoken out of turn, and struck some feeling of pain. I assure you, it was unintentional."

"I can see many of your actions are unintentional, Mrs. Pitt," Talulla snapped. "And cause pain."

There was a rustle of silk against silk as a couple of the other women moved slightly in discomfort. Someone drew breath as if to speak, glanced at Talulla, and changed her mind.

"Just as I am sure yours are not, Miss Lawless," Charlotte replied. "I find it easy to believe that every word you say is entirely both foreseen, and intended."

There was an even sharper gasp of breath. Someone giggled nervously.

"May I offer you more tea, Mrs. Pitt?" Dolina asked. Her voice was quivering, but whether with laughter or tears it was impossible to say.

Charlotte held out her cup. "Thank you. That is most kind."

"Don't be ridiculous," Talulla said tartly. "For heaven's sake, it's a pot of tea!"

"The English answer to everything," Dolina ventured. "Is that not so, Mrs. Pitt?"

"You would be surprised what can be done with it, if it is hot enough." Charlotte looked straight at her.

"Scalding, I shouldn't wonder," Dolina muttered.

CHARLOTTE RELAYED IT TO Narraway later that night, after dinner. They were alone in Mrs. Hogan's sitting room with the doors open onto the garden, which was quite small, and overhung with trees. It was a mild evening, and a moon cast dramatic shadows. In unspoken agreement they stood up and walked outside into the balmy air.

"I didn't learn anything more," she admitted finally. "Except that we are still disliked. But how could we imagine anything else? At the theater Mr. McDaid told me something of O'Neil. And O'Neil himself implied that I was here to meddle in Irish affairs—'like your friend Narraway,' as he said. It is time you stopped skirting around it and told me what happened. I don't want to know, but I have to."

He was silent for a long time. She was acutely aware of him standing perhaps a yard away from her, half in the shadow of one of the trees. He was slender, not much taller than she, but she had an impression of physical strength, as if he were muscle and bone, all softness worn away over the years. She did not want to look at his face, partly to allow him that privacy, but just as much because she did not want to see what was there.

"I can't tell you all of it, Charlotte," he said at last. "There was quite a large uprising planned. We had to prevent it."

"How did you do that?" She was blunt.

Again he did not answer. She wondered how much of the secrecy was to protect her, and how much was simply that he was ashamed of his role in it, necessary or not.

Why was she standing out here shivering? What was she afraid of? Victor Narraway? It had not occurred to her before that he might hurt her. She was afraid that she would hurt him. Perhaps that was ridiculous. If he had loved Kate O'Neil, and still been able to sacrifice her in his loyalty to his country, then he could certainly sacrifice Charlotte. She could be one of the unintended victims that Fiachra McDaid had referred to—just part of the price. She was Pitt's wife, and Narraway had shown a loyalty to Pitt, in his own way. She was also quite certain now that he was in love with her. But how naïve of her to imagine that it would change anything he had to do in the greater cause.

She thought of Kate O'Neil, wondering what she had looked like, how old she had been, if she had loved Narraway. Had she betrayed her country and her husband to him? How desperately in love she must have been. Charlotte should have despised her for that, and yet all she felt was pity. She could imagine herself in Kate's place. If she herself hadn't loved Pitt, she could easily have believed herself in love with Narraway.

"You used Kate O'Neil, didn't you?" she said.

"Yes." His voice was so soft she barely heard it.

She turned quietly and walked back the few steps into Mrs. Hogan's sitting room. There wasn't anything more to say, not here, in the soft night wind and the scents of the garden.

CHAPTER

6

PITT WAS TROUBLED. HE stood in the sun in St. Malo, leaning against the buttress edge of the towering wall, and stared out over
the sea. It was vivid blue, the light so dazzling that he found himself
squinting. Out in the bay a sailboat heeled far over.

The town was ancient, beautiful, and at any other time he would
have found it interesting. Were he here on holiday with his family, he
would have loved to explore the medieval streets and alleys, and learn
more of its history, which was peculiarly dramatic.

As it was he had the strong feeling that he and Gower were wasting time. They had watched Frobisher's house for nearly a week and
seen nothing that led them any closer to the truth. Visitors came and
went; not only men but women also. Neither Pieter Linsky nor Jacob
Meister had come again, but there had been dinner parties where at
least a dozen people were present. Deliverymen had come with baskets of the shellfish for which the area was famous. Scores of oysters had
come, shrimp and larger crustaceans like lobsters, and bags of mussels.
But then the same could be said of any of the houses in the area.

Gower wandered along the path, his face sunburned, his hair flopping forward. He stopped just inside the wall, a yard or two short of Pitt. He too leaned against the ledge as if he were watching the sailing boat.

"Where did he go?" Pitt asked quietly, without looking at him.

"Only to the same café as usual," Gower answered, referring to Wrexham, whom one or the other of them had followed every day. "I didn't go in because I was afraid he'd notice me. But I saw the same thin man with the mustache go in, then come back out again in about half an hour."

There was a slight lift in his voice, a quickening. "I watched them through the window for a few minutes as if I were waiting for someone. They were talking about more people coming, quite a lot of them. They seemed to be ticking them off, as if from a list. They're definitely planning something."

Pitt would like to have felt the same stir of excitement, but the whole week seemed too careful, too halfhearted for the passion that inspires great political change. He and Narraway had studied revolutionaries, anarchists, firebrands of all beliefs, and this had a different feel to it. Gower was young. Perhaps he attributed to them some of the vivacity he still felt himself. And he did feel it. Pitt smiled as he thought of Gower laughing with their landlady, complimenting her on the food and letting her explain to him how it was cooked. Then he told her about such English favorites as steak-and-kidney pudding, plum duff, and pickled eels. She had no idea whether to believe him or not.

"They've delivered more oysters," Pitt remarked. "It's probably another party. Whatever Frobisher's political beliefs about changing conditions for the poor, he certainly doesn't believe in starving himself, or his guests."

"He would hardly go around letting everyone know his plans . . . sir," Gower replied quickly. "If everyone thinks he's a rich man entertaining his friends in harmless idealism he never intends to act on, then nobody will take him seriously. That's probably the best safety he could have."

Pitt thought about it for a while. What Gower said was undoubtedly true, and yet he was uneasy about it. The conviction that they were wasting time settled more heavily upon him, yet he could find no argument that was pure reason rather than a niggling instinct born of experience.

"And all the others who keep coming and going?" he asked, at last turning and facing Gower, who was unconsciously smiling as the light warmed his face. Below him in the small square a woman in a fashionable dress, wide-sleeved and full-skirted, walked from one side to the other and disappeared along the narrow alley to the west. Gower watched her all the way, nodding very gently in approval.

Gower turned to Pitt, his fair face puzzled. "Yes, about a dozen of them. Do you think they're really harmless, sir? Apart from Wrexham, of course?"

"Are they all wild revolutionaries pretending very successfully to be ordinary citizens living satisfied and rather pedestrian lives?" Pitt pressed.

It was a long time before Gower answered, as if he were weighing his words with intense care. He turned and leaned on the wall, staring at the water. "Wrexham killed West for a reason," he said slowly. "He was in no present danger, except being exposed as an anarchist, or whatever he would call himself. Perhaps he doesn't want chaos, but a specific order that he considers fairer, more equal to all people. Or it may be a radical reform he's after. Exactly what it is the socialists want is one of the things we need to learn. There may be dozens of different goals—"

"There are," Pitt interrupted. "What they have in common is that they are not prepared to wait for reform by consent; they want to force it on people, violently if necessary."

"And how long will they have to wait for anyone to hand it over voluntarily?" Gower said with an edge of sarcasm. "Who ever gave up power if they weren't forced to?"

Pitt scanned his memory for the history he could recall. "None that I can think of," he admitted. "That's why it usually takes awhile. But the abolition of slavery was passed through Parliament without overt violence. Certainly without revolution."

"I'm not sure the slaves would agree with that assessment," Gower said with a twist of bitterness.

"It's time we found out what we are looking at," Pitt conceded.

Gower straightened up. "If we ask open questions it's bound to get back to him, and he may take a great deal more care. The one advantage we have, sir, is that he doesn't know we're watching him. Can we afford to lose that?" He looked anxious, his fair brows drawn together, the sunburn flushing his cheeks.

"I've been making a few inquiries," Pitt said.

"Already?" Suddenly there was an edge of anger in Gower's voice.

Pitt was surprised. It seemed Gower's easy manner hid an emotional commitment he had not seen. He should have. They had worked together for more than two months, even before the hectic chase that had brought them here.

"As to who I can ask for information without it being obvious," he replied levelly.

"Who?" Gower said quickly.

"A man named John McIver. He's another expatriate Englishman who's lived here for twenty years. Married to a Frenchwoman."

"Are you positive he's trustworthy, sir?" Gower was still skeptical. "It'll only take one careless word, one remark made idly, and Frobisher will know he's being watched. We could lose the big ones, the people like Linsky and Meister."

"I didn't choose him blindly," Pitt replied. He did not intend to tell Gower that he had encountered McIver before, on a quite different case.

Gower drew in his breath, and then let it out again. "Yes, sir. I'll stay here and watch Wrexham, and whoever he meets with." Then he flashed a quick, bright smile. "I might even go down into the square and see the pretty girl with the pink dress again, and drink a glass of wine."

Pitt shook his head, feeling the tension ease away. "I think you'll do better than I will," he said ruefully.

McIver lived some five miles outside St. Malo in the deep countryside. He was clearly longing to speak to someone in his native tongue and hear firsthand the latest news from London. Pitt's visit delighted him.

"Of course I miss London, but don't misunderstand me, sir," he said, leaning back in the garden chair in the sun. He had offered Pitt wine and little sweet biscuits, and—when he declined those—fresh crusty bread and a soft country cream cheese, which he accepted with alacrity.

Pitt waited for him to continue.

"I love it here," McIver went on. "The French are possibly the most civilized nation on earth—apart from the Italians, of course. Really know how to live, and do it with a certain flair that gives even mundane things a degree of elegance. But there are parts of English life that I miss. Haven't had a decent marmalade in years. Sharp, aromatic, almost bitter." He sighed. "The morning's *Times,* a good cup of tea, and a manservant who is completely unflappable. I used to have a fellow who could have announced the Angel of Doom with the same calm, rather mournful air that he announced the duchess of Malmsbury."

Pitt smiled. He ate a whole slice of bread and sipped his wine before he pursued the reason he had come.

"I need to make some very discreet inquiries: government, you understand?"

"Of course. What can I tell you?" McIver nodded.

"Frobisher," Pitt replied. "Expatriate Englishman living here in St. Malo. Would he be the right man to approach to ask a small service to his country? Please be candid. It is of . . . importance, you understand?"

"Oh quite—quite." McIver leaned forward a little. "I beg you, sir, consider very carefully. I don't know your business, of course, but Frobisher is not a serious man." He made a slight gesture of distaste. "He likes to cultivate some very odd friends. He pretends to be a socialist, you know, a man of the people. But between you and me, it is entirely a pose. He mistakes untidiness and a certain levity of manner for being an ordinary man of limited means." He shook his head. "He potters around and considers it to be working with his hands, as if he had the discipline of an artisan who must work to live, but he has very substantial means, which he has no intention of sharing with others, believe me."

"Are you sure?" Pitt said as politely as he could. However he said it, he was still questioning McIver's judgment.

"As sure as anyone can be," McIver replied. "Made a lot of noise about getting things done, but never done a thing in his life."

"He had some very violent and well-known people visiting him." Pitt clung to the argument, unwilling to concede that they had spent so many days here for nothing.

"See 'em yourself?" McIver asked.

"Yes. One of them in particular is very distinctive," Pitt told him. Then even as he said it, he realized how easy it would be to pretend to be Linsky. After all, he had never seen Linsky except in photographs, taken at a distance. The hatchet features, the greasy hair would not be so hard to copy. And Jacob Meister was also ordinary enough.

But why? What was the purpose of it all?

That too was now hideously clear—to distract Pitt and Gower from something else entirely.

"I'm sorry," McIver said sadly. "But the man's an ass. I can't say differently. You'd be a fool to trust him in anything that matters. And I hardly imagine you'd have come this far for something trivial. I'm not as young as I used to be, and I don't get into St. Malo very often, but if there's anything I can do, you have only to name it, you know."

Pitt forced himself to smile. "Thank you, but it would really need to be a resident of St. Malo. But I'm grateful to you for saving me from making a bad mistake."

"Think nothing of it." McIver brushed it away with a gesture. "I say, do have some more cheese. Nobody makes a cheese like the French—except perhaps the Wensleydale, or a good Caerphilly."

Pitt smiled. "I like a double Gloucester, myself."

"Yes, yes," McIver agreed. "I forgot that. Well, we'll grant the cheese equal status. But you can't beat a good French wine!"

"You can't even equal it."

McIver poured them both some wine, then leaned back in his

chair. "Do tell me, sir, what is the latest news on the cricket? Here I hardly ever get the scores, and even then they're late. How is Somerset doing?"

PITT WALKED BACK ALONG the gently winding road as the sun dropped toward the horizon. The air glowed with that faint gold patina that lends unreality to old paintings. Farmhouses looked huge, comfortable, surrounded by barns and stables. It was too early for the trees to be in full leaf, but clouds of blossom mounded like late snow, taking the delicate colors of the coming sunset. There was no wind, and no sound across the fields but the occasional movement of the huge, patient cows.

In the east, the purple sky darkened.

He went over what they knew in his mind again, carefully, all he had seen or heard himself, and all that Gower had seen and reported.

A carter passed him on the road, the wheels sending up clouds of dust, and he smelled the pleasant odor of horses' sweat and fresh-turned earth. The man grunted at Pitt in French, and Pitt returned it as well as he could.

The sun was sinking rapidly now, the sky filling with hot color. The soft breeze whispered in the grass and the new leaves on the willows, always the first to open. A flock of birds rose from the small copse of trees a hundred yards away, swirled up into the sky, and circled.

Between them Pitt and Gower had seen just enough to believe it was worth watching Frobisher's house. If they arrested Wrexham now, it would unquestionably show everyone that Special Branch was aware of their plans, so they would automatically change them.

They should have arrested Wrexham in London a week ago. He would have told them nothing, but they had learned nothing anyway. All they had really done was waste seven days.

How had he allowed that to happen? West had arranged the meeting, promising extraordinary information. Pitt could see the letter in his mind, the scrawled, misspelled words, the smudged ink.

No one else knew of it, except himself and Gower. So how had Wrexham learned of it? Who had betrayed West? It had to be one of the men plotting whatever it was that poor West had been going to reveal.

But this person had not followed West. Pitt and Gower were on his heels from the minute he began to run. If there had been anyone else running they would have seen him. Whoever it was must have been waiting for West. How had they known he would run that way? It was pure chance. He could as easily have gone in any other direction. Pitt and Gower had cornered him there, Pitt along the main street, Gower circling to cut him off.

Had West run into Wrexham by the most hideous mischance?

Pitt retraced in his mind the exact route they had taken. He knew the streets well enough to picture every step, and see the map of it in his mind. He knew where they had first spotted West, where he had started to run, and which way he had gone. There had been no one else in the crowd running. West had darted across the street and disappeared for an instant. Gower had gone after him, jabbing his arm to indicate which way Pitt should go, the shorter way, so they could cut him off.

Then West had seen Gower and swerved. Pitt had lost them both for a few minutes, but he knew the streets well enough to know which way West would go, and had been there within seconds . . . and Gower had raced up from the right to come up beside Pitt.

But the right doglegged back to the street where Pitt had run the minute before, not the way Gower had gone. Unless he had passed Wrexham? Wrexham had come from the opposite way, not following West at all. So why had West run so frantically, as if he knew death was on his heels?

Pitt stumbled and came to a stop. Because it was not Wrexham whom West was afraid of, it was either Pitt himself, or Gower. He had had no reason to fear Pitt, but Gower was a superb runner. In an uncrowded alley he could break into a full sprint in seconds. He could have been there before, ducked back into the shelter of the alley entrance, and then burst out of it again as Pitt arrived. It was he who had killed West, not Wrexham. West's blood was already pooled on the stones. Pitt could see it in his mind's eye. Wrexham was the harmless man he appeared to be, the decoy to lure Pitt to St. Malo, and keep him here, while whatever was really happening came to its climax somewhere else.

It had to be London, otherwise it was pointless to lure Pitt away from it.

Gower. In fifteen or twenty minutes Pitt would be inside the walls of St. Malo again, back to their lodgings. Almost certainly Gower would be there waiting for him. Suddenly he was no longer the pleasant, ambitious young man he had seemed only this morning. Now he was a clever and extremely dangerous stranger, a man Pitt knew only in the most superficial way. He knew that Gower slept well, that his skin burned in the sun, that he liked chocolate cake, that he was occasionally careless when he shaved himself. He was attracted to women with dark hair and he could sing rather well. Pitt had no idea where he came from, what he believed, or even where his loyalties lay—all the things that mattered, that would govern what he would do when the mask was off.

Now suddenly Pitt must wear a mask as well. His own life might depend on it. He remembered with a chill how efficiently Gower had killed West, cut his throat in one movement, and left him on the stones, bleeding to death. One error and Pitt could end the same way. Who in St. Malo would think it more than a horrific street crime? No doubt Gower would be first on the scene again, full of horror and dismay.

There was no one Pitt could turn to. No one in France even knew who he was, and London could be in another world for any help it could offer now. Even if he sent a telegram to Narraway it would make no difference. Gower would simply disappear, anywhere in Europe.

He started to walk again. The sun was on the horizon and within minutes it would be gone. It would be almost dark by the time he was within the vast city walls. He had perhaps fifteen minutes to make up his mind. He must be totally prepared once he reached the house. One mistake, one slip, and it would be his last.

He thought of the chase to the East End, and finally the railway station. He realized with acute self-blame how easily Gower had led him, always making sure they did not lose Wrexham completely, and yet the chase seemed natural enough to be real. They lost him momentarily, and it was always Gower who found him. It was Gower who stopped Pitt from arresting him, pointing out the use of watching him and learning more. Gower had had enough money in his pocket to buy tickets on the ferry.

Come to that, it was Gower who said he had seen Linsky and Meister, and Pitt who had believed it.

What was this plan that used Wrexham to lure Pitt away from London? Of course Pitt must go back, knowing now as he did that Wrexham was not West's killer. The question was what to say to Gower. What reason should he give? He would know there was no message from Lisson Grove. Had there been, it would have been delivered to the house, and simple enough to check on anyway. All Gower would have to do was ask at the post office.

The sun was already half gone, a burning orange semicircle above the purple horizon. Shadows were deepening right across the road.

Should Pitt try to elude him, simply go straight to the harbor now and wait for the next boat to Southampton? But that might not be till tomorrow morning; Gower would realize what had happened, and come after him, sometime during the night. Pitt didn't even have the rest of his clothes with him. He was wearing only a light jacket in the warm afternoon.

The idea of fighting Gower here was not to be considered. Even if he could subdue him—and that was doubtful; Gower was younger and extremely fit—what would Pitt do with him? He had no power to arrest him. Could he leave him tied up, and then escape—assuming he was successful anyway?

But Gower would not be alone here. That thought sobered him like a drench of cold water, raising goose bumps on his skin. How many of the people at Frobisher's house were part of his plan? The only answer was for Pitt to deceive him, make him believe that he had no suspicions at all, and that would not be easy. The slightest change in manner and Gower would know. Even a self-consciousness, a hesitation, a phrase too carefully chosen, and he would be aware.

How could Pitt tell him they were returning to London? What excuse would he believe?

Or should he suggest he himself return, and Gower stay here and watch Frobisher and Wrexham, just in case there was something after all? In case Meister or Linsky came back? Or anyone else they would recognize? The thought was an immense relief. A weight lifted off him as if it were a breathtaking escape, a flight into freedom. He would be alone— safe. Gower would stay here in France.

A second later he despised himself for his cowardice. When he had first gone on the beat in London, as a young man, he had expected a certain amount of violence. Indeed, now and then he had met with it. There had been a number of wild chases, with a degree of brawling at the end. But after promotion, as a detective he had almost exclusively used his mind. There had been long days, even longer nights. The emotional horror had been intense, the pressure to solve a case before a killer struck again, before the public were outraged and the police force disgraced. And after arrest there was testimony at the trial. Worst of all was the fear, which often kept him awake at night, that he had not caught the real criminal. Perhaps he had made a mistake, drawn a wrong conclusion, and it was an innocent person who was going to face the hangman.

But it was not physical violence. The battle of wits had not threatened his own life. He was chilled in the first darkness of the early evening. The sunset breeze was cold on his skin, and yet he was sweating. He must control himself. Gower would see nervousness; he would be watching for it. The suspicion that he had been found out would be the first thing to leap to his mind, not the last.

Before he reached the house, Pitt must have thought of what he would say, and then he must do it perfectly.

GOWER WAS ALREADY IN when Pitt arrived. He was sitting in one of the comfortable chairs reading a French newspaper, a glass of wine on the small table beside him. He seemed very English, very sunburned—or perhaps it was more windburn from the breeze off the sea. He looked up and smiled at Pitt, glanced then at Pitt's dirty boots, and rose to his feet.

"Can I get you a glass of wine?" he offered. "I expect you're hungry?"

For a moment Pitt was attacked by doubt. Was he being ridiculous thinking that this man had swiftly and brutally killed West, and then turned with an innocent face and helped Pitt pursue Wrexham all the way to Southampton, and across the channel to France?

He mustn't hesitate. Gower was expecting an answer, an easy and natural response to a very simple question.

"Yes I am," he said with slight grimace as he sank into the other chair and realized how exhausted he was. "Haven't walked that far in a while."

"Eight or nine miles?" Gower raised his eyebrows. He set the wine down on the table near Pitt's hand. "Did you have any luncheon?" He resumed his own seat, looking at Pitt curiously.

"Bread and cheese, and a good wine," Pitt answered. "I'm not sure red is the thing with cheese, but it was very agreeable. It wasn't Stilton," he added, in case Gower should think him ignorant of gentlemen's habit of taking port with Stilton. They were sitting with wine, like friends, and talking about etiquette, as if no one were dead and they were on the same side. He must be careful never to allow the absurdity of it to blind him to its lethal reality.

"Worth the walk?" Gower inquired. There was no edge to his voice; his lean brown hand holding the glass was perfectly steady.

"Yes," Pitt said. "Yes it was. He confirmed what I suspected. It seems Frobisher is a poseur. He has talked about radical social reform for years, but still lives in more or less luxury himself. He gives to the occasional charity, but then so do most people of means. Talking about action seems to be his way of shocking people, gaining a degree of attention for himself while remaining perfectly comfortable."

"And Wrexham?" Gower asked.

There was a moment's silence in the room. Somewhere outside a dog was barking, and much farther away someone sang a bawdy song and there was a bellow of laughter. Pitt knew it was vulgar because the intonation of the words was the same in any language.

"Obviously a different matter," Pitt replied. "We know that for ourselves, unfortunately. What he is doing here I have no idea. I hadn't

thought he knew we were after him, but perhaps I was wrong in that."
He let the suggestion hang in the air.

"We were careful," Gower said, as if turning the idea over in his
mind. "But why stay here with Frobisher if all he is doing is trying to
escape from us? Why not go on to Paris, or anywhere?" He put down
his glass and faced Pitt. "At best he's a revolutionary, at worst an anarchist wanting to destroy all order and replace it with chaos." There
was stinging contempt in his voice. If it was false then he belonged on
the stage.

Pitt rethought his plan. "Perhaps he's waiting here for someone,
and he feels safe enough not to care about us?" he suggested.

"Or whoever's coming is so important he has to take the risk?"
Gower countered.

"Exactly." Pitt settled himself more comfortably in his chair. "But
we could wait a long time for that, or possibly fail to recognize it when
it happens. I think we need a great deal more information."

"French police?" Gower said doubtfully. He moved his position
also, but to one less comfortable, as if any moment he might stand up
again.

Pitt forced himself not to copy him. He must appear totally relaxed.

"Their interests might not be the same as ours," Gower went on.
"Do you trust them, sir? In fact, do you really want to tell them what
we know about Wrexham, and why we're here?" His expression was
anxious, bordering on critical, as if it were only his junior rank that
held him from stronger comment.

Pitt made himself smile. "No I don't," he answered. "To all your
questions. We have no idea what they know, and no way of checking
anything they may tell us. And of course our interests may very well
not be the same. But most of all, as you say, I don't want them to know
who we are."

Gower blinked. "So what are you suggesting, sir?"

Now was the only chance Pitt was going to have. He wanted to
stand up, to have the advantage of balance, even of weight, if Gower
moved suddenly. He had to stiffen his muscles and then deliberately

relax to prevent himself from doing it. Carefully he slid a little farther down in the seat, stretching his legs as if they were tired—which was not difficult after his eight-mile walk. Thank heaven he had good boots, although they looked dusty and scuffed now.

"I'll go back to London and see what they have at Lisson Grove," he answered. "They may have much more detailed information they haven't given us. You stay here and watch Frobisher and Wrexham. I know that will be more difficult on your own, but I haven't seen them do anything after dark other than entertain a little." He wanted to add more, to explain, but it would cause suspicion. He was Gower's superior. He did not have to justify himself. To do so would be to break the pattern, and if Gower was clever that in itself would alarm him.

"Yes, sir, if you think that's best. When will you be back? Shall I keep the room on here for you?" Gower asked.

"Yes—please. I don't suppose I'll be more than a couple of days, maybe three. I feel we're working in the dark at the moment."

"Right, sir. Fancy a spot of dinner now? I found a new café today. Has the best mussel soup you've ever tasted."

"Good idea." Pitt rose to his feet a little stiffly. "I'll leave first ferry in the morning."

THE FOLLOWING DAY WAS misty and a lot cooler. Pitt deliberately chose the first crossing to avoid having to breakfast with Gower. He was afraid in the affected casualness of it he might try too hard, and make some slip so small Gower picked it up—while Pitt had no idea anything had changed.

Or had Gower suspected something already? Did he know, even as Pitt walked down to the harbor along ancient, now-familiar streets, that the pretense was over? He had a desperate instinct to swing around and see if anyone were following him. Would he pick out Gower's fair head, taller than the average, and know it was he? Or might he already have changed his appearance and be yards away, and Pitt had no idea?

But his allies, Frobisher's men, or Wrexham's, could be anyone:

the hold man in the fisherman's jersey lounging in a doorway taking his first cigarette of the day; the man on the bicycle bumping over the cobbles; even the young woman with the laundry. Why suppose that Gower himself would follow him? Why suppose that he had noticed anything different at all? The new realization loomed gigantic to him, filling his mind, driving out almost everything else. But how self-centered to suppose that Gower had nothing more urgent to consume his thoughts! Perhaps Pitt and what he knew, or believed he knew, were irrelevant anyway.

He increased his pace and passed a group of travelers heaving along shopping bags and tightly packed portmanteaux. On the dock-side he glanced around as if to search for someone he knew, and was flooded with relief when he saw only strangers.

He stood in the queue to buy his ticket, and then again to get on board. Once he felt the slight sway of the deck under his feet, the faint movement, even here in the harbor, it was as if he had reached some haven of safety. The gulls wheeled and circled overhead, crying harshly. Here on the water the wind was sharper, salt-smelling.

Pitt stood on the deck by the railing, staring at the gangway and the dockside. To anyone else, he hoped he looked like someone look-ing back at the town with pleasure, perhaps at a holiday well spent, possibly even at friends he might not see again for another year. Ac-tually he was watching the figures on the quay, searching for anyone familiar, any of the men he had seen arriving or leaving Frobisher's house, or for Gower himself.

Twice he thought he saw him, and it turned out to be a stranger. It was simply the fair hair, an angle of shoulder or head. He was angry with himself for the fear; he knew the danger was largely in his mind. Perhaps it was so deep because until the walk back to the town yester-day evening it had never entered his mind that Gower had killed West, and Wrexham was either a co-conspirator or even a perfectly innocent man, a tissue-paper socialist posing as a fanatic, like Frobisher himself. It was his own blindness that dismayed him. How stupid he had been, how insensitive to possibilities. He would be ashamed to tell Narraway, but he would have to; there would be no escaping it.

At last they cast off and moved out into the bay. Pitt remained where he was at the rail, watching the towers and walls of the city recede. The sunlight was bright on the water, glittering sharp. They passed the rocky outcrops, tide slapping around the feet of the minor fortress built there, guarding the approaches. There were few sailing boats this early: just fishermen pulling up the lobster pots that had been out all night.

He tried to imprint it on his mind. He would tell Charlotte about it, how beautiful it was, how it was like stepping back in time. He should bring her here one day, take her to dine where the shellfish was so superb. She hardly ever left London, let alone England. It would be fun, different. He imagined seeing her again so vividly he could almost smell the perfume of her hair, hear her voice in his mind. He would tell her about the city, the sea, the tastes and the sounds of it all. He wouldn't have to dwell on the events that had brought him to France, only on the good.

Someone bumped against him, and for a moment he forgot to be startled. Then the chill ran through him, and he realized how his attention had wandered.

The man apologized.

Pitt spoke with difficulty, his mouth dry. "It's nothing."

The man smiled. "Lost my balance. Not used to the sea."

Pitt nodded, but he moved away from the rail and went back into the main cabin. He stayed there for the rest of the crossing, drinking tea and having a breakfast of fresh bread, cheese, and a little sliced ham. He tried to look as if he were at ease.

When they reached Southampton he went ashore carrying the light case he had bought in France and looking like any other holidaymaker returning home. It was midday. The quayside was busy with people disembarking, or waiting to take the next ferry out.

He went straight to the railway station, eager to catch the first train to London. He would go home, wash, and dress in clean clothes. Then if he were lucky, he'd just have time to catch Narraway before he left Lisson Grove for the evening. Thank heaven for the telephone. At least he would be able to call and arrange to meet with him wherever was convenient. Maybe with his news about Gower, a rendezvous at Narraway's home would be better.

He felt easier now. France seemed very far away, and he had had no glimpse of Gower on the boat. He must have satisfied him with his explanation.

The station was unusually busy, crowded with people all seemingly in an ill humor. He discovered why when he bought his ticket for London.

"Sorry, sir," the ticket seller said wearily. "We got a problem at Shoreham-by-Sea, so there's a delay."

"How long a delay?"

"Can't say, sir. Maybe an hour or more."

"But the train is running?" Pitt insisted. Suddenly he was anxious to leave Southampton, as if it was still dangerous.

"Yes, sir, it will be. D'yer want a ticket fer it or not?"

"Yes I do. There's no other way to London, is there?"

"No, sir, not unless yer want ter take a different route. Some folk are doing that, but it's longer, an' more expensive. Trouble'll be cleared soon, I daresay."

"Thank you. I'll have one ticket to London, please."

"Return, sir? Would you like first, second, or third class?"

"Just one way, thank you, and second class will be fine."

He paid for it and went back toward the platform, which was getting steadily more and more crowded. He couldn't even pace backward and forward to release some of the tension that was mounting inside him, as it seemed to be for everyone else. Women were trying to comfort fretful children; businessmen pulled pocket watches out of their waistcoats and stared at the time again and again. Pitt kept glancing around him, but there was no sign of Gower, although he was not sure if he would have noticed him in the ever-increasing crowd.

He bought a sandwich and a pint of cider at two o'clock, when there was still no news. At three he eventually took the train to Worthing, and hoped to catch another train from there, perhaps to London via a different route. At least leaving Southampton gave him an illusion of achieving something. As he made his way toward a seat in the last carriage, again he had the feeling of having escaped.

The carriage was nearly full. He was fortunate there was room for him to sit. Everyone else had been waiting for some time and they were all tired, anxious, and looking forward to getting home. Even if this train did not take them all the way, at least they were moving.

One woman held a crying two-year-old, trying to comfort her. The little girl was rubbing her eyes and sniffing. It made him think of Jemima at that age. How long ago that seemed. Pitt guessed this girl had been on holiday and was now confused as to where she was going next, and why. He had some sympathy for her, and it made him engage the mother in conversation for the first two stops. Then the movement of the train and the rhythmic clatter over the connections on the rail lulled the child to sleep, and the mother finally relaxed.

Several people got off at Bognor Regis, and more at Angmering. By the time they reached Worthing and stopped altogether, there were only half a dozen people left in Pitt's carriage.

"Sorry, gents," the guard said, tipping his cap back a little and scratching his head. "This is as far as we go, till they get the track cleared at Shoreham."

There was a lot of grumbling, but the few passengers remaining got out of the carriage. They walked up and down the platform restlessly, bothered the porters and the guard asking questions to which no one had an answer, or went into the waiting room with passengers from the other carriages.

Pitt picked up someone else's discarded newspaper and glanced through it. Nothing in particular caught his eye, and he kept looking up every time someone passed, in the hope that it was news of the train leaving again.

Once or twice as the long afternoon wore on, he got up and walked the length of the platform. With difficulty he resisted the temptation to pester the guard, but he knew that the poor man was probably as frustrated as everyone else, and would have been only too delighted to have news to give people.

Finally, as the sun was on the horizon, they boarded a new train and slowly pulled out of the station. The relief was absurdly out of proportion. They had been in no hardship and no danger, yet people were smiling, talking to one another, even laughing.

The next stop was Shoreham-by-Sea, where the trouble had been, then Hove. By then it was dusk, the light golden and casting heavy shadows. For Pitt this hour of the evening had a peculiar beauty, almost with a touch of sadness that sharpened its emotional power. He felt it even more in the autumn, when the harvest fields in the country were stubble gold, the stooks like some remnant of a forgotten age that was earlier, more barbaric, without the inroads of civilization on the land. He thought of his childhood at the big house where his parents had worked, of the woods and fields, and a sense of belonging.

Suddenly the carriage enclosed him. He stood up and went to the end and through the door onto the small platform before the next carriage. It was mostly for men to light cigars without the smoke being unpleasant to other passengers, but it was a good place to stand and feel the rush of air and smell the plowed earth and the damp of the woods as they passed. Not many trains had these spaces. He had heard somewhere that it was an American invention. He liked it very much.

The air was quite cold, but there was a sweetness to it and he was happy to remain there, even though it grew darker quickly, heavy clouds rolling in from the north. Probably sometime in the night it would rain.

He considered what he would tell Narraway of what now seemed to be an abortive trip to France, and how he would explain his conclusions about Gower and his own blindness in not having understood the truth from the beginning. Then he thought with intense pleasure of seeing Charlotte, and of being at home where he had only to look up and she would be there, smiling at him. If she thought he had been stupid, she would not say so—at least not at first. She would let him say it, and then ruefully agree. That would take away most of the sting.

It was nearly dark now; the clouds had brought the night unnaturally soon.

Without any warning he was aware of it: someone behind him. With the rattle of the wheels he had not heard the carriage door open. He half turned, and was too late. The weight was there in the middle of his back, his right arm was locked in a fierce grip, his left pinned against the rail by his own body.

He tried to step backward onto the instep of the man, shock him with the pain of it. He felt the man wince, but there was no easing of the hold of him. He was being pushed forward, twisted a little. His arm was crushed on the rail and he gasped to get his breath. He was pushed so his head was far out over the speeding ground. The wind was cold on his face, smuts from the engine striking him, stinging. Any minute he was going to lose his balance and then it would be a second, two, and he would be over the edge and down onto the track. At this speed he would be killed. It would probably snap his spine. The man was strong and heavy. The weight of him was driving the breath out of Pitt's chest, and he had no leverage to fight back. It would be over in seconds.

Then there was a slam of carriage doors, and a wild shout. The pressure on Pitt's back was worse, driving the last bit of air out of his lungs. He heard a cry, and realized it was himself. The weight lifted suddenly and he gasped, hanging on to the rail, scrambling to turn around, coughing violently. The man who had attacked him was struggling with someone else, who was portly, thick-waisted. He could see only shadows and outlines in the dark. The man's hat flew off and was carried away. He was already getting the worst of the fight, backing toward the rail at the other side. In the momentary light from the door his face was contorted with anger and the beginning of terror as he realized he was losing.

Pitt straightened up and threw himself at the attacker. He had no weapon except his fists. He struck the man low in the chest, as hard as he could, hoping to wind him. He heard him grunt and he pitched forward, but only a step. The fat man slithered sideways and down onto one knee. At least that way he would not overbalance across the rail and onto the track.

Pitt followed his attacker, striking again, but the man must have expected it. He went down also, and Pitt's blow only caught the edge of his shoulder. The man twisted with it, but for no more than a moment. Then he lunged back at Pitt, his head down, catching Pitt in the stomach and sending him sprawling. The carriage door was slamming open and closed.

The fat man scrambled to his feet and charged, his face red, shouting something indistinguishable over the howl of the wind and roar and clatter of the train. He dived at Pitt's attacker, who stepped out of the way, and then swiveled around and raised himself. He grasped the fat man and heaved him over the rail to fall, screaming, arms flailing helplessly, out onto the track.

For a second Pitt was frozen with horror. Then he turned and stared at the man who had attacked him. He was only an outline in the dark, but he did not need to hear him speak to recognize him.

"How did you know?" Gower asked, curiosity keen, his voice almost normal.

Pitt was struggling to get his breath. His lungs hurt, his ribs ached where the rail had bruised him, but all he could think of was the man who had tried to rescue him, and whose broken body was now lying on the track.

Gower took a step toward him. "The man you walked eight miles to see, did he tell you something?"

"Only that Frobisher was a paper tiger," Pitt replied, his mind racing now. "Wrexham can't have taken a week to work that out, so maybe he always knew it. Then I thought perhaps he was just the same. I thought I saw him cut West's throat, but when I went over it step by step, I didn't. It just looked like it. Actually West's blood was already pooled on the stones. You were the one who had the chase, all the way to the ferry. I thought you were clever, but then I realized how easy it had been. It was always you who found him when we lost him, or who stopped us actually catching him. The whole pursuit was performed for my benefit, to get me away from London."

Gower gave a short burst of laughter. "The great Pitt, whom Narraway sets so much store by. Took you a week to work that out! You're getting slow. Or perhaps you always were. Just lucky." Then suddenly he flung himself forward, arms outstretched to grasp Pitt by the throat, but Pitt was ready this time. He ducked and charged, low, with his head down. He caught Gower in the belly just above the waist, and heard him gasp. He straightened his legs, lifting Gower off the ground. His own impetus carried him on, high over the rail and into the darkness. Pitt did not even see him land, but he knew with a violent sorrow that it had to kill him instantly. No one could survive such an impact.

He straightened up slowly, his legs weak, his body shaking. He had to cling to the rail to support himself.

The carriage door slammed shut again, then opened. The guard stood there, wide-eyed, terrified, the lantern in his hand, the carriage lights yellow behind him.

"Ye're a lunatic!" he cried, stuttering over his words.

"He was trying to kill me!" Pitt protested, taking a step forward.

The guard jerked the lantern up as if it were some kind of shield. "Don't you touch me!" His voice was shrill with terror. "I got 'alf a dozen good men 'ere 'oo'll tie yer down, so I 'ave. Ye're a bleedin' madman. Yer killed poor Mr. Summers as well, 'oo only came out there ter 'elp the other gent."

"I didn't—" Pitt began, but he didn't get to finish the sentence. Two burly men were crowding behind the guard, one of them with a walking stick, the other with a sharp-ended umbrella, both held up as weapons.

"We're gonna put yer in my van," the guard went on. "An' if we 'ave ter knock yer senseless ter do it, just gimme the excuse is all I ask. I liked Mr. Summers. 'E were a good man, an' all."

Pitt had no wish to be beaten into submission. Dazed, aching, and appalled at what he had done, he went without resisting.

CHAPTER

7

"You can't come," charlotte said vehemently. It was early afternoon and she was standing in the dining room of Mrs. Hogan's lodging house, dressed in her best spring costume, wearing the magnificent blouse. She was rather uncomfortably aware of how well it suited her. With a plain dark skirt the effect was dramatic, to say the very least. "Someone is bound to know you," she added, forcing her attention to the matter in hand.

Narraway had obviously taken care to prepare himself for the occasion also. His shirt was immaculate, his cravat perfectly tied, his thick hair exactly in place.

"I have to," he replied. "I must see Talulla Lawless. I can only see her in a public place, or she will accuse me of assaulting her. She has already tried it once, and warned me she will do it again if I attempt to see her alone. I know she is going to be there this afternoon. It's a recital. Most people will be watching the musicians."

"It will only need one person to recognize you and they will tell the others," she pointed out. "Then what will I be able to do of any value? They'll know the reason behind everything I say."

"I will not go with you. The charade of your being my sister is for Mrs. Hogan." He smiled bleakly. "You will go to the recital with Fiachra McDaid. He's coming to meet you here—" He glanced at the clock on the mantel shelf. "—in ten minutes or so. I'll go alone. I have to, Charlotte. I think Talulla is crucial to this. Too many of my investigations come back to her. She is the one thread that connects everyone involved."

"Can't I do it?" she persisted.

He smiled briefly. "Not this time, my dear."

She did not argue any further, even though she was sure he was not telling her the entire truth. But it was foolish to come here at all if they were unprepared to take any risks. She smiled back at him, just in a very tiny gesture, and gave a little nod. "Then be careful."

His eyes softened. He seemed to be about to say something half mocking, but there was a sharp tap on the door. Mrs. Hogan came in, her hair as usual falling out of its pins, her white apron crisply starched.

"Mr. McDaid is here for you, Mrs. Pitt." It was impossible to tell from her expression what her thoughts were, except that she was having an effort keeping them under control.

"Thank you, Mrs. Hogan," Charlotte said politely. "I shall be there immediately." She met Narraway's eyes. "Please be careful," she said again. Then, before he could respond, she picked up her skirt perhaps half an inch and swept out the door Mrs. Hogan was holding open for her.

Fiachra McDaid was standing in the hall next to the longcase clock, which read five minutes ahead of the one in the dining room. He was smartly dressed, but he could not manage the same casual elegance as Narraway.

"Good afternoon, Mrs. Pitt," he said pleasantly. "I hope you'll enjoy the music. It'll be another side of Dublin for you to see, and a fine day for it. And talking of the weather, have you been outside the city yet? While it's so agreeable, how about a trip to Droghada, and the ruins of Mellifont, the oldest abbey in Ireland—1142, it was, on the orders of Saint Malachy. Or if that is too recent for you, how about the Hill of Tara? It was the center of Ireland under the High

Kings, until the eleventh century when Christianity came and brought an end to their power."

"It sounds marvelous," she said with as much enthusiasm as she could manage, taking his arm and walking toward the front door. She did not look back to see if Narraway was watching her. "Are they far from the city?"

"A little distance, but it's well worth it," McDaid replied. "There's far more to Ireland than Dublin, you know."

"Of course. I appreciate your generosity in sharing it. Do tell me more about these places."

He accepted, and on the short journey to the hall where the recital was to take place, she listened with an air of complete attention. Indeed, at any other time she would have been as interested as she now pretended to be. The pride in his voice was unmistakable, and the love for his people and their history. He had a remarkable compassion for the poor and the dispossessed, which she could not help but admire.

When they arrived, the crowds were already beginning to gather, and they were obliged to find their seats if they wished to be well placed toward the front. Charlotte was pleased to do so, in order to be as far from Narraway as possible, so no one might think they were with each other—except McDaid, of course, and she had to trust in his discretion.

The other ladies were dressed very fashionably, and in the bronze-and-black-striped blouse she felt the equal of any of them. It still gave her a twinge of guilt that Narraway had paid for it, and she had no idea what words she would use to explain it to Pitt. But for the moment she indulged the pleasure of seeing both men and women glance at her, then look a second time with appreciation, or envy. She smiled a little, not too much, in case it looked like self-satisfaction, just enough to lift the corners of her mouth into a pleasant expression and return the nods of greeting from those she had met before.

She chose a chair, then sat as straight-backed as she could and affected an interest in the arrangements of the seats where the musicians were to play.

She noticed Dolina Pearse and only just avoided meeting her eyes. Next to her, Talulla Lawless was discreetly surveying the room, apparently looking for someone. Charlotte tried to follow her direction, and felt her breath catch in her throat as she saw Narraway arrive. The light was bright for a moment on the silver at his temples as he leaned forward to listen to someone. Talulla stiffened, her face set rigid. Then she smiled and turned back to the man beside her. It was a moment before Charlotte recognized him as Phelim O'Conor. He moved away and took his seat, and Talulla returned to hers.

The master of ceremonies appeared, and the babble of talk died away. The performance had begun.

For just over an hour they sat absorbed in the sound and the emotion of the music. It had a sweetness and a lilt that made Charlotte smile, and it was no effort at all to appear as if she were totally happy.

But the moment it ceased and the applause was finished, her mind returned to the reason she was here—and, more urgently, why Narraway was. She remembered the look on Talulla's face. Perhaps the greatest purpose Charlotte would serve would not be anything to do with Cormac O'Neil, but to support Narraway if Talulla should begin to create a scene.

Giving McDaid no more than a quick smile, she rose to her feet and headed for Talulla, trying to think of something reasonable to say, true or not. She reached her just as Talulla turned to walk away, and only just managed to save her balance. She looked instantly amazed.

"Oh, I am sorry," Charlotte apologized, although actually it had been Talulla who had nearly bumped into her. "I am afraid my enthusiasm rather got the better of me."

"Enthusiasm?" Talulla said coldly, her face reflecting complete disbelief.

"For the harpist," Charlotte said quickly. "I have never heard more delightful music." She was fishing desperately for anything to say.

"Then don't let me stop you from speaking to her," Talulla retorted. "I'm sure you'll find her agreeable."

"Do you know her?" Charlotte asked eagerly.

"Only by repute, and I shouldn't wish to trouble her," Talulla responded sharply. "There must be so many people eager to speak with her."

"I would be so grateful if you would introduce me," Charlotte asked, ignoring the rebuff.

"I'm afraid I cannot help you," Talulla was making it impossible to conceal her impatience. "I am not acquainted with her. Now, if you don't—"

"Oh!" Charlotte assumed an expression of dismay. "But you said she was most agreeable." She made it a challenge, not daring to look toward where she had seen Narraway talking to Ardal Barralet.

"It was the polite thing to say," Talulla snapped. "Now really, Mrs. Pitt, there is someone I wish to speak to, and I must hurry or he may leave. Excuse me." And she all but pushed Charlotte out of the way, obliging her to step aside.

Charlotte could see Narraway still talking to Barralet at the far end of the room. Talulla was heading directly toward them. Charlotte went after her, but several steps behind. They were halfway down the aisle between the chairs when Talulla stopped abruptly.

Then Charlotte saw why. A little knot of people had gathered around where Narraway had turned from Ardal Barralet and was facing Cormac O'Neil across a short open space of floor. Phelim O'Conor was looking from one to the other of them and Bridget Tyrone was just to his right.

For seconds they stood frozen. Then Cormac drew in his breath. "I never thought you'd dare show your face in Ireland again," he said between his teeth, staring at Narraway. "Who've you come back to betray this time? Mulhare is dead, or didn't you know that?" The hatred trembled in his voice; his whole body shook and his words were slurred.

A ripple of emotion ran through the gathering crowd like the passage of a storm through a field of barley.

"Yes, I know Mulhare is dead," Narraway replied, not moving backward despite Cormac's closeness to him. "Someone embezzled the money he should have had so he could go abroad and start a new life."

"Someone?" Cormac sneered. "And I suppose you have no idea who?"

"I hadn't," Narraway answered, still not moving, although Cormac was within two feet of him now. "I'm beginning to find out."

Cormac rolled his eyes. "If I didn't know you, I'd believe that. You stole the money yourself. You betrayed Mulhare just as you betrayed all of us."

Narraway was white-faced, eyes brilliant. "It was a war, Cormac. You lost, that's all—"

"All!" Cormac's face was now contorted with hate. "I lost my brother, and my sister-in-law, and my country, and you stand here and say *that's all* . . ." His voice choked.

There was a mutter from everyone around the group closest to him. Charlotte winced. She knew what Narraway meant, but he was rattled and being clumsy. He knew they were against him, and he could prove nothing. He had no backing from London now; he was alone, and losing.

"We couldn't both win." Narraway regained his self-control with an effort. "That time it was me. You wouldn't have shouted *betrayal* if it had been you."

"It's my bloody country, you arrogant ape!" Cormac shouted. "How many more of us have to be robbed, cheated, and murdered before you get some shadow of a conscience and get the hell out of Ireland?"

"I'll go as soon as I prove who took Mulhare's money," Narraway answered. "Did you sacrifice him to get your revenge on me? Is that how you know all about it?"

"Everybody knows all about it," Cormac snarled. "His body was washed up on the steps of Dublin Harbor, God damn you!"

"I didn't betray him!" Narraway's voice was shaking and growing louder despite his efforts to keep it down. "If I'd done it I'd have made a better job. I wouldn't have left the money in my own damn account for others to find it. Whatever you think of me, Cormac, you know I'm not a fool."

Cormac was stunned into momentary silence.

It was Talulla who stepped forward. Her face was white to the lips, her eyes sunken like holes in her head.

"Yes, you are a fool," she said between her teeth, facing Narraway, her back to Cormac. "An arrogant English fool who thinks we can't ever get the better of you. Well, one of us did this time. You say you didn't put the money in your own bank? Apparently someone did, and you got the blame. Your own people think you're a thief, and no one in Ireland will ever give you information again, so you'll be no use to London anymore. You have Cormac O'Neil to thank for that."

She drew in her breath, all but choking on it. "Don't you have a saying in England—'He who laughs last, laughs longest'? Well, we'll be laughing after you are a broken old man with nothing to do and no one who gives a damn about you! Remember it was an O'Neil who did that to you, Narraway!" She laughed with a brief, jagged sound, like something tearing inside her. Then she turned and pushed her way through the crowd until she disappeared.

Charlotte stared at Cormac, and Phelim O'Conor, and then at Narraway. They stood pale and shaking. It was Ardal Barralet who spoke.

"How unfortunate," he said drily. "I think, Victor, it would have been better if you had not come. Old memories die hard. It seems from what has been said as if this is one part of the war you lost. Accept it with as much grace as you expected of us, and take your leave while you can."

Narraway did not even glance at Charlotte, not drawing her into the embarrassment. He bowed very stiffly. "Excuse me." He turned and left.

McDaid took Charlotte's arm, holding her surprisingly hard. She had not even known he was near her. Now she had no choice but to leave with him.

"He's a fool," McDaid said bitterly as soon as they were sufficiently far from the nearest people that he could speak without being overheard. "Did he think anyone would forget his face?"

She knew he was right, but she was angry with him for saying so. She did not know the details of Narraway's part in the old betrayal, whether he had loved Kate O'Neil, or used her, or even both, but he was the one betrayed this time—and by a lie, not by the truth.

She was allowing emotion and instinct to replace reason in her judgment. Or maybe her belief in him was a return for the loyalty

Narraway had shown to Pitt. Pitt was not here to help, to offer any support or advice, so it was necessary that she do it for him.

Then another thought came to her, a moment of recollection as clear as lightning in a black storm. Talulla had said that Mulhare's money had been returned to Narraway's own bank in London, and now no one in London would trust him. How could she know, unless she were intimately involved in having brought that about? She was in her late twenties. At the time of Kate and Sean O'Neil's deaths she was no more than a child, perhaps six or seven years old.

Was that what Narraway had come here for: to provoke her, un-realizingly, into such self-revelation? What a desperate step to take.

She tried to free her arm from McDaid's grip, pulling sharply, but he held on.

"You're not going after him," he said firmly. "He did at least do one thing decently: He didn't involve you. As far as Talulla is concerned, you could be total strangers. Don't spoil that."

His words made it worse. It increased her debt; and to deny Narraway that would be pointless and desperately ungracious. She snatched her arm from McDaid, and this time he let go.

"I wasn't going to go after him," she said angrily. "I'm going home."

"To London?" he said incredulously.

"To Mrs. Hogan's house in Molesworth Street," she snapped. "If you would be so kind as to take me. I do not wish to have to look for an omnibus. I've no idea where I am, or where I'm going."

"That I know," McDaid agreed ruefully.

HOWEVER, AS SOON AS McDaid had left her at Mrs. Hogan's door, she waited until he had gotten back into the carriage and it was around the corner out of sight, then walked briskly in the opposite di-rection and hailed the first carriage for hire that she saw. She knew Cormac O'Neil's town address from Narraway, and she gave it to the driver. She would wait for O'Neil to return, for as long as was neces-sary.

As it transpired, it was shortly after dusk when she saw Cormac O'Neil climb out of a carriage a hundred yards down the street. He made his way a trifle unsteadily along the footpath toward his front door.

She moved out of the shadows. "Mr. O'Neil?"

He stopped, blinking momentarily.

"Mr. O'Neil," she repeated. "I wonder if I may speak with you, please? It is very important."

"Another time," he said indistinctly. "It's late." He started forward to go past her to the door, but she took a step in front of him.

"No, it's not late, it's barely supper time, and this is urgent. Please?"

He looked at her. "You're a handsome enough girl," he said gently. "But I'm not interested."

Suddenly she realized that he assumed her to be a prostitute. It was too absurd for her to take offense. But if she laughed she might sound too close to hysteria. She swallowed hard, trying to control the nervous tension all but closing her throat.

"Mr. O'Neil." She had prepared the lie. It was the only way she could think of that might make him tell her the truth. "I want to ask you about Victor Narraway . . ."

O'Neil jerked to a stop and swung around to stare at her.

"I know what he did to your family," she went on a little desperately. "At least I think I do. I was at the recital this afternoon. I heard what you said, and what Miss Lawless said too."

"Why did you come here?" he demanded. "You're as English as he is. It's in your voice, so don't try to sympathize with me." Now his tone was stinging with contempt.

She matched his expression just as harshly. "And you think the Irish are the only people who are ever victims?" she said with amazement. "My husband suffered too. I might be able to do something about it, if I know the truth."

"Something?" he said contemptuously. "What kind of something?"

She knew she must make this passionate, believable; a wound deep enough that he would see her as a victim like himself. Mentally she apologized to Narraway. "Narraway's already been dismissed from Special Branch," she said aloud. "Because of the money that was supposed to go to Mulhare. But he has everything else: his home, his friends, his life in London. My family has nothing, except a few friends who know him as I do, and perhaps you? But I need to know the truth . . ."

He hesitated a moment, then wearily, as if surrendering to something, he fished in his pocket for a key. Fumbling a little, he inserted it in the lock and opened the door for her.

They were greeted immediately by a large dog—a wolfhound of some sort, who gave her no more than a cursory glance before going to O'Neil, wagging its tail and pushing against him, demanding attention.

O'Neil patted its head, talking gently. Then he led the way into the parlor and lit the gas lamps, the dog on his heels. The flames burned up to show a clean, comfortable room with a window onto the area way and then the street. He pulled the curtain across, more for privacy than to keep out the cold, and invited her to sit down.

She did so, soberly thanking him, then waiting for him to compose himself before she began her questions. She was acutely aware that if she made even one ill-judged remark, one clumsy reaction, she could lose him completely, and there would be no opportunity ever to try again.

"It was all over twenty years ago," he said, looking at her gravely. He sat opposite her, the dog at his feet. In the gaslight it was easy to see that he was laboring to keep some control of his feelings, as if seeing Narraway again had stirred emotions he had struggled hard to bury. His eyes were red-rimmed, his face haggard. His hair stood up on end, crookedly at one side, as though he had run his fingers through it repeatedly. She could not fail to be aware that he had been drinking; these sorrows were not of the kind that drown easily.

"Yes, I know, Mr. O'Neil." She spoke quietly. "But do you find that time heals? I would like to think so, but I see no evidence of it."

She settled herself a little more comfortably in the chair and waited for his reply.

"Heals?" he said thoughtfully. "No. Grows a seal over, maybe, but it's still bleeding underneath." He looked at her curiously. "What did he do to you?"

She leapt to the future she feared, creating in her mind the worst of it.

"My husband worked in Special Branch too," she replied. "Nothing to do with Ireland. Anarchists in England, people who set off bombs that killed ordinary women and children, old people, most of them poor."

O'Neil winced, but he did not interrupt her.

"Narraway sent him on a dangerous job, and then when it turned ugly, and my husband was far from home, Narraway realized that he had made a mistake, a misjudgment, and he let my husband take the blame for it. My husband was dismissed of course, but that's not all. He was accused of theft as well, so he can't get any other position at all. He's reduced to laboring, if he can even find that. He's not used to it. He has no skills, and it's hard to learn in your forties. He's not built for it." She heard the thickening in her own voice, as if she were fighting tears. It was fear, but it sounded like distress, grief, perhaps outrage at injustice.

"How is my story going to help?" O'Neil asked her.

"Narraway denies it, of course," she replied. "But if he betrayed you as well, that makes a lot of difference. Please—tell me what happened?"

"Narraway came here twenty years ago," he began slowly. "He pretended to have sympathy with us, and he fooled some people. He looked Irish, and he used that. He knows our culture, and our dreams, our history. But we weren't fooled. You're born Irish, or you're not. But we pretended to go along with it—Sean and Kate and I." He stopped, his eyes misty, as if he were seeing something far from this quiet, sparse room in 1895. The past was alive for him, the dead faces, the unhealed wounds.

She was uncertain if she should acknowledge that she was listening, or if it would distract him. She ended up saying nothing.

"We found out who he was, exactly," Cormac went on. "We were planning a big rebellion then. We thought we could use him, give him a lot of false information, turn the tables. We had all sorts of dreams. Sean was the leader, but Kate was the fire. She was beautiful, like sunlight on autumn leaves, wind and shadow, the sort of loveliness you can't hold on to. She was alive the way other women never are." He stopped again, lost in memory, and the pain of it was naked in his face.

"You loved her," she said gently.

"Every man did," he agreed, his eyes meeting hers for an instant, as if he had only just remembered that she was there. "You remind me of her, a little. Her hair was about the same color as yours. But you're more natural, like the earth. Steady."

Charlotte was not sure if she should be insulted. There was no time now, but she would think of it later, and wonder.

"Go on," she prompted. He had not told her anything yet, except that he had been in love with his brother's wife. Was that really why he hated Narraway?

As if he had seen her thought in her eyes, he continued. "Of course Narraway saw the fire in her too. He was fascinated, like any man, so we decided to use that. God knows, we had few enough weapons against him. He was clever. Some people think the English are stupid, and surely some of them are, but not Narraway, never him."

"So you decided to use his feelings for Kate?"

"Yes. Why not?" he demanded, his eyes angry, defending that decision so many years ago. "We were fighting for our land, our right to govern ourselves. And Kate agreed. She would have done anything for Ireland." His voice caught and for a moment he could not go on.

She waited. There was no sound outside, no wind or rain on the glass, no footsteps, no horses in the road. Even the dog at Cormac's feet did not stir. The house could have been anywhere—out in the countryside, miles from any other habitation. The present had dissolved and gone away.

"They became lovers, Kate and Narraway," Cormac said bitterly. "She told us what he was planning, he and the English. At least that's what she said." His voice was thick with grief.

"Wasn't it true?" she said when he did not continue.

"He lied to her," Cormac answered. "He knew what she was doing, what we all were. Somewhere she made a mistake." The tears were running down his face and he made no effort to check them. "He fed us all lies, but we believed him. The uprising was betrayed. Stupid, stupid, stupid! They blamed Kate!" He gulped, staring at the wall as if he could see all the players in that tragedy parading in front of him.

"They saw she had led us astray," he went on. "Narraway did that to her, used her against her own people. That's why I'd see him in hell. But I want him to suffer further, here on earth, where I know it for certain. Can you make that happen, Mrs. Pitt? For Kate?"

She was appalled by the rage in him. It shook his body like a disease. His skin was blotchy, the flesh of his face wasted. He must once have been handsome.

"What happened to her?" It was cruel of Charlotte to ask, but she knew it was not the end of the story yet, and she needed to hear it from him, not just from Narraway.

"She was murdered," he replied. "Strangled. Beautiful Kate."

"I'm sorry." She meant it. She tried to imagine the woman, all passion and dreams, as Cormac had painted her, but that vision was of a man in love with an image.

"They said it was Sean who killed her," he went on. "But it couldn't have been. He knew better than to believe she would have betrayed the cause. That was Narraway again. He killed her, because she would have told them what he had done. He would never have left Ireland alive." He stared at Charlotte, his eyes brimming with tears, waiting for her to respond.

She forced herself to speak. "Why would he? Can you prove that?" she asked. "I mean, can you give me anything I can take back to London that would make them listen to me?" She was cold now too, dreading what he might say. What if he could? What would she do then? Narraway would excuse himself, of course. He would say he had had to kill her, or she would have exposed him and the uprising might have succeeded. Perhaps that was even true? But it was still ugly and terrible. It was still murder.

"He killed her because she wouldn't tell him what he wanted to know. But if I could prove it do you think he'd be alive?" Cormac asked harshly. "They'd have hanged him, not poor Sean, and Talulla'd not be an orphan, God help her."

Charlotte gasped. "Talulla?"

"She's Kate's daughter," he said simply. "Kate and Sean's. Did you not know that? After Sean and Kate died she was cared for by a cousin, so she could be protected as much as possible from the hatred against her mother. Poor child."

The dreadful, useless tragedy of it overwhelmed Charlotte. She wanted to say something that would redeem any part of the loss, but everything that came to her mind was banal.

"I'm sorry," she said. "I'm . . ."

He looked up at her. "So are you going back to London to tell someone?"

"Yes . . . yes I am."

"Be careful," he warned. "Narraway won't go down easily. He'll kill you too, if he thinks he has to, to survive."

"I will be careful," she promised him. "I think I have a little more to learn yet, but I promise I'll be . . . careful." She stood up, feeling awkward. There was nothing to say that completed their conversation. They moved from the desperate to the mundane as if it were completely natural, but what words were there that could be adequate for what either of them felt? "Thank you, Mr. O'Neil," she said gravely.

He took her to the door and opened it for her, but he did not offer to find her any transport, as if for him she ceased to be real the moment she stepped out onto the pavement.

"WHERE HAVE YOU BEEN?" Narraway demanded as soon as she came into Mrs. Hogan's sitting room. He had been standing by the window, or perhaps pacing. He looked exhausted and tense, as if his imagination had plagued him with fear. His eyes were hollow, and the lines in his face were deeper than she had ever seen them before. "Are you all right? Who's with you? Where is he?"

"Nobody is with me," she answered. "But I am perfectly all right—"

"Alone?" His voice shook. "You were out on the street alone, in the dark? For God's sake, Charlotte, what's the matter with you? Anything could have happened. I wouldn't even have known!" He put out his hand and gripped her arm. She could feel the strength of him, as if he were quite unaware how tightly he held her.

"Nothing happened to me, Victor. I wasn't very far away. And it isn't late. There are plenty of people about," she assured him.

"You could have been lost . . ."

"Then I would have asked for directions," she said. "Please . . . there is no need to be concerned. If I'd had to walk a little out of my way to get here it wouldn't have hurt me."

"You could have . . . ," he began, then stopped, perhaps realizing that his fear was disproportionate. He let go of her. "I'm sorry. I . . ."

She looked at him. It was a mistake. For an instant his emotion was too plain in his eyes. She did not want to know that he cared so much. Now it would be impossible for either of them to pretend he did not love her, and she could not pretend she did not know.

She turned away, feeling the color burning on her skin. All words would be belittling the truth.

He stood still.

"I went to see Cormac O'Neil," she said after a moment or two.

"What?"

"I was perfectly safe. I wanted to hear from him exactly what happened, or at least what he believes."

"And what did he say?" he asked quickly, his voice cracking with tension.

She did not want to look at him, to intrude into old grief that was still obviously so sharp, but evasion was cowardly. She met his eyes and repeated to him what Cormac had said, including the fact that Talulla was Kate's daughter.

"That's probably how he sees it," Narraway answered when she had finished. "I daresay he couldn't live with the truth. Kate was beautiful." He smiled briefly. In that moment she could imagine the man he had been twenty years earlier: younger, more virile, perhaps less wise.

"Few men could resist her," he went on. "I didn't try. I knew they were using her to trap me. She was brave, passionate . . ." He smiled wryly. "Perhaps a little short on humor, but far more intelligent than they realized. It sometimes happens when women are beautiful. People don't see any further than that, especially men. It's uncomfortable. We see what we want to see."

Charlotte frowned, suddenly thinking of Kate, a pawn to others, an object of both schemes and desires. "Why do you say intelligent?" she asked.

"We talked," he replied. "About the cause, what they planned to do. I persuaded her it would rebound against them, and it would have. The deaths would have been violent and widespread. Attacks like that don't crush people and make them surrender. They have exactly the opposite effect. They would have united England against the rebels, who could have lost all sympathy from everyone in Europe, even from some of their own. Kate told me what they were going to do, the details, so I could have it stopped."

Charlotte tried to imagine it, the grief, the cost.

"Who killed her?" she asked. She felt the loss touch her, as if she had known Kate more deeply than simply as a name, an imagined face.

"Sean," he replied. "I don't know whether it was for betraying Ireland, as he saw it, or betraying him."

"With you?"

Narraway colored, but he did not look away from her. "Yes."

"Do you know that, beyond doubt?"

"Yes." His throat was so tight his voice sounded half strangled. "I found her body. I think he meant me to."

She could not afford pity now. "Why are you sure it was Sean who killed her?" She had to be certain so she could get rid of the doubt forever. If Narraway himself had killed her it might, by some twisted logic of politics and terror, be what he had to do to save even greater bloodshed. She looked at him now with a mixture of new understanding of the weight he carried, and sorrow for what it had cost him: whether that was now shame, or a lack of it—which would be worse.

"Why are you sure it was Sean?" she repeated.

He looked at her steadily. "What you really mean is, how can I prove I didn't kill her myself."

She felt a heat of shame in her own face. "Yes."

He did not question her.

"She was cold when I found her," he replied. "Sean tried to blame me. The police would have been happy to agree, but I was with the viceroy in the residence in Phoenix Park at the time. Half a dozen staff saw me there, apart from the viceroy himself, and the police on guard duty. They didn't know who I was, but they would have recognized me in court, if it had been necessary. The briefest investigation showed them that I couldn't have been anywhere near where Kate was killed. It also proved that Sean lied when he said he saw me, and that by his own admission he was there." He hesitated. "If you need to, you can check it." His smile was there for a moment, then gone. "Don't you think they'd have loved to hang me for it, if they'd had the ghost of a chance?"

"Yes," she agreed, feeling the weight ease from her. Grief was one thing, but without guilt it was a passing wound, something that would heal. "I'm . . . I'm sorry I needed to ask. Perhaps I should have known you wouldn't have done it."

"I would like you to think well of me, Charlotte," he said quietly. "But I would rather you saw me as a real person, capable of good and ill, and of pity, and shame . . ."

"Victor . . . don't . . ."

He turned away slowly, staring at the fire. "I'm sorry. It won't happen again."

She left quietly, going up to her room. She needed to be alone, and there was nothing either of them could say that would do anything but make it worse.

THEY WERE AT BREAKFAST the following morning: she with a slight headache after sleeping badly; he weary, but with the mark of professionalism so graciously back in place that yesterday could have been a dream.

They were eating toast and marmalade when the messenger arrived with a letter for Narraway. He thanked Mrs. Hogan, who had brought it to him, then tore it open.

Charlotte watched his face but she could not read anything more than surprise. When he looked up she waited for him to speak.

"It's from Cormac," he said gently. "He wants me to go and see him, at midday. He will tell me what happened, and give me proof."

She was puzzled, remembering Cormac's hate, the pain that seemed as sharp as it must have been the day it happened. She leaned forward. "Don't go. You won't, will you?"

He put the letter down. "I came for the truth, Charlotte. He may give it to me, even if it is not what he means to do. I have to go."

"He still hates you," she argued. "He can't afford to face the truth, Victor. It would place him in the wrong. All he has left is his illusions of what really happened, that Kate was loyal to Ireland and the cause, and that it would all have worked, except for you. He can't give that up."

"I know," he assured her, reaching out his lean hand and touching her gently, for an instant, then withdrawing it again. "But I can't afford not to go. I have nothing left to lose either. If it was Cormac who created the whole betrayal of Mulhare, I need to know how he did it, and be able to prove it to Croxdale." His face tightened. "Rather more than that, I need to find out who is the traitor in Lisson Grove. I can't let that go."

He did not offer any rationalization, taking it for granted that she understood.

It gave her an odd feeling of being included, even of belonging. It was frightening for the emotional enormity of it, and yet there was a warmth to it she would not willingly have sacrificed.

She did not argue any further, but nodded, and decided to follow after him and stay where she could see him.

Narraway went out of the house quite casually, as if merely to look at the weather. Then, as she came to the door, he turned and walked quickly toward the end of the road.

Charlotte followed after him, barely having time to close the door behind her, and needing to run a few steps to keep up. She had a shawl on and her reticule with her, and sufficient money for as long a fare as she would be likely to need.

He disappeared around the corner into the main street. She had to hurry to make sure she saw which way he went. As she had expected, he went straight to the first carriage waiting, spoke to the driver, then climbed in.

She swung around with her back to the road and pretended to look in a shop window. As soon as he had passed she darted out into the street to look for a second carriage. It was long, desperate moments before she found one. She gave the driver the address of

Cormac O'Neil's house and urged him to go as fast as possible. She was already several minutes behind.

"I'll pay you an extra shilling if you catch up with the carriage that just left here," she promised. "Please hurry. I don't want to lose him."

She sat forward, peering out as the carriage careered down the street, swung around the corner, and then set off again at what felt like a gallop. She was tossed around, bruised, and without any sense of where she was for what felt like ages, but was probably no more than fifteen minutes. Then finally they lurched to a stop outside the house where she had been the previous evening.

She stepped out, taking a moment to find her balance after the hectic ride. She paid him more than he had asked for, and an extra shilling.

"Thank you," she said. "Please wait." Then without ensuring that he did, she walked up the same path she had trod in the evening light such a short time ago. Somehow at midday the path looked longer, the bushes more crowding in, the trees overhead cut out more of the sunlight.

She had not reached the front door when she heard the dog barking. It was an angry, frightening sound, with a note of hysteria to it, as if the wag were out of control. It had certainly not been like that yesterday evening. It had been calm, resting its head on O'Neil's feet and barely noticing her.

She was surprised Cormac did not come to see what the fuss was. He could not possibly be unaware of the noise.

She touched the door with her fingers and it opened.

Narraway was standing in the hall. He swung around as the light spread across the floor. For a moment he was startled, then he regained his presence of mind.

"I should have known," he said grimly. "Wait here."

The dog was now throwing itself at whatever barrier held it in check. Its barking was high in its throat, as if it would rip someone to shreds the moment it could reach them.

Charlotte would not leave Narraway alone. She stepped inside and looked for the umbrella stand she had noticed yesterday. She saw it, picked out a sharp-ferruled black umbrella, and held it as if it were a sword.

The barking was reaching a crescendo.

Ahead of her Narraway went to the sitting room door, to the right of where the dog was hurling itself at another door, snarling in a high, singing tone as if it scented prey close at last.

Narraway opened the sitting room door then stopped motionless. She could see over his shoulder that Cormac O'Neil was lying on the floor on his back, a pool of blood spreading on the polished wood around what was left of his head.

Charlotte gulped, trying to stop herself from being sick. Yesterday evening he had been alive, angry, weeping with passion and grief. Now there was nothing left but empty flesh lying waiting to be found.

Narraway went over and bent down, touching the skin of Cormac's face with his fingers.

"He's still warm," he said, turning back to look at Charlotte. He had to raise his voice above the noise of the dog. "We must call the police."

He had barely finished speaking when there came the bang of the front door swinging open again and hitting the wall, then footsteps.

There was no time to wonder who it was. A woman screamed with a short, shrill sound, and then seemed to choke. Charlotte swiveled to stare at Talulla Lawless. She was ashen-faced, her hand to her mouth, black eyes staring wildly past Charlotte and Narraway to the figure of Cormac on the floor.

Behind her a policeman tried to catch his breath as a wave of horror overtook him.

Talulla glared at Narraway. "I warned him," she gasped. "I knew you'd kill him, after yesterday. But he wouldn't listen. I told him! I told him!" Her voice was getting higher and higher and her body was shaking.

The policeman regained control of himself and stepped forward, looking at Charlotte, then at Narraway. "What happened here?" he asked.

"He murdered my uncle, can't you see that?" Talulla shouted at him. "Listen to the dog, damn it! For God's sake don't let it out, it'll tear that murderer apart! That's what brought me here. I heard it, poor creature."

"He was dead when we got here!" Charlotte shouted back at her. "We don't know what happened any more than you do!"

Narraway stepped forward to the policeman. "I came in first," he said. "Mrs. Pitt waited outside. She has nothing to do with this. She never met Mr. O'Neil until very recently. I've known him for twenty years. Please allow her to leave."

Talulla thrust out her hand, finger pointing. "There's the gun! Look, it's lying right there on the floor. He hasn't even had time to take it away."

"Of course he hasn't," Charlotte retorted. "We only just got here! If you ask the . . ."

"Charlotte, be quiet," Narraway said with such force that she stopped speaking. He faced the policeman. "I came into the house first. Please allow Mrs. Pitt to leave. As I said before, she had no acquaintance with Mr. O'Neil, beyond a casual introduction. I have known him for years. We have an old enmity that has finally caught up with us. Is that not true, Miss Lawless?"

"Yes!" she said vehemently. "The dog just started to bark. I can hear it from my house. I live only a few yards away, over there. If there'd been anybody else, she'd have raised this row before. Ask anyone."

The policeman looked at Cormac on the floor, at Narraway, and the blood on his shoes, then at Charlotte, white-faced by the door. The dog was still barking and trying to break down the barrier that held it in check.

"Sir, I'm sorry, but you'll have to come with me. It'll be best for you if you don't give me any trouble."

"I have no intention of giving you trouble," Narraway told him. "None of this is your fault. Will you permit me to make certain that Mrs. Pitt has sufficient funds to pay a cabdriver? She has had a very ugly shock."

The policeman looked confused. "She was with you, sir," he pointed out.

"No," Narraway corrected him. "She came after me. She was not here when I arrived. I went in and O'Neil and I quarreled. He attacked me, and I had no choice but to defend myself."

"You came deliberately to kill," Talulla accused. "He showed you for the liar and the cheat you are. He got you dismissed from your position and you wanted your revenge. You came here and shot him." She looked at Charlotte. "Can you deny that?"

"Yes, I can," Charlotte responded heatedly. "I did arrive after Mr. Narraway was already here, but only seconds behind him. He had not gone farther than the hallway. The sitting room door was closed. We discovered Mr. O'Neil's body at the same moment."

"Liar!" Talulla shouted. "You're his mistress. You'd say anything."

Charlotte gasped.

A look at once of humor and pain flickered in Narraway's eyes. He turned to the policeman. "That is not true. Please allow her to go. If you can find the cabbie who brought her, he will affirm that Mrs. Pitt arrived after I did, and he must have seen her come into the house. O'Neil was shot, as you observe. Ask the driver if he heard the shot."

The policeman nodded. "You're right, sir. Don't take the lady down with you." He turned to Talulla. "And if you'd go back home, ma'am, I'll take care o' this. An' you, ma'am." He looked at Charlotte. "You'd better go an' find a cab back to your lodgings. But don't leave Dublin, if you please. We'll be wishing to talk to you. Where are you staying?"

"Number twelve, Molesworth Street."

"Thank you, ma'am. That'll be all. Now, don't stop me doing my duty, or it'll be the worse for you."

Charlotte could do nothing but watch helplessly as another policeman arrived. Narraway was manacled and led away, to Talulla's intense delight.

Charlotte walked back down the pathway and along the road, dazed and alone.

CHAPTER

8

PITT CEASED TO STRUGGLE. At first, in the heat of the moment, there was no point. He was in the grasp of two burly constables, both convinced they had apprehended a violent lunatic who had just hurled two men, possibly strangers to him, off a fast-moving train.

The irate and terrified passengers who had witnessed half the events had seen Pitt on the platform with the first man who had gone over, and then alone with Gower just before he had been pitched over as well.

"I know what I saw!" one of them stated. He stood as far away from Pitt as he could, his face a mask of horror in the railway platform gaslight. "He threw them both over. You want to watch yourselves or he'll have you too! He's insane! He has to be. Threw them over, one after the other."

"We were fighting!" Pitt protested. "He attacked me, but I won!"

"Which one of them would that be, sir?" one of the constables asked him. "The first one, or the second one?"

"The second one," Pitt answered but he heard the note of desperation in his own voice. It sounded ridiculous, even to him.

"Maybe he didn't like it that you'd thrown the first man off the train," the constable said reasonably. "'E was tryin' to arrest you. Good citizen doin' 'is duty."

"He attacked me the first time," Pitt tried to explain. "The other man was trying to rescue me, and he lost the fight!"

"But when this second man attacked you, you won, right?" the constable said with open disbelief.

"Obviously, since I'm here," Pitt snapped. "If you undo the mana-cles, I'll show you my warrant card. I'm a member of Special Branch."

"Yes, sir," the constable said sarcastically. "They always go around throwin' people off trains. Very special, they are."

Pitt barely controlled his temper. "Look in my pocket, inside my coat, up at the top," he said between his teeth. "You'll find my card."

The constables looked at each other. "Yeah? An' why would you be pitchin' people off trains, sir?"

"Because the man attacked me," Pitt said again. "He is a danger-ous man planning violence here." He knew as he spoke how absurd that sounded, considering that Gower was dead on the track, and Pitt was standing here alive and unhurt, apart from a few bruises. "Look," he went on, trying anew. "Gower attacked me. The stranger came to my rescue, but Gower was stronger and he lost the fight. I couldn't save him. Then Gower attacked me, but this time I was ready. I won. Look for my warrant card. That'll prove who I am."

The constables exchanged glances again. Then one of them very gingerly approached Pitt and held his coat open with one hand, while the other felt inside his inner pocket.

"There in't nothin' there, sir," he said, removing his hand quickly.

"There's my warrant card and my passport," Pitt said with a sense of rising panic. It had to be. He had had them both when he got onto the train at Shoreham. He remembered putting them back, as always.

"No, sir," the constable repeated. "Your pocket's empty, sir. There in't nothin' in it at all. Now, why don't you come quietly? No use in causing a lot o' fuss. Just gets people 'urt, as I can promise you, sir, it'll be you as comes off worst." He turned to the other passenger. "Thank you for yer trouble, sir. We got yer name and address. We'll be in touch with yer when we needs more."

Pitt drew in his breath to try reasoning further, and realized the futility of it. He knew what must have happened. Either his warrant card and passport had fallen out of his pocket in the fight, which didn't seem likely—not from a deep pocket so well concealed—or else Gower had taken the precaution of picking it during the struggle. They had stood very close, struggling together. He had been thinking of saving his own life, not being robbed. He turned to the constable closest to him.

"I've just come in from France, through Southampton," he said with sudden hope. "I had to have my passport then, or they wouldn't have let me in. My warrant card was with it. Can't you see that I've been robbed?"

The constable stared at him, shaking his head. "I only know as you're on the train, sir. I don't know where you got on, or where you was before that. You just come quietly, and we'll get you sorted at the police station. Don't give us any more trouble, sir. Believe me, yer got enough already."

"Do you have a telephone at the police station?" Pitt asked, but he made no protest as they led him away. It would be pointless. As it was, a crowd was gathering watching him. At this moment it was impossible for him to feel sorry Gower was dead. The other passenger he grieved for with a dull, angry pain. "Do you have a telephone?" he demanded.

"Yes, sir, o' course we do. If yer got family, we'll call them for yer an' let 'em know where you are," he promised.

"Thank you."

But when they arrived at the police station and Pitt was led in, a constable closely at either side of him, he was put straight into a cell and the door locked.

"My phone call!" he persisted.

"We'll make it for yer, sir. 'Oo shall we call, then?"

Pitt had considered it. If he called Charlotte she would be frightened and very distressed, and there was nothing she could do. Far better he call Narraway, who would straighten out the whole hideous mess, and could tell Charlotte about it afterward. "Victor Narraway," he answered.

"'E related to yer?" the constable asked suspiciously.

"Brother-in-law," Pitt lied quickly. He gave them the Lisson Grove number. "That's his work. It's where he'll be, or they'll know where to find him."

"At this time o' night, sir?"

"There's always someone there. Please, just call."

"If that's what yer want, we'll call."

"Thank you." Pitt sat down on the hard wooden bench in the cell and waited. He must stay calm. It would all be explained in a matter of minutes. This part of the nightmare would be over. There was still Gower's treachery and his death; now, in the silence of the cell, he had time to think of it more deeply.

He should not have been surprised that Gower came after him. The pleasant, friendly face Gower had shown in France, indeed all the time they had worked together over the last few months, might have been part of his real character, but it was superficial, merely a skin over a very different man beneath.

Pitt thought of his quick humor, how he had watched the girl in the red dress, admiring her, taking pleasure in her easy walk, the swing of her skirt, imagining what she would be like to know. He remembered how Gower liked the fresh bread. He drank his coffee black, even though he pulled his mouth at its bitterness, and still went back for more. He pictured how he stood smiling with his face to the sun, watched the sailing boats on the bay, and knew the French names for all the different kinds of seafood.

People fought for their own causes for all kinds of reasons. Maybe Gower believed in his goal as much as Pitt did; they were just utterly different. Pitt had liked him, even enjoyed his company. How had he not seen the ruthlessness that had let him kill West, and then turn on Pitt so stealthily?

Except perhaps it had not been easy? Gower might have lain awake all night wretched, seeking another way and not finding it. Pitt would never know. It was painful to realize that so much was not as he had trusted, and his own judgment was nowhere near the truth. He could imagine what Narraway would have to say about that.

The constable came back, stopping just outside the bars. He did not have the keys in his hand.

Pitt's heart sank. Suddenly he felt confused and a little sick.

"Sorry, sir," the constable said unhappily. "I called the number you gave. It was a branch o' the police all right, but they said as they'd got no one there called Narraway, an' they couldn't 'elp yer."

"Of course Narraway's there!" Pitt said desperately. "He's head of Special Branch! Call again. You must have had the wrong number. This is impossible."

"It were the right number, sir," the constable repeated stolidly. "It was Special Branch, like you said. An' they told me they got no one there called Victor Narraway. I asked 'em careful, sir, an' they were polite, but very definite. There in't no Victor Narraway there. Now you settle down, sir. Get a bit o' rest. We'll see what we can do in the morning. I'll get you a cup o' tea, an' mebbe a sandwich, if yer like?"

Pitt was numb. The nightmare was getting worse. His imagination created all kinds of horror. What had happened to Narraway? How wide was this conspiracy? Perhaps he should have realized that if they removed Pitt himself to France on a pointless errand, then of course they would have gotten rid of Narraway as well. There was no purpose in removing Pitt otherwise. He was only a kind of backup: a right-hand man possibly, but not more than that. Narraway was the real threat to them.

"Yer want a cup o' tea, sir?" the constable repeated. "Yer look a bit rough, sir. An' a sandwich?"

"Yes . . . ," Pitt said slowly. The man's humanity made it all the more grotesque, yet he was grateful for it. "I would. Thank you, Constable."

"Yer just rest, sir. Don't give yerself so much trouble. I'll get yer a sandwich. Would 'am be all right?"

"Very good, thank you." Pitt sat down on the cot to show that he had no intention of causing any problem for them. He was numb anyway. He did not even know whom to fight: certainly not this man who was doing his best to exercise both care and a degree of decency in handling a prisoner he believed had just committed a double murder.

It was a long and wretched night. He slept little, and when he did his dreams were full of fear, shifting darkness, and sudden explosions of sound and violence. When he woke in the morning his head throbbed, and his whole body was bruised and aching from the fight. It was painful to stand up when the constable came back again with another cup of tea.

"We'll take yer ter the magistrate later on," he said, watching Pitt carefully. "Yer look awful!"

Pitt tried to smile. "I feel awful. I need to wash and shave, and I look as if I've slept in my clothes, because I have."

"Comes with being in jail, sir. 'Ave a cup o' tea. It'll 'elp."

"Yes, I expect it will, even if not much," Pitt accepted. He stood well back from the door so the constable could place it inside without risking an attack. It was the usual way of doing things.

The constable screwed up his face. "Yer bin in the cells before, in't yer," he observed.

"No," Pitt replied. "But I've been on your side of them often enough, as I told you. I'm a policeman myself. I have another number I would like you to call, seeing that Mr. Narraway doesn't seem to be there. Please. I need to let someone know where I am. My wife and family, at least."

"'Oo would that be, sir?" The constable put down the tea and backed out of the cell again, closing and locking the door. "You give me the number and I'll do it. Everyone deserves that much."

"Lady Vespasia Cumming-Gould," Pitt replied. "I'll write the number down for you, if you give me a pencil."

"You jus' tell me, sir. I'll write it down."

Pitt obeyed. There was no point in arguing.

The man returned ten minutes later, his face wide-eyed and a trifle pale.

"She says as she knows yer, sir. Described yer to a T, she did. Says as ye're one o' the best policemen in London, an' Mr. Narraway's 'oo yer said 'e were, but summink's 'appened to 'im. She's sending a Member o' Parliament down ter get yer out of 'ere, an' as we'd better treat yer proper, or she'll be 'avin' a word wi' the chief constable. I dunno if she's real, sir. I 'ope yer understand I gotter keep yer in 'ere till this gentleman comes, wi' proof 'e's wot 'e says 'e is, an' all. 'E could be anyone, but I know I got two dead bodies on the tracks."

"Of course," Pitt said wearily. He would not tell him that Gower was Special Branch, and Pitt had not known that he was a traitor until yesterday. "Of course I'll wait here," he said aloud. "I'd be obliged if you didn't take me before the magistrate until the man arrives that Lady Vespasia sends."

"Yes, sir, I think as we can arrange that." He sighed. "I think as we'd better. Next time yer come from Southampton, sir, I'd be obliged if yer'd take some other line!"

Pitt managed a lopsided smile. "Actually I'd prefer this one. Given the circumstances, you've been very fair."

The constable was lost for words. He struggled, but clearly nothing he could think of seemed adequate.

It was nearly two hours later that Mr. Somerset Carlisle, MP, came sauntering into the police station, elegantly dressed, his curious face filled with a rueful amusement. Many years ago he had committed a series of outrages in London, to draw attention to an injustice against which he had no other weapon. Pitt had been the policeman who led the investigation. The murder had been solved, and he had seen no need to pursue the man who had so bizarrely brought it to public attention. Carlisle had remained grateful, becoming an ally in several cases since then.

On this occasion he had with him all his identification verifying the considerable office he held. Within ten minutes Pitt was a free man, brushing aside the apologies of the local police and assuring them that they had performed their duties excellently, and he found no fault with them.

"What the devil's going on?" Carlisle asked as they walked outside into the sun and headed in the direction of the railway station. "Vespasia called me in great agitation this morning, saying you had been charged with a double murder! You look like hell. Do you need a doctor?" There was laughter in his voice, but his eyes reflected a very real anxiety.

"A fight," Pitt explained briefly. He found walking with any grace very difficult. He had not realized at the time how bruised he was.

"On the platform at the back of a railway carriage traveling at considerable speed." He told Carlisle very briefly what had happened.

Carlisle nodded. "It's a very dark situation. I don't know the whole story, but I'd be very careful what you do, Pitt. Vespasia told me to get you to her house, not Lisson Grove. In fact she advised me strongly against letting you go there at all."

Pitt was cold. The sunlit street, the clatter of traffic all seemed unreal. "What's happened to Narraway?"

"I don't know. I've heard whispers, but I don't know the truth. If anyone does, it'll be Vespasia. But I'll take you to my flat first. Clean you up a bit. You look as if you've spent the night in jail!"

Two hours later, he was washed, shaved, and dressed in a clean shirt, provided by Carlisle, as well as clean socks and underwear. Pitt alighted from the hansom cab outside Vespasia's house and walked up to the front door. She was expecting him, and he was taken straight to her favorite sitting room, which looked onto the garden. There was a bowl of fresh narcissi on the table, their scent filling the air. Outside the breeze very gently stirred the new leaves on the trees.

Vespasia was dressed in silver-gray, with the long ropes of pearls he was so accustomed to seeing her wear. She looked calm, as she always did, and her beauty still moved him with a certain awe. However, he knew her well enough to see the profound anxiety in her eyes. It alarmed him, and he was too tired to hide it.

She looked him up and down. "I see Somerset lent you a shirt and cravat," she observed with a faint smile.

"Is it so obvious?" he asked, standing in front of her.

"Of course. You would never choose a shirt of that shade, or a cravat with a touch of wine in it. But it becomes you very well. Please sit down. It is uncomfortable craning my neck to look up at you."

He would never have seated himself before she gave her permission, but he was glad to do so, in the chair opposite her. The formalities were over, and they would address the issues that burdened them both.

"Where have you been?" she asked. Her imperious tone swept

aside the possibility that the answer was confidential even though she knew more about the power and danger of secrets than most ministers of government.

"In St. Malo," he replied. He was embarrassed now by his prior failure to see through the subterfuge more rapidly. However, he did not avoid her eyes as he told her about himself and Gower chasing through the streets, their brief parting, then their meeting and almost instantly finding Wrexham crouched over the corpse of West, his neck slashed open and blood covering the stones.

Vespasia winced but did not interrupt him.

He described their pursuit of Wrexham to the East End, and then the train to Southampton, and the ferry across to France. He found himself explaining too fully why they had not arrested Wrexham until it sounded miserably like excuses.

"Thomas," she interrupted gently. "Common sense justifies your actions, as seen at the time. You were aware of a socialist conspiracy, and you believed it to be more important than one grisly murder in London. What did you learn in St. Malo?"

"Very little," he replied. "We saw one or two known socialist agitators in the first couple of days . . . at least I think we did."

"You think?" she questioned.

He explained to her that it was Gower who had made the identification, and he had accepted it.

"I see. Who did he say they were?"

He was about to say that she would not know their names, then remembered her own radical part in the revolutions of 1848 that had swept across every country in Western Europe, except Britain. She had been in Italy, manning the barricades for that brief moment of hope in a new freedom. It was possible she had not lost all interest. "Jacob Meister and Pieter Linsky," he replied. "But they didn't come back again."

She frowned. Pitt noticed how she tensed her shoulders involuntarily, the way her hands in her lap gripped each other.

"You know of them?" he concluded.

"Of course," she said drily. "And many others. They are dangerous, Thomas. There is a new radicalism awakening in Europe. The next insurrections will not be like '48. They will be of a different breed. There will be more violence; I think perhaps it will be much more. The Russian monarchy cannot last a much longer in its current state. The oppression is fearful. I have a few friends left who are able to write occasionally, old friends, who tell me the truth. There is desperate poverty. The tsar has lost all sense of reality and is totally out of touch with his people—as are all his ministers and advisers. The gulf between the obscenely rich and the starving is so great it will eventually swallow them all. The only question is when."

The thought was chilling, but he did not argue, or even question it.

"And I am afraid the news is not good here," Vespasia continued. "But you already know something of it."

"Only that Narraway is out of Lisson Grove," he replied. "I have no idea why, or what happened."

"I know why." She sighed, and he saw the sadness in her eyes. She looked pale and tired. "He has been charged with the embezzlement of a considerable amount of money, which—"

"What?" It was absurd. Ordinarily he would not have dreamed of interrupting her—it was a breach of courtesy unimaginable to him— but Pitt's disbelief was too urgent to be stifled.

A flicker of amusement sparkled in her eyes, and vanished as quickly. "I am aware of the absurdity, Thomas. Victor has several faults, but petty theft is not among them."

"You said a large amount."

"Large to steal. It cost a man's life because he did not have it. Someone engineered this very astutely. I have my ideas as to who it may have been, but they are no more than ideas, insubstantial, and quite possibly mistaken."

"Where is Narraway?" he demanded.

"In Ireland," she told him.

"Why Ireland?" he asked.

"Because he believes that whoever was the author of his misfortune is Irish, and that the culprit is to be found there." She bit her lip very slightly. It was a gesture of anxiety so deep, he could not recall having seen her do it before.

"Aunt Vespasia?" He leaned forward a little.

"He believed it personal," she continued. "An act of revenge for an old injury. At the time I thought he might have been correct, although it was a long time to wait for such perceived justice, and the Irish have never been noted for their patience, especially for revenge. I assumed some new circumstance must have made it possible . . ."

"You said *assumed*—were you wrong?" he asked.

"After what you have told me of your experience in France, and of this man Gower, who was your assistant, and of whom neither you nor anyone else in Special Branch appeared to have any suspicions, I think Victor was mistaken," she said gravely. "I fear it may have had nothing to do with personal revenge, but have been a means of removing him from command of the situation in London, and replacing him with someone either of far less competence or—very much worse—of sympathy with the socialist cause. It looks as if you were removed to France for the same reason."

He smiled with a bitter humor. "I am not of Narraway's experience or power," he told her honestly. "I am not worth their trouble to remove."

"You are too modest, my dear." She regarded him with amused affection. "Surely you would have fought for Victor. Even if you were not as fond of him as I believe you to be, you would do it out of loyalty. He took you into Special Branch when the Metropolitan Police dismissed you, and you had too many enemies to return there. He took some risk doing so, and made more enemies of his own. Most of those men are gone now, but at the time it was a dangerous act. You have more than repaid him with your ability, but you can now repay the courage. I do not imagine you think differently."

Her eyes were steady on his. "Added to which, you have enemies in Special Branch yourself, because of the favor he showed you, and your somewhat rapid rise. With Victor gone, you will be very fortunate indeed if you survive him for long. Even if you do, you will be forever watching over your shoulder and waiting for the unseen blow. If you do not know that, you are far more naïve than I think you."

"My loyalty to Narraway would have been enough, to bring me to his aid," he told her. "But yes, of course I am aware that without his protection I won't last long."

Her voice was very gentle. "My dear, it is imperative, for many reasons, that we do what we can to clear Victor's name. I am glad you see it so clearly."

He felt a sudden chill, a warning.

She inclined her head in assent. "Then you will understand why Charlotte has gone to Ireland with Victor to help him in any way she can. He will find it hard enough on his own. She may be his eyes and ears in places he is unable to go himself."

For a moment he did not even understand, as if her words were half in a foreign language. The key words were plain enough— *Charlotte, Narraway,* and *Ireland*—but the whole of it made no sense.

"Charlotte's gone to Ireland?" he repeated. "She can't have! What on earth could she do? She doesn't know Ireland, and she certainly doesn't know anything about Narraway's past, his old cases, or anyone else in Special Branch." He hesitated to tell her she had misunderstood. It would sound so rude, but it was the only explanation.

"Thomas," Vespasia said gravely. "The situation is very serious. Victor is helpless. He is closed out of his office and all access to any assistance from Special Branch. We know that at least one person there, highly placed, is a thief and a traitor. We do not know who it is. Charles Austwick is in charge . . ."

"Austwick?"

"Yes. You see how serious it is? Do you imagine that without your help he will find the traitor? Apparently none of you, including Victor, were aware of Gower's treason. Who else would betray you? Charlotte is at least in part aware of the danger, including the danger to you personally. She went with Victor partly out of loyalty to him, but mostly to save his career because she is very sharply aware that yours depends upon it also. And another element that you may not yet have had time to consider: If Victor can be made to appear guilty of theft, how difficult would it be for the same people to make you appear guilty with him?"

It was a nightmare again: frightening, irrational. Pitt was exhausted, aching with the pain of disillusion and the horror of his own violence. His body was bruised and so tired he could sleep sitting in this comfortable chair, if only he could relax long enough. And yet fear knotted the muscles in his back, his shoulders, and his neck, and his head throbbed. This last piece of news made the situation immeasurably worse. He struggled to make sense of it.

"Where is she? Is she safe . . . ?" *Safe* was a stupid word to use if she was in Ireland with Narraway.

"Thomas, Victor is out there with her. He won't let any harm come to her if he can prevent it," Vespasia said softly.

Pitt knew Narraway was in love with her, but he did not want to hear it. "If he cared, he wouldn't have . . . ," he began.

"Allowed her to go?" she finished for him. "Thomas, she has gone in order to honor her friendship and loyalty, and above all to protect her husband's career, and therefore the family's means of survival. What do you imagine he could have said or done that would have stopped her?"

"Not told her he was going in the first place!" he snapped.

"Really?" She raised her silver eyebrows. "And left her wondering why you did not come home after chasing your informant through the streets? Not that night, or the entire following week? She might have gone to Lisson Grove and asked, by which time she would be frantic with fear. And she would have been met with the news that Narraway was gone and you were nowhere to be found, and there was no one in Lisson Grove to help or support you. Do you feel that would have been preferable?"

"No . . ." He felt foolish—panicky. What should he do? He wanted to go immediately to Ireland and make sure Charlotte was safe, but even an instant's reflection told him that it was an irresponsible, hotheaded thing even to think of. By reacting thoughtlessly, he would likely be playing directly into the hands of his enemies.

"I'll go home and see Daniel and Jemima," he said more calmly. "If they have had a week of Mrs. Waterman, they may be feeling pretty desperate. She is not an easy woman. I must speak to Charlotte about that, when she gets home."

"You don't need to concern yourself—" Vespasia began.

"You don't know the woman—" he started.

"She is irrelevant," Vespasia told him. "She left."

"What? Then . . ."

Vespasia raised her hand. "That is the other thing I was going to tell you. She has been replaced by a new maid, on the recommendation of Gracie. She seems a very competent girl, and Gracie looks in on them every day. Her reports of this new girl are glowing. In fact I must say that I rather like the sound of young Minnie Maude. She has character."

Pitt was dizzy. Everything seemed to be shifting. The moment he looked at it, it changed, as if someone had struck the kaleidoscope and all the pieces had shattered and re-formed in a different pattern.

"Minnie Maude?" he said stumblingly. "For God's sake, how old is she?" To him, Gracie herself was little more than a child, despite the fact that he had known her since she was thirteen.

"About twenty," Vespasia replied. "Gracie has known her since she was eight. She has courage and sense. There is nothing to concern yourself about, Thomas. As I said—I have been there myself, and everything was satisfactory. Perhaps just as important, both Daniel and Jemima like her. Do you imagine I would allow the situation to remain if that were not so?"

Now he felt clumsy and deeply ungracious. He knew an apology was appropriate; his fear had made him foolish and rude. "Of course not. I'm sorry. I . . ." He hunted for words.

She smiled. It was a sudden, beautiful gesture that lit her face and restored everything of the beauty that had made her famous. "I would think less of you were you to take it for granted," she said. "Now, before you leave, would you like tea? And are you hungry? If you are I shall have whatever you care for prepared. In the meantime we need to discuss what is to be done next. It is now up to you to address the real issue behind all this ploy and counterploy by whoever is the traitor at Lisson Grove."

Her words were sobering. How like Vespasia to discuss the fate of revolution, murder, and treason in high places over tea and a plate of sandwiches in the withdrawing room. It restored a certain sanity to the world. At least something was as it should be. He drew in a deep breath and let it out slowly, steadying himself.

"Thank you. I should very much like a good cup of tea. The prison in Shoreham had only the most moderate amenities. And a sandwich would be excellent."

PITT ARRIVED HOME AT Keppel Street in the early afternoon. Both Daniel and Jemima were still at school. He knocked on the door, rather than use his key and startle this Minnie Maude in whom Vespasia seemed to have so much confidence.

He stood on the step shifting his weight from one foot to the other, his mind racing over what changes he might find: what small things uncared for, changed so it was no longer the home he was used to, and which he realized he loved fiercely, exactly as it was. Except, of course, Charlotte should be there. Without her nothing was more than a shell.

The door opened and a young woman stood just inside, her expression guarded.

"Yes, sir." She said it politely, but stood squarely blocking the way in. "Can I 'elp yer?" She was not pretty but she had beautiful hair: thick and curling and of a rich, bright color. And she had the freckles on her face that so often went with such vividness. She was far taller than Gracie and slender; however, she had the same direct, almost defiant gaze.

"Are you Minnie Maude?" he asked.

"Beggin' yer pardon, sir, but that in't yer business," she replied. "If yer want the master, yer gimme a card, an' I'll ask 'im to call on yer."

He could not help smiling. "I'll give you a card, by all means." He fished for one in his pocket and passed it to her, then wondered if she could read. He had become used to Gracie reading, since Charlotte had taught her.

Minnie Maude looked at the card, then up at him, then at the card again.

He smiled at her.

The blush spread up her cheeks in a hot tide. "I'm sorry, sir." She stumbled over the words. "I din't know yer."

"Don't be sorry," he said quickly. "You shouldn't allow anyone in unless you know who they are, and not just because they say so."

She stood back, allowing him to pass. He went into the familiar hallway, and immediately smelled the lavender floor polish. The hall mirror was clean, the surfaces free of dust. Jemima's shoes were placed neatly side by side under the coat stand.

He walked down to the kitchen and looked around. Everything was as it should be: blue-and-white-ringed plates on the Welsh dresser, copper pans on the wall, kitchen table scrubbed, the stove burning warm but not overhot. He could smell newly baked bread and the clean, comfortable aroma of fresh laundry hanging from the airing rail up near the ceiling. He was home again. There was nothing wrong, except that his family was not there. But he knew where Charlotte was, and the children were at school.

"Would you like a cup o' tea, sir?" Minnie Maude asked in an uncertain voice.

He did not really need one so soon after leaving Vespasia's, but he felt she would like to do something familiar and useful.

"Thank you," he accepted. He had been obliged to buy several necessities for the days he had been in France, including the case in which he now carried them. "I have a little laundry in my bag, but I don't know whether I shall be home for dinner or not. I'm sorry. If I am, something cold to eat will do very well."

"Yes, sir. Would you like some cold mutton an' 'ot bubble and squeak? That's wot Daniel an' Jemima'll be 'avin', as it's wot they like. 'Ceptin' they like eggs wif it."

"Eggs will be excellent, thank you." He meant it. Eggs sounded familiar, comfortable, and very good.

VESPASIA HAD WARNED PITT not to go to Lisson Grove, but he had no choice; he could do nothing to help Narraway and Charlotte, without information held there.

Of course there was the question of explaining what had happened to Gower. Pitt had no idea how badly he had been disfigured by the fall from the train, but every effort would be made to identify him. Indeed, by the time Pitt reached Lisson Grove he might find that it had already been done.

What should his story be? How much of the truth could he tell without losing every advantage of surprise that he had? He did not know who his enemies were, but they certainly knew him. His instinct was to affect as much ignorance as possible. The less they considered him a worthwhile opponent, the less likely they'd be to eliminate him. Feigning ignorance would be a manner of camouflage, at least for a while.

He should be open and honest about the attack on the train. It was a matter of record with the police. But it would be easy enough, highly believable in fact, to claim that he had no idea who the man was. Remove every thought that it was personal.

He had last seen Gower in St. Malo, when they agreed that Pitt should come home to see what Lisson Grove knew of any conspiracy, and Gower should remain in France and watch Frobisher and Wrexham, and anyone else of interest. Naturally he would know nothing of Narraway's disgrace, and be thoroughly shocked.

He arrived just before four o'clock. He went in through the door, past the man on duty just inside, and asked to see Narraway.

He was told to wait, as he had expected, but it was a surprisingly short time before Charles Austwick himself came down and conducted Pitt up to what used to be Narraway's office. Pitt noticed immediately that all signs of Narraway were gone: his pictures, the photograph of his mother that used to sit on top of the bookcase, the few personal books of poetry and memoirs, the engraved brass bowl from his time in North Africa.

Pitt stared at Austwick, allowing his sense of loss to show in his face, hoping Austwick would see it as confusion.

"Sit down, Pitt." Austwick waved him to the chair opposite the desk. "Of course you're wondering what the devil's going on. I'm afraid I have some shocking news for you."

Pitt forced himself to look alarmed, as if his imagination were racing. "Something has happened to Mr. Narraway? Is he hurt? Ill?"

"I'm afraid in some ways it is worse than that," Austwick said somberly. "Narraway appears to have stolen a rather large amount of money, and—when faced with the crime—he disappeared. We don't know where he is. Obviously he has been dismissed from the service, and at least for the time being I have replaced him. I am sure that is temporary, but until further notice you will report to me. I'm sorry. It must be a great blow to you, indeed it is to all of us. I don't think any-one imagined that Narraway, of all people, would give in to that kind of temptation."

Pitt's mind raced. How should he respond? He had thought it was all worked out in his mind, but sitting here in Narraway's office, sub-tly but so completely changed, he was uncertain again. Was Austwick the traitor? If so then he was a far cleverer man than Pitt had thought. But Pitt had had no idea that there was a traitor at all, and he had trusted Gower. What was his judgment worth?

"I can see that you're stunned," Austwick said patiently. "We've had a little while to get used to the idea. We knew almost as soon as you had gone. By the way, where is Gower?"

Pitt inhaled deeply, and plunged in. "I left him in France, in St. Malo," he replied. He watched Austwick's face as closely as he dared, trying to read in his eyes, his gestures, if he knew that that was only half true.

Austwick spoke slowly, as if he also was measuring what he said, and he seemed to be watching Pitt just as closely. Had he noticed Somerset Carlisle's beautifully cut shirt? Or his wine-colored cravat?

Pitt repeated exactly what he believed had happened at the time he had first notified Narraway that he had to remain in France.

Austwick listened attentively. His expression did not betray whether he knew anything further or not.

"I see," he said at last, drumming his fingers silently on the desk-top. "So you left Gower there in the hope that there might yet be something worthwhile to observe?"

"Yes . . . sir." He added the *sir* with difficulty. There was a slowly mounting rage inside him that this man was sitting there in Nar-raway's chair, behind his desk. Was he also a pawn in this game, or was he the one playing it with the opposing pieces?

"Do you think that is likely?" Austwick asked. "You say you saw nothing after that first sighting of . . . who did you say? Meister and Linsky, was it?"

"Yes," Pitt agreed. "There were plenty of people coming and going all the time, but neither of us recognized anyone else. It's possible that was coincidence. On the other hand, West was murdered, and the man who killed him, very brutally and openly, fled to that house. There has to be a reason for that."

Austwick appeared to consider it for several moments. Finally he looked up, his lips pursed. "You're right. There is certainly something happening, and there is a good chance it concerns violence that may affect us here in England, even if it begins in France. We have our allies to consider, and what our failure to warn them may do to our relationship. I would certainly feel a distinct sense of betrayal if they were to have wind of such a threat against us, and keep silent about it."

"Yes, sir," Pitt agreed, although the words all but stuck in his throat. He rose to his feet. "If you'll excuse me, I have several matters to attend to."

"Yes, of course," Austwick agreed. He seemed calm, even assured. Pitt found himself shaking with anger as he left the room, making an effort to close the door softly.

THAT EVENING HE WENT to see the minister, Sir Gerald Croxdale. Croxdale himself had suggested that he come to the house. If the matter were as private and as urgent as Pitt had said, then it would be better if their meeting were not observed by others.

Croxdale's home in Hampstead was old and very handsome, overlooking the heath. The garden trees were coming into leaf, and the air seemed to be full of birdsong.

Pitt was shown in by the butler. He found Croxdale standing in his library, which had long windows onto the lawn at the back of the house. At present the curtains were open; the evening sky beyond was pale with the last light. Croxdale turned from gazing at it as Pitt came in. He offered his hand.

"Miserable time," he said sympathetically. "Pretty bad shock to all of us. I've known Narraway for years. Difficult man, not really a team player, but brilliant, and I'd always thought he was sound. But it seems as if a man can never entirely leave his past behind." He gestured to one of the armchairs beside the fire. "Do sit down. Tell me what happened in St. Malo. By the way, have you had any dinner?"

Pitt realized with surprise that he had not. He had not even thought of eating, and his body was clenched with anxiety as different possibilities poured through his mind. Now he was fumbling for a gracious answer.

"Sandwich?" Croxdale offered. "Roast beef acceptable?"

Experience told Pitt it was better to eat than try to think rationally on an empty stomach. "Thank you, sir."

Croxdale rang the bell, and when the butler appeared again he requested roast beef sandwiches and whiskey.

"Now." He sat back as soon as the door was closed. "Tell me about St. Malo."

Pitt offered him the same edited version he had given Austwick. He was not yet ready to tell anyone the whole truth. Croxdale had known Victor Narraway far longer than he had known Pitt. If he would believe that Narraway had stolen money, why should he think any better of Pitt, who was Narraway's protégé and closest ally?

The butler brought the sandwiches, which were excellent. Pitt took an unaccustomed glass of whiskey with it, but declined a second. To have the fire inside him was good, his heart beating a little faster. However, to be fuzzy-headed could be disastrous.

Croxdale considered in silence for some time before he replied. Pitt waited him out.

"I am certain you have done the right thing," Croxdale said at length. "The situation requires very careful watching, but at this point we cannot afford your absence from Lisson Grove. This fearful business with Narraway has changed all our priorities."

Pitt was aware that Croxdale was watching him far more closely than at a glance it might seem. He tried to keep his expression respectful, concerned, but not as if he were already aware of the details.

Croxdale sighed. "I imagine it comes as a shock to you, as it does to me. Perhaps we should all have seen some warning, but I admit I did not. Of course we are aware of people's financial interests—we would be remiss not to be. Narraway has no urgent need of money, as far as we know. This whole business with O'Neil is of long standing, some twenty years or more." He looked closely at Pitt, his brows drawn together. "Did he tell you anything about it?"

"No, sir."

"Old case. All very ugly, but I thought it was over at the time. We all did. Very briefly, Narraway was in charge of the Irish situation, and we knew there was serious trouble brewing. As indeed there was. He foiled it so successfully that there was never any major news about it. Only afterward did we learn what the price had been."

Pitt did not need to pretend his ignorance, or the growing fear inside him, chilling his body.

Croxdale shook his head minutely, his face clouded with unhappiness. "Narraway used one of their own against them, a woman named Kate O'Neil. The details I don't know, and I prefer to be able to claim ignorance. The end of it was that the woman's husband killed her, rather messily, and was tried and hanged for it."

Pitt was stunned. Was Narraway really as ruthless as that story implied? He pictured Narraway's face in all the circumstances they had known each other through: success and failure; exhaustion, fear, disappointment; the conclusion of dozens of battles, won or lost. Reading Narraway defied reason: It was instinct, the trust that had grown up over time in all sorts of ways. It took him a painful and uncertain effort to conceal his feelings. He tried to look confused.

"If all this happened twenty years ago, what is it that has changed now?" he asked.

Croxdale was only momentarily taken aback. "We don't know," he replied. "Presumably something in O'Neil's own situation."

"I thought you said he was hanged?"

"Oh yes, the husband was; that was Sean O'Neil. But his brother Cormac is still very much alive. They were unusually close, even for an Irish family," Croxdale explained.

"Then why did Cormac wait twenty years for his revenge? I assume you are saying that Narraway took the money in some way because of O'Neil?"

Croxdale hesitated, then looked at Pitt guardedly. "You know, I have no idea. Clearly we need to know a good deal more than we do at present. I assume it is to do with O'Neil because Narraway went almost immediately to Ireland."

This question nagged at Pitt, but Croxdale cleared his throat and continued on, once again in his usual tones of assuredness.

"This regrettable defection of Narraway's has astounded us all, but at the same time, we must keep sight of the greater threat: the ominous socialist activity cropping up. There seem to be plots on all sides. I'm sure what you and Gower were witness to is part of some larger and possibly very dangerous plan. The socialist tide has been rising for some time in Europe, as we are all aware. I can no longer have Narraway in charge, obviously. I need the very best I can find, a man I can trust morally and intellectually, whose loyalty is beyond question and who has no ghosts from the past to sabotage our present attempts to safeguard our country, and all it stands for."

Pitt blinked. "Of course." Did that mean that Croxdale knew Austwick was the traitor? Pitt had been avoiding the issue, waiting, judging pointlessly. It was a relief. Croxdale was clever, more reliable than he had thought. Then how could he think such things of Narraway?

But what was Pitt's judgment to rely on? He had trusted Gower!

Croxdale was still looking at him intently.

Pitt could think of nothing to say.

"We need a man who knows what Narraway was doing and can pick up the reins he dropped," Croxdale said. "You are the only man who fits that description, Pitt. It's a great deal to ask of you, but there is no one else, and your skills and integrity are things about which I believe Narraway was both right and honest."

"But . . . Austwick . . . ," Pitt stammered. "He . . ."

"Is a good stopgap," Croxdale said coolly. "He is not the man for the job in such dangerous times as these. Frankly, he has not the ability to lead, or to make the difficult decisions of such magnitude. He was a good enough lieutenant."

Pitt's head swam. He had none of his predecessor's nerve, confidence, political savvy, or decision-making experience.

"Neither have I the skills," he protested. "And I haven't been in the service long enough for the other men to have confidence in me. I will support Austwick as best I can, but I haven't the abilities to take on the leadership."

Croxdale smiled. "I thought you would be modest. It is a good quality. Arrogance leads to mistakes. I'm sure you will seek advice, and take it—at least most of the time. But you have never lacked judgment before, or the courage to go with your own beliefs. I know your record, Pitt. Do you imagine you have gone unnoticed in the past?" He asked it gently, as if with a certain degree of amusement.

"I imagine not," Pitt conceded. "You will know a good deal about anyone, before taking them into the service at all. But—"

"Not in your case," Croxdale contradicted him. "You were Narraway's recruit. But I have made it my business to learn far more about you since then. Your country needs you now, Pitt. Narraway has effectively betrayed our trust and has likely fled the country. You were Narraway's second in command. This is your duty as well as your privilege to serve." He held out his hand.

Pitt was overwhelmed, not with pleasure or any sense of honor, but with great concern for Narraway, fear for Charlotte, and the knowledge that he did not want this weight of command. It was not in his nature to act with certainty when the balance of judgment was so gray, and the stakes were the lives of other men.

"We look to you, Pitt," Croxdale said again. "Don't fail your country, man!"

"No, sir," Pitt said unhappily. "I will do everything I can, sir . . ."

"Good." Croxdale smiled. "I knew you would. That is one thing Narraway was right about. I will inform the necessary people, including the prime minister, of course. Thank you, Pitt. We are grateful to you."

Pitt accepted: He had little choice. Croxdale began to outline to him exactly what his task would be, his powers, and the rewards.

It was midnight when Pitt walked outside into the lamplit night and found Croxdale's own carriage waiting to take him home.

CHAPTER

9

CHARLOTTE WALKED AWAY FROM Cormac O'Neil's home
with as much composure as she could muster, but she had the sinking
fear inside her that she looked as afraid and bewildered as she felt, and
as helplessly angry. Whatever else Narraway might have been guilty
of—and it could have been a great deal—she was certain that he had
not killed Cormac O'Neil. She had arrived at the house almost on his
heels. She had heard the dog begin to bark as Narraway went into the
house, and continue more and more hysterically, knowing there was
an intruder, and perhaps already aware of O'Neil's death.

Had Cormac cried out? Had he even seen his killer, or had he
been shot in the back? She had not heard a gun fire, only the dog
barking. That was it, of course! The dog had barked at Narraway, but
not at whoever had fired the shot.

She stopped in the street, standing rooted to the spot as the realization shook her with its meaning. Narraway could not possibly have
shot Cormac. Her certainty was not built on her belief in him but on
evidence: facts that were not capable of any other reasonable inter-

pretation. She turned on her heel and stepped out urgently, striding across the street back toward O'Neil's house, then stopped again just as suddenly. Why should they believe her? She knew that what she said was true, but would anyone else substantiate it?

Of course not! Talulla would contradict it because she hated Narraway. With hindsight, that had been perfectly clear, and predictable. She would be only too delighted if he were hanged for Cormac's murder. To her it would be justice—the sweeter now after the long delay. She must know he was not guilty because she had been close enough to have heard the dog start to bark herself, but she would be the last person to say so.

Narraway would know that. She remembered his face as he allowed the police to handcuff him. He had looked at Charlotte only once, concentrating everything he had to say in that one glance. He needed her to understand.

He also needed her to keep a very calm mind and to think: to work it out detail by detail and not act before she was certain—not only of the truth, but that she could prove it so it could not be ignored. It is very difficult indeed to make people believe what is against all their emotions: the conviction of friend and enemy years-deep, paid for in blood and loss.

She was still standing on the pavement. A small crowd had gathered because of the violence and the police just over a hundred yards away. They were staring, wondering what was the matter with her.

She swallowed, straightened her skirt, then turned yet again and walked back toward where she judged to be the best place to find a carriage to take her to Molesworth Street. There were many practical considerations to weigh very carefully. She was completely alone now. There was no one at all she could trust. She must consider whether to remain at Mrs. Hogan's or if it would be safer to move somewhere else where she would be less exposed. Everyone knew she was Narraway's sister.

But where else could she go? How long would it take anyone to find her again in a town the size of Dublin? She was a stranger, an Englishwoman, on her own. She knew no one except those Narraway had introduced her to. A couple of hours' inquiries would find her again, and she would merely look ridiculous, and evasive, as if she had something of which to be ashamed.

She was walking briskly along the pavement, trying to appear to know precisely where she was going and to what purpose. The former was true. There was a carriage ahead of her setting down a fare, and she could hire it if she was quick enough. She reached the carriage just as it began to move.

"Sir!" she called out. "Will you be good enough to take me to Molesworth Street?"

"Sure, an' I'll be happy to," the driver responded, completing his turn and pulling the horse up.

She thanked him and climbed up into the carriage, feeling intensely grateful as the wheels rumbled over the cobbles and they picked up speed. She did not turn to look behind her; she could picture the scene just as clearly as if she were gazing upon it. Narraway should still be in the house, manacled like any other dangerous criminal. He must feel desperately alone. Was he frightened? Certainly he would never show any such weakness.

She told herself abruptly to stop being so useless and self-indulgent. Pitt was somewhere in France with nobody else to rely on, believing Narraway was still at Lisson Grove. Not even in his nightmares would he suppose Narraway could be in Ireland under arrest for murder, and Lisson Grove in the hands of traitors. Whatever she felt was irrelevant. The only task ahead was to rescue Narraway, and to do that she must find the truth and prove it.

Talulla Lawless knew who had killed Cormac because it had to be someone the dog would not bark at: therefore someone who had a right to be in Cormac's home. The clearest answer was Talulla herself. Cormac lived alone; he had said so the previous evening when Charlotte had asked him. No doubt a local woman would come in every so often and clean for him, and do the laundry.

Why would Talulla kill him? He was her uncle. But then how often was murder a family matter? She knew from Pitt's cases in the past, very much too often. The next most likely answer would be a robbery, but any thief breaking in would have set the dog into a frenzy.

Still, why would Talulla kill him, and why now? Not purely to blame Narraway, surely? How could she even know that he would be there to be blamed?

The answer to that was obvious: It must have been she who had sent the letter luring Narraway to Cormac's house. She of all people would be able to imitate his hand. Narraway might recall it from twenty years ago, but not in such minute detail that he would recognize a good forgery.

That still left the question as to why she had chosen to do it now. Cormac was her uncle; they were the only two still alive from the tragedy of twenty years ago. Cormac had no children, and her parents were dead. Surely both of them believed Narraway responsible for that? Why would she kill Cormac?

Was Narraway on the brink of finding out something Talulla could not afford him to know?

That made incomplete sense. If it were true, then surely the obvious thing would be to have killed Narraway?

She recalled the look on Talulla's face as she had seen Narraway standing near Cormac's body. She had been almost hysterical. She might have a great ability to act, but surely not great enough to effect the sweat on her lip and brow, the wildness in her eyes, the catch in her voice as it soared out of control? And yet never once had she looked at Cormac's body—perhaps she already knew exactly what she would see? She had not gone to him even to assure herself that he was beyond help. There had been nothing in her face but hate—no grief, no denial.

Charlotte was oblivious to the handsome streets of Dublin as the carriage drove on. It could have been any city on earth, so absorbed was she in thought. She was startled by a spatter of cold rain through the open window that wet her face and shoulder.

How much of this whole thing was Talulla responsible for? What about the issue of Mulhare and the embezzled money? She could not possibly have arranged that.

Or was someone in Lisson Grove using Irish passion and loyalties to further their own need to remove Narraway? Whom could she ask? Were any of Narraway's supposed friends actually willing to help him? Or had he wounded or betrayed them all at one time or another, so that when it came to it they would take their revenge? He was totally vulnerable now. Could it be that at last they had stopped quarreling with one another long enough to conspire to ruin him?

Perhaps Charlotte had no right to judge Narraway's Irish enemies. What would she have felt, or done, were it all the other way around: if Ireland were the foreigner, the occupier in England? If someone had used and betrayed her family, would she be so loyal to her beliefs in honesty or impartial justice? Perhaps—but perhaps not. It was impossible to know without one's having lived that terrible reality.

Yet Narraway was innocent of killing Cormac—and she realized as she said this to herself that she thought he was no more than partially responsible for the downfall of Kate O'Neil. The O'Neils had tried to use him, turn him to betray his country. They might well be furious that they had failed, but had they the right to exact vengeance for losing?

She needed to ask help from someone, because alone she might as well simply give up and go back to London, leaving Narraway to his fate, and eventually Pitt to his. Before she reached Molesworth Street and even attempted to explain the situation to Mrs. Hogan, which she must do, she had decided to ask Fiachra McDaid for help.

"WHAT?" MCDAID SAID INCREDULOUSLY when she found him at his home and told him what had happened.

"I'm sorry." She gulped and tried to regain her composure. She had thought herself in perfect control, and realized she was much farther from it than she'd imagined. "We went to see Cormac O'Neil. At least Victor said he was going alone, but I followed him, just behind . . ."

"You mean you found a carriage able to keep up with him in Dublin traffic?" McDaid frowned.

"No, no I knew where he was going. I had been there the evening before myself . . ."

"To see O'Neil?" He looked incredulous.

"Yes. Please . . . listen." Her voice was rising again, and she made an effort to calm it. "I arrived moments after he did. I heard the dog begin to bark as he went in, but no shot!"

"It would bark." The frown deepened on his brow. "It barks for anyone except Cormac, or perhaps Talulla. She lives close by and looks after it if Cormac is away, which he is from time to time."

"Not the cleaning woman?" she said quickly.

"No. She's afraid of it." He looked at her more closely, his face earnest. "Why? What does it matter?"

She hesitated, still uncertain how far to trust him. It was the only evidence she had that protected Narraway. Perhaps she should keep it to herself.

"I suppose it doesn't," she said, deliberately looking confused. Then, as coherently as she could, but missing out any further reference to the dog, she told him what had happened. As she did, she watched his face, trying to read the emotions in it, the belief or disbelief, the confusion or understanding, the loss or triumph.

He listened without interrupting her. "They think Narraway shot Cormac? Why would he, for God's sake?"

"In revenge for Cormac having ruined him in London," she answered. "That's what Talulla said. It makes a kind of sense."

"Do you think that's what happened?" he asked.

She nearly said that she knew it was not, then realized her mistake just in time. "No." She spoke guardedly now. "I was just behind him, and I didn't hear a shot. But I don't think he would do that anyway. It doesn't make sense."

He shook his head. "Yes it does. Victor loved that job of his. In a way it was all he had." He looked conflicted, emotions twisting his features. "I'm sorry. I don't mean to imply that you are not important to him, but I think from what he said that you do not see each other so often."

Now she was angry. She felt it well up inside her, knotting her stomach, making her hands shake, her voice thick as if she were a little drunk. "No. We don't. But you've known Victor for years. Was he ever a fool?"

"No, never. Many things good and bad, but never a fool," he admitted.

"Did he ever act against his own interest, hotheadedly, all feelings and no thought?" She could not imagine it, not the man she knew. Had he once had that kind of runaway passion? Was his supreme control a mask?

McDaid laughed abruptly, without joy. "No. He never forgot his cause. Hell or heaven could dance naked past him and he would not be diverted. Why?"

"Because if he really thought Cormac O'Neil was responsible for ruining him in London, for setting up what looked like embezzlement and seeing that he was blamed, the last thing he would want was Cormac dead," she answered. "He would want Cormac's full confession, the proof, the names of those who aided—"

"I see," he interrupted. "I see. You're right. Victor would never put revenge ahead of getting his job and his honor back."

"So someone else killed Cormac and made it look like Victor," she concluded. "That would be their revenge, wouldn't it." It was a statement, not a question.

"Yes," he agreed, his eyes bright, his hands loosely beside him.

"Will you help me find out who?" she asked.

He gestured to one of the big leather chairs in his gracious but very masculine sitting room. She imagined wealthy gentlemen's clubs must be like this inside: worn and comfortable upholstery, lots of wood paneling, brass ornaments—except these were silver, and uniquely Celtic. She sat down obediently.

He sat opposite her, leaning forward a little. "Have you any idea who already?"

Her mind raced. How should she answer, how much of the truth? Could he help at all if she lied to him?

"I have lots of ideas, but they don't add up," she replied, hoping to conceal her knowledge of the facts. "I know who hated Victor, but I don't know who hated Cormac."

A moment of humor touched his face, and then vanished. It looked like self-mockery.

"I don't expect you to know," she said quietly. "Or you would have warned him. But perhaps with hindsight you might understand something now. Talulla is Sean and Kate's daughter, brought up away from Dublin after her parents' deaths." She saw instantly in his eyes that he had known that.

"She is, poor child," he agreed.

"You didn't warn Victor of that, did you?" It sounded more like an accusation than she had intended it to.

McDaid looked down for a moment, then back up at her. "No. I thought she had suffered enough."

"Another one of your innocent casualties," she observed, remembering what he had said during their carriage ride in the dark. Something in that had disturbed her, a resignation she could not share. All casualties still upset her; but then her country was not at war, not occupied by another people.

"I don't make judgments as to who is innocent and who guilty, Mrs. Pitt, just what is necessary, and that only when I have no choice."

"Talulla was a child!"

"Children grow up."

Did he know, or guess, whether Talulla had killed Cormac? She looked at him steadily and found herself a little afraid. The intelligence in him was overwhelming, rich with understanding of terrible irony. And it was not himself he was mocking: it was her, and her naïveté. She was quite certain of that now. He was a thought, a word ahead of her all the time. She had already said too much, and he knew perfectly well that she was sure Talulla had shot Cormac.

"Into what?" she said aloud. "Into a woman who would shoot her uncle's head to pieces in order to be revenged on the man she thinks betrayed her mother?"

That surprised him, just for an instant. Then he covered it. "Of course she thinks that," he replied. "She can hardly face thinking that Kate went with him willingly. In fact if he'd asked her, maybe she would have gone to England with him. Who knows?"

"Do you?" she said immediately.

"I?" His eyebrows rose. "I have no idea."

"Is that why Sean killed her, really?"

"Again, I have no idea."

She did not know whether to believe him or not. He had been charming to her, generous with his time and excellent company, but behind the smiling façade he was a complete stranger. She had no idea what was going on in his thoughts.

"More incidental damage," she said aloud. "Kate, Sean, Talulla, now Cormac. Incidental to what, Mr. McDaid? Ireland's freedom?"

"Could we have a better cause, Mrs. Pitt?" he said gently. "Surely Talulla can be understood for wanting that? Hasn't she paid enough?"

But it didn't make sense, not completely. Who had moved the money meant for Mulhare back into Narraway's account? Was that done simply in order to lure him to Ireland for this revenge? Wouldn't Talulla's rage have been satisfied by killing Narraway herself? Why on earth make poor Cormac the sacrifice? If she wanted Narraway to suffer, she could have shot him somewhere uniquely painful, so he would be disabled, mutilated, die slowly. There were plenty of possibilities.

And why now? There had to be a reason.

McDaid was still watching her, waiting.

"Yes, I imagine she has paid enough," she said, answering his question. "And Cormac? Hasn't he too?"

"Ah yes . . . poor Cormac," McDaid said softly. "He loved Kate, you know. That's why he could never forgive Narraway. She cared for Cormac, but she would never have loved him . . . mostly I suppose because he was Sean's brother. Cormac was the better man, I think. Maybe in the end, Kate thought so too."

"That doesn't answer why Talulla shot him," Charlotte pointed out.

"Oh, you're right. Of course it doesn't . . ."

"Another victim of incidental damage?" she said with a touch of bitterness. "Whose freedom do you fight for at such a cost? Is that not a weight of grief to carry forever?"

His eyes flashed for a moment, then the anger was gone again. But it had been real.

"Cormac was guilty too," he said grimly.

"Of what? Surviving?" she asked.

"Yes, but more than that. He didn't do much to save Sean. He barely tried. If he'd told the truth, Sean might have been a hero, not a man who murdered his wife in a jealous rage."

"Perhaps to Cormac he *was* a man who murdered his wife in a jealous rage," she pointed out. "People react slowly sometimes when they are shattered with grief. Cormac might have been too shocked to do anything useful. What could it have been anyway? Didn't Sean himself tell the truth as to why he killed Kate?"

"He barely said anything," McDaid admitted, this time looking down at the floor, not at her.

"Stunned too," she said. "But someone told Talulla that Cormac should have saved her father, and she believed them. Easier to think of your father as a hero betrayed than as a jealous man who killed his wife in a rage because she cuckolded him with his enemy, and an Englishman at that."

McDaid looked at her with another momentary flare of anger. Then he masked it so completely she might almost have thought it was her imagination.

"It would seem so," he agreed. "But how do we prove any of that?"

She felt the coldness sweep over her. "I don't know. I'm trying to think."

"Be careful, Mrs. Pitt," he said gently. "I would not like you to be incidental damage as well."

She managed to smile just as if she did not even imagine that his words could be as much a threat as a warning. She felt as if it were a mask on his face: transparent, ghostly. "Thank you. I shall be cautious, I promise, but it is kind of you to care." She rose to her feet, vigilant not to sway. "Now I think I had better go back to my lodgings. It has been a . . . a terrible day."

When she reached Molesworth Street again, Mrs. Hogan came out to see her immediately. She looked awkward, her hands winding around each other, twisting her apron.

Charlotte addressed the subject before Mrs. Hogan could search for the words.

"You have heard about Mr. O'Neil," she said gravely. "A very terrible thing to have happened. I hope Mr. Narraway will be able to help them. He has some experience in such tragedies. But I quite understand if you would prefer that I move out of your house in the meantime. I will have to find something, of course, until I get my passage back home. I daresay it will take me a day or two. In the meantime I will pack my brother's belongings and put them in my own room, so you may let his rooms to whomsoever you wish. I believe we are paid for another couple of nights at least?" Please heaven within a couple of days she would be a great deal further on in her decisions, and at least one other person in Dublin would know for certain that Narraway was innocent.

Mrs. Hogan was embarrassed. The issue had been taken out of her hands and she did not know how to rescue it. As Charlotte had hoped, she settled for the compromise. "Thank you, that would be most considerate, ma'am."

"If you will be kind enough to lend me the keys, I'll do it straightaway." Charlotte held out her hand.

Reluctantly Mrs. Hogan passed them over.

Charlotte unlocked the door and went inside, closing it behind her. Instantly she felt intrusive. She would pack his clothes, of course, and have someone take the case to her room, unless she could drag it there herself.

But far more important than shirts, socks, personal linen, were whatever papers he might have. Had he committed anything to writing? Would it even be in a form she could understand? If only she could at least ask Pitt! She had never missed him more. But then of course if he were here, she would be at home in London, not trying desperately to carry out a task for which she was so ill suited. She was in a foreign country where she was considered the enemy, and justly so. The weight of centuries of history was against her.

She opened the case, then went to the wardrobe and took out Narraway's suits and shirts, folded them neatly, and packed them. Then, feeling as if she were prying, she opened the drawers in the chest. She took out his underwear and packed it also, making sure she had his pajamas from under the pillow on the bed. She included his extra pair of shoes, wrapped in a cloth to keep them from marking anything, and put them in as well.

She collected the toiletries, a hairbrush, a toothbrush, razor, and small clothes brush. He was an immaculate man. How he would hate being locked up in a cell with no privacy, and probably little means to wash.

The few papers there were in the top drawer of the dresser. Thank heaven they were not locked in a briefcase. But that probably indicated that they would mean nothing to anyone else.

Back in her own room, with Narraway's case propped in the corner, she looked at the few notes he had made. They were a curious reflection on his character, a side of him she had not even guessed at before. They were mostly little drawings, very small indeed, but very clever. They were little stick men, but imbued with such movement and personality that she recognized instantly who they were.

There was one little man with striped trousers and a banknote in his hat, and beside him a woman with chaotic hair. Behind him was another woman, even thinner, her limbs poking jaggedly.

Even with arms and legs merely suggested, Charlotte knew they were John and Bridget Tyrone, and that Tyrone's being a banker was important. The other woman had such a savagery about her it immediately suggested Talulla. Beside her was a question mark. There was no more than that, except a man of whom she could see only the top half, as if he was up to his arms in something. She stared at it until it came to her with a shiver of revulsion. It was Mulhare, drowning—because the money had not been paid.

The little drawing suggested a connection between John Tyrone and Talulla. He was a banker—was he the link to London? Had he the power, through his profession, to move money around from Dublin to London and, with the help of someone in Lisson Grove, to place it back in Narraway's account?

Then who in Lisson Grove? And why? No one could tell her that but Tyrone himself.

Was it dangerous, absurd, to go to him? She had no one else she could turn to, because she did not know who else was involved. Certainly she could not go back to McDaid. She was growing more and more certain within herself that his remarks about accidental damage to the innocent were statements of his philosophy, and also a warning to her.

Was Talulla the prime mover in Cormac's death, or only an instrument, used by someone else? Someone like John Tyrone, so harmless seeming, but powerful enough in Dublin and in London even to create a traitor in Lisson Grove?

There seemed to be two choices open to her: go to Tyrone himself; or give up and go home, leaving Narraway here to answer whatever charge they brought against him, presuming he lived long enough to face a trial. Would it be a fair trial, even? Possibly not. The old wounds were raw, and Special Branch would not be on his side. So Charlotte really had no choice at all.

THE MAID WHO ANSWERED the door let her in somewhat reluctantly.

"I need to speak with Mr. Tyrone," Charlotte said as soon as she was into the large, high-ceilinged hall. "It is to do with the murder of Mr. Mulhare, and now poor Mr. O'Neil. It is most urgent."

"I'll ask him, ma'am," the maid replied. "Who shall I say is calling?"

"Charlotte Pitt." She hesitated only an instant. "Victor Narraway's sister."

"Yes, ma'am." She went across the hall and knocked on a door at the far side. It opened and she spoke for a moment, then returned to Charlotte. "If you'll come with me, ma'am."

Charlotte followed her, and the maid knocked on the same door again.

"Come in." Tyrone's voice was abrupt.

The maid opened it for Charlotte to go past her. Tyrone had obviously been working—there were papers spread across the surface of the large desk.

He stood impatiently, making no attempt to hide the fact that she had interrupted him.

"I'm sorry," she began. "I know it is late and I have come without invitation, but the matter is urgent. Tomorrow may be impossible for me to rescue what is left of the situation."

He moved his weight from one foot to the other. "I am very sorry for you, Mrs. Pitt, but I have no idea how I can help. Perhaps I should send the maid to see where my wife is." It was offered more as an excuse than a suggestion. "She is calling on a neighbor. She cannot be far."

"It is you I need to see," she told him. "And it might be more suitable for your reputation if the maid were to remain, although my inquiries are confidential."

"Then you should call at my place of business, within the usual hours," he pointed out.

She gave him a brief, formal smile. "Confidential to you, Mr. Tyrone. That is why I came here."

"I don't know what you are talking about."

It was still only a deduction from Narraway's drawings, but it was all she had left.

She plunged in. "The money for Mulhare that you transferred back into my brother's account in London, which was responsible for Mulhare's death, and my brother's professional ruin, Mr. Tyrone."

He might have intended to deny it, but his face gave him away. The shock drained the blood from his skin, leaving him almost gray. He drew in his breath sharply, then changed his mind and said nothing. His eyes flickered; and for an instant Charlotte wondered if he was going to call for some kind of assistance and have her thrown out. Probably no servant would attack her, but if any other of the people involved in the plan were—it would only increase her danger. McDaid had warned her.

Or did Tyrone imagine she had even had some hand in murdering Cormac O'Neil?

Now her own voice was shaking. "Mr. Tyrone, too many people have been hurt already, and I'm sure you know poor Cormac was killed this morning. It is time for this to end. I would find it easy to believe that you had no idea what tragedies would follow the transfer of that money. Nor do I find it hard to sympathize with your hatred of those who occupy a country that is rightfully yours. But by using personal murder and betrayal you win nothing. You only bring more tragedy on those you involve. If you doubt me, look at the evidence. All the O'Neils are dead now. Even the loyalty that used to bind them is destroyed. Kate and Cormac have both been murdered, and by the very ones they loved."

"Your brother killed Cormac," he said at last.

"No, he didn't. Cormac was already dead by the time we got there."

He was startled. "We? You went with him?"

"Just after him, but only moments after . . ."

"Then he could have killed him before you got there!"

"No. I was on his heels. I would have heard the shot. I heard the dog begin to bark as Victor entered."

He let out a long, slow sigh, as if at last the pieces had settled into a dark picture that, for all its ugliness, still made sense to him. His face looked bruised, as if some familiar pain had returned inside him.

"You had better come into the study," he said wearily. "I don't know what you can do about any of it now. The police believe Narraway shot O'Neil because they want to believe it. He's earned a long, deep hatred here. They caught him all but in the act. They won't look any further. You would be wise to go back to London while you can." He led the way across the floor into the study and closed the door. He offered her one of the leather-seated chairs and took the other himself.

"I don't know what you think I can do to change anything." There was no lift in his voice, no hope.

"Tell me about transferring the money," she answered.

"And how will that help?"

"Special Branch in London will know that Victor did not steal it." She must remember always to refer to him by his given name. One slip calling him Mr. *Narraway* and she would betray both of them.

He gave a sharp bark of laughter. "And when he's hanged in Dublin for murdering O'Neil, what will that matter to him? There's a poetic justice to it, but if it's logic you're after, the fact that he didn't steal the money won't help. O'Neil had nothing to do with it, but Narraway didn't know that."

"Of course he did!" she retorted instantly. "How do you think I know?"

That caught him off guard; she saw it instantly in his eyes.

"Then what is it you want me to tell you?" he asked.

"Who helped you? Someone in Lisson Grove gave you the account information so you could have it done. And it was nothing to do with helping you. It was to get Victor out of Special Branch. You just served their purpose." She had not thought what she was going to say until the words were on her lips. Did she really mean that it was Charles Austwick? It didn't have to be; there were a dozen others who could have done it, for a dozen other reasons, even one as simple as being paid to. But again that came back to Ireland, and who would pay, and for what reason—just revenge, or an enemy who wanted their own man in Narraway's place? Or was it simply an ambitious man, or one Narraway suspected of treason or theft, and they struck before he could expose them?

She watched Tyrone, waiting for him to respond.

He was trying to judge how much she knew, but there was also something else in his eyes: a hurt that so far made no sense as part of this old vengeance.

"Austwick?" she guessed, before the silence allowed the moment to slip.

"Yes," he said quietly.

"Did he pay you?" She could not keep the contempt from her voice.

His head came up sharply. "No he did not! I did it because I hate Narraway, and Mulhare, and all other traitors to Ireland."

"Victor is not a traitor to Ireland," she pointed out. "He's as English as I am. You're lying." She picked a weapon out of her imagination. "Did he have an affair with your wife, as well as with Kate O'Neil?"

Tyrone's face flamed, and he half rose from his chair. "If you don't want me to throw you out of my house, woman, you'll apologize for that slur on my wife! Your mind's in the gutter. But then I daresay you know your brother a great deal better than I do. If he is your brother, that is?"

Now Charlotte felt her own face burn. "I think perhaps it is your mind that is in the gutter, Mr. Tyrone," she said with a tremor in her voice, and perhaps guilt, because she knew what Narraway felt for her.

Unable to piece together a defense, she attacked. "Why do you do this for Charles Austwick? What is he to you? An Englishman who wants to gain power and office? And in the very secret service that was formed to defeat Irish hopes of Home Rule." That was an exaggeration, she knew. It was formed to combat the bombings and murders intended to terrorize Britain into granting Home Rule to Ireland, but the difference hardly mattered now.

Tyrone's voice was low and bitterly angry. "I don't give a tinker's curse who runs your wretched services, secret or open. It was my chance to get rid of Narraway. Whatever else Austwick is, he's a fool by comparison."

"You know him?" She seized the only part of what he was saying that seemed vulnerable, even momentarily.

There was a tiny sound behind her; just the brushing of a silk skirt against the doorjamb.

She turned around and saw Bridget Tyrone standing a yard from her. Suddenly she was horribly, physically afraid. She could scream her lungs out here and no one would hear her, no one would know . . . or care. It took all the strength she had to stand still, and command her voice to be level—or at least something like it.

It would be absurd to pretend Bridget had not overheard the conversation.

Charlotte was trapped, and she knew it. The fury in Bridget's face was unmistakable. Just as Bridget moved forward, Charlotte did also. She had never before struck another woman. However, when she turned as if to say something to Tyrone and saw him also moving toward her, she swung back, her arm wide. She put all her weight behind it, catching Bridget on the side of the head just as she lunged forward.

Bridget toppled sideways, catching at the small table with books on it and sending it crashing, herself on top of it. She screamed, as much in rage as pain.

Tyrone was distracted, diving to help her. Charlotte ran past, out of the door and across the hall. She flung the front door open, hurtling out into the street without once looking behind her. She kept on running, both hands holding her skirts up so she did not trip. She reached the main crossroads before she was so out of breath she could go no farther.

She dropped her skirt out of shaking hands and started to walk along the dimly lit street with as much dignity as she could muster, keeping an eye to the roadway for carriage lights in the hope of getting one to take her home as soon as it could. She would prefer to be far away from the area.

When she saw an unoccupied cab, she gave the driver the Molesworth Street address before climbing in and settling back to try to arrange her thoughts.

The story was still incomplete: bits and pieces that only partially fit together. Talulla was Sean and Kate's daughter. When had she known the truth of what had happened, or at least something like it? Perhaps more important, who had told her? Had it been with the intention that she should react violently? Did they know her well enough, and deliberately work on her loneliness, her sense of injustice and displacement, so that she could be provoked into murdering Cormac and blaming Narraway? To her it could be made to seem a just revenge for the destruction of her family. Sometimes rage is the easiest answer to unbearable pain. Charlotte had seen that too many times before, even been brushed by it herself long ago, at the time of Sarah's death. It is instinctive to feel that someone must be made to pay.

Who could have used Talulla that way? And why? Was Cormac the intended victim? Or was he a victim of incidental damage, as Fiachra McDaid had said—one of the fallen in a war for a greater purpose—and Narraway the real victim? It would be a poetic justice if he were hanged for a murder he did not commit. Since Talulla believed Sean innocent of killing Kate, and Narraway guilty, for her that would be elegant, perfect.

But who prompted her to it, gave her the information and stoked her passions, all but guided her hand? And why? Obviously not Cormac. Not John Tyrone, because he seemed to know nothing about it, and Charlotte believed that. Bridget? Perhaps. Certainly she was involved. Her reaction to Charlotte that evening had been too immediate and too violent to spring from ignorance. In fact, looking back at it now, perhaps she had known more than Tyrone himself. Was Tyrone, at least in part, another victim of incidental damage? Someone to use, because he was vulnerable, more in love with his wife than she was with him, and because he was a banker and had the means?

She could no longer evade the answer—Fiachra McDaid. Perhaps he had nothing to do with the past at all, or any of the old tragedy, except to use it. And for him winning was all, the means and the casualties nothing.

How did getting Narraway out of Special Branch help the cause of Ireland, though? He would only be replaced. But perhaps that was it. Replaced with a traitor, bought and paid for. She was still working on this train of thought when she arrived at Mrs. Hogan's door. She had promised Mrs. Hogan she would be gone by the next day. It would be very difficult to manage her own luggage and Narraway's as well, and there were other practical considerations to be taken in mind, such as the shortage of money to remain much longer away from home. She had still her tickets to purchase, for the boat and for the train.

When everything was weighed, she had little choice but to go to the police station in the morning and tell them, carefully, all that she believed. However, she had no proof she could show them. That she had arrived at Cormac's house just after Narraway but had heard no gunshot, just the dog barking—why should her story convince them?

The police would ask her why she had not given this account at the time. Should she admit that she had not thought they would believe her? Is that what an innocent person would do?

She went to sleep uneasily, waking often with the problem still unsolved.

N ARRAWAY SAT IN HIS cell in the police station less than a mile from where Cormac O'Neil had been murdered. He maintained a motionless pose, but his mind was racing. He must think—plan. Once they moved him to the main prison he would have no chance. He might be lucky to survive long enough to come to trial. And by that time memories would be clouded, people persuaded to forget, or to see things differently. But far worse even than that, whatever was being planned and for which he had been lured to Ireland, and Pitt to France, would have happened, and be irretrievable.

He sat there and remained unmoving for more than two hours. No one came to speak to him or give him food or drink. Slowly a desperate plan took shape in his mind. He would like to wait for nightfall, but he could not take the risk that they would take him into the main prison before that. Daylight would be much more dangerous, but perhaps that too was necessary. He might have only one chance.

He listened intently for the slightest sound beyond the cell door, any movement at all. He had decided exactly what to do when at last it came. It would have to, eventually.

When they put the heavy key in the lock and swung the door open Narraway was lying on the floor, sprawled in a position that looked as if he had broken his neck. His beautiful white shirt was torn and hanging from the bars on the window above him.

"Hey! Flaherty!" the guard called. "Come, quick! The stupid bastard's hung himself!" He came over to Narraway and bent to check his pulse. "Sweet Mother of God, I think he's dead!" he breathed. "Flaherty, where the devil are you?"

Before Flaherty could come, and there would be two of them to fight, Narraway snapped his body up and caught the guard under the chin so hard his head shot back. Narraway hit him again, sideways, so as to knock him unconscious, but very definitely not kill him. In fact he intended him to be senseless for no more than fifteen or twenty minutes. He needed him alive, and able to walk.

He moved the inert body to the exact spot where he himself had been lying, all but tore the man's jacket off him, and left him in his shirt. He took his keys and barely managed to get behind the door when Flaherty arrived.

Narraway held his breath in case Flaherty had the presence of mind to come in and lock the door or, even worse, stay out and lock it. But he was too horrified by the sight of the other guard on the floor to think so rationally. He covered the few paces to the fallen man, calling his name, and Narraway took his one chance. He slipped around the door, slammed it shut, and locked it. He heard Flaherty yelling almost immediately. Good. Someone would let him out within minutes. He needed them in hot pursuit.

He was very careful indeed going out of the police station, twice standing motionless on corners while people moved past him, following the shouting and the hurried footsteps.

Outside in the street, he ran. He wanted to draw attention to himself, to be remembered. Someone had to tell them which way he had gone.

He could afford no delay, no hesitation.

It was wet. The rain came down in a steady drizzle. The gutters were awash and very quickly he was soaked, his hair sticking to his brow, his bare neck cold without his shirt. People looked at him but no one stood in his way. Perhaps they thought he was drunk.

He had to go around Cormac's house, in case there were still police there. He could not be stopped now. He slowed to a walk and crossed the road away from it, then back again, without seeing anyone, and in at the gate of Talulla's house and up to the front door. If she did not answer he would have to break a window and force his way in. His whole plan rested on confronting her when the police caught up with him.

He knocked loudly.

There was no answer. What if she were not here, but with friends? Could she be, so soon after killing Cormac? Surely she would need to be alone? And she had to take care of the dog. Wouldn't she be waiting until the police left so she could take whatever she wanted, or needed to protect, of the records of her parents that Cormac had kept?

He banged again.

Again—silence.

Was she there already? He had seen no police outside. She might be upstairs here in her own house, lying down, emotionally exhausted from murder and the ultimate revenge.

He took off the jacket. Standing in the rain, bare-chested, he wrapped the jacket around his fist and with as little noise as possible broke a side window, unlocked it, and climbed inside. He put the jacket on again and walked softly across the floor to look for her.

He searched from top to bottom. There was no one there. He had not expected a maid. Talulla would have given her the day off so she could not witness anything to do with Cormac's murder, not hear any shots, any barking dog.

He let himself out of the back door and ran swiftly to Cormac's house. Time was getting short. The police could not be far behind him. Hurry! Hurry!

He wasted no time knocking on the door. She would almost certainly not answer. And he had no time to wait.

He took off the jacket again, shivering with cold now, and perhaps also with fear. He smashed another window and within seconds was inside. At once the dog started barking furiously.

He looked around him. He went into some kind of pantry. He must get as far as the kitchen before she found him. If she let the dog attack him he had to be ready. And why would she not? He had broken into the house. He was already accused of Cormac's murder. She would have every possible justification.

He opened the door quickly and found himself in the scullery, the kitchen beyond. He darted forward and grabbed at a small, hard-backed wooden chair just as Talulla opened the door from the farther side and the dog leapt forward, still barking hysterically.

She stopped, stunned to see him.

He lifted the chair, its thin, sharp legs pointed toward the dog.

"I don't want to hurt the animal," he said, having to raise his voice to be heard above it. "Call it off."

"So you can kill me too?" she shouted back at him.

"Don't be so damn stupid!" He heard the rage trembling in his own voice, abrasive, almost out of control. "You killed him yourself, to get your revenge at last."

She smiled, a hard, glittering expression, vibrant with hate. "Well, I have, haven't I? They'll hang you, Victor Narraway. And the ghost of my father will laugh. I'll be there to watch you—that I swear." She turned to the dog. "Quiet, girl," she ordered. "Don't attack him. I want him alive to suffer trial and disgrace. Ripping his throat out would be too quick, too easy." She looked back at him.

But the dog was distracted by something else now. It swung its head around and stared toward the front door, hackles raised, a low growl in its throat.

"Too easy?" Narraway heard his voice rising, the desperation in it palpable. She must hear it too.

She did, and her smile widened. "I want to see you hang, see your terror when they put the noose around your neck, see you struggle for breath, gasping, your tongue purple, filling your mouth and poking out. You won't charm the women then, will you? Do you soil yourself when you hang? Do you lose all control, all dignity?" She was screeching now, her face twisted with the pain of her own imagination.

"Actually the function of the noose and the drop of the trapdoor is to break your neck," he replied. "You are supposed to die instantly. Does that take the pleasure away for you?"

She stared at him, breathing heavily. The dog now was fully concentrated on the front door, the growl low in its throat, lips curled back off the teeth.

If she realized there was someone at the front, please God in heaven, the police, then she would stop, perhaps even claim he had attacked her. But this was the moment of her private triumph, when she could tell him exactly how she had brought about his ruin.

He made a sudden movement toward her.

The dog swung around, barking again.

He raised the chair, legs toward it, just in case it leapt.

"Frightened, Victor?" she said with relish.

"Why now?" he asked, trying to keep his voice level. He nearly succeeded, but she must have seen the sheen of sweat on his face. "It was McDaid, wasn't it? He told you something? What? Why does he want all this? He used to be my friend."

"You're pathetic!" she said, all but choking over her words. "He hates you as much as we all do!"

"What did he tell you?" he persisted.

"How you seduced my whore of a mother and then betrayed

her. You killed her, and let my father hang for it!" She was sobbing now.

"Then why kill poor Cormac?" he asked. "Was he expendable, simply to create a murder for which you could blame me? It had to be you who killed him, you're the only one the dog wouldn't bark at, because you feed her when Cormac's away. She's used to you in the house. She'd have raised the roof if it had been me."

"Very clever," she agreed. "But by the time you come to trial, no one else will know that. And no one will believe your sister, if that's who she is, because they'll all know she would lie for you."

"Did you kill Cormac just to get me?" he asked again.

"No! I killed him because he didn't raise a hand to save my father! He did nothing! Absolutely nothing!"

"You were only a child, not even eight years old," he pointed out.

"McDaid told me!" she sobbed.

"Ah yes, McDaid—the Irish hero who wants to turn all Europe upside down in a revolution to change the social order, sweep away the old, and bring in the new. And do you imagine that will bring Ireland freedom? To him you are expendable, Talulla, just as I am, or your parents, or anyone else."

It was at that point that she let go of the dog's collar and shrieked at it to attack, just as the police threw open the door to the hall and Narraway raised the chair as the dog leapt and sent him flying to land hard on his back, half winding him.

One of the policemen grabbed the animal by its collar, all but choking it. The other seized hold of Talulla.

Narraway climbed to his feet, coughing and gasping to get his breath.

"Thank you," he said hoarsely. "I hope you have been here rather longer than it would appear."

"Long enough," the elder of the two responded. "But there'll still be one or two charges for you to answer, like assaulting a policeman while in custody, and escaping custody. If I were you, I'd run like hell and never come back to Ireland, Mr. Narraway."

"Very good advice." Narraway stood to attention, gave the man a smart salute, then turned and ran, exactly as he had been told.

IN THE MORNING THERE was no alternative for Charlotte but to have a hasty breakfast, pay Mrs. Hogan the last night for which she owed her. Then, with Mrs. Hogan's assistance, she sent for a carriage to take her and all the baggage as far as the police station where Narraway was held.

It was a miserable ride. She had come up with no better solution than simply to tell the police that she had further information on the death of Cormac O'Neil, and hope that she could persuade someone with judgment and influence to listen to her.

As she drew closer and closer the idea seemed to grow even more hopeless.

The carriage was about a hundred yards away from the police station. She was dreading being put out on the footpath with more luggage than she could possibly carry, and a story she was already convinced no one would believe. Then abruptly the carriage pulled up short and the driver leaned down to speak to someone Charlotte could only partially see.

"We are not there yet!" she said desperately. "Please go farther. I cannot possibly carry these cases so far. In fact I can't carry them at all."

"Sorry, miss," the driver said sadly, as if he felt a real pity for her. "That was the police. Seems there's been an escape of a very dangerous prisoner in the night. They just discovered it, an' the whole street's blocked off."

"A prisoner?"

"Yes, miss. A terrible, dangerous man, they say. Murdered a man yesterday, near shot his head off, an' now he's gone like magic. Just disappeared. Went to see him this morning, and his cell is empty. They're not allowing any carriages through."

Charlotte stared at him as if she could barely understand his words, but her mind was racing. Escape. Murdered a man yesterday. It had to be Narraway, didn't it? He must have known even more certainly than she did just how much people hated him, how easy it would be for them to see all the evidence the way they wished to.

Who would believe him—an Englishman with his past—rather than Talulla Lawless, who was Sean O'Neil's daughter and, perhaps even more important, Kate's daughter? Who would want to believe she shot Cormac?

The driver was still staring at Charlotte, waiting for her decision.

"Thank you," she said, fumbling for words. She did not want to leave Narraway alone and hunted in Ireland, but there was no way in which she could help him. She had no idea which way he would go, north or south, inland, or even across the country to the west. She did not know if he had friends, old allies, anyone to turn to.

Then another thought came to her with a new coldness. When they arrested him, they would have taken his belongings, his money. He would be penniless. How would he survive, let alone travel? She must help him.

Please heaven he did not trust any of the people he knew in Dublin! Every one of them would betray him. They were tied to one another by blood and memory, old grief too deep to forget.

"Miss?" The driver interrupted her thoughts.

Charlotte had little money either. She was marked as Narraway's sister. She would be a liability to him. There was nothing she could do to help here. Her only hope was to go back to London and somehow find Pitt or, at the very least, Aunt Vespasia.

"Please take me to the dock," she said as steadily as she could. "I think it would be better if I caught the next steamer back to England. Whatever dock that is, if you please."

"Yes, miss." He climbed back over the box again and urged his horse forward and around. They made a wide turn in the street heading away from the police station.

The journey was not very long, but to Charlotte it seemed to take ages. They passed down the wide, handsome streets. Some of the roads would have taken seven or eight carriages abreast, but they seemed half deserted compared with the noisy, crushing jams of traffic in London. She was desperate to leave, and yet also torn with regrets. One day she wanted to come back, anonymous and free of burdens, simply to enjoy the city. Now she could only lean forward, peering out and counting the minutes until she reached the dock.

The whole business of alighting with the luggage and the crowds waiting to board the steamer was awkward and very close to desperate. She tried to move the cases without leaving anything where it could be taken, and at the same time keep hold of her reticule and pay for a ticket. In the jostling of people she was bumped and knocked. Twice she nearly lost her own case while trying to move Narraway's and find money ready to pay the fare.

"Can I help you?" a voice said close to her.

She was about to refuse when she felt his hand over hers and he took Narraway's case from her. She was furious and ready to cry with frustration. She lifted her foot with its nicely heeled boot and brought it down sharply on his instep.

He gasped with pain, but he did not let go of Narraway's case.

She lifted her foot to do it again, harder.

"Charlotte, let the damn thing go!" Narraway hissed between his teeth.

She let not only his case go but her own also. She was so angry she could have struck him with an open hand, and so relieved she felt the tears prickle in her eyes and slide down her cheeks.

"I suppose you've no money!" she said tartly, choking on the words.

"Not much," he agreed. "I borrowed enough from O'Casey to get as far as Holyhead. But since you have my luggage, we'll manage the rest. Keep moving. We need to buy tickets, and I would very much like to catch this steamer. I might not have the opportunity to wait for the next. I imagine the police will think of this. It's the obvious way to go, but I need to be back in London. I have a fear that something very nasty indeed is going to happen."

"Several very nasty things already have," she told him.

"I know. But we must prevent what we can."

"I know what happened with Mulhare's money. I'm pretty sure who was behind it all."

"Are you?" There was an eagerness in his voice that he could not hide, even now in this pushing, noisy crowd.

"I'll tell you when we are on board. Did you hear the dog?"

"What dog?"

"Cormac's dog."

"Of course I did. The poor beast hurled itself at the door almost as soon as I was in the house."

"Did you hear the shot?"

"No. Did you?" He was startled.

"No," she said with a smile.

"Ah!" He was level with her now, and they were at the ticket counter. "I see." He smiled also, but at the salesman. "Two for the Holyhead boat, please."

CHAPTER

10

Pitt was overwhelmed with the size and scope of his new responsibilities. There was so much more to consider than the relatively minor issues of whether the socialist plot in Europe was something that could be serious, or only another manifestation of the sporadic violence that had occurred in one place or another for the last several years. Even if some specific act were planned, very possibly it did not concern England.

The alliance with France required that he pass on any important information to the French authorities, but what did he know that was anything more than speculation? West had been killed before he could tell him whatever it was he knew. With hindsight now, it had presumably been Gower who was a traitor. But had there been more to it than that? Had West also known who else in Lisson Grove was—what? A socialist conspirator? To be bought for money, or power? Or was it not what they wished to gain so much as what they were afraid to lose? Was it blackmail over some real or perceived offense? Was it someone who had been made to appear guilty, as Narraway had, but this person had yielded to pressure in order to save himself?

Had Narraway been threatened, and defied them? Or had they known better than to try, and he had simply been professionally destroyed, without warning?

He sat in Narraway's office, which was now his own: a cold and extraordinarily isolating thought. Would he be ousted next? It was hard to imagine he posed the threat to them that Narraway had, whoever they were. He looked around the room. It was so familiar to him from the other side of the desk that even with his back to the wall he could see in his mind's eye the pictures Narraway used to have there. They were mostly pencil drawings of bare trees, the branches delicate and complex. There was one exception: an old stone tower by the sea, but again the foreground was in exquisite detail of light and shadow, the sea only a feeling of distance without end.

He would ask Austwick where they were, and put them back where they belonged. If Narraway ever returned, then Pitt would give them back to him. Narraway's belongings were part of the furniture of his mind, of his life. They would give Pitt a sense of his presence, and it was both sad and comforting at the same time.

Narraway would have known what to do about these varied and sometimes conflicting remnants of work that scattered the desk now. Pitt was familiar with some of them, but he had only a vague knowledge of others. They were cases Narraway had dealt with himself.

Austwick had left him notes, but how could he trust anything Austwick had said? He would be a fool to, without corroboration from someone else, and that would take time he could not afford now. And whom could he trust? There was nothing but to go on. He would have to compare one piece of information with another, canceling out the impossible and then weighing what was left.

As the morning wore on, and assistants of one sort or another came with new papers, more opinions, he became painfully aware of how isolated Narraway must have been. He was commander now; he was not permitted to reveal vulnerability or confusion. He was not expected to consult. But he badly needed to— and recognized no one he could trust with certainty.

He looked in the faces of his juniors and saw courtesy, respect for his new position. In a few he also saw envy. Once he recognized an anger that he, such a relative newcomer, should have been promoted before them. In none did he see the kind of respect he needed in order to command their personal loyalty beyond their commitment to the task. That could only exist when it had been earned.

He would have given most of what he possessed to have Narraway back. Knowing that one misjudgment could now cost him his life, Pitt desperately craved his colleague's steady, quick-thinking presence and his quiet support.

Where was Narraway now? Somewhere in Ireland, trying to clear his name of a crime he did not commit? Pitt realized with a chill that he was not certain that Narraway was innocent. Could he have lied, embezzled, betrayed his country, and broken the trust of all he knew? Pitt would never before have believed that Narraway would commit *any* crime, even out of desperation. But perhaps he would if his life were in jeopardy, or Charlotte's. That thought hurt Pitt in a way that he could not fight.

Why had she gone with him? To help fight against injustice, out of loyalty to a friend in desperate need? How like her! But Narraway was Pitt's friend, not really hers. And yet, remembering a dozen small things, he knew that Narraway was in love with her, and had been for some time.

He knew exactly when he had first realized it. He had seen Narraway turn to look at her. They had been standing in the kitchen in his own house in Keppel Street. It had been during a bad case, a difficult one. Narraway had come to see him late in the evening over something or other, a new turn in events. They had had tea. The kettle was steaming on the hob. Charlotte had been standing waiting for it to boil again. She had been wearing an old dress, not expecting anyone except Pitt. The lamplight had shone on her hair, bringing up the warm, deep color of it, and on the angle of her cheek. He could see her in his mind's eye picking up the mitt so as not to burn her hands on the kettle.

Narraway had said something, and she had looked at him and laughed. In an instant his face had given him away.

Did she know? It had taken her what seemed like ages to realize that Pitt was in love with her, years ago, in the beginning. But since then they had all changed. She had been awkward, the middle sister of three, the one her mother found so difficult to match with an acceptable husband. Now she knew she was loved. But Pitt knew that her righteous indignation over the injustice against Narraway may have spurred Charlotte to impulsive actions.

She would be furiously angry that Narraway's reputation had been damaged, and she would still feel a gratitude to Narraway for having taken Pitt into Special Branch when he so badly needed it. Life could have become very bleak indeed. And if she knew that Narraway loved her that could be an added sense of responsibility, even of debt. To think of it as a debt was ridiculous—she had not asked for his regard, but Pitt knew the fierce protectiveness she felt toward the vulnerable. It was instinctive, defensive, like an animal with cubs. She would act first and think afterward. He loved her for it. He would lose something of infinite value if she were different, more guarded, more sensible. But it was still a liability.

There were papers piled on the desk in front of him, reports waiting to be made sense of, but still his mind was on Charlotte.

Where was she? How could he find out without placing her in further danger? Who was he absolutely certain he could trust? A week ago, he would have sent Gower. Unwittingly he would have been giving them the perfect hostage.

Should he contact the Dublin police? How could he be sure that he could trust them either, in light of all the schemes and plots that seemed to be under way right in his own government branch?

Perhaps anonymity was her best defense, but his own helplessness was almost like a physical pain. He had all the forces of Special Branch at his fingertips, but no idea whom he could trust.

There was a knock on his door. The moment he answered it Austwick came in, looking grave and slightly smug. He had more papers in his hand.

Pitt was glad to be forced back into the present. "What have you?" he asked.

Austwick sat down without being asked. Pitt realized he would not have done that with Narraway.

"More reports from Manchester," Austwick replied. "It does begin to look as if Latimer is right about this factory in Hyde. They are making guns, despite their denials. And then there's the mess-up in Glasgow. We need to pay more attention to that, before it gets any bigger."

"Last report said it was just young people protesting," Pitt reminded him. "Narraway had it marked as better left alone."

Austwick pulled his face into a grimace of distaste. "Well I think Narraway's mind was hardly on the country's interests over the last while. Unfortunately we don't know how long his . . . inattention had been going on. Read it yourself and see what you think. I've been handling it since Narraway went, and I think he may have made a serious misjudgment. And we can't afford to ignore Scotland either."

Pitt swallowed his response. He did not trust Austwick, but he must not allow the man to see his doubt. All this felt like wasting time, of which he had far too little.

"What about the other reports from Europe on the socialists?" he asked. "Anything from Germany? And what about the Russian émigrés in Paris?"

"Nothing significant," Austwick replied. "And nothing at all from Gower." He looked at Pitt steadily, concern in his eyes.

Pitt kept his expression perfectly composed. "He won't risk communication unless he has something of value to report. It all has to go through the local post office."

Austwick shook his head. "I think it's of secondary importance, honestly. West may have been killed simply on principle when they discovered he was an informant. He may not have possessed the crucial information we assumed he did."

Austwick shifted his position a little and looked straight at Pitt. "There have been rumblings about great reform for years, you know. People strike postures and make speeches, but nothing serious happens, at least not here in Britain. I think our biggest danger was three or four years ago. There was a lot of unrest in the East End of London, which I know you are aware of, though much of it took place just before you joined the branch."

That was a blatant reminder of how new Pitt was to this job. He saw the flicker of resentment in Austwick's eyes as he said it. He wondered for a moment if the hostility he sensed was due to Austwick's personal ambition having been thwarted. Then he remembered Gower bending over West's body on the ground, and the blood. Either Austwick had nothing to do with it, or he was better at masking his emotions than Pitt had judged. He must be careful.

"Perhaps we'll escape it," he offered.

Austwick shifted in his chair again. "These are the reports in from Liverpool, and you'll see some of the references to Ireland. Nothing dangerous as yet, but we need to make note of some of these names, and watch them." He pushed across more papers, and Pitt bent to read them.

The afternoon followed the same pattern: more reports both written and verbal. A case of violence in a town in Yorkshire looked as if it was political and turned out not to be. A government minister was robbed in Piccadilly; and investigating it took up the rest of the day. The minister had been carrying sensitive papers. Fortunately it was not Pitt's decision as to how seriously he should be reprimanded for carelessness. It was, however, up to him to decide with what crime the thief should be charged.

He weighed it with some consideration. He questioned the man, trying to judge whether he had known his victim was in the government, and if so that his attaché case might contain government papers. He was uncertain, even after several hours, but Narraway would not have asked advice, and neither would he.

Pitt decided that the disadvantages of letting the public know how easy it was to rob an inattentive minister outweighed the possible error of letting a man be charged with a lesser crime than the one he had intended to commit.

He went home in the evening tired and with little sense of achievement.

It changed the moment he opened the front door and Daniel came racing down the hall to greet him.

"Papa! Papa, I made a boat! Come and look." He grasped Pitt's hand and tugged at him.

Pitt smiled and followed him willingly down to the kitchen, where the rich smell of dinner cooking filled the air. Something was bubbling in a big pan on the stove and the table was littered with pieces of newspapers and a bowl of white paste. Minnie Maude was standing with a pair of scissors in her hands. As usual, her hair was all over the place, pinned up over and over again as she had lost patience with it. In pride of place in the center of the mess was a rather large papier-mâché boat, with two sticks for masts and several different lengths of tapers for bowsprit, yardarms, and a boom.

Minnie Maude looked abashed to see him, clearly earlier than she had expected.

"See!" Daniel said triumphantly, pointing to the ship. "Minnie Maude showed me how to do it." He gave a little shrug. "And Jemima helped a bit . . . well . . . a lot."

Pitt felt a sudden and overwhelming warmth rush up inside him. He looked at Daniel's face shining with pride, and then at the boat.

"It's magnificent," he said, emotion all but choking his voice. "I've never seen anything better." He turned to Minnie Maude, who was standing wide-eyed. She was clearly waiting to be criticized for playing when she should have been working, and having dinner on the table for him.

"Thank you," he said to her sincerely. "Please don't move it until it is safe to do so without risk of damage."

"What . . . what about dinner, sir?" she asked, beginning to breathe again.

"We'll clear the newspapers and the paste, and eat around it," he answered. "Where's Jemima?"

"She's reading," Daniel answered instantly. "She took my *Boys' Own!* Why doesn't she read a girls' book?"

" 'Cos they're boring," Jemima answered from the doorway. She had slipped in without anyone hearing her come along the corridor. She looked past Pitt at the table, and the ship at the center. "You've got the masts on! That's beautiful." She gave Pitt a radiant smile. "Hello, Papa. Look what we made."

"I see it," he replied, putting his arm around her shoulder. "It's magnificent."

"How is Mama?" she asked, an edge of worry in her voice.

"Well," he answered, lying smoothly and holding her a little closer. "She's helping a friend in bad trouble, but she'll be home soon. Now let's help clear the table and have dinner."

Afterward he sat alone in the parlor as silence settled over the house. Daniel and Jemima had gone up to bed. Minnie Maude had finished in the kitchen and went up as well. He heard every creak of her tread on the stairs. Far from being comforting, the absence of all voices or movement made the heaviness swirl back in again like a fog. The islands of light from the lamps on the wall made the shadows seem deeper than they were. He knew every surface in the room. He also knew they were all immaculately clean, as if Charlotte had been there to supervise this new girl whose only fault was that she was not Gracie. She was good; it was only the familiarity she lacked. The papier-mâché ship made him smile. It wasn't a trivial thing; it was very important indeed. Minnie Maude Mudway was a success.

He sat in the armchair, thinking of Jemima's pride and Daniel's happiness for as long as he could. Finally he turned his mind to the following day and to the fact that he must go and tell Croxdale the truth about Gower, and the betrayal that might run throughout the service.

THE FOLLOWING DAY AT Lisson Grove was filled with the same necessary trivia as the one before. There was news from Paris that was only vaguely disturbing: a definite increase in activity among the people Special Branch was watching, though if it had any meaning he was unable to determine what it was. It was much the same sort of thing he might have done had Narraway been there, and he in his own job. The difference was the weight of responsibility, the decisions that he could no longer refer upward. Now they all came to him. Other men who had previously been his equals were now obliged to report to him, for Pitt needed to know of anything at all that might threaten the safety of Her Majesty's realm, and her government, the peace and prosperity of Britain.

Late that morning he finally obtained an interview with Sir Gerald Croxdale. He felt the urgent need to tell Croxdale of Gower's death, and how it had happened. No report had come in yet, as far as he knew, but it could not be long now.

Pitt arrived at Whitehall late in the afternoon. The sun was still warm and the air was soft as he walked across from the park and along the street to the appropriate entrance. Several carriages passed him, the women in them wearing wide hats to protect their faces from the light, their muslin sleeves drifting in the breeze. Horse brasses winked with bright reflections, and some doors carried family crests painted on them.

He was admitted without question. Apparently the footman knew who he was. He was taken straight to Croxdale's rooms and ushered into his presence after only a matter of moments.

"How are you, Pitt?" Croxdale said warmly, rising from his seat to shake Pitt's hand. "Sit down. How is it at Lisson Grove?" His voice was pleasant, almost casual, but he was watching Pitt intently. There was a gravity in him as if he already knew that Pitt had ugly news to tell him.

It was the opening Pitt needed without having to create it himself.

"I had hoped to tell you more, sir," he began. "But the whole episode of seeing West murdered and following Frobisher to France was far more serious than I thought at first."

Croxdale frowned, sitting a little more upright in his chair. "In what way? Have you learned what he was going to tell you?"

"No, sir, I haven't. At least, I am not certain. But I have a strong idea, and everything I have discovered since returning supports it, but does not provide a conclusion."

"Stop beating around the bush, man!" Croxdale said impatiently. "What is it?"

Pitt took a deep breath. "We have at least one traitor at Lisson Grove . . ."

Croxdale froze, his eyes hard. His right hand on top of the desk suddenly became rigid as if he were deliberately forcing himself not to clench it.

"I presume you mean other than Victor Narraway?" he said quietly.

Pitt made another decision. "I don't and never have believed that

Narraway was a traitor, sir. Whether he is guilty of a misjudgment, or
a carelessness, I don't yet know. But regrettably we all misjudge at
times."

"Explain yourself!" Croxdale said between his teeth. "If not Narraway, and I reserve judgment on that, then who?"

"Gower, sir."

"Gower?" Croxdale's eyes opened wide. "Did you say *Gower?*"

"Yes, sir." Pitt could feel his own temper rising. How could Croxdale accept so easily that Narraway was a traitor, yet be so incredulous
that Gower could be? What had Austwick told him? How deep and
how clever was this web of treason? Was Pitt rushing in where a wiser,
more experienced man would have been careful, laying his ground
first? But there was no time to do that. Narraway was considered a
fugitive by his former colleagues in the Special Branch and heaven
only knew if Charlotte was safe, or where she was and in what circumstances. Pitt could not afford to seek their enemies cautiously.

Croxdale was frowning at him. Should he tell him the whole
story, or simply the murder of West? Any of it made Pitt look like a
fool! But he had been a fool. He had trusted Gower, even liked him.
The memory of it was still painful.

"Something happened in France that made me realize it only appeared that Gower and I arrived together as Wrexham killed West,"
he said. "Actually Gower had been there moments before and killed
him himself."

"For God's sake, man! That's absurd," Croxdale exploded, almost
rising from his seat. "You can't expect me to believe that! How did
you fail . . ." He sat back again, composing himself with an effort. "I'm
sorry. This comes as an appalling shock to me. I . . . I know his family.
Are you certain? It all seems very . . . flimsy."

"Yes, sir, I'm afraid I am certain." Pitt felt a stab of pity for him. "I
made an excuse to leave him in France and return by myself—"

"You left him?" Again Croxdale was stunned.

"I couldn't arrest him," Pitt pointed out. "I had no weapon, and
he was a young and very powerful man. The last thing I wanted to do
was inform the local police of who we were, and that we were there
without their knowledge or permission, watching French citizens . . ."

"Yes, of course. I see. I see. Go on." Croxdale was flushed and obviously badly shaken. Pitt could have sympathized at another time.

"I told him to remain watching Wrexham and Frobisher . . ."

"Who's Frobisher?" Croxdale demanded.

Pitt told him what they knew of Frobisher, and the other men they had seen coming and going from his house.

Croxdale nodded. "So there was some truth to this business of socialists meeting, and possibly planning something?"

"Possibly. Nothing conclusive yet."

"And you left Gower there?"

"I thought so. But when I reached Southampton I took the train to London. On that train I was attacked, twice, and very nearly lost my life."

"Good God! By whom?" Croxdale was horrified.

"Gower, sir. The first time he was interrupted, and the man who did so paid for his courage with his life. Then Gower renewed his attack on me, but this time I was ready for him, and it was he who lost."

Croxdale wiped his hand across his brow. "What happened to Gower?"

"He went over onto the track," Pitt replied, his stomach knotting at that memory and the sweat breaking out on his skin again. He decided not to mention his own arrest, because then he would have to explain how Vespasia had rescued him, and he preferred to keep her name out of it altogether.

"He was . . . killed?" Croxdale said.

"At that speed, sir, there can be no doubt."

Croxdale leaned back. "How absolutely fearful." He let out his breath slowly. "You are right, of course. We had a traitor at Lisson Grove. I am profoundly grateful that it was he and not you who went over onto the tracks. Why on earth did you not tell me this as soon as you returned?"

"Because I hoped to learn who was the man behind Gower before I told you," Pitt answered.

Croxdale's face went white. "Behind . . . Gower?" he said awkwardly.

"I don't yet know," Pitt admitted. "Not for certain. I never found

evidence one way or the other whether Frobisher was the power behind a new socialist uprising, perhaps violent, or only a dilettante
playing on the edge of the real plot."

"We don't assume it is trivial," Croxdale said quickly. "If Gower . . .
I still find it hard to credit . . . but if Gower murdered two people, and
attempted to murder you also, then it is very real indeed." He bit his
lip. "I assume from what you say that you did not tell Austwick this?"

"No. I believe someone made it appear that Narraway was guilty
of embezzlement in order to get him out of the way, discredit him so
deeply that anything he said against them would be disbelieved."

"Who? Someone to do with Frobisher? Or Gower again?"

"Neither Frobisher nor Gower had the ability," Pitt pointed out.
"That has to be someone in Lisson Grove, someone with a consider-
able amount of power in order to have access to the details of
Narraway's banking arrangements."

Croxdale was staring at him, his face drawn, cheeks flushed. "I
see. Yes, of course you are right. Then this socialist plot seems very
deep. Perhaps this Frobisher is as dangerous as you first thought, and
poor West was killed to prevent you from learning the full extent of
it. No doubt Gower kept you along with him when he went to France
so you could be duped into believing Frobisher harmless, and sending
that misinformation back to London." He smiled bleakly, just for an
instant. "Thank God you were clever enough to see through it, and
agile enough to survive his attack on you. You are the right man for
this job, Pitt. Whatever else he may be guilty of, Narraway did well
when he brought you into the service."

Pitt felt he should thank him for the compliment, and for his
trust, but he wanted to argue and say how little he was really suited to
it. He ended by inclining his head, thanking him briefly, and moving
on to the more urgent problem of the present.

"We need to know very urgently, sir, what information Gower
himself may have passed back to London, and—more specifically—
to whom. I don't know who I can trust."

"No," Croxdale said thoughtfully, now leaning back again in his
chair. "No, neither do I. We need to look at this a great deal more
closely, Pitt. Austwick has reported to me at least three times since

Narraway left. I have the papers here. We need to go through all this information and you must tell me what you know to be accurate, or inaccurate, and what we still need to test. Some picture should emerge. I'm sorry, but this may very well require all night. I'll have someone fetch us supper." He shook his head. "God, what a miserable business."

There was no question of argument.

Croxdale had other notes not only of what Austwick had reported to him but, going back farther, of what Narraway also had written. It was curious looking at the different papers. Austwick's writing was neat, his notes carefully thought out and finely presented. Narraway's Pitt saw with a jolt of familiarity, and a renewed sense of his friend's absence. Narraway's penmanship was smaller, more flowing than his successor's. There was no hesitation. He had written his note with forethought, and there was no attempt to conceal the fact that he was giving Croxdale only the minimum. Was that an agreement between them, and Croxdale could read between the lines? Or had Narraway simply not bothered to conceal the fact that he was telling only part of what he knew?

Pitt studied Croxdale's face, and did not know the answer.

They read them carefully. A servant brought in a tray of light toast and pâté, then cheese and finally a heavy fruitcake—along with brandy, which Pitt declined.

It was now totally dark outside. The wind was rising a little, spattering rain against the windows.

Croxdale put down the last paper. "Narraway obviously thought there was something to this business in St. Malo, but not major. Austwick seems to disagree, and thinks that it is nothing but noise and posturing. Unlike Narraway, he believes it will not affect us here in Britain. What do you think, Pitt?"

It was the question Pitt had dreaded, but it was inevitable that it would come. There was no room for excuses, no matter how easy to justify. He would be judged on the accuracy of his answer. He had lain awake weighing everything he knew, hoping Croxdale's information would tip the balance one way or the other.

Again he answered with barely a hesitation. "I think that

Narraway was on the brink of finding out something crucial, and he was gotten rid of before he could do so."

Croxdale waited a long time before he answered.

"Do you realize that if that is true, then you are also saying that Austwick is either incompetent to a most serious degree, or else—far worse than that—he is complicit in what is going on?"

"Yes, sir, I'm afraid that has to be the case," Pitt agreed. "But Gower was reporting to someone, so we know that at least one person within the service is a traitor."

"I've known Charles Austwick for years," Croxdale said softly. "But perhaps we don't know anyone as well as we imagine." He sighed. "I've sent for Stoker. Apparently he's newly back from Ireland. He may be able to throw some light on things. Do you trust him?"

"Yes. But I trusted Gower as well," Pitt said ruefully. "Do you?"

Croxdale gave him a bleak smile. "Touché. Let's at least see what he has to say. And the answer is no, I trust no one. I am painfully aware that we cannot afford to. Not after Narraway, and not it would seem Gower also. Are you sure you won't have a brandy?"

"I'm quite sure, thank you, sir."

There was a knock on the door and, at Croxdale's word, Stoker came in. He looked tired. There were shadows around his eyes, and his face was pinched with fatigue. However, he stood to attention until Croxdale gave him permission to sit. Stoker acknowledged Pitt, but only so much as courtesy demanded.

"When did you get back from Ireland?" Croxdale asked him.

"About two hours ago, sir," Stoker replied. "Weather's a bit poor."

"Mr. Pitt doesn't believe the charge of embezzlement against Narraway," Croxdale went on. "He thinks it is possibly false, manufactured to get rid of him because he was on the verge of gaining information about a serious socialist plot of violence that would affect Britain." He was completely ignoring Pitt, his eyes fixed on Stoker so intently they might have been alone in the room.

"Sir?" Stoker said with amazement, but he did not look at Pitt either.

"You worked with Narraway," Croxdale continued. "Does that seem likely to you? What is the news from Ireland now?"

Stoker's jaw tightened as if he were laboring under some profound emotion. His face was pale as he leaned forward a little into the light. He seemed leached of color by exhaustion. "I'm sorry, sir, but I can't see any reason to question the evidence. It's amazing what lack of money can do, and how it can change your view of things."

Pitt felt as if he had been struck. The sting of Stoker's words was hard enough to have been physical. He would rather it had been.

Stoker continued, a grim weariness in his voice. "Sir, there is more. I deeply regret that I must bear this grave news, gentlemen, but yesterday O'Neil was murdered, and the police immediately arrested Narraway. He was on the scene and practically caught red-handed. He had the grace not to deny it. He is now in prison in Dublin awaiting trial."

Pitt felt as if he had been sandbagged. He struggled to keep any sense of proportion, even of reality. He stared at Stoker, then turned to Croxdale. Their faces wavered and the room seem to swim in and out of his focus.

"My word," Croxdale said slowly. "This comes as a terrible shock." He turned to Pitt. "You could have had no idea of this side of Narraway, and I admit, neither had I. I feel remiss to have had such a man in charge of our most sensitive service during my period of office. His extraordinary skill completely masked this darker, and clearly very violent side of his nature."

Pitt refused to believe it, partly because he could not bear it. Charlotte was in Ireland with Narraway. What had happened to her? How could he find out without admitting that he knew this? He would not draw Vespasia into it. She was one element he had in his favor, perhaps the only one.

Stoker gazed downward, his voice quieter, as though he too were stunned. "I am afraid it's true, sir. We were all deceived as to his character. The case against him is as plain as day. It seems Narraway quarreled with O'Neil rather publicly, making no secret of the fact that he believed O'Neil to be responsible for creating the evidence that made it seem he was guilty of embezzling the money intended for Mulhare. And to be honest, that could well be true."

"Could it? Croxdale asked, a slight lift of hope in his voice."

"From what I can make out, yes, sir, it could," Stoker replied. "Only problem is how he got the information he'd need to get it into Mr. Narraway's account. I've been trying to find the answer to that, and I think I'll get there."

"Someone at Lisson Grove?" Croxdale said.

"No, sir," Stoker answered without a flicker in his face. "Not as far as I can see."

Croxdale's eyes narrowed. "Then who? Who else would be able to do that?"

Stoker did not hesitate. "Looks like it could be someone at Mr. Narraway's bank, sir. I daresay one time and another, he's made some enemies. Or it could just be someone willing to be paid. Nice to think that wouldn't happen, but maybe a bit innocent. There'd be those with enough money to buy most things."

"I suppose so," Croxdale replied. "Perhaps Narraway found out already? That would explain a great deal. What other news have you from Ireland?"

Stoker told him about Narraway's connections, whom he had spoken to and their reactions, the confrontation with O'Neil at the soirée. Never once did he mention Charlotte. At least some of what he described was so unlike Narraway, panicky and protective, that it seemed as if his whole character had fallen apart.

Pitt listened with disbelief and mounting anger at what he felt had to be a betrayal.

"Thank you, Stoker," Croxdale said sadly. "A tragic end to what was a fine career. Give your report on Paris to Mr. Pitt."

"Yes, sir."

Stoker left, and Croxdale turned to Pitt. "I think that makes the picture clearer. Gower was the traitor, which I admit I still find hard to credit, but what you say makes it impossible to deny. We may have the disaster contained, but we can't take it for granted. Make as full an investigation as you can, Pitt, and report to me. Keep an eye to what's going on in Europe and if there is anything we should inform the French of, then we'll do so. In the meantime there's plenty of other political trouble to keep us busy, but I'm sure you know that." He rose to his feet, extending his hand. "Take care of yourself, Pitt.

You have a difficult and dangerous job, and your country needs you more than it will ever appreciate."

Pitt shook his hand and thanked him, going out into the night without any awareness of the sudden chill. The coldness was already inside him. What Stoker had said of Narraway's bank betraying him could be true, although he did not believe it. The rest seemed a curious set of exaggerations and lies. Pitt could not accept that Narraway had fallen apart so completely, either to steal anything in the first place, or to so lose the fundamental values of his past as to behave in the way Stoker had described. Pitt could not possibly believe that Narraway was a cold-blooded murderer. And surely Stoker must at the very least have noticed Charlotte?

Or was Stoker the traitor at Lisson Grove?

He was floundering, like a man in quicksand. None of his judgments was sound. He had trusted Stoker, he had even liked Gower. Narraway he would have sworn his own life on . . . He admitted, he still would. Something had to be amiss. The Narraway that Pitt had known would never kill for any reason other than self-defense.

Croxdale's carriage was waiting to take him home. He half saw the shadow of a man on the pavement who moved toward him, but he ignored it. The coachman opened the door for him and he climbed in, sitting miserable and shivering all the way back to Keppel Street. He was glad it was late. He did not want to make the intense effort it would cost to hide his disillusion from Daniel and Jemima. If he was fortunate, even Minnie Maude would be asleep.

IN THE MORNING HE was halfway to Lisson Grove when he changed his mind and went instead to see Vespasia. It was too early for any kind of social call, but if he had to wait until she rose, then he was willing to. His need to speak with her was so urgent he was prepared to break all the rules of etiquette, even of consideration, trusting that she would see his purpose beyond his discourtesy.

In fact she was already up and taking breakfast. He accepted tea, but he had no need to eat.

"Is your new maid feeding you properly?" Vespasia asked with a touch of concern.

"Yes," he answered, his own surprise coming through his voice. "Actually she's perfectly competent, and seems very pleasant. It wasn't . . ." He saw her wry smile and stopped.

"It wasn't to seek recommendation for a new maid that you came at this hour of the morning," she finished for him. "What is it, Thomas? You look very troubled indeed. I assume something new has occurred?"

He told her everything that had happened since they last spoke, including his dismay and disappointment over Stoker's sudden change of loyalties, and the brutal details with which he had described Narraway's falling apart.

"I seem to be completely incompetent at judging anyone's character," he said miserably. He would like to have been able to say it with some dry wit, but he felt so inadequate that he was afraid he sounded self-pitying.

She listened without interrupting. She poured him more tea, then grimaced that the pot was cold.

"It doesn't matter," he said quickly. "I don't need more."

"Let us sum up the situation," she said gravely. "It would seem inarguable that you were wrong about Gower, as was everyone else at Lisson Grove, including Victor Narraway. It does not make you unusually fallible, my dear. And considering that he was your fellow in the service, you had a right to assume his loyalty. At that point it was not your job to make such decisions. Now it is."

"I was wrong about Stoker," he pointed out.

"Possibly, but let us not leap to conclusions. You know only that what he reported to Gerald Croxdale seemed to blame Victor, and also was untrue in other respects. He made no mention of Charlotte, as you observed, and yet he must have seen her. Surely his omission is one you are grateful for?"

"Yes . . . yes, of course. Although I would give a great deal to know she is safe." That was an understatement perhaps only Vespasia could measure.

"Did you say anything to Croxdale about your suspicions of Austwick?" she asked.

"No." He explained how reluctant he had been to give any unnecessary trust. He had guarded everything, fearing that because Croxdale had known Austwick a long time perhaps he would be more inclined to trust him than to trust Pitt.

"Very wise," she agreed. "Is Croxdale of the opinion that there is something very serious being planned in France?"

"I saw nothing except a couple of faces," he answered. "And when I look back, it was Gower who told me they were Meister and Linsky. There was talk, but no more than usual. There was a rumor that Jean Jaures was coming from Paris, but he didn't."

Vespasia frowned. "Jacob Meister and Pieter Linsky? Are you sure?"

"Yes, that's what Gower said. I know the names, of course. But only for one day, maybe thirty-six hours, then they left again. They certainly didn't return to Frobisher's."

Vespasia looked puzzled. "And who said Jean Jaures was coming?"

"One of the innkeepers, I think. The men in the café were talking about it."

"You think? A name like Jaures is mentioned and you don't remember by whom?" she said incredulously.

Again he was struck by his own foolishness. How easily he was duped. He had not heard it himself, Gower had told him. He admitted it to Vespasia.

"Did he mention Rosa Luxemburg?" she asked with a slight frown.

"Yes, but not that she was coming to St. Malo."

"But he mentioned her name?"

"Yes. Why?"

"Jean Jaures is a passionate socialist, but a gentle man," she explained. "He was campaigner for reform. He sought office, and on occasion gained it, but he fights for change, not for overthrow. As far as I know, he is content to keep his efforts within France. Rosa Luxemburg is different. She is Polish, now naturalized German, and of a much more international cast of mind. I have Russian émigré friends who fear that one day she will cause real violence. In some places I'm afraid real violence is almost bound to happen. The oppression in Russia will end in tragedy."

"Stretching as far as Britain?" he said dubiously.

"No, only insofar as the world is sometimes a far smaller place than we think. There will be refugees, however. Indeed, London is already full of them."

"What did Gower want?" he asked. "Why did he kill West? Was West going to tell me Gower was a traitor?"

"Perhaps. But I admit, none of it makes sufficient sense to me so far, unless there is something a great deal larger than a few changes in the laws for French workers, or a rising unease in Germany and Russia. None of this is new, and none of it worries Special Branch unduly."

"I wish Narraway were here," he said with intense feeling. "I don't know enough for this job. He should have left it with Austwick—unless he knows Austwick is a traitor too?"

"I imagine that is possible." She was still lost in thought. "And if Victor is innocent, which I do not doubt, then there was a very clever and carefully thought-out plan to get both you and him out of London. Why can we not deduce what it is, and why?"

PITT WENT TO HIS office in Lisson Grove, aware as he walked along the corridors of the eyes of the other men on him, watching, waiting: Austwick particularly.

"Good morning," Austwick said, apparently forgetting the *sir* he would have added for Narraway.

"Good morning, Austwick," Pitt replied a little tartly, not looking at him but going on until he reached Narraway's office door. He realized he still thought of it as Narraway's, just as he still thought of the position as his.

He opened the door and went inside. There was nothing of Pitt's here yet— no pictures, no books—but Narraway's things were returned, as if he were still expecting the man himself to come back. When that happened he would not have to pretend to be pleased, and it would not be entirely for unselfish reasons either. He cared for Narraway, and he had at least some idea of how much the job meant to him: It was his vocation, his life. Pitt would be immensely relieved to give it back to him. It was not within Pitt's skill or his nature to perform this job. He regretted that it was now his duty.

He dealt with the most immediate issues of the day first, passing on all he could to juniors. When that was done, he told them not to interrupt him. Then he went through all Narraway's records of every crime Gower had been involved with over the past year and a half. He read all the documents, getting a larger picture concerning European revolutionary attempts to improve the lot of workingmen. He also read Stoker's latest report from Paris.

As he did so, the violence proposed settled over him like a darkness, senseless and destructive. But the anger at injustice he could not help sharing. It grieved him that it had oppressed people and denied them a reasonable life for so long that the change, when it came—and it must—would be fueled by so much hatred.

The more he read, the greater a tragedy seemed to him that the high idealism of the revolution of '48 had been crushed with so little legacy of change left behind.

Gower's own reports were spare, as if he had edited out any emotive language. At first Pitt thought that was just a very clear style of writing. Then he began to wonder if it was more: a guarding of Gower's own feelings, in case he gave something away unintentionally, or Narraway himself picked up a connection, an omission, even a false note.

Then he took out Narraway's own papers. He had read most of them before, because it was part of his duty in taking over the position. Many of the cases he was familiar with anyway, from general knowledge within the branch. He selected three specifically to do with Europe and socialist unrest, those associated with Britain, memberships of socialist political groups such as the Fabian Society. He compared them with the cases in which Gower had worked, and looked for any notes that Narraway might have made.

What were the facts he knew, personally? That Gower had killed West and made it appear it was Wrexham who had done so. All doubt left him that it had been extremely quick thinking on Gower's part. Had it been his intention all the time—with Wrexham's collaboration? Pitt recalled the chase across London and then on to Southampton. He was bitterly conscious that it had been too easy. On the rare occasions when it seemed Wrexham had eluded them, it was Gower and not Pitt who had found the trail again. The conclusion was inevitable—Gower and Wrexham were working together. To what end? Again, looked at from the result, it could only have been to keep Pitt in St. Malo—or more specifically, to keep him from being in London, and aware of what was happening to Narraway.

But to what greater purpose? Was it to do with socialist uprisings? Or was that also a blind, a piece of deception?

Who was Wrexham? He was mentioned briefly, twice, in Gower's reports. He was a young man of respectable background who had been to university and dropped out of a modern history course to travel in Europe. Gower suggested he had been to Germany and Russia, but seemed uncertain. It was all very vague, and with little substantiation. Certainly there was nothing to cause Narraway to have him watched or inquired into any further. Presumably it was just sufficient information to allow Gower to say afterward that he was a legitimate suspect.

Had he intended to turn on him in France?

The more he studied what was there, the more Pitt was certain that there had to be a far deeper plan behind the random acts he had connected in bits and pieces. The picture was too sketchy, the rewards too slight to make sense of murder. It was all random, and too small.

The most urgent question was whether Narraway had been very carefully made to look guilty of theft in order to gain some kind of revenge for old defeats and failures, or whether the real intent was to get him dismissed from Lisson Grove and out of England. The more Pitt looked at it, the more he believed it was the latter.

If Narraway had been here, what would he have made of the information? Surely he would have seen the pattern. Why could Pitt not see it? What was he missing?

He was still comparing one event with another and searching for links when there was a sharp knock on the door. He had asked not to be interrupted. This had better be something of importance, or he would tear a strip off the man, whoever he was.

"Come in," he said sharply.

The door opened and Stoker came in, closing it behind him.

Pitt stared at him coldly.

Stoker ignored his expression. "I tried to speak to you last night," he said quietly. "I saw Mrs. Pitt in Dublin. She was well and in good spirits. She's a lady of great courage. Mr. Narraway is fortunate to have her fighting his cause, although I daresay it's not for his sake she's doing it."

Pitt stared at him. He looked subtly quite different from the way he had when standing in front of Croxdale the previous evening. Was that a difference in respect? In loyalty? Personal feeling? Or because one was the truth and the other lies?

"Did you see Mr. Narraway?" Pitt asked him.

"Yes, but not to speak to. It was the day O'Neil was shot," Stoker answered.

"By whom?"

"I don't know. I think probably Talulla Lawless, but whether anyone will ever prove that, I don't know. Mr. Narraway's in trouble, Mr. Pitt. He has powerful enemies—"

"I know that," Pitt interrupted. "Apparently dating back twenty years."

"Not that," Stoker said impatiently. "Now, here in Lisson Grove. Someone wanted him discredited and out of England, and wanted you in France, gone in the other direction, where you wouldn't know what was going on here and couldn't help."

"Tell me all you know of what happened in Ireland," Pitt demanded. "And for heaven's sake sit down!" It was not that he wanted the information in detail so much as he needed the chance to weigh everything Stoker said, and make some judgment as to the truth of it, and exactly where Stoker's loyalties lay.

Stoker obeyed without comment. Possibly he knew the reason Pitt asked, but if so there was nothing in his face to betray it. "I was only there two days," he began.

"Who sent you?" Pitt interrupted.

"No one. I made it look like it was Mr. Narraway, before he went."

"Why?"

"Because I don't believe he's guilty any more than you do," Stoker said bitterly. "He's a hard man, clever, cold at times in his own way, but he'd never betray his country. They got rid of him because they knew he'd see what was going on here, and stop it. They thought you might too, in loyalty to Mr. Narraway, even if you didn't spot what they're doing. No offense, sir, but you don't know enough yet to see what it is."

Pitt winced, but he had no argument. It was painfully true.

"Mr. Narraway seemed to be trying to find out who set him up to look like he took the money meant for Mulhare, probably because that would lead back to whoever it is here in London," Stoker went on. "I don't know whether he found out or not, because they got him by killing O'Neil. They set that up perfectly. Fixed a quarrel between them in front of a couple o' score of people, then somehow got him to go alone to O'Neil's house, and had O'Neil shot just before he got there.

"By all accounts, Mrs. Pitt was right on his heels, but he swore to the police that she wasn't there at the time, so they didn't bother her. She went back to Dublin where she was staying, and that's the last I know of it. Mr. Narraway was arrested and no doubt if we don't do anything, they'll try him and hang him. But we'll have a week or two before that." He stopped, meeting Pitt with steady, demanding eyes.

The weight of leadership settled on Pitt like a leaden coat. There was no one beyond himself to turn to, no one else's opinion to listen to and use as a balance. Whoever had designed this so that it was he, and not Narraway, that they had to face, was supremely clever.

He must trust Stoker. The advantage outweighed the risk.

"Then we have ten days in which to rescue Narraway," he replied. "Perhaps whoever it is will be as aware of that as we are. It is safe to assume that by that time they will have achieved whatever it is they plan, and for which they needed him gone."

Stoker sat up a little straighter. "Yes, sir."

"And we have no idea who it is planning it," Pitt continued. "Except that they have great power and authority within the branch, so we dare not trust anyone. Even Sir Gerald himself may choose to trust this person rather than trust you or me."

Stoker allowed himself a slight smile. "You're right, sir. And that could be the end of everything, probably of you an' me, and certainly of Mr. Narraway."

"Then we are alone in working out what it is." Pitt had already made up his mind that if he were to trust Stoker at all, then it might as well be entirely. This was not the time to let Stoker believe he was only half relied on.

Pitt pulled out the papers he had been studying and placed them sideways on the desk so they could both see them.

"This is the pattern I found so far." He pointed to communications, the gun smuggling, the movements of known radicals both in Britain and on the continent of Europe.

"Not much of a pattern," Stoker said grimly. "It looks pretty much like always to me." He pointed. "There's Rosa Luxemburg in Germany and Poland in that part, but she's been getting noisier for years. There's Jean Jaures in France, but he's harmless enough. Your basic socialist reformer. Bit hard now and then, but what he's saying is fair enough, if you look at it. Nothing to do with us, though. He's as French as frog's legs."

"And here?" Pitt pointed to some Fabian Society activity in London and Birmingham.

"They'll get changes through Parliament, eventually," Stoker said. "That Keir Hardie'll do a thing or two, but that's not our bother either. Personally I wish him good luck. We need a few changes. No, sir, there is something big planned, and pretty bad, an' we haven't worked out what it is yet."

Pitt did not reply. He stared at the reports yet again, rereading the text, studying the geographic patterns of where they originated, who was involved.

Then he saw something curious. "Is that Willy Portman?" he asked Stoker, pointing to a report of known agitators observed in Birmingham.

"Yes, sir, seems like it. What's he doing here? Nasty piece of work, Willy Portman. Violent. Nothing good, if he's involved."

"I know," Pitt agreed. "But that's not it. This report says he was seen at a meeting with Joe Gallagher. Those two have been enemies for years. What could bring them together?"

Stoker stared at him. "There's more," he said very quietly. "McLeish was seen in Sheffield with Mick Haddon."

Pitt knew the names. They were both extremely violent men, and again known to hate each other.

"And Fenner," he added, putting his finger on the page where that name was noted. "And Guzman, and Scarlatti. That's the pattern. Whatever it is, it's big enough to bring these enemies together in a common cause, and here in Britain."

There was a shadow of fear in Stoker's eyes. "I'd like reform, sir, for lots of reasons. But I don't want everything good thrown out at the same time. And violence isn't the way to do anything, because no matter what you need to do in the first place, it never ends there. Seems to me that if you execute the king, either you end up with a religious dictator like Cromwell who rules over the people more tightly than any king ever did, and then you only have to get rid of him anyway—or else you end up with a monster like Robespierre in Paris, and the Reign of Terror, then Napoleon after that. Then you get a king back in the end anyway. At least for a while. I prefer us as we are, with our faults, rather than all that."

"So do I," Pitt agreed. "But we can't stop it if we don't know what it is, and when and how it will strike. I don't think we have very long."

"No, sir. And if you'll excuse me spelling it out, we haven't any allies either, least of all here in Lisson Grove. Whoever blackened Mr. Narraway's name did a very good job of it, and nobody trusts you, because you're his man."

Pitt smiled grimly. "It's a lot more than that, Stoker. I'm new to this job and I don't know the history of it and none of the men will trust me above Austwick, for which you can hardly blame them."

"Is Austwick a traitor, sir?"

"I think so. But he may not be the only one."

"I know that," Stoker said very quietly.

CHAPTER

11

Narraway was intensely relieved to see the familiar coast of Ireland slip away over the horizon with no coast guard or police boat in pursuit of them. At least for a few hours he could turn his attention to what he should do once he arrived at Holyhead. The obvious thing would be to catch the next train to London. Would it be so obvious a move that he might be apprehended? On the other hand, a delay might give anyone still bent on catching him a better chance to cross the Irish Sea in a lighter, perhaps faster boat, and arrest him before he could get any help.

He was standing on the deck gazing westward. Charlotte was beside him. She looked weary, and the marks of fear were still drawn deep into her face. Even so, he found her beautiful. He had long ago grown tired of unspoiled perfection. If that was what one hungered for—the color, the proportion, the smooth skin, the perfect balance of feature—there were works of art all over the world to stare at. Even the poorest man could find a copy for himself.

A real woman had warmth, vulnerability, fears, and blemishes of her own—or else how could she have any gentleness toward those of her mate? Without experience, one was a cup waiting to be filled—well crafted perhaps, but empty. And to a soul of any courage or passion, experience also meant a degree of pain, false starts, occasional bad judgments, a knowledge of loss. Young women were charming for a short while, but very soon they bored him.

He was used to loneliness, but there were times when its burden ached so deeply he could never be unaware of it. Standing on the deck with Charlotte, watching the wind unravel her hair and blow it across her face, was one such time.

She had already told him what she had learned of Talulla, of John Tyrone and the money, and of Fiachra McDaid. It was complicated. Some of the situation he had guessed from what O'Casey had told him, but he had not understood Talulla's place in it. Had Fiachra not convinced her that her parents were innocent, she would not have blamed Cormac. She would still have blamed Narraway, of course, but that was fair. Kate's death was as much his fault as anyone's, insofar as it was foreseeable. He had known how Sean felt about her.

What did Talulla imagine Cormac could have done to save Sean? Sean was a rebel whose wife gave him up to the English. Was that betrayal treason to the spirit of Ireland, or just a practical decision to avoid more pointless, heartbreaking bloodshed? How many people were still alive who would not have been if it had happened? Perhaps half the people she knew.

But of course she wouldn't see it that way. She couldn't afford to. She needed her anger, and it was justified only if her parents were the victims.

And Fiachra? Narraway winced at his own blindness. How desperately he had misread him! He had concealed the passion of his Irish nationalism inside what had seemed to be a concern for the disenfranchised of all nations. The more Narraway thought about it, the more it made sense. Odd how often a sweeping love for all could be willing to sacrifice the one, or the ten, or the score, almost with indifference. Fiachra would see the glory of greater social justice, freedom for Ireland—and the price would slip through his fingers uncounted. He was a dreamer who stepped over the corpses without even seeing them. Under the charm there was ice—and by God he was clever. In law he had committed no crime. If justice ever reached him, it would be for some other reason, at another time.

Narraway looked at Charlotte again. She became aware of his gaze and turned to him.

"There's no one anywhere on the whole sea," she said with a slightly rueful smile. "I think we're safe."

The inclusion of herself in his escape gave him a sort of warmth that he was aware was ridiculous. He was behaving like a man of twenty.

"So far," he agreed. "But when we get on the train at Holyhead you would be safer in a different carriage. I doubt there will be anyone looking for me, but it's not impossible."

"Who?" she said, as if dismissing the idea. "No one could have gotten here ahead of us." Before he could answer she went on. "And don't tell me they anticipated your escape. If they had, they'd have prevented it. Don't be naïve, Victor. They wanted you hanged. It would be the perfect revenge for Sean."

He winced. "You're very blunt."

"I suppose you just noticed that!" She gave a tiny, twisted smile.

"No, of course not. But that was unusual, even for you."

"This is an unusual situation," she said. "At least for me. Should I be trite if I asked you if you do it often?"

"Ah, Charlotte!" He brushed his hand through his heavy hair and turned away, needing to hide the emotion in his face from her. He needed it to be private, but—far more than that—he knew that it would embarrass her to realize how intense were his feelings for her.

"I'm sorry," she said quickly.

Hell, he swore to himself. He had not been quick enough.

"I know it's serious," she went on, apparently meaning something quite different.

A wave of relief swept over him, and, perversely, of disappointment. Did some part of him want her to know? If so, it must be suppressed. It would create a difficulty between them that could never be forgotten.

"Yes," he agreed.

"Will you go to Lisson Grove?" Now she sounded anxious.

"No. I'd rather they didn't even know I was back in England, and certainly not where." He saw the relief in her face. "There's only one person I dare trust totally, and that is Vespasia Cumming-Gould. I shall get off the train one or two stops before London and find a telephone. If I'm lucky I'll be able to get hold of her straightaway. It'll be long after dark by then. If not, I'll find rooms and wait there until I can."

His voice dropped to a more urgent note. "You should go home. You won't be in any danger. Or else you could go to Vespasia's house, if you prefer. Perhaps you should wait and see what she says." He realized as he spoke that he had no idea what had happened to Pitt, even if he was safe. To send Charlotte back to a house with no one there but a strange maid was possibly a cruel thing to do. She had said before that her sister Emily was away somewhere, similarly her mother. God! What a mess. But if anything had happened to Pitt, no one would be able to comfort her. He could not bear to think of that.

Please heaven whoever was behind this did not think Pitt a sufficient danger to have done anything drastic to him. "We'll get off a couple of stops before London," he repeated. "And call Vespasia."

"Good idea," she agreed, turning back to watch the gulls circling over the white wake of the ship. The two of them stood side by side in silence, oddly comforted by the endless, rhythmic moving of the water and the pale wings of the birds echoing the curved line of it.

NARRAWAY WAS CONNECTED WITH Vespasia immediately. Only when he heard the sound of her voice, which was thin and a little crackly over the line, did he realize how overwhelmingly glad he was to speak with her.

"Victor! Where on earth are you?" she demanded. Then an instant later: "No. Do not tell me. Are you safe? Is Charlotte safe?"

"Yes, we are both safe," he answered her. She was the only woman since his childhood who had ever made him feel as if he were accountable to her. "We are not far away, but I thought it better to speak to you before coming the rest of the journey."

"Don't," she said simply. "It would be far better if you were to find some suitable place, which we shall not name, and we shall meet there. A very great deal has happened since you left, but there is far more that is about to happen. I do not know what that is, except that it is of profound importance, and it may be tragically violent. But I daresay you have deduced that for yourself. I rather fear that your whole trip to Ireland was designed to take you away from London. Everything else was incidental."

"Who's in charge now?" he asked, the chill seeping into him, even though he was standing in a very comfortable hotel hallway, looking from left to right every few moments to make sure he was still alone and not overheard. "Charles Austwick?"

"No," she answered, and there was a heaviness in her voice, even over the wires. "That was only temporary. Thomas is back from France. That trip was entirely abortive. He has replaced Austwick, and is now in your office, and hating it."

Narraway was so stunned for a moment he could think of no words adequate to his emotions—certainly none that he could repeat in front of Vespasia, or Charlotte, were she close enough to hear.

"Victor!" Vespasia said sharply.

"Yes . . . I'm here. What . . . what is going on?"

"I don't know," she admitted. "But I have a great fear that he has been placed there precisely because he cannot possibly cope with whatever atrocity is being planned. He has no experience in this kind of leadership. He has not the deviousness nor the subtlety of judgment to make the necessary unpleasant decisions. And there is no one there whom he can trust, which at least he knows. I am afraid he is quite appallingly alone, exactly as someone has designed he should be. His remarkable record of success as a policeman, and as a solver of crimes within Special Branch jurisdiction, will justify his being placed in your position. No one will be held to blame for choosing him . . ."

"You mean he's there to take the blame when this storm breaks," Narraway said bitterly.

"Precisely." Her voice cracked a little. "Victor, we must beat this, and I have very little idea how. I don't even know what it is they plan, but it is something very, very wrong indeed."

She was brave; no one he knew had ever had more courage; she was clever and still beautiful . . . but she was also growing old and at times very much alone. Suddenly he was aware of her vulnerability: of the friends, and even the loves she had cared for passionately, and lost. She was perhaps a decade or so older than he. Suddenly he thought of her not as a force of society, or of nature, but as a woman, as capable of loneliness as he was himself.

"Do you remember the hostelry where we met Somerset Carlisle about eight years ago? We had the most excellent lobster for luncheon?" he asked.

"Yes," she said unhesitatingly.

"We should meet there as soon as possible," he told her. "Bring Pitt . . . please."

"I shall be there by midnight," she replied.

He was startled. "Midnight?"

"For heaven's sake, Victor!" she said tartly. "What do you want to do, wait until breakfast? Don't be absurd. You had better reserve us three rooms, in case there is any of the night left for sleeping." Then she hesitated.

He wondered why. "Lady Vespasia?"

She gave a little sigh. "I dislike being offensive, but since I assume that you escaped from . . . where you were, you have little money, and I daresay are in less than your usually elegant state. You had better give my name, as if you were booking it for me, and tell them that I shall settle when I arrive. Better if you do not give anyone else's name, your own, or Thomas's."

"Actually Charlotte had the foresight to pack my case for me, so I have all the respectable attire I shall need," he replied with the first flash of amusement he had felt for some time.

"She did what?" Vespasia said coolly.

"She was obliged to leave the lodgings," he exclaimed, still with a smile. "She did not wish to abandon my luggage, so she took it with her. If you don't know me better than that, you should at least know her!"

"Quite so," she said more gently. "I apologize. Indeed, I also know you. I shall see you as close to midnight as I am able to make it. I am very glad you are safe, Victor."

That meant more to him than he had expected, so much more that he found himself suddenly unable to answer. He replaced the receiver on its hook in silence.

PITT WAS AT HOME, sitting at the kitchen table beginning his supper when Minnie Maude came into the room. Her face was pink, her eyes frightened, her usually untamed hair pulled even looser and badly pinned up at one side.

"What's the matter?" Pitt said, instantly worried as well.

Minnie Maude took a deep breath and let it out shakily. "There's a lady 'ere ter see yer, sir. I mean a real lady, like a duchess, or summink. Wot shall I do wif' 'er, sir?"

"Oh." Pitt felt a wave of relief wash over him, like warmth from a fire on cold flesh. "Show her in here, and then put the kettle on again."

Minnie Maude held her guard. "No, sir, I mean a real lady, not jus' some nice person, like."

"Tall and slender, and very beautiful, despite the fact that she isn't young anymore," Pitt agreed. "And eyes that could freeze you at twenty paces, if you step out of line. Lady Vespasia Cumming-Gould. Please ask her to come into the kitchen. She has been in here before. Then make her a cup of tea. We have some Earl Grey. We keep it for her."

Minnie Maude stared at him as if he had lost his wits.

"Please," he added.

"Yer'll pardon me, sir," Minnie Maude said shakily. "But yer look like yer bin dragged through an 'edge backward."

Pitt pushed his hand through his hair. "She wouldn't recognize me if I didn't. Don't leave her standing in the hall. Bring her here."

"She in't in the 'all, sir. She's in the parlor," Minnie Maude told him with disgust at his imagining she would do anything less.

"I apologize. Of course she is. Bring her here anyway."

Defeated, she went to obey.

Pitt ate the last mouthful of his supper and cleared the table as Vespasia arrived in the doorway.

"I always liked this room," she observed. "Thank you, Minnie Maude. Good evening, Thomas. I am sorry to have interrupted your dinner, but it is unavoidable."

Behind him Minnie Maude skirted her and put the kettle onto the hob. Then she began to wash out the teapot in which Pitt's tea had been, and prepare it to make a different brew for Vespasia. Her back was very straight, and her hands shook just a little.

Pitt did not interrupt Vespasia. He held one of the hard-backed kitchen chairs for her to be seated. She declined to take off her cape.

"I have just heard from Victor," she told him. "On the telephone, from a railway station not far from the city. Charlotte was with him, and perfectly well. You have no need to concern yourself about her health, or anything else. However there are other matters of very great concern indeed. Matters that require your immediate and total attention."

"Narraway?" His mind raced. She was being discreet, no doubt aware that Minnie Maude could hear all they said. It would be cruel, pointless, and possibly even dangerous to frighten her unnecessarily. Certainly she did not deserve it, apart from the very practical matter that he needed her common sense to care for his household and, most important, his children—at least until Charlotte returned. And, he admitted, he rather liked her. She was good-natured and not without spirit. There was something about her not totally unlike Gracie.

"Indeed." Vespasia turned to Minnie Maude. "When you have made the tea, will you please go and pack a small case for your master, with what he will need for one night away from home. Clean personal linen and a clean shirt, and his customary toiletries. When you have it, bring it downstairs and leave it in the hall by the bottom step."

Minnie Maude's eyes widened. She blinked, as if wondering whether she dare confirm the orders with Pitt, or if she should simply obey them. Who was in charge?

They were giving the poor girl a great deal to become accustomed to in a very short while. He smiled at her. "Please do that, Minnie Maude. It appears I shall have to leave you. But also, I shall return before too long."

"You may be extremely busy for some time," Vespasia corrected him. "It is a very good thing that Minnie Maude is a responsible girl. You will need her. Now let us have tea and prepare to leave."

As soon as the tea was poured and Minnie Maude was out of the room Pitt turned to Vespasia. The look on his face demanded she explain.

"It is a conclusion no longer avoidable that both you and Victor were drawn away from London for a very specific purpose," she said, sipping delicately at her tea. "Victor was put out of office, with an attempt to have him at least imprisoned in Ireland, possibly hanged. You were lured away from London before that, so you, as the only person at Lisson Grove with an unquestionable personal loyalty to him, and the courage to fight for him, would not be there. He would be friendless, as indeed he was."

Pitt would have interrupted Narraway to ask why, but he would not dare interrupt Vespasia.

"It appears that Charles Austwick is involved," she continued. "To what degree, and for what purpose, we do not yet know, but the plot is widespread, dangerous, and probably violent."

"I know," he said quietly. "I think I can rely on Stoker, but so far as I can see, at the moment, he is the only one. There will be more, but I don't know who they are, and I can't afford any mistakes. Even one could be fatal. What I don't understand is why Austwick made so little fuss at being removed from the leadership. It makes me fear that there is someone else who knows every move I make and who is reporting to him."

She set her cup down. "The answer is uglier than that, my dear," she said very quietly. "I think that what is planned is so wide and so final in its result that they wish you to be there to take the blame for Special Branch's failure to prevent it. Then the branch can be recreated from the beginning with none of the experienced men who are there now, and be completely in the control of those who are behind this. Or alternatively, it might be disbanded altogether, as a force that has served its purpose in the past but is now manifestly no longer needed."

The thought was so devastating that it took him several moments to grasp the full import of it. He was not promoted for merit, but as someone completely dispensable, a Judas goat to be sacrificed when Special Branch took the blame for failing to prevent some disaster. He should have been furiously angry, and he would be, eventually, when he absorbed the enormity of it and had time to think of himself. Now all he could deal with was the nature of the plot, and who was involved. How could they ever begin to fight against it?

He looked at Vespasia. He was startled to see the gentleness in her face, a deep and hurting compassion.

He forced himself to smile at her. In the same circumstances she would never have spent time pitying herself. He would not let her down by doing so.

"I'm trying to think what I would have been working on had I not gone to St. Malo," he said aloud. "I don't know if poor West was actually going to tell me anything that mattered, such as that Gower was a traitor, or if he was killed only to get me chasing Wrexham to France. I thought it was the former, but perhaps it wasn't. Certainly that was the end of my involvement over here."

"If you had been here you might have prevented Victor from having been removed from office," she concluded. "On the other hand, you might have been implicated in the same thing, and removed also . . ." She stopped.

He shrugged. "Or killed." He said what he knew she was thinking. "Sending me to France was better, much less obvious. Also, it seems they wanted me here now, to take the blame for this failure that is about to descend on us. I've been trying to think what cases we were most concerned with, what we may have learned had we had time."

"We will consider it in my carriage on the way to our appointment," she said, finishing her tea. "Minnie Maude will have your case packed any moment, and we should be on our way."

He rose and went to say good night and—for the very immediate future—good-bye to his children. He gave Minnie Maude last instructions, and a little more money to ascertain that she had sufficient provisions. Then he collected his case and went outside to Vespasia's carriage where it was waiting in the street. Within seconds they were moving briskly.

"I've already looked over everything that happened shortly before

I left, and in Austwick's notes since," he began. "And in the reports from other people. I did it with Stoker. We saw something that I don't yet understand, but it is very alarming."

"What is it?" she asked quickly.

He told her about the violent men who had been seen in several different parts of England, and watched her face grow pale and very grave as he told her how old enemies had been seen together, as if they had a common cause.

"This is very serious," she agreed. "There is something I also have heard whispers of while you have been away. I dismissed it at first as being the usual idealistic talk that has always been around among dreamers, always totally impractical. For example, certain social reformers seem to be creating plans as if they could get them through the House of Commons without difficulty. Some of the reforms were radical, and yet I admit there is a certain justice to them. I assumed they were simply naïve, but perhaps there is some major element that I have missed."

They rode in silence for the length of Woburn Place toward Euston Road, then turned right with the stream of traffic and continued north until it became the Pentonville Road.

"I fear I know what element you have missed," Pitt said at last.

"Violence?" she asked. "I cannot think of any one man, or even group of men, who would pass some of the legislation they are proposing. It would be pointless anyway. It would be sent back by the House of Lords, and then they would have to begin again. By that time the opposition would have collected its wits, and its arguments. They must know that."

"Of course they do," he agreed. "But if there were no House of Lords . . ."

The street lamps outside seemed harsh, the rattle of the carriage wheels unnaturally loud. "Another gunpowder plot?" she asked. "The country would be outraged. We hung, drew, and quartered Guy Fawkes and his conspirators. We might not be quite so barbaric this time, but I wouldn't risk all I valued on it." Her face was momentarily in the shadows as a higher, longer carriage passed between them and the nearest street lamps.

Nearly an hour later they arrived at the hostelry Narraway had chosen, tired, chilly, and uncomfortable. They greeted one another briefly, with intense emotion, then allowed the landlord to show them to the rooms they would occupy for the night. Then they were offered a private lounge where they might have whatever refreshments they wished, and be otherwise uninterrupted.

Pitt was filled with emotion to see Charlotte; joy just at the sight of her face, anxiety that she looked so tired. He was relieved that she was safe when she so easily might not have been; frustrated that he had no opportunity to be alone with her, even for a moment; and angry that she had been in such danger. She had acted recklessly and with no reference to his opinion or feelings. He felt painfully excluded. Narraway had been there and he had not. His reaction was childish; he was ashamed of it, but that did nothing to lessen its sharpness.

Then he looked at Narraway, and despite himself his anger melted. The man was exhausted. The lines in his face seemed more deeply cut than they had been just a week or two before; his dark eyes were bruised around the sockets, and he brushed his hair back impatiently with his thin, strong hands as if it were in his way.

They glanced at each other, no one knowing who was in command. Narraway had led Special Branch for years, but it was Pitt's job now. And yet neither of them would preempt Vespasia's seniority.

Vespasia smiled. "For heaven's sake, Thomas, don't sit there like a schoolboy waiting for permission to speak. You are the commander of Special Branch. What is your judgment of the situation? We will add to it, should we have something to offer."

Pitt cleared his throat. He felt as if he were usurping Narraway's place. Yet he was also aware that Narraway was weary and beaten, betrayed in ways that he had not foreseen, and accused of crimes where he could not prove his innocence. The situation was harsh; a little gentleness was needed in the few places where it was possible.

Carefully he repeated for Narraway what had happened from the time he and Gower had seen West murdered until he and Stoker had put together as many of the pieces as they could. He was aware that he was speaking of professional secrets in front of both Vespasia and

Charlotte. It was something he had not done before, but the gravity of the situation allowed no luxury of exclusion. If they failed to restore justice, it would all become desperately public in a very short time anyway. How short a time he could only guess.

When he had finished he looked at Narraway.

"The House of Lords would be the obvious and most relevant target," Narraway said slowly. "It would be the beginning of a revolution in our lives, a very dramatic one. God only knows what might follow. The French throne is already gone. The Austro-Hungarian is shaking, especially after that wretched business at Mayerling." He glanced at Charlotte and saw the puzzlement in her face. "Six years ago, in '89," he explained, "Crown Prince Rudolf and his mistress shot themselves in a hunting lodge. All very messy and never really understood." He leaned forward a little, his face resuming its gravity. "The other thrones of Europe are less secure than they used to be, and Russia is careering toward chaos if they don't institute some sweeping reforms, very soon. Which is almost as likely as daffodils in November. They're all hanging on with their fingers."

"Not us," Pitt argued. "The queen went through a shaky spell a few years ago, but her popularity's returning."

"Which is why if they struck here, at our hereditary privilege, the rest of Europe would have nothing with which to fight back," Narraway responded. "Think about it, Pitt. If you were a passionate socialist and you wanted to sweep away the rights of a privileged class to rule over the rest of us, where would you strike? France has no ruling nobility. Spain isn't going to affect the rest of us anymore. They used to be related to half Europe in Hapsburg times, but not now. Austria? They're crumbling anyway. Germany? Bismarck is the real power. All the great royal houses of Europe are related to Victoria, one way or the other. If Victoria gets rid of her House of Lords, then it will be the beginning of the end for privilege by birth."

"One cannot inherit honor or morality, Victor," Vespasia said softly. "But one can learn from the cradle a sense of the past, and gratitude for its gifts. One can learn a responsibility toward the future, to guard and perhaps improve on what one has been given, and leave it whole for those who follow."

His face pinched as he looked at her. "I am speaking their words, not my own, Lady Vespasia." He bit his lip. "If we are to defeat them, we must know what they believe, and what they intend to do. If they can gain the power they will sweep away the good with the bad, because they don't understand what it is to answer only to your conscience rather than to the voice of the people, which comes regardless whether or not they have the faintest idea what they are talking about."

"I'm sorry," she said very quietly. "I think perhaps I am frightened. Hysteria appals me."

"It should," he assured her. "The day there is no one left to fear it we are all lost." He turned to Pitt. "Have you any idea as to what specific plans anyone has?"

"Very little," Pitt admitted. "But I know who the enemy is." He relayed to Narraway what he had told Vespasia about the different violent men who loathed one another, and yet appeared to have found a common cause.

"Where is Her Majesty now?" Narraway asked.

"Osborne," Pitt replied. He felt his heart beating faster, harder. Other notes he had seen from various people came to mind: movements of men that were small and discreet, but those men's names should have given pause to whoever was reading the reports. Narraway would have seen it. "I believe that's where they'll strike. It's the most vulnerable and most immediate place."

Narraway paled even further. "The queen?" He gave no exclamation, no word of anger or surprise; his emotion was too consuming. The thought of attacking Victoria herself was so shocking that all words were inadequate.

Pitt's mind raced to the army, the police on the Isle of Wight, all the men he himself could call from other duties. Then another thought came to him: Was this what they were supposed to think? What if he responded by concentrating all his resources on Osborne House, and the actual attack came somewhere else?

"Be careful," Narraway said quietly. "If we cause public alarm it could do all the damage they need."

"I know." Pitt was aware of Charlotte and Vespasia watching him as well. "I know that. I also know that they have probably a large space of time in which to strike. They could wait us out, then move as soon as we have relaxed."

"I doubt it." Narraway shook his head. "They know I escaped and they know you are back from France. I think it's urgent, even immediate. And the men you named here in England, together, won't wait. You should go back to Lisson Grove and—"

"I'm going to Osborne," Pitt said, cutting across him. "I don't have anyone else I can send, and if you're right, we could already be late."

"You're going to Lisson Grove," Narraway repeated. "You are head of Special Branch, not a foot soldier to be going into battle. What happens to the operation if you are shot, captured, or simply where no one can reach you? Stop thinking like an adventurer and think like a leader. You need to find out exactly whom you can trust, and you need to do it by the end of tomorrow." He glanced at the ormolu clock on the mantel. "Today," he corrected. "I'll go to Osborne. I can at least warn them, perhaps find a way of holding off whatever attack there is until you can send men to relieve us."

"You may not be let in," Vespasia pointed out to him. "You have no standing now."

Narraway winced. Clearly he had forgotten that aspect of his loss of office.

"I'll come with you," Vespasia said, not as an offer but as a statement. "I am known there. Unless I am very unfortunate, they will admit me, at least to the house. If I explain what has happened, and the danger, the butler will give me audience with the queen. I still have to decide what to tell her once I am in her company."

Pitt did not argue. The logic of it was only too clear. He rose to his feet. "Then we had better return and begin. Charlotte, you will come with me as far as Keppel Street. Narraway and Aunt Vespasia had better take the carriage and set out for the Isle of Wight."

Vespasia looked at Pitt, then at Narraway. "I think a couple of hours' sleep would be wise," she said firmly. "And then breakfast before we begin. We are going to make some very serious judgments, and perhaps fight some hard battles. We will not do it well if we are mentally or physically so much less than our best."

Pitt wanted to argue with her, but he was exhausted. If it was in any way acceptable he would like to lie down for an hour or two and allow his mind to let go of everything. He couldn't remember when he had last relaxed totally, let alone had the inner peace of knowing that Charlotte was beside him, that she was safe.

He looked at Narraway.

Narraway gave a bleak smile. "It's good advice. We'll get up at four, and leave at five." He glanced toward Vespasia to see that it met with her agreement.

She nodded.

"I'm coming with you," Charlotte said. There was no question in her voice, just a simple statement. She turned to Pitt. "I'm sorry. It is not a question of not wanting to be left out, or of any idea that I am indispensable. But I can't let Aunt Vespasia travel alone. It would be remarked on, for a start. Surely the servants at Osborne would consider it very odd?"

Of course she was right. Pitt should have thought of it himself. It was a large omission on his part that he had not. "Of course," he agreed. "Now let's retire while we still have a couple of hours left."

When they were upstairs and the door closed Charlotte looked at him with gentleness and intense apology. "I'm sorry . . . ," she began.

"Be quiet," he answered. "Let's just be together, while we can."

She walked into his arms and held him close. He was so tired that he was almost asleep on his feet. Moments later, when they lay down, he was dimly aware that she was still holding him.

IN THE MORNING PITT left to return to Lisson Grove. Charlotte, Vespasia, and Narraway took the coach south along the main road to the nearest railway station to catch the next train to Southampton, and from there the ferry to the Isle of Wight.

"If nothing is happening yet we may have a little trouble in gaining an audience with the queen," Narraway said when they were sitting in a private compartment in the train. The soothing rattle of the wheels over the rails rhythmically clattered at every joint. "But if the enemy are there already, we will have to think of a better way of getting inside."

"Can we purchase a black Gladstone bag in Southampton?" Charlotte suggested. "With a few bottles and powders from an apothecary, Victor could pose as a doctor. I shall be his nurse." She glanced at Vespasia. "Or your lady's maid. I have no skills in either, but am sufficiently plainly dressed to pass, at least briefly."

Vespasia considered for only a moment. "An excellent idea," she agreed. "But we should get you a plainer gown, and an apron. A good white one, without ornament, should serve for either calling. I think Victor's nurse would be better. The staff will be very familiar with lady's maids; nurses they might know less. Do you agree, Victor?"

There was a flash of amusement in his eyes. "Of course. We will arrange it all as soon as we arrive at the station."

"You think we are late already, don't you?" Charlotte said to him.

He made no pretense. "Yes. If I were they, I would have acted by now."

An hour and a half later they approached the spacious, comfortable house in which Queen Victoria had chosen to spend so many years of her life, particularly since the death of Prince Albert. Osborne seemed to offer her a comfort she found nowhere else in the more magnificent castles and palaces that were also hers.

The house looked totally at peace in the fitful spring sun. Most of the trees were in leaf, in a clean, almost gleaming translucency. The grass was vivid green. There was blossom on the blackthorn, and the hawthorn was in heavy bud.

Osborne was set in the gently rolling parkland that one would expect of any family mansion of the extremely wealthy. Much of the land was wooded, but there were also wide, well-kept sweeps of grass that gave it a feeling of great space and light. The house had been designed by Prince Albert himself, who had clearly much admired the opulent elegance of the Italian villas. It had two magnificent square towers, which were flat-topped and had tall windows on all sides. The main building copied the same squared lines, and the sunlight seemed to reflect on glass in every aspect. One could only imagine the beauty of the inside.

Their carriage pulled up and they alighted, thanking the driver and paying him.

"You'll be wanting me to wait," the cabbie said with a nod. "You can look, but that's all. Her Majesty's in residence. You don't get no closer than this."

Vespasia paid him generously. "No thank you. You may leave us."

He shrugged and obeyed, turning his vehicle around and muttering to the horse about tourists with no sense.

"There is nothing for us to wait for either," Narraway said ruefully. "I can't tell anything from the outside, can you? It all looks just as I imagine it should. There's even a gardener at work over there." He did not point but inclined his head.

Charlotte glanced in the direction he indicated and saw a man bent over a hoe, his attention apparently on the ground. The scene looked rural and pleasantly domestic. Some of her anxiety eased. Perhaps they had been more frightened than necessary. They were in time. Now they must avoid looking foolish, not only for the sake of pride, but so that when they gave the warning the royal household staff would take them seriously. Anyway, it would not be long before Pitt would send reinforcements who were trained for just this sort of duty, and the danger would be past.

Unless, of course, they were mistaken, and the blow would strike somewhere else. Was this yet another brilliant diversion? Narraway forced himself to smile in the sunlight. "I feel a trifle ridiculous carrying this case now."

"Hold on to it as if it were highly valuable to you," Vespasia said very quietly. "You will need it. That man is no more a gardener than you are. He doesn't know a weed from a flower. Don't look at him, or he will become alarmed. Doctors called out to the queen are not concerned with men hoeing the heads off petunias."

Charlotte felt the sun burn in her eyes. The huge house in front of them seemed to blur and go fuzzy in her vision. Ahead of her,

Vespasia's back was ruler-straight. Her head with its fashionable hat was as high and level as if she were sailing into a garden party as an honored guest.

They were met at the door by a butler whose white hair was scraped back from the high dome of his forehead as if he had run his hands through it almost hard enough to pull it out. He recognized Vespasia immediately.

"Good afternoon, Lady Vespasia," he said, his voice shaking. "I am afraid Her Majesty is a little unwell today, and is not receiving any callers whatever. I'm so sorry we didn't know in time to advise you. I would invite you in, but one of our housemaids has a fever that we would not wish anyone else to catch. I'm so sorry."

"Most unpleasant for the poor girl," Vespasia sympathized. "And for all the rest of you also. You are quite correct to take it seriously, of course. Fortunately I have brought Dr. Narraway with me and I'm sure he would be happy to see the girl and do whatever can be done for her. Sometimes a little tincture of quinine helps greatly. It might be wise for Her Majesty's sake as well. It would be dreadful if she were to catch such a thing."

The butler was lost for words. He drew in his breath, started to speak, and stopped again. The sweat stood out on his brow and his eyes blinked rapidly.

"I can see that you are distressed for her." Vespasia spoke as reassuringly as she could, although her voice wavered a trifle also. "Perhaps in humanity, as well as wisdom, we should have Dr. Narraway look at her. If all your staff became infected you will be in a serious and most unpleasant situation."

"Lady Vespasia, I cannot . . ."

Before he could finish, another, younger man appeared, also dressed as a servant. He was dark-haired, perhaps in his mid-thirties, and heavier set.

"Sir," he said to the butler. "I think perhaps the lady is right. I just had word poor Mollie is getting worse. You'd better accept their offer and have them in."

The butler looked at the man with loathing, but after one desperate glance at Vespasia, he surrendered.

"Thank you." Vespasia stepped across the threshold; Charlotte and Narraway followed her.

The moment they were inside and the front door closed, it was apparent that they were prisoners. There were other men at the foot of the sweeping staircase and at the entrance to the kitchens and servants' quarters.

"You didn't have to do that!" the butler accused the other man.

"Oh, decidedly, we did," the other contradicted. "They'd 'ave gone away knowing there was something wrong. Best we keep all this quiet. Don't want the old lady upset."

"No you don't," Vespasia agreed tartly. "If she has an attack and dies, you will be guilty not only of murder but of regicide. Do you imagine there is anywhere in the world that you could hide from that? Not that you would escape. We may have many ideas about the liberty or equality that we aspire to, even fight for, but no one will countenance the murder of the queen who has been on our throne longer than the lifetime of most of her subjects around the face of the earth. You would be torn apart, although I daresay that matters less to you than the complete discrediting of all your ideas."

"Lady, keep a still tongue in yer head, or I'll still it for yer. Whatever people feel about the queen, no one cares a jot if yer survive this or not," the man said sharply. "Yer pushed yer way in here. Yer've no one but yerself to blame if it turns bad for yer."

"This is . . . ," the butler began. Then, realizing he was only offering another hostage to fate, he bit off his words.

"Is anyone sick?" Vespasia inquired of no one in particular.

"No," the butler admitted. "It's what they told us to say."

"Good. Then will you please conduct us to Her Majesty. If she is being held with the same courtesy that you are offering us, it might still be as well for Dr. Narraway to be close to her. You don't want her to suffer any unnecessary ill effects. If she is not alive and well I imagine she will be of little use to you as a hostage."

"How do I know ye're a doctor?" the man said suspiciously, looking at Narraway.

"You don't," Narraway replied. "But what have you to lose? Do you think I mean her any harm?"

"What?"

"Do you think I mean her any harm?" Narraway repeated impatiently.

"Of course not! What kind of a stupid question is that?"

"The only kind that needs an answer. If I mean her no harm then it would be of less trouble to you to keep us all in the same room rather than use several. This is not so very large a house, for all its importance. I will at least keep her calm. Is that not in your interest?"

"What's in that bag? Yer could have knives, even gas for all I know."

"I am a physician, not a surgeon," Narraway said tartly.

"Who's she?" the man glanced at Charlotte.

"My nurse. Do you imagine I attend female patients without a chaperone?"

The man took the Gladstone bag from Narraway and opened it up. He saw only the few powders and potions they had bought from the apothecary in Southampton, all labeled. They had been careful, for precisely this reason, not to purchase anything that was an obvious weapon, not even small scissors for the cutting of bandages. Everything was exactly what it purported to be.

The man shut the bag again and turned toward his ally at the foot of the stairs. "Yer might as well take 'em up. We don't want the old lady passing out on us."

"Not yet, anyway," the other man agreed. He jerked his hand toward the flight of stairs. "Come on, then. Yer wanted to meet Her Majesty—this is yer lucky day."

It was the butler who conducted them up and then across the landing and knocked on the upstairs sitting room door. At the order from inside, he opened it and went in. A moment later he came out again. "Her Majesty will receive you, Lady Vespasia. You may go in."

"Thank you," Vespasia accepted, leading the way while Narraway and Charlotte followed a couple of steps behind her.

Victoria was seated in one of the comfortable, homely chairs in the well-used, very domestic living room. Only the height and ornate decoration of the ceiling reminded one that this was the home of the queen. She herself was a small, rather fat, elderly woman with a beaky nose and a very round face. Her hair was screwed back in an unflatteringly severe style. Her large eyes were pale and she was dressed entirely in black, which drained every shred of color from her skin. When she saw Vespasia for a second she blinked, and then she smiled.

"Vespasia. How very agreeable to see you. Come here!"

Vespasia went forward and dropped a graceful curtsy, her head slightly bowed, her back perfectly straight. "Your Majesty."

"Who are these?" Victoria inquired, looking beyond Vespasia to Narraway and Charlotte. She lowered her voice only slightly. "Your maid, presumably. The man looks like a doctor. I didn't send for a doctor. There's nothing the matter with me. Every fool in this household is treating me as if I'm ill. I want to go for a walk in the garden, and I am being prevented. I am empress of a quarter of the world, and my own household won't let me go for a walk in the garden!" Her voice was petulant. "Vespasia, come for a walk with me." She made to rise to her feet, but she was too far back in the chair to do so without assistance, and rather too fat to do it with any grace.

"Ma'am, it would be better if you were to remain seated," Vespasia said gently. "I am afraid I have some very harsh news to tell you . . ."

"Lady Vespasia!" Narraway warned.

"Be quiet, Victor," Vespasia told him without turning her eyes away from the queen. "Her Majesty deserves to know the truth."

"I demand to know it!" Victoria snapped. "What is going on?"

Narraway stepped back, surrendering with as much dignity as possible.

"I regret to say, ma'am," Vespasia said frankly, "that Osborne House has been surrounded by armed men. Of what number I do not know, but several of them are inside and have taken your household prisoner."

Victoria stared at her, then glanced past her at Narraway. "And who are you? One of those . . . traitors?"

"No, ma'am. Until very recently I was head of your Special Branch," he replied gravely.

"Why are you not still so? Why did you leave your post?"

"I was dismissed, ma'am, by traitors within. But I have come now to be of whatever service I may until help arrives, as it will do. We have seen to it."

"When?"

"I hope by nightfall, or shortly after," Narraway replied. "First the new head of the branch must be absolutely certain whom he can trust."

She sat very still for several moments. The ticking of the long-case clock seemed to fill the room.

"Then we had best wait with some composure," Victoria said at last. "We will fight if necessary."

"Before that we may have some chance to attempt escape . . . ," Narraway began.

Victoria glared at him again. "I am Queen of England and the British Empire, young man. In my reign we have stood our ground and won wars in every corner of the earth. Am I to run away from a group of hooligans in my own house? In Osborne!"

Narraway stood a little more uprightly.

Vespasia held her head high.

Charlotte found her own back ramrod-straight.

"I should think so!" Victoria said, regarding them with a very slight approval. "To quote one of my greatest soldiers, Sir Colin Campbell, who said at the battle of Balaclava, 'Here we stand, and here we die.' She smiled very slightly. "But since it may be some time, you may sit, if you wish."

Pɪᴛᴛ ʀᴇᴛᴜʀɴᴇᴅ ᴛᴏ ʟɪssᴏɴ Grove knowing that he had no
allies there except probably Stoker, and that the safety of the queen,
perhaps of the whole royal house, depended upon him. He was surprised, as he walked up the steps and in through the doorway, how intensely he felt about his responsibility. There was a fierce loyalty in
him, but not toward an old woman sitting in lonely widowhood in a
house on the Isle of Wight, nursing the memories of the husband she
had adored.

It was the ideal he cared about, the embodiment of what Britain
had been all his life. It was the whole idea of unity greater than all the
differences in race, creed, and circumstance that bound together a
quarter of the earth. The worst of society was greedy, arrogant, and
self-serving, but the best of it was supremely brave, it was generous,
and above all it was loyal. What was anybody worth if they had no
concept of a purpose greater than themselves?

This was very little to do with Victoria herself, and most certainly
nothing to do with the Prince of Wales. The murder at Buckingham
Palace was very recent in his mind. He could not forget the selfishness

of the prince, his unthinking arrogance, and the look of hatred he had directed at Pitt, nor should he. Soon the prince would be King Edward VII, and Pitt's career as a servant of the Crown would rest at least to some degree in his hands. Pitt would have wished him a better man, but his own loyalty to the throne was something apart from any personal disillusionment.

All his concentration now was bent on controlling Austwick. Whom did he dare to trust? He could not do this alone, and he must force himself not to think of Charlotte or Vespasia, or even of Narraway, except insofar as they were allies. Their danger he must force from all his conscious thoughts. One of the burdens at the core of leadership was that you must set aside personal loyalties and act in the good of all. He made himself think of how he would feel if others in command were to save their own families at the cost of his, if Charlotte were sacrificed because another leader put his wife's safety ahead of his duty. Only then could he dismiss all questions from his mind.

As he passed along the familiar corridors he had to remind himself again not to go to his old office, which was now occupied by someone else, but to go back to the one that used to be Narraway's, and would be again as soon as this crisis was past. As he closed the door and sat at the desk, he was profoundly glad that he had retrieved Narraway's belongings and never for a moment behaved as if he believed this was permanent. The drawings of trees were back on the walls, and the tower by the sea, even the photograph of Narraway's mother, dark and slender as he was, but more delicate, the intelligence blazing out of her eyes.

Pitt smiled for a moment, then turned his attention to the new reports on his desk. There were very few of them, just pedestrian comments on things that for the most part he already knew. There was no information that changed the circumstances.

He stood up and went to find Stoker rather than sending for him, because that would draw everyone's attention to the fact that he was singling him out. Even with Stoker's help, success would be desperately difficult.

"Yes, sir?" Stoker said as soon Pitt had closed the door and was in front of him. He stared at Pitt's face, as if trying to read in it what he was thinking.

Pitt hoped that he was a little less transparent than that. He remembered how he had tried to read Narraway, and failed, at least most of the time.

"We know what it is," he said quietly. There was no point in concealing anything, and yet even now he felt as if he were standing on a cliff edge, about to plunge into the unknown.

"Yes, sir . . ." Stoker froze, his face pale. On the desk, still holding the paper he had been reading, his hands were stiff.

Pitt took a breath. "Mr. Narraway is back from Ireland." He saw the relief in Stoker's eyes, too sharp to hide, and went on more easily, a darkness sliding away from him also. "It seems we are right in thinking that there is a very large and very violent plan already begun. There is reason to believe that the people we have seen together, such as Willy Portman, Fenner, Guzman, and so on, intend to attack Her Majesty at Osborne House—"

"God Almighty!" Stoker gasped. "Regicide?"

Pitt grimaced.

"Not intentionally. We think they mean to hold her ransom in return for a bill to abolish the hereditary power of the House of Lords— a bill that of course she will sign before, I imagine, her own abdication . . ."

Stoker was ashen. He looked at Pitt as if he had turned into some nightmare in front of his eyes. He swallowed, then swallowed again. "And then what? Kill her?"

Pitt had not taken it that far in his mind, but perhaps it was the logical end, the only one they could realistically live with. In the eyes of Britain, and most of the world, as long as Victoria was alive she would be queen, regardless of what anyone else said or did. He had thought things could not get worse, but in one leap they had.

"Yes, I imagine so," he agreed. "Narraway and Lady Vespasia Cumming-Gould have gone to Osborne, to do what they can, until we can send reinforcements to deal with whatever we find."

Stoker half rose in his seat.

"But not until we know whom we can trust," Pitt added. "The group must be small enough to be discreet. If we go in with half an army it will be far more likely to provoke them to violence immediately. If they know they are cornered and cannot escape, they'll hold her for ransom—their freedom for her life." He felt his throat tighten as he said it. He was fighting an enemy of unknown size and shape. Moreover, elements of it were secret from him, and lay within his own men. For a moment he was overwhelmed. He had no idea even where to begin. Every possibility seemed to carry its own failure built into it.

"A few men, well armed and taking them by surprise," Stoker said quietly.

"That's our only hope, I think," Pitt agreed. "But before we do that, we need to know who is the traitor here in Lisson Grove, and who else is with him. Otherwise they may sabotage any effort we make."

Stoker's hand on the desk clenched into a fist. "You mean you think there's more than one?"

"Don't you?"

"I don't know." Stoker pushed his hand through his hair, scraping it back off his forehead. "God help me, I don't know. And there's no time to find out. It could take us weeks."

"It's going to have to take us a lot less than that," Pitt replied, pulling out the hard-backed chair opposite the desk and sitting on it. "In fact we must make a decision by the end of today."

Stoker's jaw dropped. "And if we're wrong?"

"We mustn't be," Pitt told him. "Unless you want a new republic born in murder, and living in fear. We'll start with who set up the fraud that got rid of Narraway and made it all connect up with Ireland, so he would be in an Irish prison when all this happened."

Stoker took a deep breath. "Yes, sir. Then we'd better get started. And I'm sorry to say this, but we'll have to consider whoever Gower worked with as well, because getting you out of the way has to be part of it."

"Of course it has," Pitt agreed. "But Gower worked with me, and I reported to Narraway."

"That's the way it looked to all of us," Stoker agreed. "But it can't be what it was. I'll get his records from the officer who keeps all the personal stuff. We'll have to know who he worked with before you. You don't happen to know, do you?"

"I know what he said," Pitt replied with a twisted smile. "I'd like to know rather more than that. I think we'd better take as close a look as we can at everyone."

They spent the rest of the day going through all the records they could find going back a year or more, having to be discreet as to why.

"What are you looking for, sir?" one man asked helpfully. "Perhaps I can find it. I know the records pretty well."

Pitt had his answer prepared. "It's a pretty serious thing that we were caught out by Narraway," he replied grimly. "I want to be sure, beyond any doubt at all, that there's nothing else of that kind, in fact nothing at all that can catch us out again."

The man swallowed, his eyes wide. "There won't be, sir."

"That's what we thought before," Pitt told him. "I don't want to leave it to trust—I want to know."

"Yes, sir. Of course, sir. Can I help . . . or . . ." He bit his lip. "I see, sir. Of course you can't trust any of us."

Pitt gave him a bleak smile. "I don't mind your help, Wilson. I need to trust all of you, and equally you need to trust me. It was Narraway who embezzled the money, after all, not one of the juniors here. But I have to know who helped him, if anyone, and who else might have had similar ideas."

Wilson straightened up. "Yes, sir. Is anyone else allowed to know?"

"Not at the moment." Pitt was taking a chance, but time was growing short, and if he caught Wilson in a lie, it would at least tell him something. In fact perhaps fear would be a better ally than discretion, as long as that too was used secretly.

He loathed this. At least in the police he had always known that his colleagues were on the same side as he. He had not realized then how infinitely valuable that was. He had taken it for granted.

By the middle of the afternoon, they had found the connection between Gower and Austwick. They discovered it more by luck than deduction.

"Here," Stoker held out a piece of paper with a note scrawled across the bottom.

Pitt read it. It was a memorandum of one man, written to himself, saying that he must see Austwick at a gentlemen's club, and report a fact to him.

"Does this matter?" he asked, puzzled. "It's nothing to do with socialists or any kind of violence or change, it's just an observation of someone that turned out to be irrelevant."

"Yes, sir," Stoker agreed. "But it's this." He handed another note with something written on the bottom in the same hand.

Gave the message on Hibbert to Gower to pass on to Austwick at the Hyde Club. Matter settled.

The place was a small, very select gentlemen's club in the West End of London. He looked up at Stoker. "How the devil did Gower get to be a member of the Hyde Club?"

"I looked at that, sir. Austwick recommended him. And that means that he must know him pretty well."

"Then we'll look a lot more closely at all the cases Gower's worked on, and Austwick as well," Pitt replied.

"But we already know they're connected," Stoker pointed out.

"And who else?" Pitt asked. "There are more than two of them. But with this we've got a better place to start. Keep working. We can't afford even one oversight."

Silently Stoker obeyed. He concentrated on Gower while Pitt looked at every record he could find of Austwick.

By nine o'clock in the evening they were both exhausted. Pitt's head thumped and his eyes felt hot and gritty. He knew Stoker must feel the same. There was little time left.

Pitt put down the piece of paper he had been reading until the writing on it had blurred in front of his vision.

"Any conclusions?" he asked.

"Some of these letters, sir, make me think Sir Gerald Croxdale was just about on to him. He was pretty close to putting it together," Stoker replied. "I think that might be what made Austwick hurry it all up and act when he did. By getting rid of Narraway he shook everybody pretty badly. Took the attention away from himself."

"And also put him in charge," Pitt added. "It wasn't for long, but maybe it was long enough." The last paper he had read was a memorandum from Austwick to Croxdale, but it was a different thought that was in his mind.

Stoker was waiting.

"Do you think Austwick is the leader?" he asked. "Is he actually a great deal cleverer than we thought? Or at any rate, than I thought?"

Stoker looked unhappy. "I don't think so, sir. It seems to me like he's not making the decisions. I've read a lot of Mr. Narraway's letters, and they're not like this. He doesn't suggest, he just tells you. And it isn't that he's any less of a gentleman, just that he knows he's in charge, and he expects you to know it too. Maybe that wasn't how he spoke to you, but it's how he did to the rest of us. No hesitation. You ask, you get your answer. I reckon that Austwick's asking someone else first."

That was exactly the impression Pitt had had: a hesitation, as if checking with the man in control of the master plan.

But if Croxdale was almost on to him, why was Narraway not?

"Who can we trust?" he asked aloud. "We have to take a small force, no more than a couple of dozen men at the very most. Any more than that and we'll alert them. They'll have people watching for exactly that."

Stoker wrote a list on a piece of paper and passed it across. "These I'm sure of," he said quietly.

Pitt read it, crossed out three, and put in two more. "Now we must tell Croxdale and have Austwick arrested." He stood up and felt his muscles momentarily lock. He had forgotten how long he had been sitting, shoulders bent, reading paper after paper.

"Yes, sir. I suppose we have to?"

"We need an armed force, Stoker. We can't go and storm the queen's residence, whatever the reason, without the minister's approval. Don't worry, we've got a good enough case here." He picked up a small leather satchel and put into it the pages vital to the conclusions they had reached. "Come on."

AT OSBORNE, CHARLOTTE, VESPASIA, and Narraway were kept in the same comfortable sitting room with the queen. One terrified lady's maid was permitted to come and go in order to attend to the queen's wishes. They were given food by one of the men who kept them prisoner, and watched as they availed themselves of the necessary facilities for personal relief.

The conversation was stilted. In front of the queen no one felt able to speak naturally. Charlotte looked at the old lady. This close to her, with no distance of formality possible, she was not unlike Charlotte's own grandmother, someone she had loved and hated, feared and pitied over the years. As a child she had never dared to say anything that might be construed as impertinent. Later, exasperation had overcome both fear and respect, and she had spoken her own mind with forthrightness. More recently she had learned terrible secrets about that woman, and loathing had melted into compassion.

Now she looked at the short, dumpy old lady whose skin showed the weariness of age, whose hair was thin and almost invisible under her lace cap. Victoria was in her seventies, and had been on the throne for nearly half a century. To the world she was queen, empress, defender of the faith, and her numerous children had married into half the royal houses of Europe. However, it was not the responsibility to her country that wore her down; it was the bitter loneliness of widowhood.

Here at Osborne, standing looking out of the upstairs window across the fields and trees in the waning afternoon light, she was a tired old woman who had servants and subjects, but no equals. She would probably never know if any of them would have cared a jot for her if she were a commoner. The loneliness of it was unimaginable.

Would they kill her, those men in the hallway with guns and violent dreams of justice for people who would never want it purchased this way? If they did, would Victoria mind so very much? A clean shot through the heart, and she would join her beloved Albert at last.

Would they kill the rest of them too: Narraway and Vespasia, and Charlotte herself? What about all the servants? Or did the hostage-takers consider the servants to be ordinary people like themselves? Charlotte was sure the servants didn't think anything of the sort.

Charlotte had been sitting quietly on a chair at the far side of the room. On a sudden impulse she stood up and walked over toward the window. She stopped several feet short of the queen. It would be disrespectful to stand beside her. Perhaps it was disrespectful to stand here at all, but she did so anyway.

The view was magnificent. She could even see a bright glint of sunlight on the sea in the distance.

The hard light picked out every line on Victoria's face: the marks of tiredness, sorrow, ill temper, and perhaps also the inner pain of emotional isolation. Was she afraid?

"It is very beautiful, ma'am," Charlotte said quietly.

"Where do you live?" Victoria asked.

"In London, in Keppel Street, ma'am."

"Do you like it?"

"I have always lived in London, but I think I might like it less if I had the choice of living where I could see something like this, and just hear the wind in the trees, instead of the traffic."

"Can you not be a nurse in the country?" Victoria asked, still staring straight ahead of her.

Charlotte hesitated. Surely this was a time for the truth? It was only conversation. The queen did not care in the slightest where she lived. Any answer would do. If they were all to be shot, what sort of an answer mattered? An honest one? No, a kind one.

She turned and looked quickly at Vespasia.

Vespasia nodded.

Charlotte moved half a step closer to the queen. "No, ma'am. I'm afraid I'm not a nurse at all. I told the man at the door that I was in order for them to allow me in."

Victoria twisted her head to stare at Charlotte with cold eyes. "And why was that?"

Charlotte found her mouth dry. She had to lick her lips before she could speak. "My husband is in Special Branch, ma'am. Yesterday he became aware what these men planned to do. He returned to

London to get help from among those we can trust. Lady Vespasia, Mr. Narraway, and I came here to warn you, hoping we were in time. Clearly we were not, but now that we are here, we will do all we can to be of help."

Victoria blinked. "You knew that those . . . creatures were here?" she said incredulously.

"Yes, ma'am. Lady Vespasia realized that the man pretending to be a gardener was actually taking the heads off the petunias. No real gardener would do that."

Victoria looked beyond Charlotte to Vespasia, still at the far side of the room.

"Yes, ma'am." Vespasia answered the unspoken question.

Narraway moved at last. He came forward, bowed very slightly, just an inclination of his head. "Ma'am, these men are violent and we believe they are seeking reform of all hereditary privilege in Europe—"

"All hereditary privilege?" she interrupted. "You mean . . ." Her voice faltered. ". . . like the French?" From the pallor of her face she had to be thinking of the guillotine, and the execution of the king.

"Not as violently as that, ma'am," Narraway told her. "We believe that when they are ready they will ask you to sign a bill abolishing the House of Lords . . ."

"Never!" she said vehemently. Then she gulped. "I do not mind dying so much, for myself, if that is what they have in mind. But I do not wish it for my household. They have been loyal, and do not deserve this repayment. Some of them are . . . young. Can you negotiate . . . something . . . that will spare them?"

"With your permission, ma'am, I will attempt to prevaricate long enough for help to arrive," he replied.

"Why does Special Branch not call in the army or, at the very least, the police?" she asked.

"Because if they come in with force, these people may react violently," he explained. "They are tense now. In their own way they are frightened. They know the cost of losing. They will certainly be hanged. We cannot afford to panic them. Whatever we do, it must be so stealthy that they are unaware of it. Everything must appear normal, until it is too late."

"I see," she said quietly. "I thought I was being brave when I said *Here we die*. It looks as if I was more accurate than I intended. I will remain here in this room, where I have been so happy in the past." She gazed out of the window. "Do you suppose heaven is like that, Mr. . . . what is your name?"

"Narraway, ma'am. Yes, I think it may well be. I hope so."

"Don't humor me!" she snapped.

"If God is an Englishman, ma'am, then it certainly will be," he said drily.

She turned and gave him a slow, careful look. Then she smiled.

He bowed again, then turned away and walked to the door.

Outside in the landing he saw one of the armed men halfway down the stairs.

The man must have caught the movement in the corner of his vision. He spun around, raising the gun.

Narraway stopped. He recognized Gallagher from Special Branch photographs, but he did not say so. If any of them realized who he was they might shoot him, on principle.

"Get back there!" Gallagher ordered.

Narraway stood where he was. "What do you want?" he asked. "What are you waiting for? Is it money?"

Gallagher gave a snort of contempt. "What do you think we are—bloody thieves? Is that as far as your imagination goes? That's all your sort thinks of, isn't it! Money, all the world's money, property. You think that's all there is, property and power."

"And what's yours?" Narraway asked, keeping his voice level, and as emotionless as he could.

"Get back in there!" Gallagher jerked the gun toward the upstairs sitting room again.

Again Narraway remained where he was. "You're holding Her Majesty hostage, you must want something. What is it?"

"We'll tell you that when we're ready. Now unless you want to get shot, get back in there!"

Reluctantly Narraway obeyed. There was an edge of fear in Gallagher's voice, a jerkiness in his movements that said he was as tight as a coiled spring inside. He was playing for the highest stakes he could imagine, and this was the only chance they would have. This was win, or lose it all.

Back in the sitting room Vespasia looked at Narraway the moment the door was closed.

"They're waiting for something," he said quickly. "Whoever it is here, he's not in charge. Someone will come with a proclamation for Her Majesty to sign, or something of the sort." He gritted his teeth. "We may be here for some time—this has been put to the prime minister—if they are arguing this thing in the cabinet. We'll have to keep our heads. Try to keep them calm, and possibly even convince them they have a hope of success. If they lose that, they may just kill us all. They'll have nothing to lose." He looked at her white face. "I'm sorry. I would prefer not to have had to tell you that, but I can't do this alone. We must all stay steady—the household staff as well. I wish I could get to them to persuade them of the need for calm. One person in hysterics might be enough to panic them all."

Vespasia rose to her feet a trifle unsteadily. "Then I will ask this lunatic on the stairs for permission to go and speak with the household staff. Perhaps you will be good enough to help me persuade him of the necessity. Charlotte will manage here very well."

Narraway took her arm, holding it firmly. He turned to Victoria.

"Ma'am, Lady Vespasia is going to speak with your staff. It is imperative that no one loses control or behaves with rashness. I shall try to persuade the men who hold us hostage to permit her to do this, for all our sakes. I am afraid we may be here for some little time."

"Thank you." Victoria spoke more to Vespasia than to Narraway, but the comment included them both.

"Perhaps they could serve everyone food?" Charlotte suggested. "It is easier to be busy."

"An excellent idea," Vespasia agreed. "Come, Victor. If they have any sense at all, they will see the wisdom of it."

They went to the door, and he held it open for her.

Charlotte watched them go with her heart pounding and her stomach clenched tight. She turned to Victoria, who was staring at her with the same fear bright in her eyes.

Out on the landing there was still silence . . . no sound of gunfire.

A LITTLE BEFORE MIDNIGHT Pitt and Stoker sat in a hansom cab on its way to the home of Sir Gerald Croxdale. With them in the satchel was the main evidence to prove Austwick's complicity in the movement of the money that had made Narraway appear guilty of theft and had resulted in the murder of Mulhare. Also included were the reports of the leading revolutionary socialists prepared to use violence to overthrow governments they believed to be oppressive, who were now gathered together in England, and had been seen moving south toward Osborne House and the queen. Also, of course, were the names of the traitors with Special Branch.

It took nearly five minutes of ringing and knocking before they heard the bolts drawn back in the front door. It was opened by a sleepy footman wearing a coat over his nightshirt.

"Yes, sir?" he said cautiously.

Pitt identified himself and Stoker. "It is an extreme emergency," he said gravely. "The government is in danger. Will you please waken the minister immediately." He made it a request, but his tone left no doubt that it was an order.

They were shown to the withdrawing room. Just over ten minutes later Croxdale himself appeared, hastily dressed, his face drawn in lines of anxiety. As soon as he had closed the door, he spoke, looking from Pitt to Stoker and back again.

"What is it, gentlemen?"

There was no time for any more explanation than necessary to convince him. "We have traced the money that was placed in Narraway's account," Pitt said briefly. "It was Charles Austwick behind it, and the consequent murder of Mulhare, and also behind Gower's murder of West. Far more important, we know the reason for both. It was to place Austwick in charge of Special Branch, so no one else would notice the violent radical socialists coming into Britain, men who have been idealogical enemies until now, suddenly cooperating with one another and all moving down toward the Isle of Wight."

Croxdale looked startled. "The Isle of Wight? For God's sake, why?"

"Osborne House," Pitt said simply.

"God Almighty! The queen!" Croxdale's voice was all but strangled in his throat. "Are you sure? No one would . . . why? It makes no sense. It would unite the world against them." He waved one hand and shook his head, as if to push away the whole idea.

"Not to kill her," Pitt told him. "At least not to start with, perhaps not at all."

"Then what?" Croxdale peered at him as if he had never really seen him before. "Pitt, are you sure you know what you are talking about?"

"Yes, sir," Pitt said firmly. He was not surprised Croxdale doubted him. If he had not seen the proof himself he would not have believed it. "We traced the money that was supposed to go to Mulhare. The information he gave was very valuable. He gave up Nathaniel Byrne, one of the key men responsible for several bombings in Ireland and in London. Very few people knew that, even in Special Branch, but Austwick was one of them. Narraway arranged the payment so Mulhare could escape. That was a condition of his giving the information."

"I knew nothing about it!" Croxdale said sharply. "But why would Austwick do such a thing? Did he take some of it himself?"

"No. He wanted Narraway out of Special Branch, and me too, in case I knew enough of what Narraway had been working on to piece it together."

"Piece what?" Croxdale said sharply. "You haven't explained anything yet. And what has this to do with socialist violence against the queen?"

"Passionate idealism gone mad," Pitt answered. "Hold the queen for ransom to abolish the House of Lords, and then probably to abdicate. The end of rule by hereditary privilege, then likely a republic, with only elected representation of the people."

"Good God." Croxdale sank into the nearest armchair, his face ashen, his hands shaking. "Are you certain, man? I can't act on this without absolute proof. If I have to mount a force of armed men to take Osborne House, I'd better be bloody sure I'm doing the right thing—in fact the only thing. If you're wrong, I'll end up in the Tower, and it'll be my head on the block."

"Mr. Narraway is already at Osborne, sir," Pitt told him.

"What?" Croxdale sat up with a jerk. "Narraway's in . . ." He stopped, rubbing his hand over his face. "Do you have proof of all this, Pitt? Yes or no? I have to explain this to the prime minister before I act: immediately, tonight. I can have Austwick arrested—I'll do that first, before he gets any idea that you know what he's done. I'll do that now. But you must give me more than your word to take to the prime minister."

"Yes, sir." Pitt indicated the case he had with him. "It's in here. Reports, instructions, letters. It takes a bit of piecing together, but it's all there."

"Are you certain? My God, man, if you're wrong, I'll see you go down with me!" Croxdale rose to his feet. "I'll get it started. There's obviously no time to waste." He walked slowly from the room, closing the door behind him.

Stoker was standing where he had been throughout the conversation. There was a very slight frown on his face.

"What is it?" Pitt asked.

Stoker shook his head. "I don't know, sir."

Pitt had the case in his hand with the papers. Why had Croxdale not asked to see them, at least check over them? With the possibility of treachery inside Special Branch, and his belief earlier that Narraway himself was a thief, why had he not asked to see it? Pitt was known to be Narraway's man. In his place, Pitt would have been skeptical, at the very least.

"Do you think he suspected Austwick all along?" Stoker asked.

"Of what? If he was part of setting up the forgeries to blame Narraway, then he was part of the plot to attack the queen. If Croxdale knew that, then he's part of it too." As he spoke the pieces fell together in his mind. Austwick was reporting to someone else, they were certain of that. Croxdale himself?

Then he remembered something else: Croxdale had said he did not know about Austwick sending the money for Mulhare—but Croxdale had had to countersign it. It was too large an amount for one signature alone.

He turned to Stoker. "He's going to get rid of Austwick, and blame him for all of it," he said. "Then the queen."

Stoker was hollow-eyed in the lamplight; Pitt knew he must look the same. Could they possibly be right? The price would be total ruin if they were wrong. And ruin for the country if they were right, and did nothing.

Pitt nodded.

Stoker went to the door and opened it very quietly, not allowing the latch to click back. Pitt came behind him. Across the hallway the study door was ajar and there was a crack of light across the dark floor.

"Wait till he comes out," Stoker said under his breath. "I'll get over the far side, in the other doorway. You hold his attention, I'll be behind him. Be prepared. He'll fight."

Pitt could feel his heart pounding so hard his whole body must be shaking with it. Had his promotion gone to his head? He was doing the wildest thing of his life, perhaps throwing away everything he had in a gesture that in the light of day would look like the act of a madman, or a traitor. He should wait, act with moderation, ask someone else's opinion.

What if Stoker was the traitor, and deliberately provoking Pitt to this? What if he was Austwick's man, about to arrest the one person who stood in their way?

What if it were all a plan to ruin Special Branch? Discredit it into oblivion?

He froze.

Ahead of him Stoker tiptoed across the hall to stand, little more than a shadow, in the doorway next to the study, where Croxdale would have his back to him when he came out to go back to Pitt.

The seconds ticked by.

Was Croxdale speaking to the prime minister? What could he tell him over a telephone? Would he have to go and see him in person in order to raise a force of men to relieve Osborne House? No—this was an emergency, no time to argue, or plead a case. Was he arranging to have Austwick arrested?

The study door opened and Croxdale came out. Now was the time for decision, as Croxdale walked across the unlit hall, before he reached the sitting room door.

Pitt stepped forward. "Sir Gerald, Austwick is not the leader in the attempted coup."

Croxdale stopped. "What the devil are you talking about? If there's somebody else, why in God's name didn't you tell me before?"

"Because I didn't know who it was," Pitt said honestly.

Croxdale was in the shadow, his face all but invisible. "And now you do?" His voice was soft. Was it in disbelief, or understanding at last?

"Yes," Pitt said.

Stoker moved silently forward until he was a yard behind Croxdale. He had deliberately chosen an angle from which he cast no shadow.

"Indeed. And who is it?" Croxdale asked.

"You," Pitt answered.

There was total silence.

Croxdale was a big man, heavy. Pitt wondered if he and Stoker would be able to take him, if he fought back, if he called for the footman who must be waiting somewhere. Please God he was in the kitchen where he would only hear a bell. But he would not go back to bed while his master was up and there were visitors in the house.

"You made a mistake," Pitt pointed out, as much to hold Croxdale's attention from any slight sound Stoker might make as for any reasoning.

"Really? What was that?" Croxdale did not sound alarmed. In seconds he had regained his composure.

"The amount of money you paid Mulhare."

"He was worth it. He gave us Byrne," Croxdale replied, the contempt undisguised in his voice. "If you were up to your job, you would know that."

"Oh, I do know it," Pitt answered, keeping his eyes on Croxdale so he did not waver even once and glance at Stoker behind him. "The point is not whether Mulhare was worth it, it is that that amount had to be authorized by more than one man. It has your signature on it."

"What of it?" Croxdale asked. "It was a legitimate payment."

"It was used to get rid of Narraway—and you said you didn't know anything about it," Pitt reminded him.

Croxdale brought his hands out of his pockets. In the left one there was a small gun. The light from the sitting room behind Pitt gleamed on the metal of the barrel as Croxdale raised it.

Pitt swung around as if Stoker were behind him, just as Stoker slammed into Croxdale, kicking high and hard at his left elbow.

The gun flew in the air. Pitt lunged for it, just catching it as it arced over to his left.

Croxdale swung around and grabbed at Stoker, twisting his arm and turning him so he half fell and Croxdale had him in a stranglehold.

"Give me back the gun, or I'll break his neck!" Croxdale said in a grating voice, just a little high-pitched.

Pitt had no doubt whatever that he would do it. The mask was off: Croxdale had nothing to lose. Pitt looked at Stoker's face, which was already turning red as his neck was crushed by Croxdale's hold. There was no choice. Stoker was still only half in front of Croxdale, but slipping forward and sideways. A minute more and he would be unconscious and form a perfect shield. He aimed the gun and cocked the trigger.

Pitt shot Croxdale in the head, making a single wound.

Croxdale fell backward. Stoker, sprayed with blood, staggered and collapsed onto the floor. Pitt was alarmed by his own accuracy, though the distance to his target had been short enough. Of course he was surprised; he had never shot a man to death before.

He dropped the gun and held out his hand, hauling Stoker to his feet again.

Stoker looked at the gun.

"Leave it!" Pitt said, startled to find his voice almost level. "The minister shot himself when he realized we had proof of his treason. We didn't know he had a gun, so we weren't able to prevent him from doing it." Now he was shaking, and it took all his control to keep even reasonably steady. "What the hell did you think you were doing?" he snarled at Stoker suddenly. "He would have killed you, you fool!"

Stoker coughed and rubbed his hand over his throat. "I know that," he said huskily. "Just as well you shot him, or I'd have been the one on the floor. Thank you, sir."

Pitt was about to tell Stoker that he was incompetent to have allowed Croxdale to grasp hold of him like that. However, with a shock like a physical blow, he realized that Stoker had done it on purpose, risking his own life to force Pitt to shoot Croxdale. He stared at him as if seeing him for the first time.

"What could we have done with him, sir?" Stoker said pragmatically. "Tie him up here, for his servants to find and let go? Take him with us, in a hansom cab or one of us stay and sit—"

"All right!" Pitt cut in. "Now we have to get to the Isle of Wight and rescue the queen—and Narraway and Lady Vespasia, and my wife." His mind raced, picturing the men he knew were going to be there: violent, fanatical men like Portman, Gallagher, Haddon, Fenner, and others with the same distorted idealism, willing to kill and to die for the changes they believed would bring a new era of social justice.

Then another idea came to him. "If he had Austwick arrested, where would he be taken to? Quickly?"

"Austwick?" Stoker sounded confused.

"Yes. Where would he be now? Where does he live, do you know? How can we find out?"

"Kensington, sir, not far from here," Stoker replied. "It'd be the Kensington police—if Croxdale really called anyone."

"If he didn't, we will," Pitt said, now knowing exactly what he was going to do. "Come on, we've got to hurry. We don't know who Croxdale actually spoke to. It won't have been the prime minister." He started toward Croxdale's study.

"Sir!" Stoker said, bewildered.

Pitt turned. "If one of the servants comes down, tell him Sir Gerald shot himself. Do what you can to make it look right. I'm going to call the Kensington police." In Croxdale's study there was no time to search. He picked up the receiver and asked the operator to connect him, as an emergency. Perhaps Croxdale had done the same.

As soon as they answered he identified himself and said that there had been a practical joke suggested concerning the arrest of Mr. Austwick. It should be disregarded.

"Are you sure, sir?" the man at the other end said doubtfully. "We've 'ad nothing 'ere."

"Mr. Austwick lives in your area?" Pitt had a sudden sinking in the pit of his stomach.

"Oh yes, sir."

"Then we'd better make certain he's safe. What is his address?"

The man hesitated a moment, then told him. "But we'll send men there ourselves, sir, if you'll pardon me, seein' as 'ow I don't really know 'oo you are."

"Good. Do that," Pitt agreed. "We'll be there as soon as I can get a cab." He replaced the receiver and went to find Stoker. The other man was waiting by the front door, anxiously moving his weight from one foot to the other.

"Right, find a hansom," Pitt told him.

"We'll have to walk as far as the main road," Stoker warned, opening the door and slipping out with immense relief. They strode along at as rapid a pace as possible, short of breaking into a run.

It was still several minutes before they found a cab. They gave Austwick's address, with orders to make the best speed possible.

"What are we going to do with Austwick, sir?" Stoker asked. He had to raise his voice above the clatter of the hooves and the rattle and hiss of wheels over the cobbles.

"Get him to help us," Pitt replied. "They're his men down there. He's the one person who might be able to call them off without an all-out shooting battle. We won't have achieved much in capturing them if they kill the queen in the process." He did not mention Narraway or Vespasia, or Charlotte.

"Do you think he'll do that?" Stoker asked.

"It's up to us to persuade him," Pitt said grimly. "Croxdale's dead, Narraway's alive. I doubt the queen will sign anything that reduces the power or dignity of the Crown, even in fear of her life."

Stoker did not reply, but in the light of the next street lamp they passed, Pitt saw that he was smiling.

When they reached Austwick's house there were police outside it, discreetly, well in the shadows.

Pitt identified himself, showing them his new warrant card, and Stoker did the same.

"Yes, sir," the sergeant said smartly. "How can we help, sir?"

Pitt made an instant decision. "We are going to collect Mr. Austwick, and we are all going to travel to Portsmouth, as rapidly as possible."

The sergeant looked bemused.

"Use Austwick's telephone. Hold the night train," Pitt told him. "It's imperative we get to the Isle of Wight by morning."

The sergeant came to attention. "Yes, sir. I'll . . . I'll call immediately."

Pitt smiled at him. "Thank you." Then he nodded to Stoker. They went to the front door of Austwick's house and knocked hard and continuously until a footman in his nightshirt opened it, blinking and drawing in breath to demand an explanation.

Pitt told him sharply to step back.

The man saw the police beyond Pitt, and Stoker at his elbow, and did as he was told. Ten minutes later Austwick was in the hall, hastily dressed, unshaven, and very angry.

"What the hell is going on?" he said furiously. "Do you know what time it is, man?"

Pitt looked at the long-case clock at the far side of the hall. "Coming up to quarter to two," he answered. "And we must make Portsmouth by dawn."

Austwick paled visibly, even in the dim light of the hall with its main chandelier unlit. If anything could tell Pitt that he knew of Croxdale's plan, it was the fear in his face now.

"Croxdale is dead," Pitt said simply. "He shot himself when we faced him with his plans. It's all over. Narraway's back. He's at Osborne now, with the queen. You've got two choices, Austwick. We can arrest you now, and you'll be tried as a traitor. You'll hang, and your family will never live it down. Your grandchildren, if you have any, will still carry the stigma of your name." He saw Austwick's horror, but could not afford to pity him. "Or you can come with us and call off your men from Osborne," he went on. "You have two minutes to choose. Do you wish to hang as a traitor, or come with us, to live or die as a hero?"

Austwick was too paralyzed with fear to speak.

"Good," Pitt said decisively. "You're coming with us. I thought you'd choose that. We're going for the night train to Portsmouth. Hurry."

Stoker grasped Austwick by the arm, holding him hard, and they stumbled out into the night.

They half heaved him into the waiting hansom, then sat with one on either side of him. Two uniformed police followed in another cab, ready to clear traffic if there should be any and to confirm that the night train was held.

They raced through the streets in silence toward the river and the railway station beyond, where they could catch the mail train to the coast. Pitt found his fists clenched and his whole body aching with the tension of not knowing whether the sergeant he had instructed had been able to hold the train there. It could only have taken a telephone call from Austwick's house to his own police station, and then a call from there to the railway. What if the stationmaster on night duty did not believe them, or realize the urgency of it? What if he was simply incompetent for such a crisis?

They swayed and lurched along the all-but-deserted streets, then over the river at the Battersea Bridge, and sharp west along the High Street. One moment he was desperate that they were going too slowly, the next, as they slewed around a corner, that they were going too fast and would tip over.

At the station they leapt out, Pitt wildly overpaying the driver because he could not wait for change. They ran into the station, dragging Austwick with them. The sergeant showed his warrant card and shouted at the stationmaster to direct them to the train.

The man obeyed with haste, but was clearly unhappy about it all. He looked at Austwick's ashen face and dragging feet with pity. For a moment Pitt feared he was going to intervene.

The train was waiting, the engine belching steam. A very impatient guard stood at the door of his van, his whistle in one hand ready to be raised to his lips.

Pitt thanked the sergeant and his men, happy to be able to give them some idea of how intensely grateful he was. He made a mental note to commend the sergeant if they survived the night. He was doubly glad that his own reputation was such that his appreciation was a blessing, not a curse.

As soon as they were in the guard's van, the whistle blew. The train lurched forward like a horse that had been straining at the bit.

The guard was a small, neat man with bright blue eyes.

"I hope all this is worth it," he said looking at Pitt dubiously. "You've a lot of explaining to do, young man. Do you realize you have kept this train waiting ten minutes?" He glanced at his pocket watch and then replaced it. "Eleven minutes," he corrected himself. "This train carries the Royal Mail. Nobody holds us up. Not rain nor floods nor lightning storms. And here we stood around the platform for the likes of you."

"Thank you," Pitt said a little breathlessly.

The guard stared at him. "Well . . . nice manners are all very good, but you can't hold up the Royal Mail, you know. While it's in my care, it belongs to the queen."

Pitt drew in his breath to reply, and then the irony of the situation struck him. Smiling, he said nothing.

They continued on to the rear carriage and found seats. Stoker remained next to Austwick, as if he feared the man might make a run for it, although there was nowhere for him to go.

Pitt sat silently trying to make the best plans possible for when they arrived. They would have to commandeer a boat—any sort would do—to get them across the narrow strip of water to the Isle of Wight.

He was still thinking of it when about fifteen minutes into the journey the train slowed. Then, with a great panting of steam, it stopped altogether. Pitt shot to his feet and went back to the guard's van.

"What's the matter?" he demanded. "Why have we stopped? Where are we?"

"We stopped to put off the mail, o' course," the guard said with elaborate patience. "That's what we came for. Now you just go an' sit down in your seat and be quiet, sir. We'll be on our way when we're ready."

"How many places do you stop?" Pitt asked. His voice was louder and harsher than he meant it to be, but it was sliding out of his control.

The guard stood very straight, his face grim.

"Every place where we got to pick up mail, or set it down, sir. Like I said, that's what we do. Jus' you go an' sit back down, sir."

Pitt pulled out his warrant card and held it for the guard to see. "This is an emergency. I'm on the queen's business, and I need to get to the Isle of Wight by sunrise. Drop off the mail on the way back, or let the next train through pick it up."

The guard stared at Pitt with both pride and disgust. "I'm on the queen's business too, sir. I carry the Royal Mail. You'll get to Portsmouth when we've done our job. Now, like I said, go an' sit down an' we'll get on with the mail. Ye're just holding us up, sir, an' I won't have that. You've caused enough trouble already."

Pitt felt exasperation well up inside him so he could almost have hit the man. It was unfair; the guard was doing his duty. He had no idea who Pitt was, other than some kind of policeman.

Could Pitt tell him any part of the truth? No. He would find himself held in charge as a lunatic. He could prove nothing, and it would only delay them even more. With a chill he remembered his helplessness on his last train ride, the horror and absurdity of it—and Gower's mangled body on the tracks. Thank God, at least he had not seen it.

He returned to the carriage and sat down in his seat.

"Sir?" Stoker said.

"We have to stop at all the stations," Pitt answered, keeping his voice level this time. "Without telling him the truth I can't persuade him not to." He smiled lopsidedly. "It's the Royal Mail. Nothing stands in its way."

Stoker started to say something, then changed his mind. Everything he meant to express was in the lines of his face.

The journey seemed achingly slow. None of them spoke again until finally they pulled into Portsmouth station as the dawn was lightening the eastern sky. Austwick caused no trouble as they went through the barely wakening streets and found a large rowing boat to take them across the water.

There was a brisk wind and the sea was choppy, the wave caps translucent, almost mirroring the high, rippling clouds shot through by the rising wind. It was hard work, and they were obliged to bend their backs to make headway.

They landed, shivering, at the wharf and set off toward Osborne House, which was just in sight above the tangle of the still-bare trees. They walked as fast as they could, since there was no one around from whom to beg or hire any kind of transport.

The sun was above the horizon and glittering sharp in a clear morning when they approached the boundaries. The rolling parkland and the splendid stone mansion were spread before them, broad and magnificent, as if still sleeping in the hushed land, which was silent but for the birdsong.

Pitt had a moment of terrible doubt. Was this whole thing no more than a vast nightmare, without reality at all? Had they misunderstood everything? Was he about to burst in on the queen and make the ultimate fool of himself?

Stoker strode forward, still gripping Austwick by the arm.

Nothing at Osborne stirred. Surely there had to be a guard of some sort, whatever the circumstances, even if the entire conspiracy was Pitt's delusion?

As they reached the gate, a man stepped forward. He was in livery, but it fitted him poorly. He stood straight, but not like a soldier. There was an arrogance in his eyes.

"You can't come in here," he said curtly. "This is the queen's house. You can look, of course, but no farther, understand?"

Pitt knew his face. He tried to remember his name, but it eluded him. He was so tired his vision swam a little. He must stay alert, keep his mind sharp, his judgment steady. He was a little behind Austwick, so he pushed him hard in the small of the back.

"It's all right, McLeish," Austwick said, his voice shaky and a little rough. "These gentlemen are with me. We need to come in."

McLeish hesitated.

"Quickly," Pitt added. "There are others behind us. It'll all be over in an hour or two."

"Right!" McLeish responded, turning on his heel and leading the way.

"Ask about the queen!" Pitt hissed at Austwick. "Don't slip up now. Hanging is not a nice way to die."

Austwick stumbled. Stoker yanked him up.

Austwick cleared his throat. "Is Her Majesty still all right? I mean . . . I mean, will she be able to sign papers?"

"Of course," McLeish answered cheerfully. "Three people turned up unexpectedly. We had no choice but to let them in, or they'd have gone away and raised the alarm. A man and two women. But they're no trouble. It's all going well."

They were nearly at the front doors.

Austwick hesitated.

The sun was dazzling through a break in the trees. There was no sign of life inside, no sound, but then the weight of the doors would have muffled anything.

Someone must have been watching. The door opened and a heavyset man stood barring the way, a shotgun hanging on his arm.

Austwick stepped forward, his head high. His voice cracked at first, then gained strength.

"Good morning, Portman. My name is Charles Austwick. I represent Gerald Croxdale and the socialist people of Britain."

"About damn time you turned up!" Willy Portman said sharply. "Have you got the documents?"

"We're taking them to the queen," Pitt said quickly. "Get everybody in. It's nearly over." He tried to put some excitement in his voice.

Portman smiled. "Right. Yes!" He raised his arm with the gun in it, giving a salute of victory.

Stoker stepped forward and hit him as hard as he could, with all the force of his weight. He caught him in the vulnerable point of the solar plexus, driving him backward and inside. Portman doubled up in agony, the gun flying from his hand. Stoker spun around and picked it up.

Austwick stood as if paralyzed.

Pitt started up the stairs as another man came out of the servants' quarters with a gun at the ready.

Narraway emerged onto the landing and struck the man at the top of the stairs, sending him pitching forward and down, his gun flying out of his grasp. He landed at the bottom, his neck broken.

The man in the hall raised his gun and aimed at Pitt.

Austwick stepped in front of him. There was the roar of an explosion and Austwick collapsed slowly, crumpling to the ground in a sea of blood.

Stoker shot the man with the gun.

Narraway came down the stairs and picked up the gun from the man at the bottom

"There are five more," he said calmly. "Let's see if we can get them without any further bloodshed."

Pitt looked at him. Narraway sounded totally in control, but his face was haggard, hollow-eyed. There was a rough edge to his voice as if he held it level with an effort that cost him all he had.

Pitt glanced at Stoker, who was now armed with the gun that had killed Austwick.

"Yes, sir," Stoker said obediently, and set off toward the servants' quarters.

Narraway looked at Pitt. He smiled very slightly, but there was a warmth in his eyes Pitt had never seen before, even in the best of their past triumphs. "Would you like to go up and tell Her Majesty that order is restored?" he said. "There will be no papers to sign."

"Are you . . . all right?" Pitt asked. Suddenly he found he cared very much.

"Yes, thank you," Narraway replied. "But this business is not quite finished yet. Is that Charles Austwick on the floor?"

"Yes," Pitt answered. "I think it might be better all around if we say he died giving his life for his country."

"He was the head of this God damn conspiracy," Narraway said between his teeth.

"Actually he wasn't," Pitt told him. "Croxdale was."

Narraway looked startled. "Are you sure?"

"Absolutely. He more or less admitted it."

"Where is he?"

"Dead. We'll say he took his own life." Pitt found he was shivering. He tried to control it, and couldn't.

"But he didn't?"

"I shot him. He had Stoker by the neck. He was going to break it." Pitt passed him on the stairs.

"I see," Narraway said slowly. He broke into a companionable smile. "Croxdale underestimated you, didn't he?"

Pitt found himself blushing. Embarrassed, he turned and went on up the stairs. At the top he crossed the landing and knocked on the door.

"Come!" a quiet voice commanded.

He turned the handle and went inside. Victoria was standing in the middle of the room, Charlotte to one side of her, Vespasia to the other. As Pitt looked at them, the emotion welled up inside him until he felt the tears of relief prickle in his eyes. His throat was so tight the words were difficult to say.

"Your Majesty." He cleared his throat. "I am pleased to inform you that Osborne House is now back in the hands of those to whom it belongs. There will be no further trouble, but I would advise you to remain here until a little clearing up has been done."

Vespasia's face was radiant with relief, all the past weariness slipping from her.

Charlotte smiled at him, too happy, too proud even to speak.

"Thank you, Mr. Pitt," Victoria said a trifle hoarsely. "We are most obliged to you. We shall not forget."

For more high-stakes murder and mystery

in Victorian England, turn the page to sample

DORCHESTER TERRACE

The newest Charlotte and Thomas Pitt novel
from Anne Perry

CHAPTER

1

It was mid-february and growing dark outside. Pitt stood up from his desk and walked over to turn the gas up on the wall lamps one by one. He was becoming used to this office, even if he was not yet comfortable in it. In his mind it still belonged to Victor Narraway. When he turned back to his desk he half expected to see the pencil drawings of bare trees that Narraway used to keep on the walls, instead of the watercolors of skies and seascapes that Charlotte had given him. His books were not so different from Narraway's. There was less poetry, fewer classics perhaps, but similar titles on history, politics, and law.

Narraway had of course taken with him the large, silver-framed picture of his mother. Today, Pitt had finally put in its place his favorite photograph of his family. In it, Charlotte is smiling; beside her stands thirteen-year-old Jemima, looking very grown-up, and ten-year-old Daniel, still with the soft face of a child.

After the fiasco in Ireland at the end of last year, 1895, Narraway had not been reinstated as head of Special Branch, though he had been exonerated of all charges, of course. Instead, Pitt's temporary status as head had been made official. Even though it had happened several months earlier, he still found it hard to get used to. And he knew very well that the men who had once been his superiors, then his equals, and now his juniors, also found the new situation trying at best. Rank, in and of itself, meant little. His title commanded obedience, but not loyalty.

So far they had obeyed him without question. But he had had several months of very predictable events to deal with. There had been only the usual rumblings of discontent among the various immigrant populations, particularly here in London, but no crises. None of the difficult situations that endangered lives and tested his judgment. If such a crisis were to occur, it was then, he suspected, that he might find his men's trust in him strained and tenuous.

Pitt stopped by the window, staring out at the pattern of the opposite rooftops and the elegant wall of the nearby building, just able to discern their familiar outlines in the fading light. The bright gleam of streetlamps was increasing in all directions.

He pictured Narraway's grave face as it had been when they last spoke: tired and deeply lined, the effect of his difficult escape from total disgrace and from the emotional toll of his experiences in Ireland. Pitt knew that Narraway had accepted, at last, the existence of his feelings for Charlotte; but as always, Victor's coal-black eyes had given little away as they talked.

"You will make mistakes," he had said to Pitt in the quietness of this room, with its view of sky and rooftops. "You will hesitate to act when you know it could hurt people or destroy a life. Do not hesitate too long. You will misjudge people; you've always thought better of your social superiors than you should have. For God's sake, Pitt, rely on your instincts. Sometimes the results of your decisions will be serious. Live with it. The measure of your worth is what you learn from the errors you make. You cannot opt out; that would be the worst mistake of all." His face had been grim, shadowed by memories. "It is not only the decision you make that counts, but that you make it at the right moment. Anything that threatens the peace and safety of Britain can come under your jurisdiction."

Narraway had not added "God help you," though he might as well have. Then a dry humor had softened his eyes for a moment. Pitt had seen a flicker of compassion there for the burden that lay ahead, and also a hint of envy, regret for the excitement lost, the pounding of the blood and the fire of the mind that Narraway was being forced to give up.

Of course, Pitt had seen him since then, but only briefly. There had been social events here and there, conversations that were polite, but devoid of meaning beyond the courtesies. The questions as to how each of them was learning to bend, to adapt and alter his stride to a new role, remained unspoken.

Pitt sat down again at his desk and turned his attention to the papers in front of him.

There was a brief knock on the door.

"Come in," he said.

The door opened at once, and Stoker entered. Thanks to the events in Ireland, he was the one man in the Branch that Pitt knew for certain he could trust.

"Yes?" he said as Stoker came to stand in front of Pitt's desk. He looked worried and uncomfortable, his lean face more expressive than usual.

"Got a report in from Hutchins in Dover, sir. Seen one or two unusual people coming over on the ferry. Troublemakers. Not the usual sort of political talkers—more like the ones who really do things. He's pretty sure at least one of them was involved in the murder of the French prime minister the year before last."

Pitt felt a knot tighten in his stomach. No wonder Stoker looked so worried. "Tell him to do all he can to be absolutely sure of their identities," he replied. "Send Barker down as well. Watch the trains. We need to know if any of them come up to London, and who they contact if they do."

"It may be nothing," Stoker said without conviction. "Hutchins is a bit jumpy."

Pitt drew in his breath to say that it was Hutchins's job to be overcautious, then changed his mind. Stoker knew that as well as he did. "Still, we should keep our eyes open. We've enough men in Dover to do that, with Barker."

"Yes, sir."

"Thank you."

Stoker turned and left. Pitt sat without moving for a moment or two. If it really was one of the French prime minister's assassins, would the French police or secret service get in touch with him? Would they want his help, or prefer to deal with the man themselves? They might hope to get information about other anarchists from him. Or, on the other hand, they might simply contrive for him to meet with an accident, so the whole matter would never reach the public eye. If the latter were the case, it would be better if the British Special Branch pretended not to be aware of the situation. Pitt would have to make the decision about whether to involve the Special Branch, and to what extent, later, when he had more information. It was the type of decision Narraway had referred to: a gray area, fraught with moral difficulties.

Pitt bent back to the papers he had been reading.

There was a reception that evening. A hundred or so people of social and political importance would be gathered, ostensibly to hear the latest violin prodigy playing a selection of chamber pieces. In truth it would be a roomful of people attempting to observe and manipulate any shifts in political power, and to subtly exchange information that could not be passed in the more rigid settings of an office.

Pitt walked through the front door of his house in Keppel Street just after seven o'clock, with plenty of time to get ready for the reception. He found himself smiling at the immediate warmth, a relief after the bitter wind outside. The familiar smells of baked bread and clean cotton drifted from the kitchen at the far end of the passage. Charlotte would be upstairs dressing. She was not yet used to being back in the glamour arnd rivalry of the high society into which she had been born. She had found it shallow when she was younger, and then, after marrying Pitt, it had been out of her reach. Now he knew, although she had never once said so, that at times she had missed the color and wit of it all, however superficial it was.

Minnie Maude was in the kitchen preparing Welsh rarebit for him, in case the refreshments at the event were meager. Her hair was flying out of its pins as usual, her face flushed with exertion, and perhaps a certain excitement. She swung around from the big stove as soon as she heard his footsteps.

"Oh, Mr. Pitt, sir, 'ave yer seen Mrs. Pitt? She looks a proper treat, she does. I never seen anyone look so . . ." She was lost for words, so instead held out the plate of hot savory cheese on toast. Then, realizing the need for haste, she put it on the kitchen table, and fetched him a knife and fork. "I'll get yer a nice cup o' tea," she added. "Kettle's boiled."

"Thank you," he said, hiding at least part of his amusement. Minnie Maude Mudway had replaced Gracie Phipps, the maid who had been with the Pitts almost since they were married. He was still not entirely used to the change. But Gracie had her own home now, and he was happy for her. Minnie Maude had been hired on Gracie's recommendation, and it was working out very satisfactorily, even if he missed Gracie's forthright comments about his cases, and her loyal and highly independent support.

He ate in silence, with considerable appreciation. Minnie Maude was rapidly becoming a good cook. With a more generous budget at her disposal than Gracie had ever had, she had taken to experimenting—on the whole, with great success.

He noticed that she had made enough for herself, although her portion was much smaller. However, she seemed unwilling to eat it in front of him.

"Please don't wait," he said, gesturing toward the saucepan on the stove. "Have it while it's hot."

She gave an uncertain smile and seemed about to argue, then changed her mind and served it. Almost at once she was distracted by a stack of clean dishes waiting to be put away in the Welsh dresser, and her meal went untouched. Pitt decided he should speak to Charlotte about it; perhaps she could say something to make Minnie Maude feel more comfortable. It was absurd for her to feel that she could not eat at the kitchen table just because he was there. Now that she had taken Gracie's place, this was her home.

When he had finished his tea he thanked her and went upstairs to wash, shave, and change.

In the bedroom he found Jemima as well as Charlotte. The girl was regarding her mother with careful appreciation. Pitt was startled to see that Jemima had her long hair up in pins, as if she were grown-up. He felt proud, and at the same time, felt a pang of loss.

"It's wonderful, Mama, but you are still a little pale," Jemima said candidly, reaching forward to straighten the burgundy-colored silk of Charlotte's gown. Then she flashed Pitt a smile. "Hello, Papa. You're just in time to be fashionably late. You must do it. It's the thing, you know."

"Yes, I do know," he agreed, then turned to look at Charlotte. Minnie Maude was right, of course, but it still caught him by surprise sometimes, how lovely Charlotte was. It was more than the excitement in her face, or the warmth in her eyes. Maturity became her. She had an assurance now, at almost forty, that she had not had when she was younger. It gave her a grace that was deeper than the mere charm that good coloring or straight features offered.

"Your clothes are laid out for you," Charlotte said, in answer to his glance. "Fashionably late is one thing; looking as if you mistook the arrangements, or got lost, is another."

He smiled, and did not bother to answer. He understood her nervousness. He was trying to counter his own anxiety over suddenly being in a social position that he had not been born into. His new situation was quite different in nature from being a senior policeman. Now he was the head of Special Branch and, except in the most major of cases, entirely his own master. There was no one with whom to share the power, knowledge, or responsibility.

Pitt was even more aware of the change in his circumstances as he alighted from the hansom and held out his arm for Charlotte, steadying her for an instant as she stepped down. The night air was bitterly cold, stinging their faces. Ice gleamed on the road, and he was careful not to slip as he guided Charlotte over to the pavement.

A coach with four horses pulled up a little ahead of them, a coat of arms painted on the door. The horses' breath was visible, and the brass on their harnesses winked in the light as they shifted their weight. A liveried footman stepped down off the box to open the door.

Another coach passed by, the sound of iron-shod hoofs sharp on the stones.

Charlotte gripped his arm tightly, though it was not in fear that she might slip. She wanted only a bit of reassurance, a moment to gather her strength before they ventured in. He smiled in the dark and reached over with his other hand to touch hers for an instant.

The large front doors opened before them. A servant took Pitt's card and conducted them to the main hall, where the reception had already begun.

The room was magnificent. Scattered columns and pilasters stretching up to the painted ceiling gave it an illusion of even greater height. It was lit by four massive, dazzling chandeliers hanging on chains that seemed to be solid gold, though of course they weren't.

"Are you sure we're in the right place?" Pitt whispered to Charlotte.

She turned to him with a wide-eyed look of alarm, then saw that he was deliberately teasing her. He was nervous. But he was also proud that this time she was here because he was invited, rather than because her sister, Emily, or her aunt, Lady Vespasia Cumming-Gould, had been. It was a small thing to give her, after all the years of humble living, but it pleased him.

Charlotte smiled and held her head a little higher before sailing down the small flight of steps to join the crowd. Within moments they were surrounded by a swirl of color and voices, muted laughter, and the clink of glasses.

The conversation was polite and most of it meaningless, simply a way for everyone to take stock of one another while not seeming to do so. Charlotte appeared perfectly at ease as they spoke to one group, then another. Pitt watched her with admiration as she smiled at everyone, affected interest, passed subtle compliments. There was an art to it that he was not yet ready to emulate. He was afraid he would end up looking as if he were trying too hard to copy those born into this social station, and they would never forget such a slip.

Some junior minister of the government spoke to him casually. He could not remember the man's name, but he listened as if he were interested. Someone else joined in and the discussion became more serious. He made the odd remark, but mostly he just observed.

Pitt noticed an accute difference in the way people behaved toward him now, as compared to a few months ago, although not everyone knew who he was yet. He was pleased to be quite drawn into another conversation, and saw Charlotte smile to herself before turning to a rather large lady in green and listening to her with charming attention.

". . . Complete ass, if you ask me," an elderly man said heartily. He looked at Pitt, raising an eyebrow in question. "No idea why they promoted the fellow to the Home Office. Must be related to someone." He laughed. "Or know a few secrets, what?"

Pitt smiled back. He had no idea who they were referring to.

"I say, you're not in Parliament, are you?" the man went on. "Didn't mean to insult you, you know."

"No, I'm not," Pitt answered him with a smile.

"Good job." The man was clearly relieved. "My name's Willoughby. Got a little land in Herefordshire. Couple of thousand acres." He nodded.

Pitt introduced himself in turn, hesitated a moment, then decided against stating his occupation.

Another man joined them, slim and elegant with slightly protruding teeth and a white moustache. "Evening," he said companionably. "Rotten business in Copenhagen, isn't it? Still, I dare say it'll blow over. Usually does." He looked at Pitt more carefully. "Suppose you know all about it?"

"I've heard a thing or two," Pitt admitted.

"Connections?" Willoughby asked.

"He's head of Special Branch!" the other man said tartly. "Probably knows more about either of us than we know about ourselves!"

Willoughby paled. "Oh, really?" He smiled but his voice rasped as if his throat were suddenly tight. "Don't think there's much of any interest to know, ol' boy."

Pitt's mind raced to think of the best way to reply. He could not afford to make enemies, but neither would it be wise to belittle his importance, or allow people to assume that he was not the same master of information that Narraway had been.

He made himself smile back at Willoughby. "I would not say you are uninteresting, sir, but you are not of concern to us, which is an entirely different thing."

Willoughby's eyes widened. "Really?" He looked mollified, almost pleased. "Really?"

The other man looked amused. "Is that what you say to everyone?" he asked with the ghost of a smile.

"I like to be courteous." Pitt looked him directly in the eye. "But I can't deny that some people are less interesting than others."

This time Willoughby was very definitely pleased and made no attempt to hide it. Satisfaction radiated from him as he took a glass of champagne from a passing footman.

Pitt moved on. He was more careful now of his manner, watching but speaking little, learning to copy the polite words that meant nothing. It was not an art that came to him easily. Charlotte would have understood the nuances within what was said, or unsaid. Pitt would have found direct openness much more comfortable. However, this form of socializing was part of his world from now on, even if he felt like an intruder, even if he knew that beneath the smiles, the smooth, self-assured men around him were perfectly aware of how he felt.

A few moments later he saw Charlotte again. He made his way toward her with a lift of spirits, even a pride he thought was perhaps a little silly after all these years, but nevertheless was quite real. There were other women in the room with more classic beauty, and certainly more sumptuous gowns, but for him they lacked warmth. They had less passion, less of that certain indefinable grace that comes from within.

Charlotte was talking to her sister, Emily Radley, who was wearing a pale blue-green silk gown with gold embroidery. Emily's first marriage had been a match to make any mother proud. Lord George Ashworth had been the opposite of Pitt in every way: handsome, charming, of excellent family, and in possession of a great deal of money. After his death, it was held in trust for his and Emily's son, Edward. A suitable time later, Emily had married Jack Radley. He was another handsome man, even more charming, but with no money at all. His father had been a younger son, and something of an adventurer.

It was Emily who had persuaded Jack to enter politics and aspire to make something of himself. Perhaps some of Emily's hunger to affect other people's lives had come from her observation of Charlotte and her involvement in several of Pitt's earlier cases. To be fair, at times Emily had also helped Charlotte, with both flair and courage. The sisters had exasperated and embarrassed Pitt, driving him frantic with fear for their safety, but they had also very thoroughly earned his respect and gratitude.

Looking at Emily now, the light from the chandeliers gleaming on her fair hair and on the diamonds around her neck, he thought back with a little nostalgia to the adventure and emotion of those times. He could no longer share information about his cases, even with Charlotte. It was a loss he felt with surprising sadness. Now his assignments were not merely confidential, but completely secret.

Emily saw him looking at her and smiled brightly.

"Good evening, Thomas. How are you?" she said cheerfully.

"Well, thank you. And I can see that you are," he responded. Emily was naturally pretty, with her golden hair and wide, dark blue eyes. More important, she knew exactly how to dress to complement the best in herself, whatever the occasion. But, perhaps because it was his job to watch people and read the emotions behind their words, he could see at once that Emily was uncharacteristically tense. Could it be that she was wary of him, too? The thought chilled him so much that he could barely gather himself enough to acknowledge Jack Radley.

"My lord, may I introduce my brother-in-law, Thomas Pitt?" Jack said very formally, as Pitt turned automatically toward the man with whom Jack had been speaking. "Thomas, Lord Tregarron."

Jack did not mention Tregarron's position. Presumably he considered the man important enough that Pitt should have been familiar with his title.

It was then that Pitt remembered Charlotte telling him of Jack's promotion to a position of responsibility within the government, a position that finally gave him some real power. Emily was very proud of it. So perhaps it was defensiveness, then, that he could see in her quick eyes and in the slight stiffness of her shoulders. She was not going to let Pitt's promotion overshadow Jack's.

It came to Pitt suddenly; Tregarron was a minister in the Foreign Office, close to the Foreign Secretary himself.

"How do you do, my lord?" Pitt replied, smiling. He glanced at Charlotte, and saw that she too understood Emily's tension.

"Lord Tregarron was telling us about some of the beautiful places he has visited," Emily said brightly. "Especially in the Balkans. His descriptions of the Adriatic Coast are breathtaking."

Tregarron gave a slight shrug. He was a dark, stocky man with thick, curling hair and a highly expressive face. No one could have thought him comely, and yet the strength and vitality in him commanded attention. Pitt noticed that several women in the room kept glancing at him, then looking away.

"That a Cornishman admires anyone else's coast has impressed Mrs. Radley greatly," Tregarron said with a smile. "As so it should. We have had our share of troubles in the past, between shipwreck and smuggling, but I have no time for separatists. Life should be about inclusion, not everyone running off to his own small corner and pulling up the drawbridge. Half the wars in Europe have started out of that type of fear. The other half, out of greed. Don't you agree?" He looked directly at Pitt.

"Liberally helped with misunderstanding," Pitt replied. "Intentional or not."

"Well put, sir!" Tregarron commended him instantly. He turned to Jack. "Right, Radley? A nice distinction, don't you think?"

Jack signaled his approval, smiling with the easy charm he had always possessed. He was a handsome man, and wore it with grace.

Emily shot Pitt a swift glance and there was a distinct chill in it. Pitt hoped Jack had not seen it, lest it upset him. Pitt knew he himself would dislike it if Charlotte were so defensive of him. In his experience, you do not guard anyone so closely, unless you fear they are in some way vulnerable. Did Emily doubt that Jack had the steel in his nature—or perhaps the intelligence—to fill his new post well?

And had Tregarron chosen Jack, or had Emily used some connection of her own, from her days as Lady Ashworth, in order to obtain the position for him? Pitt could not think of anyone Emily knew who was powerful enough to do that, but then, the whole world of political debt and preferment was one he was unfamiliar with. Narraway had been excellent at figuring out the truth in this type of situation. It was a skill Pitt needed to arm himself with, and quickly.

He felt a sudden, powerful empathy with Jack; they were both swimming with sharks in unfamiliar seas. But Jack was used to using his charm and instinctive ability to read people. Perhaps he would manage to survive, and survive well.

The conversation had moved from the Adriatic Coast to a discussion about the Austro-Hungarian Empire in general, and from there went on to Berlin, and finally to Paris, that city of elegance and gaiety. Pitt said little, content to listen.

The musical interlude for the evening began. Much of its exquisite beauty was wasted on the audience, who were not so much listening as waiting in polite silence until it was over and they could resume their own conversations.

But Charlotte heard the haunting beauty of the pieces and wished the musician could play all evening. However, she understood the rhythm of such gatherings; this break was to allow a regrouping of forces. It was a time in which to weigh what one had observed and heard, and to consider what to say next, whom to approach, and what gambit to play next.

She was sitting beside Pitt, a hand resting lightly on one arm. She could see Emily, seated in a gold-painted chair several rows in front of her, between Lord Tregarron and Jack.

Charlotte had known Jack's promotion was important, but she had not realized until now how steep a climb it had truly been. And tonight she had recognized that, under Emily's usual charming manner, lurked fear for Jack in his new position.

Was it because Emily knew Jack too well, was aware of a fundamental weakness in him that others did not see? Or could it be that she did not know him well enough and so was unable to see the strength of will beneath his easy manner, his charisma that seemed so effortless?

Charlotte suspected that the real truth was that, after a decade of marriage, Emily was finally realizing that she was not only in love with Jack, but that she also cared about his ability to succeed not just for what it might bring her, but also for what it could give Jack.

Emily had been the youngest and prettiest of the three Ellison sisters, and the most single-mindedly ambitious. Sarah, the eldest, had been dead for fifteen years. Her death now seemed a lifetime ago. The fear and pain of that time had receded into a distant nightmare, one Charlotte seldom revisited. Their father had also died, about four years ago, and some time later their mother had remarried. This was another subject fraught with mixed emotions, though Charlotte had completely accepted her mother's choice, and Emily largely so. Only their grandmother remained horrified. But then, Mariah Ellison had made a profession out of disapproving. Caroline's second husband, Joshua Fielding, belonged to an acting troupe, was Caroline's junior by many years, and was Jewish to boot. Caroline's marriage to him gave Grandmama more than ample opportunity to express all her pent-up prejudices. That Caroline was thoroughly happy with Joshua only added insult to the injury.

It made Charlotte happy to think that Emily seemed to be learning how to love in a different, more unselfish way, a way that was more protective, more mature. It meant she herself was becoming more mature. Not that the ambition was gone! It was very much present, woven into the fiber of Emily's character.

Charlotte also understood the defensive posture Emily had adopted earlier. Charlotte felt the same tigress-like instinct to protect Pitt; but she also knew that in his new position, there was little with which she could help. He was on far more unfamiliar ground than even Jack was; though Jack's family had had no money, it did have aristocratic connections in half the counties in England. Pitt was the mere son of a gamekeeper.

But if Charlotte were to attempt to protect him, she would not signal it as clearly as Emily had done earlier. Charlotte knew Pitt would hate that! She wasn't sure whether Jack would too.

When the performance was over and the applause died down, the conversations resumed, and Charlotte soon found herself talking to a most unusual woman.

She was probably in her late thirties, like Charlotte herself, but in all other ways she was quite different. She was dressed in a huge-skirted gown the color of candlelight through brandy, and she was so slender as to look fragile. The bones of her neck and shoulders appeared as if they might break if she were bumped too roughly. There were blue veins just visible beneath her milk-white skin, and her hair was so dark as to be nearly black. Her eyes were dark-lashed and heavy-lidded above her high cheekbones, her mouth soft and generous. To Charlotte it was a face that was instantly likeable. She felt that the mysterious woman had a great strength the moment their eyes met.

She introduced herself as Adriana Blantyre. Her voice was very low, just a trifle husky, and she spoke with an accent so slight that Charlotte had to strain her ears to make certain she had really heard it.

Adriana's husband was tall and dark, and he too had a remarkable face. At a glance he was handsome, yet there was far more to him than a mere balance or regularity of feature. Once Charlotte had met his eyes, she kept looking back at him because of their intelligence, and the fierceness of his emotion. There was a grace in the way he stood, but no ease. She felt Pitt watching her curiously as she looked at the man, and yet she did not stop herself.

Evan Blantyre was an ex-diplomat, particularly interested in the eastern Mediterranean.

"A marvelous place, the Mediterranean," he said, facing Charlotte, and yet speaking almost to himself. "Part of Europe, and yet at the gateway to a world far older, and civilizations that prefigure ours and from which we are sprung."

"Such as Greece?" Charlotte asked, not having to feign interest. "And maybe Egypt?"

"Byzantium, Macedonia, and before that Troy," he elaborated. "The world of Homer, imagination and memory at the root of our thoughts, and the concepts from which they rise."

Charlotte could not let him go unchallenged, not because she disbelieved him but because there was an arrogance in him that she was compelled to probe.

"Really? I would have thought Judea was the place at the root of our thoughts," she argued.

He smiled widely, seizing on her interest. "Judea certainly, for the roots of faith, but not of thought, or, if you prefer, philosophy, the love of wisdom rather than commanded belief. I chose my words with care, Mrs. Pitt."

Now she knew exactly what he meant, and that he had been deliberately baiting her, but she also saw that there was intense conviction behind what he said. There was no pretense in the passion of his voice.

She smiled at him. "I see. And which of our modern civilizations carry the torch of that philosophy now?" It was a challenge, and she meant him to answer.

"Ah." Now he was ignoring the others in their group. "What an interesting question. Not Germany, all brightly polished and looking for something brave and brash to do. Not really France, although it has a uniquely piquant sophistication. Italy has sown the seeds of much glory, yet it is forever quarrelling within itself." He made a rueful and elegant gesture.

"And us?" Charlotte asked him, her tone a little sharper than she had meant it to be.

"Adventurers," he replied without hesitation. "And shopkeepers to the world."

"So no present-day heirs?" she said, with sudden disappointment.

"Austro-Hungary," he replied too quickly to conceal his own feelings. "It has inherited the mantle of the old Holy Roman Empire that bound Europe into one Christian unity after the fall of Rome itself."

Charlotte was startled. "Austria? But it is ramshackle, all but falling apart, isn't it? Unless all we are told of it is nonsense?"

Now he was amused, and he allowed her to see it. There was warmth in his smile, but also a bright and hard irony.

"I thought I was baiting you, Mrs. Pitt, and I find instead that you are baiting me." He turned to Pitt. "I underestimated your wife, sir. Someone mentioned that you are head of Special Branch. If that is indeed true, then I should have known better than to imagine that you would choose a wife purely for her looks, however charming."

Pitt was smiling now too. "I was not head of Special Branch at the time," he replied. "But I was ambitious, and hungry enough to reach for the best with no idea of my own limitations."

"Excellent!" Blantyre applauded him. "Never allow your dreams to be limited. You should aim for the stars. Live and die with your arms outstretched and your eyes seeking the next goal."

"Evan, you are talking nonsense," Adriana said quietly, looking first at Charlotte, then at Pitt, judging their reactions. "Aren't you ever afraid people will believe you?"

"Do you believe me, Mrs. Pitt?" Blantyre inquired, his eyes wide, still challenging.

Charlotte looked at him directly. She was quite sure of her answer.

"I'm sorry, Mr. Blantyre, because I don't think you mean me to, but yes, I do believe you."

"Bravo!" he said quietly. "I have found a sparring partner worth my efforts." He turned to Pitt. "Does your position involve dealing with the Balkans, Mr. Pitt?"

Pitt glanced at Jack and Emily—who had now moved farther away and were engaged in conversation elsewhere—then back at Blantyre.

"With anyone whose activities might threaten the peace or safety of Britain," he replied, the levity wiped from his face.

Blantyre's eyebrows rose. "Even if in northern Italy, or Croatia? In Vienna itself?"

"No," Pitt told him, keeping his expression agreeable, as if they were playing a parlor game of no consequence. "Only on British soil. Farther afield would be Mr. Radley's concern. As I'm sure you know."

"Of course." Blantyre nodded. "That must be challenging for you, to know when you can act, and when you must leave the action to someone else. Or am I being unsophisticated? Is it actually more a matter of how you do a thing rather than what you do?"

Pitt smiled without answering.

"Does your search for information ever take you abroad?" Blantyre continued, completely unperturbed. "You would love Vienna. The quickness of wit, and the music. There is so much music there that is new, innovative in concept, challenging to the mind. I daresay they are musicians you have never heard of, but you will. Above all, there is a breadth of thought in a score of subjects: philosophy, science, social mores, psychology, the very fundamentals of how the human mind works. There is an intellectual imagination there that will very soon lead the world in some areas."

He gave a slight mocking shrug, as if to deny the heat of his feelings. "And of course there is the traditional as well." He turned to look at Adriana. "Do you remember dancing all night to Mr. Strauss's music? Our feet ached, the dawn was paling the sky, and yet if the orchestra had played into the daylight hours, we could not have kept still."

The memory was there in Adriana's eyes, but Charlotte was certain she also saw a shadow cross her face.

"Of course I do," Adriana answered. "No one who has waltzed in Vienna ever completely forgets it."

Charlotte looked at her, fascinated by the romance of dancing to the music of the Waltz King. "You actually danced when Mr. Strauss conducted the orchestra?" she asked with awe.

"Indeed," Blantyre responded. "No one else can give music quite the same magic. It makes one feel as if one must dance forever. We watched the moon rise over the Danube, and talked all night with the most amazing people: princes, philosophers, artists, and scientists."

"Have you met the emperor Franz Josef?" Charlotte pursued. "They say he is very conservative. Is that true?" She told herself it was to keep the conversation innocuous, but she was caught up in this dream portait of Vienna, the new inventions and new ideas of society. It was a world she herself would never see, but—at least as Blantyre had told it—Vienna was the heart of Europe. It was the place of the genesis of new ideas that would spread throughout the whole continent one day, and beyond.

"Yes, I have, and it is true." Blantyre was smiling but the emotion in his face was intense. There was a passion in him that was urgent, electric.

"A grim man, with a devil on his shoulder," he went on, watching her face as closely as she was watching his. "A contradiction of a man. More disciplined than anyone else I know. He sleeps on an army bed and rises at some ungodly hour long before dawn. And yet he fell madly in love with Elisabeth, seven years younger than himself, sister of the woman his father wished him to marry."

"The empress Elisabeth?" Charlotte said with even sharper interest. There was a vitality in Blantyre that intrigued her. She was unsure whether he spoke with such intensity merely to entertain, or possibly to impress, or whether his passion for his subject was really so fierce that he had no control over it.

"The very same," Blantyre agreed. "He overrode all opposition. He would not be denied." Now the admiration in his face was undisguised. "They married, and by the time she was twenty-one she had given birth to her third child, her only son."

"A strange mixture of rigidity and romance," she said thoughtfully. "Are they happy?"

She felt Pitt's hand touching her arm, but it was too late to withdraw the remark. She glanced at Adriana and saw in her eyes an emotion she could not read at all: a brilliance, a pain, and something she was trying very hard to conceal. Becoming aware of Charlotte's gaze on her, she looked away.

"No," Blantyre said frankly. "She is somewhat bohemian in her tastes, and highly eccentric. She travels all over Europe wherever she can."

Charlotte wanted to make some light remark that would ease the tension and turn the conversation away from her misjudged question, but she thought now that such a thing would be obvious, and only make matters worse.

"Perhaps it was a case of falling in love with a dream that one did not really understand," she said quietly.

"How very perceptive of you. You are rather alarming, Mrs. Pitt." Blantyre said this with pleasure, and a distinct respect. "And very honest!"

"I think you mean 'indiscreet,' " she said ruefully. "Perhaps we had better return to Mr. Strauss and his music. I believe his father was a noted composer as well?"

"Ah, yes." He drew a deep breath and his smile was a little wry. "He composed the 'Radetzky March.' "

PHOTO: © JONATHAN HULME

ANNE PERRY is the bestselling author of two acclaimed se-
ries set in Victorian England: the Charlotte and Thomas
Pitt novels, most recently *Dorchester Terrace* and *Treason at
Lisson Grove*, and the William Monk novels, including *Ac-
ceptable Loss* and *Execution Dock*. She is also the author of
the World War I novels *No Graves As Yet*, *Shoulder the Sky*,
Angels in the Gloom, *At Some Disputed Barricade*, and *We
Shall Not Sleep*, as well as nine Christmas novels, most re-
cently *A Christmas Homecoming*. Her stand-alone novel
The Sheen on the Silk, set in the Byzantine Empire, was a
New York Times bestseller. Anne Perry lives in Scotland.

www.AnnePerry.net